The
WEIGHT
of
CROWNS

ALSO BY ALINA BELLCHAMBERS

The Order of Masks

ABOUT THE AUTHOR

Alina Bellchambers grew up in her family's bookstore and spent a childhood immersed in fantastical worlds. She now writes twisty thrillers and dark fantasies that reflect her love of fierce protagonists, villainous romances and moral complexities. Alina has a university degree in psychology and writes on a forty-acre hobby farm in the picturesque Adelaide Hills of South Australia. When not typing in her study and drinking copious amounts of tea, Alina enjoys hiking with her feisty dog Scamp and travelling abroad. She can be found on social media under @alinabellwrites and loves connecting with readers.

ALINA BELLCHAMBERS

The WEIGHT of CROWNS

HODDERSCAPE

First published in Great Britain in 2025 by Hodderscape
An imprint of Hodder & Stoughton Limited
An Hachette UK company

The authorised representative in the EEA is Hachette Ireland,
8 Castlecourt Centre, Dublin 15, D15 XTP3, Ireland (email: info@hbgi.ie)

1

A CIP catalogue record for this title is available from the British Library

Hardback ISBN 978 1 399 73083 9
Trade Paperback ISBN 978 1 399 73084 6
ebook ISBN 978 1 399 73085 3

Typeset in Baskerville

Printed and bound in Great Britain by Clays Ltd, Elcograf S.p.A.

Hodder & Stoughton policy is to use papers that are natural, renewable
and recyclable products and made from wood grown in sustainable forests.
The logging and manufacturing processes are expected to conform
to the environmental regulations of the country of origin.

Hodder & Stoughton Limited
Carmelite House
50 Victoria Embankment
London EC4Y 0DZ

www.hodderscape.co.uk

For all the wonderful readers who have found your way here:
It's a dream come true to be able to share Mira and Scarlett's stories with you.

And for Dad:
You are my rock. I love you forever
(even after you tried to convince me to take out the steamy scenes).

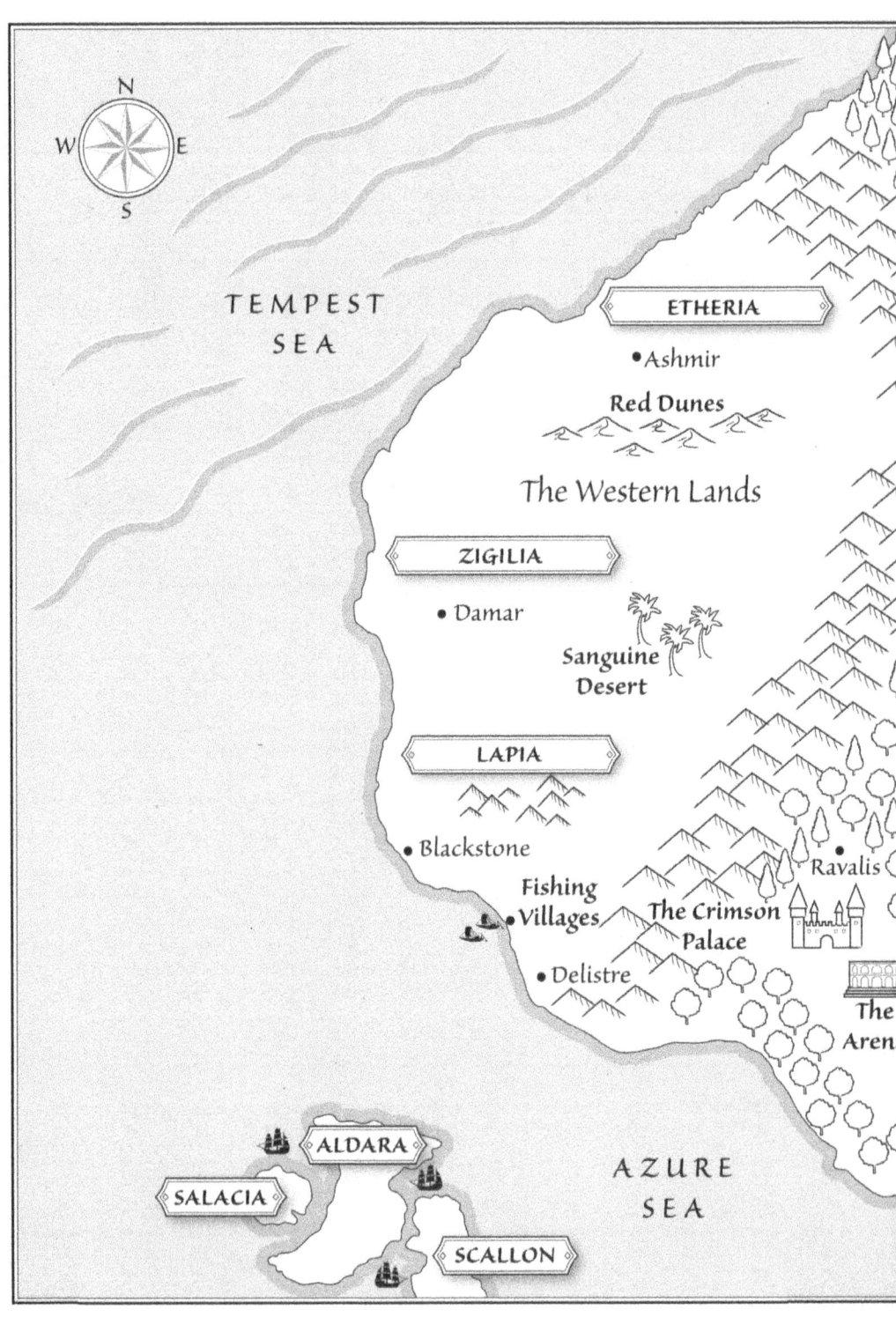

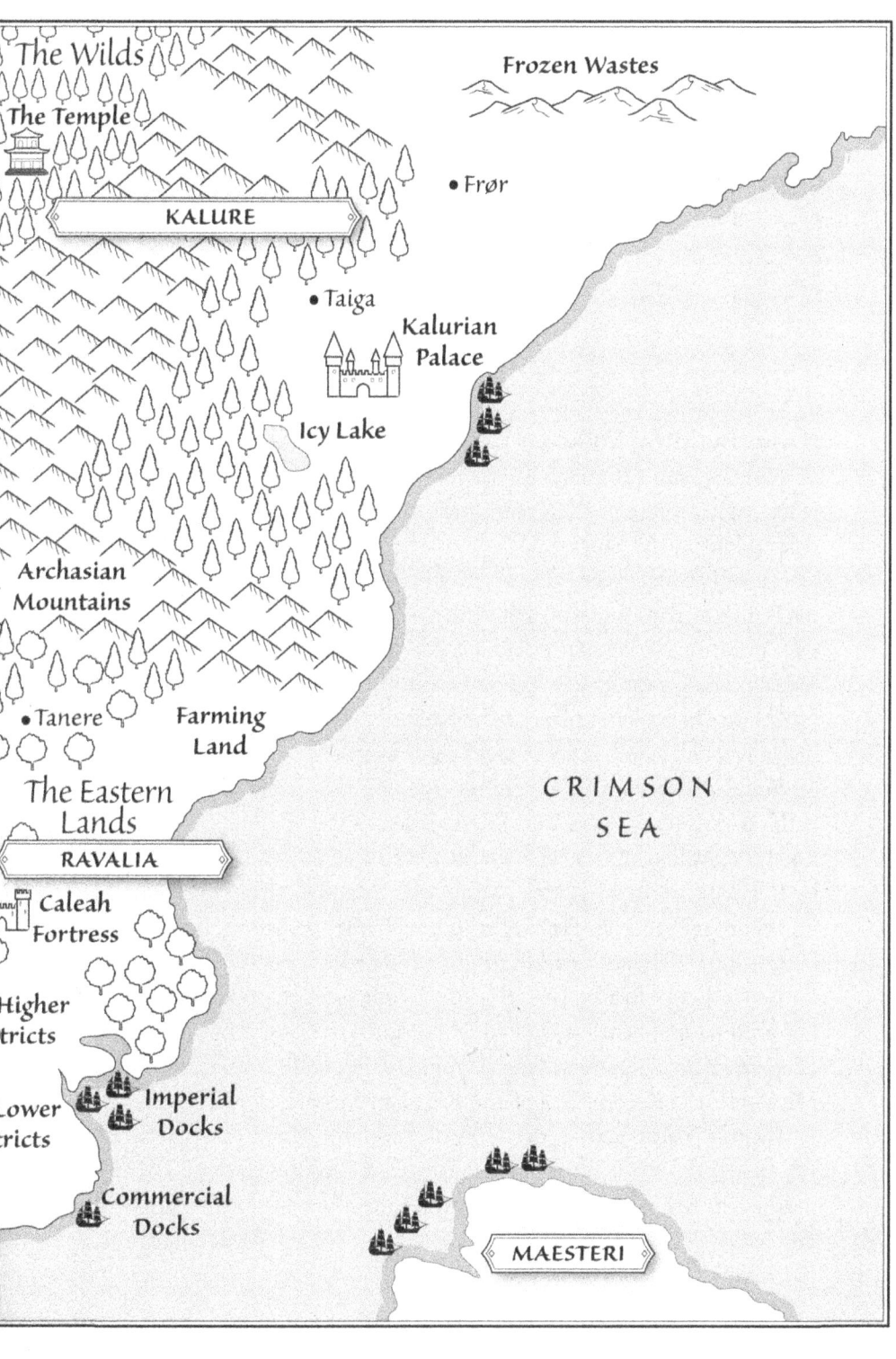

Character List

Kasmira (Mira) Volaris – Daughter of Adalyn, a former member of the Ravalian Order of Masks, and King Arioch of Kalure. Mira is the rightful queen of Kalure and inherited magical abilities as a descendant of the Sorceress.

To avoid being executed as a traitor like her mother, Mira competed in the Ravalian Trials and won a place in the Order of Masks. Mira schemed with Princess Scarlett and Prince Cassius for vengeance on the emperor, but ultimately gave up revenge to be with her lover Aric. Forced to flee to Kalure, she took her place as the Kalurian queen, vowing to embrace her magic and lead her people into battle against the Ravalian Empire.

Scarlett Valerian – Illegitimate daughter of Emperor Kalias and ruthless sorceress Zandri, and a descendant of the Sorceress. Ambitious for the Ravalian throne, she survived multiple assassination attempts by her half-brothers, Prince Roran and Prince Cassius. Has natural illusion magic and developed death magic after drowning.

During the Trials, Scarlett disguised herself as a contestant named Sabine to help Mira survive. But Mira's engagement to Cassius made her a threat and Scarlett worked with Zandri to frame Mira for killing Emperor Kalias. Scarlett plans to eliminate her half-brothers, deal with Mira and become empress of the Ravalian Empire.

Roran Valerian – Eldest son of Emperor Kalias and Empress Ivalene, and Crown Prince of the Ravalian Empire. Executed Mira's mother on the emperor's orders, tried to murder his brother Cassius and half-sister Scarlett and is now next in line for the Ravalian throne. Currently fighting to subjugate Kalure.

Cassius Valerian – Youngest son of Emperor Kalias and Empress Ivalene, brother to Roran and half-brother to Scarlett. Conspired with Mira in his own grab for power, tricking her into implicating his fiancée's family as traitors and forcing Mira into a political engagement with him. Was taken hostage by Mira and transported to Kalure as a prisoner.

Aric – Mira's childhood friend, combat trainer and lover. Originally from the Elusive Isles, he competed in the Trials with Mira and became a Warrior. Sought revenge against Prince Roran for killing his brother Kain, but chose to be with Mira instead. Mistakenly believes Mira betrayed him and was responsible for his sister Lillian's death. Now loyal to Scarlett and intends to kill Roran for her.

Severin – Scarlett's secret lover, a powerful seer from the Western Lands and the head of the Order of Artisans. Zandri decided to murder him to maintain her own control over Scarlett, and Severin allowed himself to die, hoping that one day Scarlett would learn the truth and turn against her mother.

Zandri – Scarlett's mother and Mira's aunt, responsible for the assassination of King Arioch of Kalure, her brother. Descended from the Sorceress, Zandri possesses powerful blood magic which she uses to control the magical Ravalian Orders.

Velanthe – Kalurian high priestess of the Temple dedicated to the Sorceress, the last stronghold of the Kalurian rebels.

Odessa Tiran – Formerly engaged to Cassius and a member of the Order of Masks. Wrongly imprisoned until Mira aided her escape and brought her to Kalure.

The Sorceress – An immortal deity whose whereabouts are unknown. The first queen of Kalure, worshipped by the Temple and its priestesses.

Lillian – Aric's sister and Mira's best friend. She was killed during Emperor Kalias's assassination but resurrected by Scarlett, and is now magically tied to her.

Darius – Leader of the rebels in Ravalia and friend to Mira's mother. Mira broke him out of the Ravalian dungeons and he helped her escape to Kalure.

Jadis and Elian – Twins and orphans, part of the Ravalian resistance. Fled with Mira and Darius to Kalure.

CHAPTER ONE

Mira

Ice whipped across my face like hundreds of tiny blades. The Kalurian winter was merciless – as cruel and unforgiving as the wrath building in my throat.

I gripped the hilt of my sword with frostbitten fingers, itching to draw it and run the man in front of me through.

My mother's murderer. And the butcherer of my people.

Roran smiled faintly, fully aware of my warring impulses. He towered over me just as he had in the arena a year ago. And though I didn't fear him as I had then, I would be lying if I didn't feel a chill as I took in the blood darkening his golden armour, or the hellish, raised scar bisecting his face.

'Not pretty, is it?' Roran traced the scar with an idle finger, but his hard green eyes were fixed on me. Predatory. Assessing. 'Healers offered to remove it, but I like the reminder.'

The last thing I wanted was to indulge him. 'What reminder?' I gritted out.

Roran moved forward, his boots thudding against the frozen, rocky ground. We had met halfway between the Kalurian capital and the boundary of the Wilds, on a desolate mountain plateau. His delegation – twenty black-garbed killers from the Order of Warriors – looked on from behind a white banner of truce. I felt their longing to end this war with a single, bloody strike.

For once, we were of the same mind.

I resisted the urge to glance behind me – to where twenty of my best fighters watched from a nearby ridge, mounted atop their horses.

If Roran attacked me, I would retaliate, and so would they. And perhaps my mother would finally be avenged.

But Roran stopped a slight distance from me and murmured, 'A reminder to raze the Wilds to the ground.'

'And here I believed that you wanted to negotiate.'

'Oh, I'm prepared to negotiate.' His breath was hot on my face. 'Surrender now, and I'll offer you a good death. Quick and clean, like the one I would have given you in the arena.'

Staring up into his pitiless face, I had to swallow down rising bile. 'Never,' I breathed back. And then, more loudly: 'I'll *never* surrender to you.'

'Suit yourself.' Roran's tone was dismissive. 'You don't have the numbers to pose a threat to me, and when you *do* come out of hiding, I'll skewer you along with your so-called army. Perhaps I'll mount your head on a spike after I'm done, and fix it to the gates of the Kalurian palace. A fitting homecoming.'

'If you're threatening me,' I said coldly, 'then I must be doing *something* right. What was it that cut the deepest, Roran? Was it when my people burned your army's stores? Raided their camps? Slit their throats?'

His smile was a terrible thing. 'Not without casualties.'

'Always higher for you, I hear. That's the thing about guerrilla warfare: it's easier to do damage on my end. After all, we have a large target to work with. It isn't hard to make you bleed.'

'You've landed a few cuts, I'll give you that. But I'm not the one who's about to bleed, Mira.' Roran stepped closer, until his armoured breastplate brushed mine. '*You* are.'

This close, his features were highlighted in familiar, terrifying detail. With his red hair and emotionless face, Roran could have been Emperor Kalias brought back to life.

My heart pounded a jagged rhythm against my chest, so loud that I wondered if he could hear it.

And a terrible suspicion began to take root.

Roran's eyes glittered as understanding dawned on my face. I never should have accepted his truce. He had come here for one reason, and one reason alone: to torment me.

'You could have . . . sent me their bodies,' I managed to say, my voice hoarse. 'You didn't need to arrange this farce.'

'Ah,' Roran grinned, flashing his teeth, 'but where is the fun in that? Every one of my soldiers you killed, every piece of machinery and grain of food you destroyed . . . I added all of it to your tally. And now it's time for you to pay.' He nodded to his Warriors.

They parted like a dark sea, revealing the two bound captives at the heart of Roran's contingent. A morbid centrepiece.

Darius looked up at me from his knees. His face was coated in dried blood, and one of his sea-green eyes was swollen shut. Beside him, Nari seemed to have fared better, though the Kalurian warrior favoured her right side. I made an involuntary move towards them.

'You can see perfectly well from here,' Roran said, holding up a hand.

As if it was a signal, two Warriors stepped forward. Though neither drew their sword, the threat was clear.

'How should I do it, do you think?' Roran asked. 'A beheading, like your mother? That has sentimental value, I suppose, but it's positively merciful. Too good for cowards who attack under the cover of darkness.'

I tried to block out his words, but I still felt the horror of them. 'What can I give you in exchange for their lives?'

He pretended to consider. Then he said, 'Nothing. I've already told you what I want: your surrender.'

'In return for a quick death,' I reiterated.

A curt nod.

'*And* their lives?'

Darius shook his head at me, his expression anguished. The cloth in his mouth made talking impossible, but if he could, I knew he would beg me not to do this. So would Nari, who believed wholeheartedly in protecting the Wilds.

'Two grunts in exchange for a queen?' Roran said. 'I'm willing to make that deal.'

I kept looking at Darius and Nari – at the conviction burning in their eyes. They were willing to die for me, just like the Kalurian Governor had been. Didn't I owe it to Søren Halvor, and to the countless Kalurians who had died in this war, to continue fighting?

'I heard about your military conquest in Etheria,' I said, shifting to face Roran once more. 'The courtiers laughed about it back in Ravalia. The long line of slaves snaking down to the mines. The ones you strung up on posts along the way, as reminders.' I paused, sucking in a steadying breath. 'I can't allow you to do that here, even if it means watching my friends die. But I have another proposition for you.'

'And what might that be?' Roran asked, twirling a dagger in his hand.

'I have your brother in my dungeons.' I could only imagine the damage Cassius could do if he was reunited with his older brother, but it couldn't be helped. 'If you give me Darius and Nari, I will return Cassius to you unharmed.'

'*Cassius?*' Roran released a booming laugh. 'You think I care about that little deviant? I'm grateful you locked him up.' Still chortling, Roran caught the dagger and pointed with it back towards the encampment. 'How about this: you can pick one of them to survive. I'll allow whoever you choose one minute to run to your side. If they reach you in that time, I will let them live.'

'What's the catch?'

'No catch. I'll keep my word. But whichever you *don't* choose, I will feed to my hounds.'

Tears welled in my eyes, but I refused to let them fall. Roran's offer wasn't a mercy – far from it. But if it meant I could save one of them . . .

I gazed from Darius to Nari and back again. Darius had survived so much back in Ravalia, rising up to lead the Ravalian resistance. He had proved equally valuable here in Kalure, but more than that, he had become something of a father figure to me. I couldn't look at him without being reminded of all the stories we'd shared about my mother. Letting him die would be like watching her die all over again.

But Nari wasn't merely a Kalurian warrior or the head of clan Völsung. She was also the sister of Vølund, the warlord the clans had chosen as their leader. If I chose a Ravalian over her, I risked alienating Vølund and losing the support of his warriors – which meant losing this war against Roran.

I can't do it, I realised, looking at Darius with blurry eyes. *I can't save you.*

Darius blinked once, as if telling me that he understood.

'I choose . . .' My gaze was drawn to Nari, who was watching me intently. Despite her fierceness, despite her resolve to die with honour, she wanted to live. '. . . Darius,' I finished. 'I choose Darius.'

Nari's expression turned as cold and distant as the snow-capped mountains around us. I had dangled hope in front of her and then snatched it away – the cruellest torment of all.

She couldn't possibly hate me more than I hated myself. But I didn't try to reverse my decision. I couldn't.

'Release him,' Roran called, and his Warriors complied.

Darius stumbled forward, and I gasped at the mottled bruising and raised scars criss-crossing his pale chest. It had only been two days since I'd lost contact with him. *Two days—*

'Shouldn't you be running?' Roran asked mildly.

Panic flared in Darius's eyes. He lurched forward with all the grace of a drunk person, and I realised with a surge of terror that Roran hadn't merely had Darius beaten, or deprived of food and water. He had weakened him with some toxin or drug.

'I thought Ravalians prided themselves on honour,' I spat at Roran.

'There is no honour in war.' He kept his voice low, so that only I could hear him. 'Every true leader knows that, Kasmira. It's time you learnt it, too.'

Furious tears flowed down my cheeks. Darius was making ground, but he wasn't moving fast enough. His own body was betraying him; a body that he had trained and honed and relied upon for decades. Watching him lurch sideways only to right himself temporarily and push on was more than I could bear.

Then he fell.

Blood poured from his nose as he struggled to rise, using his single arm to push off the ground.

My legs tensed, preparing to run to him—

'You do that,' Roran said, the point of his blade pressing against my sternum, 'and this truce is over. I will have the excuse I need to kill you and the rest of your people.'

I looked up at Roran, hating him more than I had ever hated anyone in my life. Even Emperor Kalias.

'I *will* kill you for this,' I vowed. 'And when I do, I will show you as much mercy as you've shown today.'

'I look forward to it.'

Both Roran and I were watching Darius now. We all knew what this was, but still Darius staggered towards me. Still, he refused to give up.

His love for me was bright in his one open eye. I hoped he saw the answering love in my own.

Roran brushed his thumb across my tear-stained cheek. I wanted to slap it away, but my body was frozen in place.

And then he let his hand fall.

'Close,' he announced, advancing on Darius – one slow, deliberate step after another. 'But not close enough.'

Roran's sword pierced Darius's heart. A clean, fatal strike. Darius was dead before he even hit the ground. Less than five metres away from me.

I fell to my knees. When I had watched my mother die, I had been consumed by grief and hatred. But staring at the vacant face of the man I had come to love like a father, there was only numbness.

'Now *this* feels familiar, Kasmira,' Roran said, and I was dimly aware of him standing over me. 'I wonder how many more loved ones you'll lose before this war is done. Fortunately, I have a long list to choose from.'

His shadow retreated, the dying light of the sun reaching me once more. But its warmth didn't touch me.

'Enough of this theatre,' I heard Roran shout to his Warriors. 'Release the Kalurian.'

Another trick. It had to be.

I raised my head to watch Nari crossing the stretch of plain that had claimed Darius's life. Flakes of snow drifted down from above, but even tired and freezing, Nari kept her head held high, her kohl-darkened eyes locked on Roran.

As she passed him, Roran grasped her arm. She and I both tensed, readying ourselves for the killing blow.

But he merely said, 'Return to your brother with my blessing and this offer: if Vølund surrenders Kasmira Volaris to me, I will consider the Wilds an independent territory, under his jurisdiction.' I stared at Nari in shock, willing her to look at me. But she only had eyes for Roran as he continued, 'You have seen how little regard your so-called queen has for Kalurian lives. I will give you until the end of the month to decide.'

He strode back to his encampment without sparing me another glance. There was no need to torment me further. He had already landed the crippling blow.

Nari crouched beside Darius's body and pressed two fingers to his brow – a Kalurian gesture of respect to honour a fallen warrior. When she rose, I couldn't remain silent any longer.

'I'm so sorry,' I told her, my voice breaking. 'I never meant to—'

At last Nari looked at me. She was so tall I had to crane my neck to meet her dark eyes, a striking contrast with her long, braided blonde hair. As the wind picked up, the bones woven into her braids jangled – an eerie, discordant sound.

'My life is irrelevant, Kasmira.' Though she spoke without inflection, I heard the accusation in her words. 'But what I represent isn't.'

'You can't take Roran's offer to your brother.' It was the wrong thing to say – I was making all the wrong decisions, one after another, and I sensed Nari's respect for me draining away. But I had to convince her. I had to *try*. 'You've seen what Roran is. He's a monster, and he won't keep his word.'

I felt even more diminished under the weight of Nari's disappointed stare. 'It is up to Vølund and the clans to decide whether to accept Roran's offer. But you will have the chance to plead your case.'

I watched Nari walk back to her warriors, recognisable as berserkers by the bones in their hair and the animal pelts over their chain mail. They greeted her with far more affection than they had ever shown me, and as I looked on from a distance, I was reminded that there was a very good reason why Vølund had empowered Nari to act in his stead. She might not have been descended from the Sorceress like I was, but she *looked* like a warrior queen – and I had no doubt that Vølund was her male equivalent. A physical embodiment of the fearsome, ancient Kalurian kings who had ruled long before the Sorceress's line.

Given the distrust between the clans and the Temple, given their wariness of blood magic and a half-Ravalian ruler . . . I was terrified that was *exactly* what Vølund would become. A Kalurian king, with no need for the Temple – or for me.

I slumped back onto the hard ground, studying Darius's ravaged face, the frost clinging to his closed eyelids. I tried to imagine him at peace, finally reunited with my mother, but it didn't work. Despite all the Temple services I had attended, I still didn't believe in an afterlife.

'Come on, Mira.' Jadis and her brother, Elian, helped me stand. Tear-tracks gleamed on Jadis's dark skin, and I remembered Darius telling me that he had taken Jadis and Elian in as children, after their parents were killed by Ravalian Warriors. 'We're no longer protected by the banner of truce – we can't stay here.'

'The berserkers will defend us—'

'No,' Jadis said, an edge to her voice. 'They won't.'

I glanced at the spot where the Kalurian warriors should have been, but saw only an empty ridge. They had left for the Wilds without waiting for my order. Without giving any thought to their queen.

Icy fear speared my heart.

'It will be dark soon,' Jadis pressed, but I didn't need her to convince me of the danger we were in.

Between the three of us, we carried Darius's body across the mountain pass, one painstaking step after another.

The bloodcurdling howls of Roran's hounds followed us all the way back to the Temple.

CHAPTER TWO

Mira

At dawn, the full extent of my failure would become known. Three thousand Kalurian warriors.

Three thousand.

For months they had been stationed in a nearby field for our protection, maintaining a respectful distance. Now they encircled the Temple like a ring of steel, their hands on their swords. Fully prepared to cut down anyone who tried to resist Vølund's authority.

I met their eyes as I passed through their ranks. Most were warriors I had sparred with, warriors who had pledged their loyalty to me and listened as I outlined military campaigns. I hoped they remembered that now. I hoped they looked at me and felt the shame of their actions.

From ruler to glorified prisoner, I thought bitterly. *How quickly loyalty shifts.*

'No one else in or out,' Thoren told me, his voice a harsh rasp. 'Nari's orders.'

I paused on the well-worn sandstone steps. Behind me, I felt Jadis and Elian move closer – guarding my back.

'Surely the priestesses can—'

'No exceptions.'

I held Thoren's gaze, refusing to be intimidated by his hulking build or the emerald tattoos on his pale cheeks, marking him as chieftain of clan Asbjørn. 'Until Vølund makes his decision, I am still your queen. And as your queen,' I said loudly, my words carrying to his companions, 'I am ordering you to make an exception. Those people out there—' I nodded at the makeshift dwellings spanning from the Temple walls to the forest beyond— 'depend on food and water from the Temple stores. Are you willing to have their deaths on your conscience?'

'Vølund will be here soon enough.' Thoren folded his muscular arms. 'He can decide what happens to them then.'

I was so angry I could have taken his axe and gutted him. The Kalurian refugees had been ousted from their homes in the capital – men and women and children who had come here for my help, my *protection*, and now . . .

I had failed them. Just like I had failed Darius.

But I would fix it. Even if it meant crossing a line I had hoped not to.

Straightening my shoulders, I entered the Temple complex. Large doors inlaid with bronze carvings opened into a pillared courtyard, surrounded by colonnades. During the day, the banquet hall and work spaces were filled with cooks busily preparing meals, artisans crafting wood and metal in their workshops, and servants filling store rooms with grain and other necessities. But at night everything was dark and still, people having retired to their living quarters on the level above.

'You should get some rest, Mira,' Jadis said to me, her exhaustion obvious. Her hands were covered in dirt; she and Elian had helped me bury Darius in the forest close to the Temple. 'There's nothing that can be done tonight.'

She was wrong. High above, in the Inner Sanctum, Velanthe would be waiting for me. It had been bad enough seeing the disappointment in Nari's face. It would be even worse to see it in the high priestess's.

But if tonight had shown me anything, it was that Velanthe was right. If I was going to be a true queen, I needed to embrace every advantage at my disposal. Even the ones I found unpalatable.

'Go on without me,' I told Jadis, already turning away from her and Elian. 'I'll see you both tomorrow.'

A set of double doors barred the way to the main domed Temple – almost as tall as the mountain it was built into and fashioned from dark basalt stone. The inside wasn't any more inviting. A faint smell of sulphur wafted from the cavernous chamber far below, where priestesses cleansed themselves in the hot springs before ceremonies. Firelit wall sconces illuminated my way as I followed the curving staircase upwards.

The whisper of silk alerted me before the priestesses came into view, their youthful faces cast in a faint reddish glow. They bowed their heads as I passed into the Inner Sanctum – an imposing expanse of polished black stone, with towering columns holding up a high ceiling.

It had been designed to dwarf those who entered, but as I walked through the echoey chamber, I felt even more insignificant than usual. The Sorceress's life-sized statue dominated the space, a reminder of the legacy I had to live up to. A legacy I was falling short of.

Velanthe was waiting for me at the base of the statue. She raised her hands in ceremonial greeting and the material of her dress moved with her, attached to her arms by fitted black bracelets. As high priestess, she was the only member of the Temple permitted to wear the Sorceress's colour, striking ebony silk criss-crossing her chest before falling to the floor in slitted panels. In front of her was an obsidian altar, usually overflowing with blood offerings.

Tonight, a person was laid out on it instead.

Swallowing down apprehension, I asked, 'Did anyone see you take him from the dungeons?'

'No.' Velanthe set the small bowl on the altar, her auburn braids snaking over her shoulders. 'I made sure there were no witnesses.'

The words chilled me, because there was only one reason she needed to be concerned with witnesses. But I had faced enough death today that the prospect of sending one more soul to the afterlife . . . well, it was still horrifying, but no longer unthinkable.

Not like it had been months earlier, when Velanthe had first informed me of the price blood magic demanded.

I watched the faint rise and fall of the man's chest. As I did, I noticed the smudged, bloody line across his forehead.

My eyes flicked to the bowl Velanthe had set down. The liquid inside was dark and thick.

'I have tried to be patient with you, Kasmira,' Velanthe said, each word as sharp as the blades she kept hidden on her person. 'But we're out of time. Your actions tonight may well have cost us everything.'

I didn't try to make excuses. The simple truth was this: Roran had outplayed me. He had bargained on me choosing to act with my heart, rather than my head. By choosing Darius, I had lost sight of my position as queen. And I had lost Darius anyway – along with Nari and quite possibly any chance I had at saving the Kalurian people.

'I'm glad you appreciate the severity of the situation.' Velanthe's reddish wrist tattoos caught the light as she picked up a ceremonial dagger. She offered it to me, palm up. 'Perhaps now you will be willing to take the necessary steps to *win*.'

Even though I had known it would come to this, I hesitated to take the dagger. 'There has to be another way.'

Velanthe's eyes met mine, as dark and unfathomable as the Sorceress's statue. 'There isn't.'

I stared down at the unconscious Ravalian Warrior. He looked nothing like the Kalurian I had killed during the third Trial, but for a moment that was who I saw in front of me: Governor Halvor, his face filled with resolve as he begged me to end it, to survive another day and find a way to help his – *our* – people.

Fight for them, Kasmira. Promise me.

By killing this man, I would be keeping my promise. But if that was the case, why did I feel as though I was moving further and further away from the ruler I had wanted to be? The ruler my mother had envisioned?

'You're doing the right thing, Kasmira,' Velanthe murmured, placing a reassuring hand on my shoulder.

I wished I could believe that. I wished I had another choice.

But now that Roran had offered Vølund what he had always wanted – the Wilds acknowledged as an independent territory, under his leadership – how long would it be until he handed me over to Roran for execution?

That thought frightened me less than the next. What would happen to the priestesses and refugees who had sought shelter at the Temple? Would Vølund show them mercy, or would he turn them over to Roran as well?

It almost didn't matter. Even if Vølund *did* show them mercy, it would buy the priestesses and refugees time – nothing more. Roran would go back on his promises and destroy the Wilds, unless I was strong enough to stop him.

Satisfaction gleamed in Velanthe's eyes as I took the dagger and sliced it across my palm.

I knelt at the Warrior's side, trying not to notice his dark hair and lightly tanned skin. Trying – and failing – not to be reminded of Aric. But this man was a killer, not my former lover. He was every bit as responsible for the deaths of my people as Roran was.

I have to do this, I thought as I cut his hand and brought our bleeding palms together.

The moment our blood touched, my eyes fluttered closed, hazy images forming in my mind. Flashes of memory. *Not mine,* I told myself, forcing them down as guilt threatened to swallow me.

When my eyes reopened, it was as if I could see *through* his skin. Reddish tendrils were everywhere, infesting his blood. I was connected to all of them; his body and mind under my complete control.

As if from a long distance away, I heard Velanthe's voice. 'Remember, it's all about control and intention.'

I held onto her words, willing myself to focus. My gaze went to the pulse pounding in his neck. His heart – pumping blood through his veins.

I willed it to slow.

That was all it took – one thought. His heartbeat stuttered, its natural rhythm faltering—

Emotion crashed over me like a wave, the man's mind waking up to what was happening a second too late to stop it. Panic, fear, confusion – I felt everything he did as he fought me uselessly for control, his heart straining, fighting to keep beating even as I willed it to stop completely.

The wave of emotion crested, and the current swept us both under.

I dreamt in red.

'Drink this.'

Velanthe's pale face swam into view. She was holding something to my lips – something smoking.

I spluttered at the resulting burn and shifted into a seated position. I was still in the Inner Sanctum, though it was no longer night-time; sunlight filtered through the balcony at the far end of the cavernous space.

'How long was I out?'

'Almost a full day,' Velanthe said. 'I warned you; blood magic demands much from the wielder. I'll make up more tonic and have it sent to your chambers to help with the after-effects. But don't rely on it. Its numbing properties can be addictive.'

I nodded, biting back a gasp at the pain in my skull. 'Did it work? Is he . . .'

'His soul is at peace,' Velanthe said, her voice soft. 'And now that the sacrifice has been made, you will be able to use your blood magic at will. The priestesses would be more than eager to play a role in your training – I'm sure I can find a few volunteers.'

Of that, I had no doubt. The priestesses were desperate for me to embrace my magic – not just because of their Temple ideology, but because they believed Kalure's survival depended on it. Still—

'No volunteers,' I said firmly. 'Not after what I did to Odessa.'

A trace of impatience entered Velanthe's voice. 'Odessa would be the first to thank you. You took away her emotional pain – and replaced it with purpose.'

I thought of how I had tried to comfort her in the wake of her parents' deaths – of how uncontrollably my blood magic had risen up. Trying to impress on Odessa that she was safe, that she had finally found somewhere she belonged.

Purpose? I wondered, recalling how deferential she was to Velanthe now, how deeply she believed in the Sorceress and the Temple. How fiercely she believed in *me. Or servitude?*

'We only have a short window to rectify your mistake with Nari,' the high priestess continued. 'Vølund is already on his way, and he *must* stand with us – or Kalure will fall, the Wilds and the Temple along with it.'

My throat went dry, because I understood what she was really asking. 'You know how the clans feel about blood magic. If I use it and Vølund even *suspects*—'

'If you use your magic properly, he won't know you've influenced him.' Velanthe straightened, the firelight catching on her dress and sending it sparkling. 'There's something else,' she said. 'Vølund is aware that we have Roran's brother in the dungeons. He specifically requested an audience.'

'With *Cassius?*'

A terse nod. 'There are rumours you and Cassius were responsible for Emperor Kalias's assassination. Perhaps the clan leader wishes to speak to you both about your reasons.' Velanthe paused. 'Or perhaps his motive is more personal. You were engaged to Cassius. Vølund might wonder about your relationship, and what that says about your character.'

Judging by her slightly pained expression, my choice to lock up my ex-fiancé and alleged partner in crime didn't paint me in the best light. Ordinarily I wouldn't care, but I was counting on Roran's history of conquering and absorbing countries into the Ravalian Empire to count against him. I couldn't risk coming off equally untrustworthy and losing whatever chance I had at salvaging this alliance.

'Can we deny that Cassius is here? Tell Vølund some lie?'

'Too many Kalurians saw Cassius when you first arrived. But this meeting could work in our favour. While Vølund is unlikely to believe anything you tell him about Roran's character, it will be harder to dismiss testimony from a family member.'

'Fine.' I sighed. 'Accept Vølund's terms. I'll speak to Cassius – I know he's eager to be let out of the dungeons. With any luck, the threat of a return visit will keep him in line.' I smiled wryly. 'The idea of meeting a clan leader and foiling Roran's plans might be enough motivation on its own. He thrives on political intrigue.'

I turned, but Velanthe's voice called me back. To my surprise, a smile curved her red lips.

'And Kasmira? If Cassius can't be controlled by ordinary means, remember, you have other methods at your disposal.'

Though she made it sound like an afterthought, I knew it wasn't. I paused, staring into Velanthe's glittering eyes.

'I thought I made myself clear,' I said, a bite of anger in my voice.

'I listened to every word,' Velanthe replied, holding up her hands in a pacifying gesture. 'There will be no priestess volunteers. But perhaps there is no need for them. Sometimes, all that's needed is the right motivation.'

Like a country hanging in the balance. And my reluctance to risk a life-saving alliance on the word of a duplicitous Ravalian prince.

If ever there was a good reason to use my magic, it was to help Kalure. And what better way to hone my abilities than by practising on someone who despised me? Someone whose personality I didn't mind altering, because quite frankly, any alteration would be an improvement?

Maybe Velanthe was right.

Maybe this was exactly the motivation I needed.

CHAPTER THREE

Scarlett

I barely noticed the wounded and dying men as I strode past. After years of shadowing the emperor on his military campaigns, corpses and bloodstains had ceased to bother me.

It was a pity I couldn't say the same for Lillian.

She hurried to keep up with my longer stride, her white skirts – entirely impractical for a battlefield – caked in blood and dirt.

'How do you stand it?' she asked, her voice faint. 'It's horrible.'

'It's war,' I said, without looking at her. 'It's not meant to be pleasant.'

I hadn't listened to Zandri when she recommended I stay behind, safe inside the palace walls. My father had been a lot of things, but never a coward. Who would respect a future empress who didn't fight her own battles?

So instead, I had made the arduous journey to the Western Lands. Had endured three days of blistering heat to reach Zigilia, only to spend another two months camped outside Damar, repelling skirmishes and waiting for the insurgents to run out of what seemed to be an endless supply of food and water.

I clenched my jaw as I stared at the fortified walls of Damar, hating them more than I had ever hated anything. Under different circumstances, I might have found my surroundings beautiful: the green oasis where my army had set up camp, the rocky mountains silhouetted behind Damar's high walls, and the reddish sand dunes of the Sanguine Desert.

But the sand dunes weren't the only thing encircling the city.

It was also surrounded by a moat of corpses. A tangible sign of my continuing failure to take Damar.

'It's him, isn't it? Severin.' A frown puckered Lillian's dainty brows. 'You think he might have fled here. That's why you walk amongst the bodies; you're checking to make sure he's not one of them.'

I hadn't expected Lillian to make the connection, and it irritated me. But I tried to suppress the emotion, knowing that Lillian would feel that, too – which seemed exceedingly unfair, since I couldn't magically perceive *her* emotions.

'It doesn't matter,' I said sharply. 'Severin left the Ravalian Court. *If* he came here, to muster forces against me and my family, then he's committed treason and will need to be punished for it. It might be better if he *is* dead.'

Wisely, Lillian remained silent – though I doubted she believed me. She had been by my side when I'd scoured the Ravalian palace for Severin, sending out search parties every morning. She had felt the same pain I had when I'd been informed, again and again, that it was useless. Severin had vanished.

Lillian stopped abruptly and crouched down, peering intently at the body of a Warrior. I waved a hand in front of my face, trying to dispel the crowd of flies buzzing around the corpses.

'He's alive,' Lillian announced, her face pale but determined. 'Look – see? His chest is moving.'

'If he is alive, the healers will carry him back on a stretcher.' I started walking, but Lillian's voice called me back.

'We can't just *leave* him here.'

'And what do you suggest we do?' I asked with fraying patience. '*Drag* him back to camp? That would defeat the purpose of trying to save his life, don't you think?'

Lillian narrowed her eyes stubbornly. 'At the very least, we should tell the healers where he is. Maybe I can wait here, and—'

'I have a strategy meeting in an hour. I can't be distracted, worrying about you and some random soldier.'

'You can be cruel sometimes,' Lillian said softly. Even in their softness, her words were cutting.

I strode away, not bothering to check that Lillian was following.

Ever since I had brought her back to life, I always knew exactly where she was.

'Those men fought and died for *you*,' Lillian muttered.

'They fought and died for the empire,' I corrected, and tried not to think about how many men I'd lost today.

Even a costly victory is better than a defeat, I reminded myself. But they weren't my words.

They were my father's.

The crimson pavilion was surrounded by four armed men – two outfitted in Warrior black, and two wearing the golden armour of normal soldiers. I had insisted upon it.

The custom was for royals to be guarded by the Order of Warriors – men and women with magical strength and speed – but I couldn't trust them. Roran had been their royal patron, after all. Now, as our father's heir, he was only a formal coronation away from becoming emperor.

It was a dangerous edge to balance on, overseeing a war in my half-brother's name. I wore a crown and commanded immense resources, but I was constantly looking over my shoulder – and so were the Masks Zandri had sent with me for protection. Yet Roran seemed content to leave me alive for now.

If Zandri's spies were correct, and they usually were, he was wholly focused on his military campaign in Kalure. No doubt his arrogance demanded that he assert full control over the country before returning, victorious, to officially claim the Ravalian throne.

Which couldn't happen. If Roran ever returned to Ravalia, it would have to be in a coffin. Because if he returned and was crowned—

One battle at a time, I told myself. *Focus on the enemies* inside *your borders*. Then *the ones in the North*.

General Harte and his officers had already begun the meeting inside, seated around a circular wooden table with a map spread out in front of them. Disrespectful, but I wasn't surprised. The general was a bullish, unpleasant man who had no love for me – or any woman in a position of power. Only Aric and Avril – whose presence I had personally requested – were truly on my side.

Chairs scraped back at my arrival. Led by the grim-faced General Harte, the officers bowed their heads, with murmurs of, 'Princess.'

'I invited you here,' I said, taking a seat at the head of the table, 'to advise on our next move.'

'We simply wait them out,' General Harte said, his voice a low rumble.

'We've been here for two months without progress, General. The army is restless, and I'm losing patience.'

'It's important that we all hold our nerve, Your Highness.' This was said with an edge of condescension, but his statement was ambiguous enough that I couldn't challenge him on it. 'The Zigilians rely on water and food sources outside their city walls. Now that we've seized those, they don't have the resources to withstand a siege indefinitely.'

'Neither do *we*,' I said impatiently. 'Yes, we have access to the oasis, to their livestock and their date palm farms. But feeding an army is no small task, and the Zigilians know that. We've been waiting them out for months now, and we're no closer to stopping this rebellion.'

'War takes time, Your Highness,' General Harte said, in the same indulgent tone he had used when I was a child. 'With all due respect, I've served the emperor well on many battle campaigns. It may be best to leave strategy to me.'

'Every day,' I said, fighting to keep my voice calm, 'more Warriors die outside Damar's walls—'

'—and the losses are always heavier on our enemy's side. You yourself refer to them as minor skirmishes.'

I referred to them as *skirmishes* rather than *battles* because that was what my father had always done. A skirmish was a minor act of rebellion, a tantrum that could be put down by our superior forces. But with continuing losses, and no sign of action, it wouldn't matter what I called them. I would lose the support of my army, and if that happened, I would never rule the Ravalian Empire – even if I was the last of my siblings still standing. Conspiring with Zandri to kill my father, framing Mira and Cassius for his death, losing Severin in the process . . . it would all have been for nothing.

And that was unacceptable.

'Emperor Kalias's assassination has emboldened the insurgents,'

I continued, 'and they're not the only ones. Dozens of other countries are watching this war with interest, deciding whether to follow suit and rebel. We need to make an example of Zigilia.' I turned my attention to the rest of the officers. They might be loyal to the general, but surely they could see the flaws in his plan. 'This can't be a slow war, fought with endurance and rations. It must be a fast and decisive victory. Otherwise, we'll face rebellion on multiple fronts.'

Avril leant forward, bracing her forearms against the table. Her dark, braided hair was pulled back, accentuating her deep brown eyes and sharp cheekbones.

'Not all Zigilians are against us,' she pointed out. 'Many were content to live peacefully under Ravalian rule. Perhaps they can be convinced to turn against the insurgents.'

'A convenient suggestion,' General Harte said coldly, 'considering your Zigilian heritage.'

'That heritage,' Avril retorted, 'is what makes my opinions valuable. Unlike you, General Harte, I know the Zigilian culture. I'm sure you can agree it's better to understand your opponent in war.'

'It's also important to know your enemies.' General Harte's face was hard. 'And I don't trust operatives from the Order of Masks. Let alone Zigilian ones.'

'How dare you.' The muscles in Avril's bare arms flexed, and I suspected she was imagining wrapping her hands around General Harte's throat. I sympathised with the impulse. 'I took the same oath of loyalty as you did. I can no more betray the Ravalian Empire than—'

'No one is doubting your loyalty,' I cut in. 'Zandri herself recommended you as the next governor of Zigilia, and I hold your strategic insights in high esteem. Particularly as there are no other useful suggestions.' This last part was said for General Harte's benefit, whose face hardened even further. A few of the other officers visibly bristled.

Across the table, Aric frowned at me. *Don't push him*, that frown said.

'Leave us.' At my order, the officers rose and filed out. When General Harte moved to follow, I shook my head. 'I would prefer that you stay. Aella?' My attendant rushed over, her head bowed. 'Please organise some refreshment for General Harte.' More quietly, I said, 'And tell Avril to send a Mask operative to his tent. I want to know his latest correspondence with Roran.'

Aella nodded and retreated, her copper plait bouncing.

As the interior of the pavilion darkened, servants lit fire braziers, casting General Harte's face into harsh relief. From the perspiration beading on his forehead, I knew that the fire had made the already warm space uncomfortably hot. Several servants had fainted from heatstroke today alone – but my skin remained unnaturally pale and cool, just as it had since I had drowned and come back to life.

To General Harte, however, my pristine appearance only served as proof that I was better suited to a pampered life amongst the ladies of the Ravalian Court. I wondered whether his perspective would change if he knew I had murdered my father.

Aella set cool pitchers of water in front of us. The General gulped his down, unconcerned with appearances.

I watched him, conscious of Aric's earlier warning. But I was tired of playing politics, and I suspected we both appreciated candour.

'You're being deliberately difficult,' I accused him while Aella refilled the pitcher. 'I know you don't like me, General Harte, but a win in Zigilia is a win for the entire Ravalian Empire.'

'Personal feelings have no place in battle, Your Highness. While I understand you're unhappy with the war, it's—'

'It's an *embarrassment*, that's what it is!'

'May I speak frankly?'

I drummed my steel nail guards against the table, imagining the lethal points slicing through General Harte's skin. 'Of course.'

'I worked with your father on many campaigns. I am respected amongst the men, and my track record is not in question here. Whereas *you* . . .' He paused, then continued more diplomatically, 'This is your first time in a leadership capacity. The army tolerates your presence, but they follow me.'

This wasn't an exaggeration. Without General Harte's support – such as it was – I risked losing the already tenuous support of the Warriors, who attributed this disastrous campaign to my leadership and lack of experience.

'Forgive me, General,' I said with a simpering smile – the kind that suited the court lady he believed me to be. 'I didn't mean to question your authority. I am simply anxious for this war to end.'

'As are we all, Princess,' General Harte said, magnanimous now that he had won. Without waiting to be dismissed, he stood. 'Why don't you retire to your tent and allow your servants to tend to you? Leave the bloody business of war to me.'

General Harte turned his back on me like it was nothing. I watched him walk away, tracking his movements with narrowed eyes.

He had made a mistake, believing he could push me so far without consequences.

A mistake that may well prove fatal.

CHAPTER FOUR

Scarlett

I closed my eyes, revelling in the sensation of the wind whipping through my hair and the feeling that I was leaving the entire world far behind.

'Faster,' I instructed, raising my voice to be heard over the pounding of the horse's hooves. Sand plumed behind us under the starry night sky.

I couldn't see Aric's face, but I suspected he was grinning. The Zigilian stallion lunged forward, propelled to new speeds. My hands tightened around Aric's waist, hanging on for dear life.

As we galloped through the red dunes, I thought that few things could match this. For a handful of glorious seconds, I was truly free.

'Faster,' I said again, letting out an exhilarated gasp that neither of us heard.

I wanted to reach a speed fast enough to leave reality behind. I wanted to forget all about General Harte and the officers waiting for me to fail. I wanted to forget Roran and Zandri and my guilt around Severin's disappearance.

I wanted to forget *everything*.

'Easy there, princess,' Aric called over his shoulder, amusement thick in his voice.

'I didn't think of you as the cautious type,' I retorted, leaning in until my lips were against the back of his neck.

He chuckled, but the horse was already slowing. I glanced back as we reached the crest of a dune. The Ravalian camp was no longer visible except for the faint glow of fire torches – pinpricks of light from here. They reminded me of fireflies.

Aric slid off the stallion and reached up for me. I allowed him to help me down, his hands steady on my waist. The warmth of his body settled against mine as my boots sank into the sand. I gazed up into Aric's golden-brown eyes, conscious of how close we were.

'Thank you,' I said, softer than I'd intended. 'I needed that.'

'My pleasure,' Aric said, flashing his teeth in a smile. 'I'm here if you ever need a distraction.'

It sounded like an invitation for a different kind of distraction. I tilted my head, considering him in the moonlight.

Like Severin, Aric seemed born for the Western sun, his skin having darkened to a deep brown. Two months of battle and death hadn't dimmed the fierce energy about him.

Never again, I had told Aric the last time. But I had never been particularly good at practising restraint.

I tilted his chin to mine, not breaking eye contact. This time, when I kissed him, it was with less finesse and more demand. He didn't seem to mind. His lips yielded to mine, his arms pulling me closer. The desert breeze swirled around us, and as my hair broke free of its braid, so did something inside of me.

I pushed back against the weight of him, shameless in my want, my *need*, as I slid his tunic up. Aric pulled it over his head, until he was standing before me in nothing but those tight leather breeches. So tight they fitted him like a second skin, allowing me to see exactly how much he wanted me.

I ran my hands over the contoured muscles of his chest, tracing the long scar that ran from his sternum to his navel. My desire softened along with my hands, transforming into something else. Something close to tenderness.

'I would do it again,' Aric murmured against my lips. 'In a heartbeat.'

My pulse quickened at his words even more than his bruising kiss. I had no doubt that he meant it. Aric had proven his devotion when he stepped in front of that swordsman for me. Shielding me with his own body.

And such devotion should be rewarded.

I pushed Aric onto the warm sand and rose to straddle him. Smiling with feline satisfaction at the look in his eyes, I kissed my way down the scar he had earned for me, revelling in the sound of his soft gasp.

But impatience was something we had in common. The desert heat ghosted over my bare skin as Aric shifted into a seated position, untying the strings of my blouse.

And then it was my turn to gasp. Fire spread across my icy skin, coaxed to life by his mouth – even as his fingers worked to remove the last barriers between us, until his skin was pressed against mine.

My legs wrapped around his waist, guiding him into me. Pleasure sparked between us, a flint turning into a flame, until I could barely think for how much I wanted this. Wanted *him*.

I let my head fall back, my worries along with it. I had done terrible things to get to this point.

But it was hard to regret my decisions when Aric was my reward.

I lingered on the dune for as long as I dared.

A stolen moment in time – that was what this was. Bittersweet and slightly too familiar.

But I allowed Aric to stroke my hair, even as my mind drifted to another moment. Another man.

At last, I said, 'You know nothing can come of this. We can never have a real relationship.'

Aric's fingers stilled in my hair. When he spoke, however, there was no anger in his voice – only amusement. 'I don't have any expectations, Scarlett. I certainly don't have any designs on a crown.'

'Well, that makes this easier,' I drawled, but the smile quickly slid off my face. 'What are you doing?'

'We've stayed too long already,' Aric said, standing.

I watched him, caught between irritation and admiration. Though it was dark, I hadn't seen him completely naked before – and it was difficult not to look. Even more difficult not to act on all the things I still wanted to do with him. *To* him.

Aric smiled, as if he knew exactly what I was thinking. But he merely offered me his hand.

I took it with an exasperated sigh. As I stood, I swept my hair back over my shoulder, allowing him the opportunity to admire *me—*

A wasted effort, it seemed. My eyes narrowed as I watched Aric hunt for our clothes.

'The perils of sleeping with my personal guard, I suppose,' I remarked, as I accepted my blouse and breeches from him.

Aric's soft laugh was my only answer. But I felt the way his touch lingered as he helped me mount the horse.

A smile upturned my lips. *Not all business after all.*

The stallion snorted and tossed its head, impatient to return to camp. I didn't share its eagerness, and I suspected that Aric didn't either. Neither of us pushed the horse to go faster than a smooth canter.

I was close enough to Aric that I felt him stiffen.

My eyes searched the blackness, though I already knew what had captured his attention. Every night, under the cover of darkness, a long line of carts carried bodies out into the desert – where Ravalian soldiers were buried with respect, and Zigilian soldiers were left exposed to the elements. It was an unnecessary cruelty that both Aric and I had argued against, but our opinions had been dismissed.

The carts were little more than dark smudges, making it difficult to see the piles of bodies. Still, I could *feel* them: there were so many that, even from a distance, I could sense the presence of death. Oddly enough, I could sense the carrion birds too. They were native to the Western Lands – skeletal birds with bright red talons and a maw of razor-sharp teeth.

As we rode past, the metallic taste of blood flooded my mouth. It should have been repulsive, but I was used to it. My affinity for death had grown since bringing Lillian back to life.

My tent came into view, visible thanks to its torches and the guards stationed outside. We slowed to a trot, and then to a walk. Aric nodded to my guards as he pulled back on the reins.

Courteous as ever, he dismounted first and lifted me down from the saddle. I reluctantly stepped out of his arms, but my eyes remained on his. With my father dead, and Roran in Kalure, there was no one to punish Aric if I invited him to spend the night in my tent.

Stay. That was all I needed to say, and for an instant, I considered it. The strength of my own yearning caught me by surprise.

But the flickering fire cast strange shadows on Aric's face, and I knew who that yearning was really for. Sometimes it was a little too easy to pretend he was Severin.

'Goodnight, Aric.' I softened the dismissal with a smile.

I opened the flap of my tent. The interior was lit with torches and covered with cushions. But the desk in the middle of the space was already occupied.

Avril glanced up at my arrival. We hadn't spoken since after my meeting with General Harte, when she had warned me that I couldn't kill him. I understood her reasons, but unless she provided me with another alternative, I wouldn't have a choice.

Thankfully, it seemed she was here to give me one.

'You found something?'

'More of the usual.' Avril gestured to the table. 'I made copies. I knew you would want to see them.'

The latest message from Roran to General Harte was short and to the point:

Continue stalling. Contain the insurgents but don't defeat them. I'll deal with them upon my return.

−R

'He doesn't mention me this time,' I said with a wry smile. 'No "well done making Scarlett look incompetent in the eyes of the army". I thought he'd take the opportunity to gloat, since that was his goal all along.'

Avril didn't laugh. She was the serious sort, but her single-minded focus would serve her well as the Zigilian governor. 'After your meeting, General Harte composed a new message to Roran. I intercepted it before it could be sent. You might find it interesting.'

I glanced down at the message, written in General Harte's blocky handwriting. *Scarlett is getting restless. I'm worried she might return to the Ravalian Court if something isn't done. How would you like me to proceed?*

'Can you imitate Roran's handwriting?' I asked.

'One of the other Masks is skilled at creating forgeries.'

'Perfect.' For the first time all week, my smile was completely genuine. 'I think it's time we sent General Harte some orders of our own.'

CHAPTER FIVE

Mira

The market in the courtyard was thriving.

Priestesses pressed coins into vendors' hands with warm smiles, while privileged men and women haggled over prices as though there weren't desperate refugees outside our walls. I understood the reason for the pretence; we needed to keep up morale, to pretend that we weren't surrounded by thousands of Vølund's fighters. But it reminded me too much of the Ravalian Court; the sickening divide between the rich nobles in the palace and the desperate people in the Lower Districts.

'You're scowling, Mira.'

I didn't flinch at the sound of Odessa's soft voice. As a member of the Order of Masks, she had a talent for disappearing into the shadows – and Velanthe had been quick to take advantage of it, asking Odessa to keep an eye on me. A job that she took very seriously, when she wasn't kneeling before the Sorceress's altar with the rest of the priestesses.

'I haven't had the best morning,' I replied. 'I've been fielding constant questions about Nari's return, which means lying through my teeth – all while worrying that Vølund will accept Roran's deal.'

'He won't.' This time, Odessa's voice was like steel. 'The Temple will never let that happen.'

So certain. So unwavering in her dedication.

But Odessa's expression softened as she gazed across the market, and as I noticed the direction of her gaze, I also noticed that she looked particularly beautiful today. Her hair was braided back from her face, but she had left half of it loose, allowing it to cascade down her shoulders in white-blonde waves.

'Are you going to talk to her?' I asked, nodding towards where Jadis was speaking with two other female warriors.

Odessa started guiltily. 'Why would I do that?'

'You're friends, aren't you?' I said with careful nonchalance. 'The two of you were practically inseparable when we first arrived.'

'Jadis distrusts the Temple. She didn't agree with my decision to become a priestess.'

I thought Jadis had a point, but I didn't say so. Nothing I said would make a difference – not unless I admitted to using blood magic on Odessa, and even that might not be enough to dissuade her.

As if to reinforce the thought, Odessa said, 'You should have more faith. Why don't you join me at the next service? You always keep yourself so separate.'

'I'm busy,' I hedged. 'I have a lot of responsibilities that take up my time.'

Odessa made a soft sound of agreement. 'Particularly when Cassius is one of those responsibilities.'

I frowned. 'Did Velanthe tell you that?'

She shrugged, casting a discerning eye over the market. The wooden stalls were stacked with items: clothes, shawls, and jewels caught my eye, but I was drawn to the weapons too. Most were on the daintier side, clearly targeted towards the priestesses.

Odessa picked up a thin, ornamental knife. I watched her weigh it in her palm, thinking of our time in the Order of Masks. Back then, she had worn revealing clothes and walked with a swagger that faintly imitated Cassius's. It was difficult to reconcile the young woman I'd known with the one in front of me, dressed in the breezy material of a Temple acolyte. Without makeup or the flashy jewellery she used to favour, she seemed years younger. Almost vulnerable.

'Cassius will still be under guard,' I reassured her. 'I'm not freeing him. I'm just—'

'Using him.' Odessa set down the knife with more force than necessary. 'That's how it always starts, Mira. Someone goes to Cassius because they need something, and they think they know the price of his help. But they never do.'

A thrill of foreboding darted down my spine, because she could have been referring to the deal I'd made with Cassius in the Ravalian Court. A deal that had cost me my freedom and Odessa's parents their lives.

Yet another secret I was keeping from her. One I would have to take to my grave.

'Velanthe mentioned the clan leader's request for an audience,' Odessa continued tightly. 'I presume that's why you're here – looking for a gift to make Cassius more malleable?'

'The thought had occurred to me,' I replied. 'But I haven't seen anything that stands out.'

'You're looking in the wrong place.' Odessa grabbed my arm and drew me away from the weapons. 'If you want to win Cassius over, there's no point buying him some trinket. He'll see through such an obvious tactic in a heartbeat.'

'So what would you suggest? Turn up empty-handed?'

'I'm sure Cassius can be tempted into a deal regardless. But that's not what I'm suggesting.' Odessa paused in front of a stall, and I sucked in a startled breath.

Memories of Lillian resurfaced as I stared down at the dresses, which resembled the flowing designs my friend had created in the Elusive Isles. For a moment, it was a pleasant reminder of a simpler time.

But only for a moment.

She died *for you.* Aric's parting words echoed in my mind, vicious and cold and filled with heart-wrenching pain. *And it is only because of that, Mira, that I'm here right now. That I'm willing to let you leave.*

Suddenly, I couldn't stand to be here. Not for another second.

But the two women were already bowing to me, and leaving too quickly would be seen as an insult. I forced a smile, noting the familial resemblance between them – not enough to make me think of siblings, but perhaps cousins.

Like me and Scarlett, except entirely different. I doubted either of *them* would impersonate the other and frame them for murder.

'That's the dress,' Odessa said with a grimly satisfied smile. The gown that had captured her attention wasn't the same as the ones that reminded me of Lillian. This dress was black and fitted with a tight bodice, no sleeves, and gold stencilling through the skirt. 'Cassius won't be able to look away.'

'He's in a cell. He won't be able to look away regardless.'

'If you don't want my advice—'

'I didn't say that. Of course I do.' I sighed as I turned to address the vendors. 'How much?'

I took a deep breath, revelling in the silence.

Since arriving in Kalure, I was rarely alone: guards dogged my every step, ordinary citizens petitioned me on a daily basis, and then there were my lessons with Velanthe on the Sorceress's teachings, Kalurian history and magic.

There was never a complete respite from being queen, but entering the dungeons came close.

Taking Odessa's advice, I'd worn the gown I purchased from the market, and left my hair down and unbraided. I'd ordered the guards to leave half an hour earlier, which should have piqued Cassius's interest. Two goblets dangled from my hand, along with a bottle of red wine – spiked with my blood.

According to Velanthe, once Cassius ingested enough of my blood, I should be able to sense and influence his emotional ties. Mixing our blood together would be more effective, but unless I was prepared to physically restrain Cassius, this was the most practical course of action.

Not that I felt entirely comfortable with this plan. It felt too calculated. Premeditated.

Like something Cassius would do.

The irony wasn't lost on me. Here I was, worrying about the morality of using magic on someone who wouldn't give it a second thought. If Cassius could have used a similar power to compel me to stay in the Ravalian Court and marry him, I had no doubt that he would have.

I straightened my shoulders, refusing to entertain second thoughts. But as I descended into the bowels of the Temple, I was reminded uncomfortably of my time in the Ravalian dungeons. Had I done the right thing, condemning Cassius to two months alone in the dark?

Then his cell came into view, and my sympathy evaporated. If anyone could turn punishment into a reward, it was Cassius.

I stared at the tapestries and rugs with begrudging amusement.

The guards had even dragged a divan down here, which Cassius was currently reclining on, eating dates from a nearby table. His golden-blond hair was longer, but he was as clean-shaven as I remembered – most likely another request granted by his guards. Gone were the perfectly tailored dress pants and high-collared tunics, replaced by brown leather breeches and a coarse linen shirt. Somehow, even that managed to look infuriatingly good on him. Almost *princely*.

'Why don't you join me?' Cassius motioned carelessly to the plush chairs opposite his divan. 'Sometimes the guards do. For Kalurians, they seem to like me well enough.'

'It certainly seems like you've settled in,' I said sweetly.

'Don't gloat. It's unbecoming.' He shot me a narrow-eyed stare. 'I never did anything this terrible to you.'

'No. You just promised the Kalurians freedom, without ever intending to follow through on that promise.'

Cassius said nothing for a moment, which was as good as a confession. 'I was hoping that by the time we were married, you wouldn't want to give them their independence. It's difficult to relinquish power once you have it.' His gaze shifted to my head – to the emerald crown that rested there. It was shaped into a wreath, primal and beautiful, matching the symbol emblazoned on my mother's locket.

'It isn't just Kalure.' I approached the bars. 'You lied to me about what would happen to Odessa and her family after we discredited General Tiran. You did all of that just to make me your fiancée instead, because *I* could give you a *country*. Then you tried to kill Aric—'

'That, I *didn't* do.'

'The hunt was your idea!'

'I don't deny that.'

'But you *do* deny bribing a stableboy to incorrectly saddle Aric's horse? He nearly died from that fall, which I'm sure would have suited you just fine. You knew how I felt about him.'

Cassius shrugged. 'I wouldn't have mourned Aric's death, but when *I* try to kill someone, I don't choose a method that leaves so many things to chance. My sister, on the other hand . . . she can be a little more *theatrical*.'

Scarlett had tried to kill Aric? No – not kill him, I realised. She had only wanted to scare me away from Cassius and the Ravalian Court. And she had succeeded, because of my desperation to protect Aric.

My chest tightened at the thought, and I was surprised by how much it hurt. I still didn't know exactly what had happened the night I fled Ravalia, but I knew that *someone* had impersonated me and Cassius. Someone who had gone to great pains to keep us away from the palace, and who had access to powerful illusion magic.

It shouldn't have surprised me that Scarlett was behind Aric's accident as well. Whatever had been between the three of us – whatever trust and friendship we had established – no longer mattered. Ambition and power had won out in the end.

Cassius smiled at whatever expression was on my face. 'Very clever, wasn't she? Even I didn't see her betrayal coming.'

I bit back a scathing comment about his duplicitous family. Cassius had made plenty of horrible decisions, but right now, I needed him on my side.

'Would you like some wine?' I asked, raising the goblets so he could see them.

'That depends. Will you come inside, Mira?'

It was disconcerting, hearing my preferred name on his lips. And I didn't like the edge of amusement in his sensuous voice – or the way he stood and approached the bars, turning his question into a challenge.

'I notice you have the key.' His gaze dipped – from my eyes down to my neck. 'I was surprised to see you wearing it like a trophy. Does it make you feel powerful, having such control over me?'

'It wasn't a deliberate choice,' I said defensively. 'It was just convenient. I don't have pockets.'

'And I suppose that dress is another convenient choice?' His amused gaze raked over me. 'What about the bottle of wine and the absence of my guards?' Before I could respond, he said, 'Believe me when I say that I appreciate the effort, but if you want my help, all you have to do is *ask*.'

My face flushed, his words bringing back memories of the first Trial – when I had seduced him in order to steal his crown. *If you wanted to meet with me privately, Kasmira*, he had murmured, *all you had to do was ask.*

'Fine,' I admitted. 'I have an agenda. If anyone should understand that, it's you.'

Cassius drew back from the bars, still smiling. He motioned to the door. 'The first rule of negotiation – each party has to give *something*. You can't have all the control, Mira. No matter how much it suits you.'

Ignoring his backhanded compliment, I reluctantly removed the necklace. Even as I inserted the key in the lock, I suspected that I was making a mistake. But I'd come this far – and I refused to let Cassius believe I was afraid of him. He was in Kalure, and here, *I* made the rules.

Yet somehow, he had managed to burrow under my skin. *Like a parasite.*

I locked the door behind me, a decision that made Cassius's smile widen – and my heart flutter with the knowledge that both of us were now trapped inside. But it was Cassius who should be nervous.

My grip tightened on the wine bottle. I was no longer the desperate girl he had met in the Ravalian Court. I was every bit as dangerous as Cassius and his siblings.

And every bit as willing to play the game.

CHAPTER SIX

Mira

'You didn't need to dress up for me,' Cassius remarked as I walked further into the cell. 'But I'm glad you did.'

'I'm glad you like the outfit,' I replied, 'since I bought it with you in mind.'

As I'd expected, Cassius seemed pleased by my honesty. Subterfuge appealed to him – but he respected boldness more.

He leant back in one of the plush chairs and I took the seat next to him. All that separated us was a small table; I set down the bottle and two glasses, pouring a decent amount of wine into both.

'So,' I said, crossing my legs, 'how about that drink?'

Suspicion and intrigue battled for dominance in his midnight-blue eyes. He didn't trust me much more than I trusted him. But that was what made this so entertaining.

He reached for the glass closest to my end of the table. I raised an eyebrow. 'Worried I'm trying to poison you?'

'Are you?' He swirled the red liquid in his glass.

'No,' I replied, matching his nonchalance. 'If I was going to kill you, I think I would do it with a blade. If memory serves, I've already had that chance.'

'How could I forget?' Cassius's tone was light, but he still hadn't taken a sip.

'You're not really afraid of me, are you?' There it was again: that disconcerting, misplaced sympathy. 'I know Odessa told you that the Kalurians wanted you executed, but I never considered killing you.' Not seriously, anyway.

'You locked me up for months.' It was impossible to tell what Cassius was thinking; there was no inflection in his voice.

'I was angry. You betrayed me – in so many ways.'

'So this was your idea of punishment?' Cassius looked almost curious. As if he genuinely wanted to know the answer.

'I didn't know what to do with you.' I threw my hands in the air. 'You're an enemy prince in an enemy nation. What would *you* have done in my position?'

'A set of proper chambers might have been a bit more palatable.'

'Except I *know* you. How long would it have been until you found a way to correspond with Roran or Scarlett? I couldn't risk that.'

'I've told you that I don't trust my siblings. *Especially* Roran.'

'And I've told you that I don't trust you. You've lied too many times.'

Cassius stood abruptly. His sudden movement caught me by surprise, as did the emotion simmering beneath the surface. 'I couldn't tell you the truth about Odessa. You never would have helped me implicate the general if you'd known her parents would be executed – and we never could have gotten my father out of the way without removing General Tiran.'

'It was more than that, though, wasn't it?' I said, sipping the wine. I couldn't taste my blood, but my stomach churned with the knowledge that it was there. 'You said it yourself – what use was Odessa in comparison to me?'

'That comment really bothered you, didn't it?' Cassius's smile – more of a smirk – greeted me as he sank back into his seat.

I ignored his remark. 'There was another reason I left you down here. Even if I could have trusted your motives, I didn't trust the Kalurians not to hurt you. They tolerate the other Ravalians, but as Roran's brother . . . this was the best solution I could think of.'

Cassius sipped the wine, but his eyes remained on my face. 'So you had my best interests at heart.'

'Your safety was something I considered,' I replied, keeping my tone level. He was trying to get a rise out of me, and I refused to give him the satisfaction. 'One of *many* factors in my decision.'

'And can that decision be reversed?'

I set down my goblet.

Cassius took another sip. I had the sense he was thinking very intently, but his voice was measured. 'You haven't visited me since my imprisonment. Coming here, dressed like that—' he waved a hand over my outfit— 'bringing wine, being *pleasant* . . . you want something from me. Do you expect me to guess what that is? Or will you tell me?'

'Don't you want to spend more time reminiscing first? Looking back on all the good times?'

Where my voice had been sugary sweet, his was deadpan. 'If that's what you prefer.'

I sighed and stood, even though it meant acknowledging he'd called my bluff. I crossed the cell to stand in front of the tapestries, assuming it would be easier to look at them than it would be to face Cassius.

'Forest scenes?' They were strangely simple – and wholesome – for someone who had a reputation for throwing luxurious and debauched parties back in the Ravalian Court.

Cassius strolled over to my side. 'I find them . . . soothing.' An edge of amusement entered his voice. 'Do you disagree?'

'No. I just – I didn't think *you*—'

'You didn't think that I might like to stare at something that resembles the outside world, when I'm stuck in a ten-metre cell, day in and day out?' His words were barbed. Designed to cut.

'I'm sorry,' I said, and meant it. 'I didn't think.'

'No. You didn't.' Silence stretched between us. 'There's another reason I like these. My father used to take me hunting in the forest. Usually Roran and Scarlett would come along, but there were times when it was just us. Those were some of the happiest memories of my childhood.'

I blinked – startled by his uncharacteristic vulnerability. I had noticed hunting scenes in his chambers back in Caleah Fortress, but I'd assumed they were there to intimidate. It hadn't occurred to me that they held sentimental value.

'I'm not the monster you think I am, Mira,' Cassius said softly. 'Or at least, I don't want to be. I'm flawed – but I'm not evil. Not like Roran.'

I thought of how Roran had dangled Darius and Nari's lives in front of me. Only the worst kind of monster *delighted* in causing pain. Cassius was a lot of things, but he wasn't sadistic.

My eyes dropped to the scar encircling Cassius's throat – the scar that Roran had inflicted, when he'd whipped his younger brother at Emperor Kalias's request. For as long as I'd known Cassius, he had kept that scar concealed, wearing high-necked collars that had become something of a fashion statement. It was strange to see it on display now, and I felt myself soften towards him.

'What was it like? Growing up in the Ravalian Court?'

'If it wasn't for Scarlett, I probably wouldn't have survived. Half-siblings or not, we looked out for each other. When I was young, I relied on her more than I . . .' Cassius's face suddenly hardened. 'It doesn't matter. She proved I was right not to trust her in the end.'

I had my own issues with Scarlett, so I was happy to let that one lie. But I sensed their relationship was more complicated than I could fathom.

'I knew Emperor Kalias was cruel,' I said, 'but I didn't think he would be cruel to his own children.'

'I don't think he saw us as children. We were heirs – a pragmatic necessity, nothing more. In his eyes, only the son who inherited his throne was worth anything at all.'

'Roran, you mean.'

'Roran,' Cassius agreed. 'Sometimes I wonder if he was just a boy once, like me, before our father trained him to become a monster. But I can't remember him well enough to know for certain. Scarlett might, but I've never asked her.'

'So you really have no intention of helping Roran? Even if he offered you a position in his Court?'

'Anything Roran offered me would be short-lived. He would kill me the moment I was no longer useful.'

I recalled Roran's laughter when I had tried to make a trade for Cassius, and I didn't doubt it. But it was Cassius's matter-of-fact tone that really hit home. I felt as though I was getting a real glimpse into his world – a world in which family were reluctant allies at best and mortal enemies at worst.

For someone who had grown up like that, always fearing for his life . . . was it any wonder that Cassius had lied and schemed and betrayed? What would *I* be like, if I'd grown up in the Ravalian Court?

'What are you thinking about so intently?'

I told him.

Cassius laughed lightly. 'I can't imagine you being as ruthless as me or Roran, so put it out of your mind.'

'How can you say that?' I was genuinely shocked. 'I crossed so many lines in the Ravalian Court, made so many decisions that I regret, and—'

'And you made a different choice in the end. I didn't understand it at the time, but I do now.' Cassius smiled at my confusion. 'Mira, you turned away from revenge. You let go of your hatred for Emperor Kalias and chose to sail to Kalure.'

'It didn't make a difference, though,' I said sadly. 'Aric and Lillian were still caught in the crossfire.'

'I heard that boy yelling at you.' Cassius tilted his head, the light of the single fire brazier flickering across his angular cheek. 'He's a fool – or maybe Scarlett has his emotions all twisted up and confused. She's good at that. Either way, you made the right choice. You need to stop punishing yourself for it. And maybe it wouldn't hurt to tap into some of the anger you felt towards my father. Channel it into defeating Roran.'

I glanced at the bottle of red wine. Cassius followed the direction of my gaze.

'Velanthe thinks I should use blood magic. That embracing it will allow me to defeat Roran.'

'And what do you think?' Cassius asked steadily.

'That it feels like losing myself.'

'Doesn't sound like much of a solution, then.'

I frowned. 'I was certain you would encourage me to use it. That you'd say the end justifies the means.'

'Maybe I'm reassessing some of my old philosophies,' Cassius replied. 'One advantage to being imprisoned for two months – I've had endless time to think.'

'I thought you'd be furious with me. That you'd hate me for leaving you down here.'

Another shrug. 'I told you – I've had plenty of time to think. Plenty of time to cycle through rage, too. But even when I was furious with you . . . I never hated you, Mira. I don't think I'm capable of hating you.'

He looked at me with such disturbing sincerity that I had to glance away, my heart beating erratically.

Cassius reached for the bottle of wine, but I stopped him.

'Don't,' I said, placing my hand over his – and then quickly letting go, as if his touch had burned me.

Those striking dark blue eyes met mine. I had the sense that he saw more than I wanted him to, but he didn't question me. Merely released the bottle and smiled that casual, disarming smile of his, as if things hadn't changed between us. As if the world didn't feel like it had tilted on its axis.

'What do you want from me, Mira?' he asked lightly. 'Advice on ruling? Tips on how to beat Roran?'

'Actually,' I said, 'the Kalurian clan leader is on his way here. Roran offered him a deal that I can't afford for him to take, and Vølund requested a meeting with you. I was hoping—'

'That you could convince me to behave.' Cassius's smile seemed frozen, and it no longer reached his eyes. I hadn't realised how much I had been enjoying his openness until it was gone – like a door that had been slammed in my face.

'You knew I wanted something when I came here,' I said, hating that I was trying to justify my actions.

'I did,' Cassius said, more to himself than to me. 'But I was starting to think . . .'

'What?'

He didn't answer. If possible, his expression became even more remote. And I wondered if he'd started to think I wanted his company. That I had been as lonely as he clearly was.

'I might have come here for political reasons, but I've enjoyed talking to you. Far more than I thought I would.' Inwardly, I winced. *Not helping, Mira.*

'Since you want something from me,' Cassius continued, ignoring my comment, 'I assume you're offering something in exchange?'

'That's usually how negotiations work, isn't it?' I said, echoing his earlier words. 'Both parties have to give something.'

'And in your case, that would be . . .?'

'Chambers above ground. With guards stationed on your door.'

'*One* guard,' Cassius said immediately. 'And the option to leave my rooms – with an escort.'

'Fine.'

'You're not going to haggle?' A hint of amusement entered his voice.

'I wouldn't give you the pleasure.'

'Then we have a deal.' Cassius's tone was all business. 'Do you have a strategy in mind for the clan leader?'

I fidgeted in my seat, unwilling to explain that Velanthe's preferred strategy was blood magic. Cassius's sharp eyes noticed my hesitation.

'Roran offered Vølund control over the Wilds,' I said finally. 'I would have to offer something just as enticing.'

'Ah.' Cassius didn't outwardly react, but the way he looked at me made my pulse spike. 'You're angling for a marriage proposal.'

'No,' I said quickly. 'That's not—'

'It's the most efficient means to convince him to back you,' Cassius interrupted. 'I'm sure I can help nudge him in the right direction, if that's what you want. Though I might have to smooth over some of the finer details of our engagement. Maybe this time you'll actually go through with the wedding.'

He stood and crossed over to the door. Despite the fact that *he* was the one locked in a cell, the dismissal was clear.

After the tentative warmth we'd shared, his coldness bothered me. It made me feel guilty – as though I'd done something wrong. Which was utterly *infuriating*, considering everything he'd put me through.

'You have no right to be angry.'

'What makes you think I'm angry?' Cassius asked, in a voice as dead as his face. 'I agreed to help you. Unless you intend to take me to my new chambers tonight, it would seem our business is done.'

I wanted to argue with him. No – I wanted to hit him, but I suppressed the unsettling urge.

'Leave the bottle,' he said, when I reached for the wine.

I hesitated. This was my chance. All he had to do was drink it – and

I could return later to smooth all this over. To turn him into someone more *malleable*.

Which was precisely what I should want. To change him.

But even in the midst of my anger, a part of me rebelled against the idea. Before I could think better of it, I snatched up the bottle and two glasses. Let him think I was being petty – I couldn't care less.

I unlocked the cell and re-locked it on the other side, deliberately avoiding Cassius's gaze. I thought I saw his eyes linger on the wine bottle gripped in my hands, but he said nothing more.

And neither did I.

CHAPTER SEVEN

Scarlett

Aric cast me a curious glance as I strode into view, my Warriors clearing a respectful path to the pavilion. He wasn't sure what this spectacle was, and I tried to adopt a similar expression of surprise.

'You summoned me, General?' It wasn't difficult to make my voice haughty. I was born to give orders, not take them.

Thanks to Avril, soon enough I wouldn't have to. This entire army would be mine. And so would this war.

Mine to win or lose.

The tent flaps were open, allowing the occupants of the pavilion to address the crowd outside. General Harte was at the front, a piece of parchment in his hand. The forgery Avril's Mask had created.

'Yes, Your Highness. Thank you for coming.' General Harte smiled thinly. 'I called you all here,' he said, raising his voice as he turned to the audience, 'to honour Princess Scarlett. Her brother, our future emperor, contacted me with orders that I will read out.'

The gathering went still, waiting eagerly to hear Roran's words. Words he never would have written.

'I, Roran Valerian, task my sister to put down this rebellion. In my absence, she is to be given all the respect and authority you would give me. You may consider her my eyes, ears, and hands here.'

It felt oddly anticlimactic, watching General Harte read out his own demise. In the forged message, I had instructed him to keep me at the Western front. *Under no circumstances*, the Mask had written, *can Scarlett return to Ravalia. Make her feel powerful by holding a public ceremony in front of the army. Appeal to her vanity.*

And General Harte, who constantly underestimated me, had taken Roran at his word. The fool thought a little flattery would be enough to appease me, and he could continue as he had before, opposing me at every turn. He thought his popularity within the army made him safe. That I wouldn't risk challenging him.

That I wouldn't *dare*.

General Harte bowed his head, and the other officers followed suit. A show of obedience.

Which was all it was meant to be – a show.

But General Harte had read out Roran's decree, and in doing so, he had given me the tools I needed to finally dispense with him.

'I am humbled by my brother's faith in me,' I said, addressing the crowd rather than General Harte. 'And with my newfound power, I order General Harte to Ravalia, where he can ensure the security of our home.'

General Harte's brows drew together. 'The capital is secure, Your Highness.'

'That's not what I've heard,' I said with a cool smile. 'My sources say there's growing unrest. Hardly surprising, since our forces have been away for so long.'

'Your Highness, I must protest—'

I held up a hand, the lethal points of my silver nails glinting in the sun. General Harte faded to silence, and I delighted in watching the first traces of realisation enter his eyes as I asked pointedly, 'Are you refusing to protect the Ravalian capital? As important as this war is, it means nothing if my brother's throne is lost.'

'I'm your senior general,' General Harte said stubbornly, his eyes filled with cold threat. 'I belong here, leading my men.'

'No. You belong where *I* send you. And you will serve me best as a military governor.' I smiled – the same simpering smile I had given him during our last meeting. This time, I knew he could see the knife lurking behind it.

By accident, I caught Aric's gaze. Though his expression was carefully unreadable, his eyes were appreciative.

'This task is of the utmost importance,' I continued, now playing to the crowd. 'Zandri has personally requested the assistance of

General Harte and his most esteemed officers.' I rattled off the names of men I knew were fiercely loyal to the general, and likely to cause me no end of trouble.

Murmurs broke out amongst the assembled officers. This wasn't a popular decision, but they had their orders.

'You're dismissed,' I told them. 'I wish you all a speedy journey, and thank you for your service to the empire. As does my mother.'

The mention of my mother made their expressions pale. Zandri had quite a reputation, and no matter what they thought of me, no one wanted to incur her displeasure.

'Wait,' I said, before General Harte could leave. 'Your dagger, please.'

The crowd went still. Even the officers I had dismissed paused, staring at me in shocked disbelief.

General Harte's shadowed eyes slowly rose to mine. A Warrior's dagger was a sacred personal item, inscribed with their victories. Asking him to relinquish it was akin to dragging him to the whipping post and having him publicly flogged.

He had two options: disobey my direct order, and face whatever punishment I deemed appropriate, or follow my order and lose face in front of the army he had spent his life leading. Even I wasn't sure which he would choose.

General Harte approached, one heavy, thudding step after another. I tensed, resisting the urge to reach for my own dagger. My guards drew their swords—

He threw his dagger at my feet. It landed with a clatter that reverberated through my bones.

Without even the pretence of respect, General Harte turned on his heel. His loyal men flanked him as he strode away, straight-backed and forbidding.

'I have one last announcement,' I said, once the whispering had subsided. 'And that is General Harte's replacement.'

Avril and her Masks took positions at my back, guarding me from attack. Aric was already by my side, so I only had to turn slightly to face him. I hadn't told him what I had planned, but I hoped he would take it in stride.

I offered him General Harte's dagger.

The silence held for one more, deafening minute. Everyone knew Aric was technically unqualified for the position – but he was a quick learner with a mind for battle strategy, and had spent months working alongside General Harte. And I wanted someone who was loyal. Someone I could depend on to follow *my* orders and not issue their own.

I met Aric's gaze. *Trust me.*

Slowly, almost tentatively, his hand enclosed around the blade—

The gathering dissolved into chaos.

'I will not tolerate dissent!' I shouted, but my voice was lost over the din. 'My decision is final!'

The crowd pressed closer, filled with restless energy. It made my skin prickle, and I wondered if I had pushed them too far. Perhaps I had been too optimistic about Ravalian duty and obedience.

'Come on,' Aric called, drawing his sword. 'We can escape through the back of the tent.'

I stayed where I was. 'I'm not going to run from my own people.'

'Scarlett—' Aric's protest was cut off by a shout from behind me.

'Langton!' The harsh voice reverberated through the gathering. 'Do you support the princess's decision?'

I narrowed my eyes as I located the speaker – an imposing Warrior at the front of the army. He was close enough to address me directly, but his attention was focused on the officers guarding the pavilion. Officer Langton was amongst them; one of the most experienced officers I had left. Already, the crowd was following this Warrior's lead, looking to Langton as though his opinion mattered more than mine.

I'm losing them.

That realisation slammed into me, crushing the air from my lungs. It didn't matter what Langton said. Even if he supported me, this Warrior had shifted the balance of power in Langton's favour. If I didn't do something – and fast – no one would obey my commands, and certainly not Aric's.

If my father was here, I thought bitterly, *they wouldn't dare question his authority. They would be too afraid to speak a word against him.*

Just like that, a plan started to form. I stepped forward, but Aric grabbed my arm, his fingers digging into my skin.

'Scarlett,' he said urgently, 'I won't be able to protect you if—'

'I don't need your protection.' My voice was like ice.

Striding across the pavilion, I pushed past the officers shielding me from the rest of the army. Hundreds of eyes tracked my approach, perhaps expecting me to appeal to Langton for support. But I walked past Officer Langton without a glance, my head held high, my shoulders back.

I kept walking until I was facing the burly Warrior who had challenged me. Standing on the pavilion steps, I was taller than he was, but our eyes were still level. To me, he was my entire army wrapped up into one: all the ordinary soldiers and Warriors who would either obey or rise up against me.

My hand tightened around the sword strapped to my hip. The desire to run him through was overwhelming. I could almost *feel* my blade slipping between bone and muscle, could almost *see* him toppling to the ground, never to question me again. It was what my father would have done.

I unsheathed my sword.

'I could kill you right here,' I said, in a powerful voice designed to carry. 'But what sport is there in that? I am Ravalian, like you. I grew up watching the fighting matches in the arena. And I would answer your challenge – not with words, but with arms.'

Tension rippled through my army. I felt it in the stiffening of shoulders and the shifting of feet, but the silence held. There was no risk of the crowd losing control now. They were united in their shock, and even if they weren't, every Ravalian was taught to respect the old traditions.

For I had challenged this Warrior according to the custom of the icy North. A colder, harsher time long before the Sorceress, when our ancestors had fought to the death and our rulers had held the throne through their own blood, might and cunning.

'I accept your challenge, Your Highness.' My opponent cut his palm with his dagger, the traditional acceptance required, but his eyes never left mine. They were filled with a fierce, hawk-like intensity.

The blood fever, our people used to call it.

I wondered whether the same expression was echoed on my face as I followed suit, but I didn't think so. I wasn't like this Warrior, fuelled by fire. I had been forged from something colder and crueller. Ice.

As I returned to the pavilion – to Aric and the other loyal Warriors and Masks I trusted to prepare me for this challenge – I sensed the crowd watching me. Appraising me.

I hoped they looked at me differently now. That they saw my deathly pale skin, my red hair, and the bone crown I wore, and thought of my fierce ancestors from the North, who my father had revered.

Those long-ago kings had been the most powerful and deadly of us, not to mention utterly merciless.

And if I was going to rule, I would need to be exactly the same.

CHAPTER EIGHT

Scarlett

'Again,' Aric barked as he withdrew his sword from my neck.

I shook my head, too exhausted to speak. My breath came in ragged pants, and my vision was so blurred I could barely see the sand in front of me. I only felt its heat as I collapsed to my knees.

'This is counterproductive,' I managed to say, reaching for my discarded sword and climbing to my feet. 'I need to be at my best tomorrow – which I won't be if you run me into the ground.'

'You think I've been pushing you too hard?' he challenged. 'This is the bare *minimum*, Scarlett, if you want to survive against someone like Cade. Even Mira might struggle against a Warrior—'

My frustration boiled over. It had become an unspoken rule that neither of us mentioned Mira, and I didn't appreciate Aric breaking that rule at the very moment I needed his support the most.

'What does *Mira* have to do with any of this?' I asked in a dangerous voice.

'You're nowhere close to her standard of fighting!' Aric exploded. 'I saw you spar against her in the Ravalian Court. She *decimated* you, and she wasn't imbued with unnatural strength and reflexes. Do you have any idea how dangerous the senior Warriors can be?'

'Of course I do. My mother *created* the Orders.'

'Then you know Zandri would have worked her magic on Cade, making him as invincible as possible.' Aric turned away, running a hand through his hair. 'General Tiran used to hold him in reserve until a mission was dire enough to send him in. Even *I* would be nervous about facing Cade.'

I touched Aric's arm gently. He turned to face me, a harsh line between his brows. Fear – for me.

'I'll be fine,' I said, wrestling my emotions back under control. 'I have other abilities – abilities Cade knows nothing about.'

'Magic.' The frown slowly smoothed out between Aric's brows. 'We've never really discussed what you can do. If I know the strengths and limitations of your abilities, I can help you formulate a plan—'

'I appreciate that,' I said, taking his calloused hand in mine. 'Truly. But I've already considered how to use magic in this fight. What I need right now is rest – and to know that you trust me.'

'I do.' Aric squeezed my hand. 'Of course I do.'

I smiled back at him, ignoring the sour taste in my mouth. Trust had been the wrong word to use. It brought back memories of all my lies, just as Mira's name brought back memories of the way I had betrayed her. Aric's trust wasn't earned. It was stolen.

The irony of it wasn't lost on me. Here he was, worrying about whether I would survive tomorrow's fight, when he should be the one who wanted to slide a blade into my heart.

'Are you sure about this?' Aric asked, drawing me back to reality.

I glanced up, realising that I had led him to my tent. The guards stood watching us, their faces eerie in the reddish glow of the torches. For a second, I could have sworn their eyes were a bottomless black. Then I blinked, and their eyes were normal once more.

'Yes,' I said, before I could change my mind. 'I don't want to be alone tonight.'

I swept into the tent ahead of Aric, irritated with myself for blurring the boundaries even further. It wasn't him I really wanted, I reminded myself. I wanted the familiarity and comfort that Severin had always provided. Except Severin had left me, and only now, when it was far too late, was I beginning to realise that perhaps I had loved him all along.

Perhaps I still did.

But I allowed Aric to take me in his arms, because if there was one thing I was good at, it was lying to myself.

And when he kissed me, I kissed him back with everything I had. Embracing the distraction his lips offered.

*

When Aric was fast asleep, I slipped out of my tent. One of the Warriors frowned at the movement of the tent flap but dismissed it, turning back to his colleague.

I walked past, careful not to touch them. My illusions were optical only – they didn't extend to the other senses. How useful *that* would be, I thought as I made my way through the camp.

The stallion nickered at my approach. Riding was a risk – I could make us invisible, but my illusions wouldn't mask the sound of its hoof-beats. Still, I had absolutely no intention of traversing the desert on foot.

I reached for its bridle—

'Going somewhere?' a soft voice asked from behind me.

I whirled on my heel. Lillian was standing in the shadows, an apple in her palm. A palomino mare nibbled at it eagerly, already bridled and saddled.

'What are you—?'

'I had a sudden urge to go out riding.' Lillian wiped her palm on the hem of her dress. 'And I know that urge wasn't mine. I'm getting better at recognising the difference.'

I didn't know which was stranger – the fact that she'd anticipated what I was about to do *before* I did it, or that she had gone to the effort of sourcing a double saddle.

'And before you tell me that you're going alone,' Lillian continued, 'let me remind you that whatever you're doing relies on secrecy. The last thing you want is for me to tell my brother.'

I glared at her. 'You do realise that your life is literally in my hands. I can snap the tether between us at any time.'

Lillian stepped closer. Under the light of the brazier, her blonde hair was almost as red as mine, and her expression was infinitely more stubborn. 'Empty threats won't work, Scarlett. I *know* you – possibly better than you know yourself.'

With that disconcerting statement, she climbed into the saddle. She even had the nerve to take the front spot, though I doubted she was much of a rider – a suspicion that was confirmed when she slipped and almost tumbled off.

'Move back,' I told her, rolling my eyes as I mounted and took the reins, urging the horse into a smooth canter. Lillian's arms wrapped around my waist, clinging to me so tightly that her nails dug into my skin.

Five minutes passed. Then ten.

'Do you actually *know* where you're going?'

I couldn't resist calling back, 'Aren't you supposed to be the expert in what I'm feeling? Perhaps you should tell me.'

'*Scarlett—*'

'Relax,' I interrupted, hearing the nervous edge to her voice. 'We're nearly there.'

The presence of death was now so strong that I was surprised Lillian couldn't smell it. But she showed no hesitation as I helped her dismount, just led the horse obediently after me. Moonlight illuminated the shadowed husk of an overturned cart, bodies dumped in a pile next to it. All Zigilian, I knew, because the Ravalians would have been buried.

'Is that . . .' Lillian trailed off, raising a hand to her mouth. She was even flightier than the horse; every step towards the bodies brought her closer to bolting.

'Why don't you wait for me in front of the cart?' I suggested. 'You don't have to watch this.'

Lillian didn't move. I wasn't entirely sure that she could.

Brushing past her, I approached the mound of bodies. They weren't all stacked neatly on top of each other – a few had fallen or rolled nearby, saving me the trouble of digging through the morbid pile.

Thank the Gods for small mercies, I thought as I walked towards the closest. But when I turned him over, I didn't feel thankful at all. I stared down at the youthful face in front of me – then leant over and retched.

Cool fingers pulled my hair back from my face. When I was done, I grasped Lillian's hand with mine.

'Did you see him?'

'Yes.' Her voice was soft. 'He doesn't look much older than fourteen.'

I swallowed past a sudden lump in my throat, thinking of the boy I had watched die in the Ravalian infirmary. The one I had chosen not to save.

'It's not your fault,' Lillian said, even softer.

'I never said that it was,' I said sharply, rising to my feet.

'But you're thinking it all the same,' she whispered. 'You're wondering whether this war is worth the cost. Whether the Ravalian Empire is worth so much death – and whether you're any better than your brother or your father.'

'*Shut up!*' I snarled, rounding on her. 'You don't know what I'm thinking. You have no idea.'

I didn't give Lillian the chance to respond. Forcing myself to face the boy, I reached for his white arm. It was limp and cold beneath my fingers.

Behind me, Lillian breathed, 'You're resurrecting him.'

'No,' I replied. 'I'm not.'

I watched the hope drain from Lillian's face – the hope that I wasn't the monster I seemed to be. I almost hated her in that moment. But no more than I hated myself.

If Severin was here, he would look at me like that, too. But I still sliced the boy's wrist with a sharp fingernail.

Blood answered my call. Not red – black.

I heard Lillian gasp. Black veins wound up my arms as I took death into me, and as I embraced its cold power, I no longer felt hollow or afraid of what was to come.

When I was finished, the boy's youth no longer bothered me. Neither did the sight of his eyes – nothing more than empty husks, drained of everything that had made them human. Every bit as black and unnatural as mine.

But that was my little secret – for now.

By the time I faced Lillian, my illusion was firmly in place: black veins concealed by smooth skin, my eyes returned to their previous blue. She took my hand with only a slight hesitation, allowing me to pull her to her feet.

I walked with her back to the palomino horse, which reared up at the sight of me but stilled immediately at my touch.

I smiled faintly at its reaction. It knew better than to cross me, and soon others would learn the same lesson.

I had spent my life hiding – my ambitions, my magic, my ruthlessness. But the time for hiding was over. With this power at my disposal, I could make my enemies bow down before me.

I could make the entire world tremble at my feet.

CHAPTER NINE

Mira

'This was a mistake,' I said, hesitating outside the banquet hall.

Cassius folded his arms. He was dressed in a gold-trimmed tunic, and seeing him outfitted in such a courtly fashion didn't help my nerves. 'You've faced worse than this. Remember the day we met? When I escorted you to the great hall to be introduced to the Ravalian Court?'

'How could I forget?' I muttered through gritted teeth. It had been hours after I'd watched my mother murdered, and it had been all I could do not to attack Emperor Kalias in front of the hundreds of lords and ladies in attendance.

'Well, there you have it,' Cassius said. 'I'm sure you'll do fine. Though it might have been wise to practise beforehand, if you're this worried about playing politics.'

'I'm not worried about politics,' I snapped. 'I'm worried about walking in with *you*.'

'Ah.' Cassius shrugged, irritatingly blasé. 'I did wonder about that. But it's too late to change your strategy now.'

Infuriating. He was utterly *infuriating*.

'Try not to embarrass me tonight,' I said sideways to Cassius, and after taking a deep breath, pushed open the towering carved doors.

Pillared statues of the Sorceress held up the ceiling, which was decorated with murals that I had no time to appreciate. My attention darted to the long tables, where Kalurian clansmen sat, each with weapons strapped to their sides – at least a hundred warriors, and that wasn't counting the imposing table at the head of the hall.

A few priestesses stood to one side, including Velanthe – and the sight of her diminished position only increased my foreboding. The clan leader had claimed the centre seat for himself, the heads of clans Völsung, Asbjørn and Skjöldr in places of honour close to his side: his sister Nari, Thoren and a bearded man I could only assume must be Ulrik.

Their kohl-darkened eyes were already intent on the double doors. But they weren't studying me or the traditional woollen dress I wore, handwoven with the colours of the three Kalurian clans: black, emerald and sapphire.

No – their attention was on Cassius, who couldn't have looked more Ravalian if he'd tried.

I barely heard the herald call out my title. I was more focused on Velanthe's thunderous face. This definitely *wasn't* the entrance she'd envisioned.

But if Vølund was concerned about how I'd treated my ex-fiancé, what better way than to present a united front? The other option I'd considered – having Cassius escorted to the banquet hall by armed guards – would surely have set the wrong tone. At least Cassius had enough sense to walk behind me as we approached, making it seem like I had some semblance of control over him.

I wove my way between the long tables, keeping my gaze straight ahead – even as I felt the intent appraisal of the clansmen. They had never been allowed inside the Temple before, and for good reason. The tension between them and the priestesses was so thick that it would be a miracle if we made it through tonight without bloodshed.

Vølund stood at my approach, towering over me much like his sister had done. His fur mantle made his shoulders seem even broader, and it was all I could do to avoiding looking at the sword and axe he wore. But I couldn't stop myself from staring at the ebony tattoos continuing from his brow to just below his dark green eyes: two thick lines that resembled daggers.

'Be welcome amongst me and mine, Kasmira Volaris,' Vølund said, his voice deep and surprisingly pleasant, considering his warlike appearance. I was startled to realise that he couldn't be more than ten years older than I was, placing him in his late twenties – but his youth only made him that much more dangerous. How many warriors must he have defeated, in order to prove himself as clan leader?

And then there was his choice of words, and their very clear meaning: that the Temple was effectively under *his* control. Not mine.

'I accept your hospitality.' That was the formal response Velanthe had taught me, and I didn't miss the subtle arch of Vølund's brows.

'It's gratifying to see you have learnt some of our customs.' The silver in Vølund's braided dark hair jangled as he folded his muscular arms. 'Some amongst us worried that our new queen was more Ravalian than Kalurian.'

'Not at all,' I said, relieved by such a positive start to our conversation. 'I am my father's daughter, and I'm always eager to discover more about his homeland. I'm sure we have much to learn from one another.'

'Indeed,' Vølund agreed, but his expression hardened as it fell on Cassius. 'Though it appears I may have spoken too soon in regard to your loyalties. I am unused to dining with Ravalian princes. I believe this one was your betrothed?'

Hostility radiated from Thoren and Ulrik. I knew the rules for a gathering like this one: no weapon could be drawn without severe consequences. But if *Vølund* gave the order—

'Until recently,' Nari interrupted, 'the Ravalian prince was locked up in the Temple dungeons. That he roams freely tonight is most likely a gesture of good faith. I passed on your request for an audience.'

Vølund pulled out the chair on his left. 'Sit,' he told me, in a tone that left me unsure if it was an order or an invitation. 'You imprisoned your betrothed?'

'Cassius didn't come here willingly,' I said, taking a seat, 'and though he despises his brother, I didn't feel comfortable letting him wander around the Temple as he pleased. But we've agreed to put aside past issues in favour of our common goal: defeating Roran.'

'Interesting,' Vølund said, his gaze on Cassius. 'If you were to defeat Roran, is it your intention to take his place?'

What a good question. I glanced sideways at Cassius. Undoubtedly he still had designs on the Ravalian throne – but I could never allow him to have it, considering he had no desire to give Kalure its independence.

'It's a possibility,' Cassius said, his tone noncommittal. His ease was surprising, considering he was seated between the hulking figures of Thoren and Ulrik. 'Of course, there's also Scarlett to consider.'

'Yes,' Vølund said after a pause. 'I have heard a great deal about the Ravalian princess. Does she share your reservations where Roran is concerned?'

'Certainly.' Cassius lifted a goblet of mead to his lips. 'There is no love lost between Scarlett and Roran. Our distrust for our elder brother is the one thing we agree on.'

There was a lull in conversation as plates of seafood were set in front of us. Cassius turned his attention to one of the female Kalurian servers, saying something that made her laugh – a pretty, rich sound that I immediately despised.

'Is the princess with Roran in Kalure?'

I quickly returned my attention to Vølund. 'No. Our latest information places Scarlett in the Western Lands.' I delighted in telling the clan leader, 'Apparently she's putting down their most recent rebellion.'

His slight frown said that my words had hit their mark. I could only hope that Vølund would be reconsidering Roran's offer now, with Cassius by my side and news of unrest under Ravalian rule.

I pressed my advantage. 'That's the issue with commanding such a large empire. It's an ongoing task just to keep the countries in line.'

The frown between Vølund's eyebrows deepened, and I wondered if he was thinking of the terrible methods the Ravalians employed to keep said countries in line.

'Yet you competed for a place in the Ravalian Orders.' A probing statement.

I met Vølund's gaze steadily. 'After Emperor Kalias executed my mother, he intended to kill me as well. The Trials were my only chance at survival.'

Beneath the kohl, Vølund's green eyes were vivid – and surprisingly perceptive. 'We have a similar system, when choosing our clan leader,' he said, 'but we do not kill each other for sport. The Council of Ancients wouldn't support a leader who demonstrated such a disregard for human life.'

'I thought the Council of Ancients chose your clan leader.' That was what Velanthe had told me.

'In a way, they do.' Vølund's gaze was far away as he said, 'Our chosen candidate must meet with the council before the clans will answer to them. It is considered a great honour. They do not welcome interference, and will not show themselves to anyone unless they wish to.'

I had heard that as well. It was one of the reasons I hadn't pushed for an audience, even though I knew the council held great sway over the clans. That, and Velanthe's warning that the council had severed ties with the Temple long ago, no longer recognising its authority or supporting the traditional rule of the Sorceress's descendants.

By unspoken agreement, we moved on to lighter topics. The fish and steamed shellfish – all freshly caught – prompted me to ask about traditional Kalurian fare. Vølund softened as he shared stories of Valheim, describing the rectangular longhouses of the settlement, its grazing fields and the proud fleet within its natural harbour.

'I usually only have cause to visit the traditional clan settlements,' Vølund continued, 'but the rest of the Wilds are beautiful as well. On my way here, I couldn't help but admire the tree-top villages.'

His words tempted a genuine smile from me. 'Would you like to visit one? I could take you.'

'I would like that. Perhaps we—'

The double doors burst open, displaying a dozen Kalurian warriors. One of their number approached the main table and bowed to me.

'Your Majesty,' Bane said in a deep baritone, 'Prince Roran was apprehended at the Temple gates, demanding an audience. We have him detained in the portico.'

I could hardly believe my luck. The sheer *arrogance* of it was astounding.

No doubt Roran had heard of my meeting with the clans, and had come here to derail the negotiations – or to secure the alliance for himself. But he had finally overplayed his hand.

'Execute him,' I said immediately.

The warrior turned on his heel, but Vølund called, 'Hold.'

Bane paused, his attention on me. Unlike the majority of the warriors inside the hall, Bane was from Kalure – not the Wilds. He had no allegiance to the clans.

'Roran is an enemy ruler during wartime,' I said coolly to Vølund. 'I understand that such methods may seem unpalatable to you, but since he has entered my territory uninvited—'

'He *was* invited,' Vølund interrupted. 'By me.'

Dead silence descended in the banquet hall. Bane was still looking at me, awaiting my order. I wanted to give it. My heart was pounding, adrenaline flowing through my veins.

This was my chance to kill Roran. Kill him, and his army would crumble. Kill him, and—

Vølund would become my enemy.

'I had meant to raise it more diplomatically over dinner, but circumstances have conspired against me.' Though Vølund's voice was carefully light, there was nothing light about the way he was watching me. 'I had Nari issue an invitation, but I had no idea that Prince Roran had accepted, or that he would arrive so soon.'

'Your fighters might encircle the Temple,' I said tightly, 'but you don't have the authority to invite Roran here. *I* do, and I don't want him in the Wilds.'

'I understand,' Vølund said with apparent sincerity. 'It was never my intention to escalate tensions. I simply prefer to bring all parties together in a negotiation – particularly a negotiation as important as this one.'

I glanced at Velanthe, who had been observing my interaction with Vølund from a slight distance. Her face was smooth and unreadable, giving nothing away. Still, she had advised me to do whatever it took to win the clans to my side.

Even if I executed Roran, I couldn't be certain that this war would end with him. There was still Scarlett to consider, not to mention Zandri and the Ravalian generals. And if Vølund and the clans decided to take up arms against me, the Temple would be facing a battle waged on multiple fronts.

A battle that would destroy us.

'Belay that order,' I told Bane firmly, and the clan warriors relaxed.

My eyes locked with Cassius's midnight-blue ones. It was impossible to tell whether he thought I was making a mistake, but it was too late to regret my decision now.

I issued my final order:

'Bring Roran in.'

CHAPTER TEN

Mira

'Crown Prince Roran Valerian, of the Ravalian Empire—'

'It's Emperor,' Roran corrected coldly, striding past the herald and the warriors guarding the entrance.

I watched him enter the banquet hall, marking his every movement. Roran didn't seem concerned to find himself surrounded by Kalurians. He only had eyes for me, smiling a little at my retinue of armed guards.

'Don't come any closer,' one warned.

'There's no need for unpleasantness,' Roran remarked, ignoring the directive. 'I come in peace.'

Yet I noticed that he wore black and silver – a deliberate colour choice, chosen to mock the priestesses and the Temple.

Roran strode over to Cassius. Without looking at his younger brother, he speared a slice of apple with his fork and lifted it to his mouth. 'Well done on your plan to kill Father,' he said. 'I didn't think you had it in you. Though you chose your accomplice poorly – how long has Kasmira kept you locked up for? Two months?'

I expected Cassius to deny his role in Emperor Kalias's death, but perhaps Cassius – like me – had realised the futility of it. Better to be regarded as ruthless than a liar.

'An improvement, I'm sure,' Cassius drawled, 'on the quick death *you* would have offered me.'

'I doubt I would have any allies left, if all I offered them was a quick death.' His reptilian gaze rose to lock with mine. 'It's good of you to allow my brother to participate in these negotiations, Kasmira. I do hope you offered him something decent in exchange for his cooperation.'

I ignored the barb – and its implication: that I had coerced Cassius's support. 'You took quite a risk coming here.'

'Did I?' Roran's lip curled. 'I was under the impression that you were desperate for this alliance. You certainly wouldn't achieve that by throwing me out, and as for ordering my execution . . . well, I feel confident that the clans would retaliate against such a grievous injustice. Even if Vølund *hadn't* promised that I was under his protection, allowing the murder of other rulers sets a dangerous precedent.'

'You're not even crowned yet!' I said, my voice shaking with rage. 'Technically, you're not ruler of anything.'

'And you have no palace, and by the looks of it . . .' Roran eyed my priestesses and few remaining non-clan warriors, 'not much of an army, either. Yet the clans are prepared to negotiate with *you*.' He smiled at my expression. 'But we're being rude, sniping at each other and ignoring our host. I am willing to set my personal feelings aside in favour of a pleasant evening. Are you?'

'Of course, *Prince* Roran,' I replied.

Roran's eyes sparked with anger, but only I seemed to notice. After exchanging polite pleasantries with the clan leader, he turned his attention to Nari. And no one – not even Vølund – tried to stop him as he offered her his arm.

My teeth ground together, thinking of how Roran had captured Nari and Darius, dangling their lives in front of me for sport. Surely Nari wouldn't allow him to touch her, to get within even a foot of her.

But Roran hadn't hurt *Nari*, had he? It had been Darius with the wounds, the evidence of his beatings—

Nari glanced at her brother. Vølund gave her a small nod.

She threaded her arm though Roran's, allowing him to lead her across the hall. At his sharp glance, the musicians hurriedly struck up a song – a jaunty tune that didn't suit the severity of the situation. A funeral march would have been more appropriate.

Cool hands brushed my bare shoulder. And then a voice whispered in my ear, 'You're shaking, Mira.' Pulling back from me, Cassius said more loudly, 'We can't let Roran and Nari have all the fun. Shall we?'

I hesitated, but only for a moment. Cassius waited patiently with his hand outstretched, and when I finally placed my hand into his, he offered me a faint, darkly amused smile.

'What are you doing?' I hissed as we approached Roran and Nari, who were elegantly matching the beat of the musicians' song.

'With Roran here, you can't afford to be seen as weak – not by him, and certainly not by the Kalurian clans. In politics, everything is a show. So,' he murmured, 'let's *give* them a show.'

Cassius wound his arms around my waist, drawing me scandalously close. And then we were moving.

Where Roran's movements were slower and heavier, Cassius and I twirled around the hall in tandem. I had forgotten how it felt to dance with him – forgotten the way his body seemed to meld with mine, tempting me to surrender myself to the music and this exhilarating, all-consuming sense of *oneness*.

Like a panther in human skin, I had once thought Cassius, and that panther-like grace was on full display now.

The music grew deeper, resonating through me like a heartbeat, until even I forgot about Roran and Nari. Cassius's movements were fast and impossible to anticipate, forcing me to give over control and trust him to lead. How thrilling it was – this familiar, dangerous push and pull between us.

'You're doing wonderfully,' Cassius told me after a few songs had passed. 'The clan leader hasn't taken his eyes off you.'

I didn't have the chance to answer before he unwound me. I twirled around the dance floor until his arms caught me once more.

A brief glance over Cassius's shoulder showed me that we had quite an audience. Even Roran was watching from where he had rejoined Vølund and the clan heads, who were standing in a huddle while servants brought them refreshments.

'Relax,' Cassius said when I tensed. 'You can join them in a minute. For now, try to enjoy yourself.'

It shouldn't have been possible. Not with Roran standing so close, his hateful stare focused on us. But somehow, I felt lighter, calmer, more centred.

I wasn't the only one. Priestesses twirled around the dance floor now, taking their cue from their queen.

'Roran must be hating this,' I said with satisfaction. 'Seeing my people enjoying themselves.'

Cassius's lips upturned in a wry smile. 'I'm sure.'

The song drew to a close and I stepped out of his embrace. At the last moment, I linked my arm through his, earning myself a surprised – but approving – glance.

In our hatred of Roran, at least, we were united. An alliance of two.

Whatever lightness I'd felt while dancing disappeared as we approached the main table. Seeing Roran laughing and sipping wine, as though this was *his* party, and these were *his* allies, made me want to reach for the dagger strapped to my thigh.

Cassius shot me a warning glance. I tried out a smile instead.

He nodded. *Better.*

'Nice of you to join us, Kasmira,' Roran said smoothly. I resisted the urge to throttle him. 'We were just discussing my generous deal. It's unfortunate you don't have more to offer potential allies.'

'At least I don't threaten their lives,' I said, with a pointed glance at Nari.

'Nari was treated with the upmost respect whilst in my care.' Roran smiled thinly. 'As for my threat . . . that was to prove my point: that you don't value Kalurian lives. How ironic that I showed more respect for her station than her own queen.'

'I let my personal feelings cloud my judgement. I'm sorry for that,' I said, looking first at Nari and then at Vølund. 'But an alliance with me offers something Roran cannot: security. If Roran kills me, he *will* invade the Wilds.'

'Not if we reach an agreement,' Roran replied, waving away a servant's offer of refreshment with an impatient hand.

Thoren and Ulrik shifted uneasily, having noticed the same thing I had: Roran's lack of a denial.

'Any agreement you make will be meaningless,' I said, directing my words to Vølund. 'You know Roran's history; he learnt warfare at Emperor Kalias's knee, and he's helped conquer three countries since then. Is *that* the kind of person you want as an ally? Is that the kind of person you can trust with Kalure?'

'A stirring speech,' Roran drawled, 'but fearmongering aside, it is well known that Ravalians value honour.'

'Where was *your* honour, brother,' Cassius broke in, 'when you tried to assassinate children?'

Nari exhaled a sharp breath. 'Is that true?'

Roran's calm expression didn't falter. 'Cassius is referring to himself and our sister. The Ravalian Court believes in survival of the fittest – there is nothing dishonourable about weeding out the weak. If they die, then they have proven their inferiority.'

It was clear that the clan heads strongly disagreed with this. Roran must have realised that too, because he quickly moved on.

'Regardless, there is a way I can prove my good intentions.' Roran's gaze shifted to Nari. My stomach sank even before he said, 'Were we to marry, our fates would be intertwined. Your brother would be free to rule the entirety of Kalure – not just the Wilds – and there would be a lasting peace between our countries. You could both be certain that I would never invade, and reap the benefits of being associated with the Ravalian Empire. As I'm sure you're aware, its resources are immense.'

And there it was. The blow that Roran had come all this way to deliver.

It made sense now, why he had come in person. He had wanted the opportunity to make his case in front of the clans – and to discredit me and Cassius. But most importantly, he had upped the stakes. Judging by Vølund's intent stare, this was an offer he might not be able to refuse.

Roran's eyes gleamed with victory. 'I will leave you to consider my terms.'

'I'll walk you out,' I said, slipping my arm from Cassius's.

'Are you sure?' Cassius asked quietly, his body tense. 'Perhaps I should accompany you.'

'Roran knows that he can't kill me in my own Temple, surrounded by witnesses. Besides, it would be dishonourable.' My eyes bored into Roran's. 'And I know how much you value *honour*.'

Roran smiled in response. A shark's smile.

A handful of warriors flanked us as we crossed the banquet hall. Everyone was staring but pretending not to.

'My younger brother is quite besotted with you,' Roran remarked, his tone conversational.

'I doubt that very much,' I said tersely. 'But I don't want to talk about me. I want to talk about *you*.'

'Oh?'

'You're not really going to marry Nari. I know you better than that – you have no interest in sharing power.'

A soft breeze ruffled my hair as we stepped outside. Roran surveyed the courtyard and surrounding colonnades intently, his gaze rising to the living quarters on the second level. I didn't like his focused stare: as if he was committing every balcony, statue and mural to memory.

'Marriage isn't a terrible idea,' he said at last. 'Obviously a queen or princess would be the long-term option, but for now . . . well, bringing Kalure to heel has proven to be a costly endeavour. Promising my hand to Nari is the most efficient way to take your country and your head.'

'And what happens to her once I'm dead?'

Roran shrugged, clearly losing interest. 'An emperor needs an heir. Perhaps we will grow to like each other.'

'Or perhaps,' I said coldly, 'she'll meet with a convenient accident.'

Roran smiled faintly, but didn't respond. 'I suppose this is goodbye, then, Kasmira,' he said. 'In more ways than one.'

Rather than accompanying my warriors towards the Temple steps, he walked past them – to where Nari stood beneath a sandstone archway. Even though she had every reason to distrust him, she still watched Roran with interest. Still allowed him to bring her hand to his lips.

Gods, she couldn't actually be *considering* this.

'Their engagement can never happen.' Cassius came up behind me, watching Roran and Nari with narrowed eyes. 'If it comes to that, you'll have to kill her.'

'And give the clans an even greater reason to turn against me? I don't think so.'

'I'm not suggesting a blatant assassination attempt. I'm suggesting—'

'A convenient accident?' I folded my arms. Cassius might hate Roran, but it seemed both brothers thought alike.

'That was my first instinct. Though perhaps there is a better option.' Slowly, Cassius said, 'Even the clans are aware of the division within the Ravalian royal family. Both Scarlett and Zandri are known for their ruthlessness – and your priestesses stock poisons in the Temple. Some of them are Ravalian in origin.'

I wished his words shocked me. They didn't. 'You're asking me to poison an innocent woman.'

'Nari is Roran's leverage,' he corrected, without missing a beat. 'She's no longer innocent.'

I stared at him, feeling sick to my stomach.

'Do you think I *like* suggesting this?' Cassius asked, his face flushed – not with heat or embarrassment, but with the strength of his conviction. 'I have nothing against Nari. She's intelligent and interesting to talk to, for a Kalurian. But the clans can't ally with Roran. Not if you want to stay breathing.'

I knew he was right, but my heart rebelled at the thought. I turned away from Cassius, unable to face him.

'Either you lose your head,' he called after me, 'or she loses hers. It's that simple.'

CHAPTER ELEVEN

Scarlett

'The blade is poisoned. All it will take is one cut—'

'You want me to cheat?' I asked idly, twirling the dagger in my palm.

'It will ensure your victory,' Avril replied. 'I doubt Zandri could have anticipated you challenging a Warrior to a duel, but had she known, this is the sort of strategy she would employ.'

'No poison,' I told her. 'I might not have the enhanced strength and speed of the court Warriors, but I can win this fight.'

Avril frowned, but said nothing. The other Masks – all female, all fiercely loyal to my mother, and all tasked with protecting me – shifted uneasily behind her. Their lives hung in the balance too. My mother's reputation for ruthlessness was well earned, and if I died, she would make sure these women suffered for it.

But I wasn't going to die. I was going to *win*.

Across the pavilion, Aric was pacing. He had pledged to protect me, and I knew how seriously he took that vow. It must be tearing him up that he couldn't help me now. But he would have felt far worse had he known how my decision impacted Lillian.

'I'm surprised you haven't tried to talk me out of this,' I murmured, approaching her. She stood apart from the others, and though the sun was bright in the sky, she had somehow managed to blend into the shadows.

'Would it make any difference?' she asked, softening the question with a faint smile.

Her compassion surprised me. It seemed strange that anything kind could be left after everything Lillian had experienced: her death, her resurrection, Mira's apparent betrayal. But Lillian's compassion was part of her personality, and she clung onto it with everything she had.

I still hadn't decided whether that was a weakness or a strength.

'You know what this means, don't you? If I die, my magic will no longer be able to sustain your life. You'll . . .'

'Die all over again,' Lillian finished, that soft smile still on her lips. 'I know I'm living on borrowed time, Scarlett. Aric doesn't believe that – he doesn't *want* to believe it – but I've never allowed hope to blind me. Whatever happens, I'm thankful for the additional months you've given me.'

A foreign emotion twisted my stomach. I hadn't saved Lillian out of kindness. I hadn't even done it out of affection for Aric, though that was what she believed. I had done it because I'd wanted to take something away from Mira, because I had wanted to test the limits of my abilities, and because I had wanted to use Lillian for my own ends.

'Let's hope for years,' I replied, and the gratitude in Lillian's face made my throat tighten.

I returned to the main table, where the others had gathered to discuss strategy. Aric had taken his place at its head, embracing his role as my senior general.

'Cade's strength is impressive,' Aric was saying. 'I warned Scarlett that he has a reputation.'

Avril lowered her voice. 'Without a poisoned blade, how will Scarlett fare? Is victory even possible?'

'Not unless we find a way of evening the playing field. We could—'

'No,' I said, stepping into view. Aric and Avril started guiltily – they didn't know about my power of illusion, and they were clearly wondering how they could have missed my presence. 'I appreciate your concern. I do. But if I'm going to win the respect of my army, I need to succeed on my own merits.'

Aric moved away from the table. 'Scarlett,' he said, low and intimate, 'you don't have to do this. Let me fight as your champion. You're in this situation because you appointed me as your general. *I'm* the one who should be proving myself.'

'I won't allow anyone to fight my battles for me, Aric. Not even you.'

Aric clearly didn't like it, but he nodded. Wordlessly, he checked me over. I knew I looked good in the black fighting ensemble, which had been tailored especially for me. But if Aric noticed, he didn't let on. His touch was careful and professional as he tightened the straps holding my dagger and sword, the only two weapons I was allowed.

When he finished, his eyes met mine. But I already knew there would be no drawn-out goodbyes, no emotional declarations. Sharing last night together had been enough.

'Don't die,' Aric told me with a brief smile. 'Your Majesty.'

It was the first time he had said those words to me. The first time anyone had, and they filled me with a potent mixture of conviction and determination.

Empress, I told myself as I strode from the pavilion. *I am their future empress.*

And they will *see me victorious.*

I was disappointed when I saw my arena. It was nothing like the one in Ravalia, surrounded by towering stands and steeped in centuries of tradition. Instead, it was a large patch of red sand, encircled by officers and Warriors.

I half expected them to cheer as I walked through their ranks, but there was only silence. Watchfulness.

This will still need to be a show, I reminded myself. There were too many eyes on me for it to be anything else.

The last few onlookers parted, and I saw that Cade was already in position on the other side of the circle. Behind him were the officers and Warriors who supported him – including Officer Langton, who seemed to have chosen a side. The wrong one.

My people arranged themselves at the front of the crowd: Aric and a handful of loyal officers, Avril and her Masks. Lillian and my attendants were still inside the pavilion. The placement made sense, but Lillian's distance distracted me in a way I hadn't anticipated.

I strode to meet Cade, who was dressed in the black of court Warriors, though he was bare-chested. The gold armbands on his muscled arms were a chilling reminder of his status as a senior Warrior – and I had no idea what additional magical abilities my mother might have granted him.

But I had formidable abilities of my own.

'Princess.' Cade grinned at me, displaying teeth filed to sharp points.

'Cade.' I kept my voice cool, as if this challenge didn't bother me. 'May your blood be spilled with honour.'

He echoed the words, though they held a sarcastic edge.

And we began to circle.

I wasn't sure exactly what I had expected – some sort of mad charge, probably – but Cade engaged me like a swordsman rather than relying on brute strength. Somehow that was more unnerving: his graceful, elegantly honed skill.

Parry, block, feint. My movements were instinctual, a result of years of practice. Fighting wasn't so different to Court politics, really. My eyes remained on Cade, searching for a weakness I could exploit. He was doing the same, but I could feel something shifting. His strikes became faster and more fluid, the strength behind his blows increasing.

Never retreat, the captain of the guard had told me during my training sessions. *Never give up momentum.*

Easier said than done, I thought as I narrowly blocked Cade's next swing, the force behind it making me stagger backwards. Before I could regain my composure, he stabbed at my ribs with his dagger.

I'd forgotten to watch both his weapons. Though I twisted out of the way, it sliced through my clothes and into my stomach. Was it deep? I resisted the urge to check, knowing that was what Cade was hoping for.

Hurling myself out of the way of his next strike, I rolled across the hot sand and rose onto one knee. Hunger burned in Cade's eyes as he watched me, but he seemed content to wait for me to rise.

'You're not bad,' he acknowledged, stalking closer. 'But it was foolish of you to challenge me. Foolish, and arrogant.' Cade tossed his dagger into the air and caught it. 'Roran always said your arrogance would be your downfall.'

'Roran's one to talk,' I snapped, rising to my feet and lunging. Cade – overconfident and still playing with the blade in his hand – avoided my sword but not my dagger. I smiled as it sank into an unprotected section of his armour, biting into flesh.

The instant blood welled, Cade grew taller and larger. And his eyes—

No longer brown, but blood-red. The colour of rage. Of *murder*.

I backed away from the mountainous man in front of me, heedless of my pride or the watching audience. But though my eyes were on Cade, I wasn't focusing on him. My attention was on the carrion birds nearby, feasting on the bodies in no-man's-land—

Cade's sword flashed in the sun, and I moved to meet it with my own – a terrible decision. Locked body-to-body like this, I couldn't compete with his unnatural strength. His muscles bulged as he forced me back, my sword dropping inch by inch.

But already, I could feel the death in my veins surging. The silver of my blade darkened as my magic moved *through* it—

Too late.

My sword went flying as Cade broke through my defences, sending my death magic surging back into me. I gasped at the sensation – like being immersed in an icy bath.

Cade's sword descended, but before he could complete the killing strike, a swarm of skeletal birds speared towards him.

I raced for my sword as Cade's frustrated grunts rang out behind me. But when I turned, weapon in hand, it was to see Cade wielding his sword in a vicious arc, leaving black blood and grey feathers in his wake.

Then he was bearing down on me, bloodlust in his eyes. I blocked his first vicious thrust and dodged the second, slamming the hilt of my sword against his collarbone.

Cade didn't react. Didn't even blink. Then he jabbed his elbow into my bleeding stomach.

I instinctively hunched over – just for a second, but a second was all Cade needed. He kicked me to the ground in a plume of red sand.

Vaguely, I could hear Avril screaming my name, Aric shouting something I couldn't make out, and the audience roaring, their respectful silence dispelled. I wondered dizzily whether they were excited to watch me bleed, or whether some of the spectators remained loyal to their princess.

Cade thrust his sword forward, preparing to run me through, when he paused. My illusion was desperate and clumsy, but he dropped his weapon in shock, seeing a striking viper wrapped around the blade.

Jeers rang out from the audience, who saw no logical explanation for his actions.

Before he could regain the upper hand, I slashed at him with my dagger and then whirled to the side, using my illusions to confuse him. He swung at me, but I was never exactly where he thought I was, and I managed to dodge his blows.

'Fight fair,' he growled.

I didn't reply, relying on every scrap of focus to plan and maintain my illusions. My stomach was burning, and my right arm felt like it was on fire, but I had learnt to fight almost as well with my left.

And I was fast.

I danced around Cade, landing a few lucky cuts to his side. As my confidence increased, the slices became deeper, sending him into a snarling rage.

But right when I was relying on my illusions to shield me, he hurled his dagger. It careened through the air and sliced into my shoulder, making me stumble. Cade advanced on me, his face contorted, and I knew that my illusion had faltered. He no longer had a weapon, but his fury was enough. He would rip me limb from limb if that was what it took.

I lunged in the direction of my fallen sword, trying to summon another illusion, even though it was useless. My concentration was in tatters.

Cade's fist connected with my face, knocking me off my feet. In a daze, I went to roll out of the way, but he anticipated it, his meaty hands fastening around my neck.

Touching my skin—

I grinned.

My death magic responded instantly, black veins spidering underneath his skin. Infecting him.

Air flooded into my lungs as Cade released me, tearing his dagger from my shoulder. I gritted my teeth against the pain, watching intently as Cade staggered back, seeming smaller and weaker than he had a few seconds before. Whatever abilities my mother had granted him would be useless soon, my death magic sapping his strength and reflexes.

With the circling carrion birds still providing a distraction, I wiped any trace of my death magic from view. In place of black veins, I visualised red slashes on his arms – cuts inflicted by my own hand.

Cade's yells were balm to my ears as I reached for my dagger.

He didn't notice. His blade was angled over his chest, as if he might try to cut the veins out of his body.

As Cade debated, I drew up behind him.

Blood sprayed as I sliced my dagger across his throat.

The last of the carrion birds flew off, squawking their displeasure, and as they cleared, so did my view of the onlookers.

For a second we were all united watching Cade, his face white with shock as he raised a hand to his throat. It came away slick with red, and more blood bubbled out of the side of his mouth as he gurgled something unintelligible.

I could have left him to topple forward. But this *was* supposed to be a show.

My booted foot slammed into his back, knocking the muscled Warrior into the sand. He didn't rise again.

Forcing down the pain and exhaustion that threatened to overwhelm me, I retrieved my sword. With my blood still dripping steadily to the sand, I stood tall, envisioning myself as one of those fierce ancient rulers from the icy North. Staring down at my people and daring them to challenge me.

I raised my sword in victory.

My army cheered for me, their princess who had beaten the odds and survived. There was nothing a crowd loved more than being surprised, and what a surprise I had given them.

'I *will* win this war,' I vowed when their cheers had finally died down. 'But to do that, I need your obedience. Do I have it?'

And while I might not have been my father or brothers, the Warriors around me dropped to their knees.

One by one, they bowed to me, as deeply as if Emperor Kalias himself was standing before them.

CHAPTER TWELVE

Scarlett

'Scarlett?'

At the sound of Aric's voice, I raised my head, running a hand through my matted red hair. Dried blood coated the ends, which had faded to white after I had resurrected Lillian. Subtly, I shifted to hide my trembling hands, but Aric had already seen them. He was trained to notice detail.

He took a seat on the edge of my pallet. 'How are you feeling?'

I tried to summon the conviction that had held me together in the arena, allowing me to return to my tent without assistance. But I was too tired, and in too much pain, to pretend to be invincible now. And with Aric, I didn't have to.

'Honestly? Terrible.' I smiled weakly. 'How long were the healers working on me?'

'Almost five hours.'

'That long. It must have been serious.' I tried to sit up, but Lillian was there in an instant, a delicate hand pressed against my chest to stop me from moving.

'You'll tear your stitches,' she told me, her face set in a frown. 'You're in so much pain. You shouldn't have refused the verdine root.'

'It's addictive. And even if it wasn't, I won't have medications clouding my mind. I need to stay sharp.'

'You need to stay in bed,' Lillian said with unexpected authority.

I expected Aric to chastise her – she *was* addressing her princess, after all – but he only smiled, his eyes crinkling with amusement. And something else. Relief.

He was relieved to see proof of Lillian's spirit, I realised. It had been months since she had died and been brought back to life, but I suspected it would take years before he stopped looking at her like a miracle. If he ever did.

To my surprise, Lillian avoided her brother's eyes. It must be difficult being treated like spun glass, something beautiful and fine that could shatter under the slightest pressure.

Someone – most likely Aella – had removed my bloodstained clothes. I lifted my chemise and peeled back one of the bandages covering my stomach. The stitches were small and neat, almost unnaturally so, as though they had been done by—

'I hope you don't mind,' Lillian said anxiously. 'Perhaps I should have let the healer stitch you up, but they can be a little . . . inelegant, and I didn't want it to scar.'

I looked up at her. 'You didn't have to do that.'

'I wanted to.' Lillian met my gaze boldly. 'I know I question your methods sometimes, but I am alive because of you. Consider this a small expression of my gratitude.'

'Thank you.' It was all I could think to say. Even though Lillian's friendship was based on a lie, and Aric's too, it still warmed my heart.

It doesn't matter, I thought, moving to sit up. This time, Lillian didn't try to stop me. *Sentimentality is something I can't afford.*

'Where are we with the Zigilians?' I asked, trying to conceal my wince as the stitches pulled. Lillian, feeling it too, gave me a sharp glance. I ignored her.

'No important decisions have been made during your absence. I've been focusing on establishing my authority as General Harte's replacement.' Aric's mouth turned downwards, and I wondered what kind of pushback he had received. But his voice was self-assured as he continued, 'That task will be easier once you're recovered. You won the respect of your army by defeating Cade; when the other officers see you at my side, they will fall into line.'

'What about Langton? I saw him standing with Cade during the fight.'

'I'm sure he regrets that now. Langton's an opportunist, and he made the wrong call. If anything, he's been one of the easiest officers to deal with. I think he believes that by supporting me, he can redeem himself with you.'

'It'll take more than that,' I muttered, thinking of how quickly he had turned against me.

'Good. I'd hate for you to make it easy for him.' Aric smiled, but it was short-lived. 'It would be wise to make a public appearance soon. There are rumours that your wounds could prove fatal.'

'The healer recommended a few days of bed rest,' Lillian said, then sighed at my expression. 'You remind me of Mira. She was stubborn too.'

Was. As if Mira had died – or perhaps Lillian, like Aric, believed she hadn't truly known Mira at all.

When I looked at Aric, his face was grim. Lillian went quiet, probably regretting making the comparison. Or perhaps she was reading my emotions even now, reacting to my own unease.

We moved on to discussing strategy, but Aric had to stop regularly to gather his thoughts. The third time he did this, my eyes went to the sweat glistening on his forehead.

'Perhaps you should take a break,' Lillian said to him with concern. 'You've been pushing yourself too hard as it is.'

Aric rose to his feet – only to groan and double over. Lillian was at his side before he could fall, and I noticed the way his head lolled forward as she eased him back down.

'I'm fine,' he tried to say, but his voice was thick, the words sluggish.

Fear speared through me. Lillian's eyes darted to mine, her face almost as drawn as her brother's.

'What is it?' she asked urgently. 'What's wrong with him?'

I touched his forehead. It was searing hot.

'It might just be a fever,' I said at last. 'But Aric wasn't a popular choice to replace General Harte, and his new position comes with enemies. There are plenty of toxic plants native to Zigilia, and there's always the possibility that someone could have brought poison from the Ravalian Court.'

'Poison?' Lillian's voice was high and thin. 'Are you sure?'

'I'm not sure of anything. All I have are suspicions.'

I checked Aric over, taking note of his dilated pupils and rapid breathing. He tried to push me away, mumbling something about this being unnecessary, but I persisted. Only my grip on his shoulders kept him from toppling over.

'We should call for a healer,' Lillian said, standing.

I grabbed her wrist. 'No. Not yet.' Ignoring Lillian's protests, I asked Aric, 'Have you eaten?'

He blinked rapidly, as if he was trying to focus on my face. 'No.'

So it wasn't food. That left water, which wasn't a good choice for most poisons. But if it *was* water, the poisoner would have had to use something that was clear and easily dissolvable. I ran through what Zandri had taught me about poisons, trying to think of one that might fit.

'Scarlett!' I glanced reflexively up at Lillian. 'Aric drank from this,' she said, passing over the water pitcher.

My water pitcher.

Perhaps Aric hadn't been the assassin's target at all. I cast my mind back, thinking of how no one except the healers had been allowed in to see me. Thinking of how they had poured me water and even helped me drink it—

It had to have been one of them. Which meant I had been exposed to the poison too.

My body was a little warmer than usual, and the pain was bad – but it would be, given my wounds. Could that pain be clouding the true impact of the poison? Or perhaps it hadn't been the water at all, and I was wasting precious moments while Aric became steadily weaker.

I studied the water pitcher. Then I pushed through the tent flap and addressed the Warriors stationed outside.

'I want every healer to be brought to my tent, under armed guard. Do not let them leave for any reason. Do not provide them with any food or water except for this.' I gestured to the pitcher.

If the Warriors thought my request was strange, they didn't comment on it. 'Yes, Your Highness,' they said, bringing their arms to their chests in the Ravalian gesture of obedience.

I helped Aric to his feet. He was lucid enough to stand on his own, which was a relief. I wasn't strong enough to carry him out of here, even with Lillian's help.

'Steady him,' I told Lillian when Aric swayed.

I didn't feel much better. The wound in my stomach was throbbing, and I was dizzy and light-headed. It occurred to me that it might be safest to summon the Masks and rely on them to fix this. But though Zandri had blood rubies for everyone in the Orders, Mira's mother had once found a way around her magical control. Right now, I couldn't afford to trust anyone.

'What did you say to them?' Lillian asked, her arms wrapped around Aric. Her stare burned into me as I retrieved my dagger and sliced through the back of the tent.

'I ordered the healers held here, with only my pitcher for water.' I didn't look at Lillian. 'My Warriors will observe them. If it's poisoned, and a healer *is* responsible, they will avoid drinking it. Given the heat, that should narrow down our suspects quite well.'

'Scarlett, they have families.' Lillian sounded aghast, but surely this was nothing worse than the bodies piled up outside Damar's walls. 'Most of them are loyal. They worked night and day to help you, and you're talking about *murdering*—'

I climbed outside, deliberately muffling Lillian's last words. My order could condemn innocent people to death, but I didn't have time for a crisis of conscience. I needed to focus on survival.

Lillian and Aric stumbled out of the tent after me, but I didn't turn. My eyes went to the Zigilian stallion tethered just outside. With night falling, and no fire braziers around the back of my tent, at least we had the cover of darkness on our side.

Which didn't mean we were safe. My would-be assassin could still be close – and they might decide to take a more active role in killing me. I didn't like my chances of fighting an assailant in my weakened condition in the middle of the desert. But I liked the idea of staying here even less.

I mounted the stallion first, before helping Lillian hoist Aric into the saddle. He swayed, but remained upright.

'Hold onto my waist,' I told him, and his hands tightened instinctively around me.

'Your turn,' I told Lillian, who climbed up as well.

'Are you sure about this?' she asked, holding Aric tightly. 'He's getting worse. We need to get him somewhere safe. Somewhere he can be looked after properly.'

'I am looking after him,' I said, and jammed my heels into the stallion's side.

I clutched its mane as it moved into a canter, directing it between the tents and towards the desert beyond. It wouldn't be easy to locate the tribal people of the Red Dunes, but I remembered Severin's descriptions of their camps. More importantly, I remembered how he had praised their knowledge of medicine and ancient remedies.

If anyone could save Aric, it would be them. The only problem would be giving them incentive to do so.

And staying alive long enough to find them.

CHAPTER THIRTEEN

Mira

I doubled the guard on Cassius, just to be safe. We hadn't spoken since the night of Roran's unexpected arrival, but I hadn't forgotten the ruthless pragmatism in his eyes when he'd advised me to kill Nari.

Velanthe had been equally vocal on the subject – though her answer, as usual, was to turn to blood magic.

But so far, things were progressing surprisingly well. Vølund had taken to life in the Temple with ease. He had even accepted my invitation to distribute much needed food, water and supplies to the war-torn refugees.

The sunlight played across his face, softening the harshness of his features. My eyes went to the sacks of wheat he carried, slung over his broad shoulders, and something in me softened too. I'd never seen a leader – a *ruler* – who was willing to get their hands dirty. Who actually seemed to enjoy helping and interacting with their people, not out of duty or for some political scheme, but because they truly cared.

Vølund caught me looking and raised a dark brow. 'What is it?'

'They love you,' I said, nodding at the refugees, who thronged the path between their makeshift dwellings. They ventured close as we passed, brushing my skirts with their hands and staring up at Vølund with adoring faces.

'I wouldn't go that far. Capital-dwellers are usually wary of the clans.'

'Do they look wary to you?' I asked as a group of children raced forward. The warriors behind me shifted, but I held up a hand and they remained where they were.

Bending down to their level, I smiled as I accepted a flower from a little girl.

'It's black,' she told me in her high, sweet voice. 'Black for the Sorceress.'

'Thank you,' I said, moved by the gesture. She darted off in the way children often do, taking her giggling friends with her – but not before I saw the admiring glances they shot in Vølund's direction.

Yet the clan leader's expression appeared troubled. 'I shouldn't have accompanied you.'

His words cut. I rarely had company on excursions like these – not beyond the warriors and priestesses, and they always kept a discreet distance. Having him with me had made the weight of my responsibilities feel a little lighter.

'It's my fault.' I tried to keep the disappointment from my voice. 'I shouldn't have burdened you with this. These are my people. My responsibility.'

'That's not what I mean.' Vølund's gaze was on the black-petalled flower. 'Seeing us together like this . . . it sets up certain expectations.'

When he glanced back up, I saw his concern. Not for himself – but for these people.

'And you're worried you won't be able to fulfil those expectations.' *Because you're already planning to hand me over to him.*

'I haven't decided anything yet, Kasmira.'

But the fact that we were even having this conversation . . . 'You'll tell me if you accept Roran's offer, won't you?'

'Of course.' He hesitated. 'I hope you understand that it isn't anything personal. As leaders . . . we have to make the best choice for our people.'

'That we do,' I said as we walked, stopping to hand out food and greet the men, women and children who rushed forward to meet us. 'But do you really believe Roran is what's best for *them*?'

I allowed the silence to stretch on, knowing that Vølund's doubts would stretch along with it.

'Come on,' I told him, approaching the saddled stallions waiting for us at the edge of the thick forest. 'If I recall, I promised you a visit to the treetop villages. Consider it a reward for all your help this morning.'

Vølund smoothly mounted – far more at ease in the saddle than I was. But my horse-riding skills had improved over the last few months, and I waved away the priestess who hurried over to help me.

As we turned our horses away from the Temple, I noticed Vølund cast one last glance at the refugees behind us.

Hope. That was what I saw on their faces – what he would see too. Hope for a brighter future.

My legs dangled out over empty space.

Far below, I could see wooden bridges and dwellings, artfully constructed around the ancient trees of the Wilds. Beyond them was the forest floor, distantly illuminated by mottled sunlight.

I closed my eyes as the warmth of the sun fell on my face, listening to the creak of the wooden bridge to my left, the chittering and chirping of the colourful birds, and the sigh of the wind in the trees.

When I opened my eyes, it was to see Vølund watching me with unexpected intensity.

Vølund shifted back from me – he had been leaning in, I realised now – and retreated to the centre of our treetop lookout. I followed, reclining next to him on the thick, handwoven rug.

'You've hardly touched your food,' I said, glancing at the picnic the chieftain had arranged for us: grained bread and an assortment of fruits and nuts. 'I can ask for something else.'

'I was hoping to save some for your people – the capital-dwellers outside the Temple walls.'

It was a wonderful idea. But . . .

'Why this distinction between the Wilds and the rest of Kalure? I've never really understood it.'

Vølund took the black-petalled flower from my hand, rolling it in his palm. 'What did your high priestess tell you about the deaths of Queen Rúna and her consort?'

I blinked in surprise. 'Only that Zandri was involved. I assumed that was why Arioch banished her from Kalure – as punishment for killing their parents and attempting to take the throne.'

'I wondered why you were so quick to embrace Temple teachings. It makes sense if you didn't know the full extent of it.'

'The full extent of *what?*'

'Of how your grandparents died. The Sorceress,' he continued, 'was beloved in the cities and throughout the Wilds. It was under her benevolent rule that Kalure was united. But over time, her descendants started being ruled by Temple rhetoric. They stopped visiting the Wilds, losing touch with the natural, pure core of their magic and turning to darker powers instead.'

'Blood magic,' I said quietly.

'Blood magic,' Vølund agreed. 'As I'm sure you know, it comes with a steep cost. If you push too hard, it pushes back – and it isn't always possible to know your limits. Fighting broke out between the Wilds and the capital during your great-great-grandmother's reign. She used blood magic to win, costing many lives – including her own. Queen Rúna grew up without a mother as a result, and when she came to power, she turned against the Temple and banned blood magic. But Zandri disobeyed her edict, and was stripped of her position as heir. The priestesses retaliated on her behalf and cut down the very queen they had once sworn to protect.'

The hostility between the clansmen and priestesses made sense now. Velanthe had told me they were wary of blood magic, but she'd never mentioned—

'Was – did *Velanthe* . . .' I couldn't bring myself to ask. Didn't know what I would do if the answer was yes.

'No one knows exactly who gave the order,' Vølund replied. 'I only know that Velanthe is the high priestess now. It's possible that the high priestess at the time was cut down during the assassination.'

That sounded more likely; Velanthe would have been young when my grandparents were killed. Probably too young to be high priestess. But not too young to be a priestess. Not too young to have taken part in—

I cut off the thought. If I started doubting Velanthe now, then where would I be?

'Your father had many advisers,' Vølund said, his words slow and careful. 'Admittedly he turned against the Temple, so there were no priestesses on his council. But he tried to give everyone a voice.'

'Did you . . .' My voice was soft, tentative. 'Did you know him?'

'I met him a few times. From what I saw, King Arioch was a good man. My father was one of the clansmen on his council. He always spoke highly of him.'

I looked away, not wanting Vølund to see the raw emotion on my face. 'I wonder what would have happened,' I murmured, 'if Emperor Kalias hadn't invaded. If we had met under different circumstances.'

'I would have courted you,' Vølund replied, his emerald eyes intent on mine. 'I am certain of that much.'

There it was again: that fierce, warrior-like intensity – except it was focused entirely on me. And even though I had wanted to draw him in, was *relying* on it, I wasn't nearly as unaffected as I needed to be.

Vølund smiled slightly at my expression. He wasn't quick to smile, but when he did, his smiles were always warm and genuine. After my experiences in the Ravalian Court, his openness took me by surprise.

'Do you go by Mira, as you used to in Ravalia?' he asked, breaking the comfortable silence. 'Or do you prefer Kasmira?'

I frowned, wondering if there was a deeper meaning behind his question. Was this an attempt to assess my loyalties?

Which are you, princess? Emperor Kalias had asked me once. *Ravalian or Kalurian? Because you can't be both.*

'Call me Kasmira,' I said firmly. 'I left my past in Ravalia behind when I came here.'

'I see.' A delicate pause. 'Yet two Ravalians act as your personal attendants, or perhaps bodyguards. And the priestess who rarely leaves your side is Ravalian as well.'

'I am half Ravalian,' I acknowledged, choosing my words with care. 'I suppose it's only natural that I have some remaining ties with Ravalia. But I hope you can see that I have great love and appreciation for Kalure. And . . . I am learning, Vølund. I want to do better – to create a lasting peace between the Wilds and the rest of Kalure.' I paused, then admitted, 'Circumstances have forced me to be heavily reliant on the Temple, but I am not blindly led by their beliefs. If I have the chance, I would establish a council, as my father did. I would like to be able to connect with my people, to embrace every part of this beautiful country and its history.'

A shadow briefly clouded Vølund's face. I'd seen this expression a few times – usually when Roran was mentioned. The clan leader wasn't convinced that allying with Ravalia was the right decision.

'If I may,' I began slowly, 'what do you think about Roran's offer?'

'It doesn't matter what I think.' Vølund leant back on his forearms, allowing me to admire his tanned muscles. The silver pieces in his dark braids gleamed as they caught the light. 'The clan heads are tired of this war. An opportunity for peace . . . well, that is an attractive prospect.'

'But the final decision is yours,' I pressed. 'The clans chose you as their leader for a reason.'

'They chose me because I fought and bested the other contenders. That does not mean I wish to impose my will on them.' Vølund was silent for a moment. When he next spoke, his tone was guarded. 'Even if Ravalians have a history of reneging on their promises. Even if . . . I have started to admire you. The kindness you show others. The fierceness of your spirit.'

Vølund cupped the black flower in his palm. He held it with heart-breaking tenderness, and I felt for him. He wanted to protect me, like he protected his sister and the rest of his people. But he had to honour their wishes and make the best choice for the clans.

Even if that choice cost me my life.

I took the flower from him, laying it gently on the wooden boards. Then, with a surge of daring, I took his hand in mine – calloused, from years of training. Vølund, I was coming to discover, was not a hard man. But he was fiercely capable, and I respected that. I respected *him*.

'I won't blame you. If you accept Roran's offer.' I smiled sadly. 'I don't want us to be on opposite sides of this war, but I will understand. We all make sacrifices for our people.'

He reached up to cup my cheeks, his face suddenly inches from mine. It should have been intimidating to be so close to someone clearly built for war, but even the dagger-like tattoos that pierced his dark brows were intriguing rather than frightening.

Staring up into Vølund's green eyes, I was reminded of the forest canopy around us. Bright. Luminous.

'Kasmira,' he murmured, 'I—'

I kissed him.

I hadn't planned on it, and I was surprised at my own daring. My heart pounded a thunderous rhythm against my ribcage as I braced myself for Vølund's reaction.

Strong hands came to rest on my waist, anchoring me in place. And then Vølund deepened the kiss, his lips soft and firm against mine. His muscular arms holding me close without making me feel trapped.

In the unexpected gentleness of his touch, I felt everything he wanted to say: his affection for me, his empathy and sadness for our people, and perhaps a trace of longing – that this might not have to end.

That longing was what I had been hoping for.

I pulled back but remained staring into his face. 'What if there was another way?'

Vølund clearly didn't believe that there was. But he humoured me, leaning back slightly and waiting for me to continue.

'Am I correct in saying that neither you nor the clans trust Roran? And that allying with me would be your preferred option?'

He slowly nodded. 'Yes. But there isn't enough that you can offer us. Standing with you is simply not worth the lives it will cost.'

I thought of what Roran had offered Vølund: the chance to rule over Kalure. The opportunity for Nari to stand at Roran's side and reap the benefits of an association with the Ravalian Empire.

It always came down to the Ravalian Empire, didn't it? Even here, in Kalure, where the Ravalians were hated . . . it was still the ultimate prize.

I took a deep breath. And then I said the words that I had been leading up to ever since I first met Vølund. 'What if I took Roran's place as empress of Ravalia? Would you stand with me *then*?'

Vølund stared at me in shocked disbelief.

'Roran cannot be allowed to live,' I continued. 'And the Ravalian Court values strength above all else. If I defeat Roran and remove Cassius and Scarlett – the last of Emperor Kalias's descendants – then I will have proven myself worthy of his crown.'

'You've given this a great deal of thought.'

'I have.' I met his stare evenly. 'The Ravalian Empire is broken. It is cruel to the countries it conquers, and Emperor Kalias's reign spread terror and war. It's time for a new ruler to rise. One with the ability to forge peace between two warring nations.'

Vølund frowned, though he seemed to be considering my proposal. 'What exactly are you offering?'

'The same terms as Roran,' I said promptly. 'Except my marriage would be to you. And our marriage would allow us to rule over both Ravalia and Kalure – together. There would be no need to rely on Roran's goodwill, to hope that Nari could keep him in line. You and I would have equal power. The full might of the empire would be behind us, ensuring Kalure will never again be threatened. We could give the people what they desperately want, what my father and yours wanted. True and lasting peace.'

I ignored the tightness of my chest. I had said the words, made the offer: it was too late to change course now.

'I will have to discuss this with the clans,' Vølund said at last. 'And my sister.'

'I understand.'

'But those matters are just formalities.' A smile broke over his face, shattering the guarded exterior. 'This offer – it's everything they could have wanted, Kasmira. Everything *I* could have wanted.'

He brought my hand to his lips, honouring our agreement with a kiss.

Sealing it.

CHAPTER FOURTEEN

Mira

This banquet was nothing like the last one.

It was a feast and a celebration – a rowdy, enthusiastic celebration, the Kalurian clansmen already deep in their cups. Vølund and I surveyed it all from the main table, the heavy drumbeats making talking difficult. But I preferred it like this: there was a quiet ease between us, and I knew we were both enjoying the sight of our people – warriors and priestesses alike – finally united.

Then Vølund stood, and the hall went abruptly silent.

'As you know,' he said, addressing me rather than our audience, 'the Kalurian custom is not to exchange rings and vows. But I would like to offer you an engagement gift all the same.'

Velanthe had told me about this custom. I braced myself for Vølund to call one of his warriors up to the main table, and offer me their sword. Instead—

I went still as he slid his own blade free of its sheath.

'I had modifications made,' Vølund said, extending it to me.

I took it with reverent fingers, testing the weight and balance – lighter than I would have expected. Given the significance of a sword to Kalurian warriors, I could barely believe that he would be willing to part with it, let alone have it altered to better suit me.

'You are a warrior too,' Vølund said, 'and deserving of a proper blade. These runes—' he indicated the symbols along the sword— 'tell of my previous battles. They are your victories now. As your victories will in turn be mine.'

I gazed up at him, unexpectedly touched. But—

'I don't know how to read them,' I admitted.

To my surprise, Vølund smiled. 'They're ancient symbols, only used in the Wilds. I will teach you how to read them.'

I ran a finger over the indents of the runes. No one had ever given me a gift like this before. But here Vølund was, a proud Kalurian clan leader, entrusting something intensely personal to me – and showing all the warriors in attendance just how much he held my abilities in esteem. For no warrior would give their sword to an inferior fighter.

'I watched you,' Vølund said softly, offering me his arm. I took it, allowing him to pull me to my feet. 'Every morning in the training courtyard. You fight well – even if your technique is a little too Ravalian for my liking.'

'Perhaps you would like to join me next time,' I said, keeping pace with him as we strode back through the hall. The drums started up again, almost drowned out by a roar of laughter and overly loud conversation. 'You can teach me a more Kalurian approach.'

'I look forward to it,' Vølund replied.

We stepped out into the courtyard. Before the doors shut behind us, I caught a final glimpse of the feast – or what was left of it. The Kalurian warriors clearly cared nothing for cleanliness; the food had been devoured, wine goblets spilled, and I was startled to see a few priestesses in their laps. I had never thought – never dared hope – that the tension between our peoples could be resolved this easily.

'Perhaps tonight is something of a new beginning,' Vølund said softly.

I glanced up. Under the colonnades, his face was cast in shadow – but the firelight played across his jawline, highlighting the strong angles of his face. I took in his solid fighter's build, his steady gaze. Gods, what would it be like to rely on Vølund? To rule – not by myself, floundering and afraid, but with a seasoned leader at my side?

'You're no longer alone, Kasmira,' Vølund murmured. Because he *knew*, didn't he? He knew the weight of that loneliness, that responsibility—

'Neither are you,' I murmured back.

His fingers brushed the hair back from my face. Fingers that were strong and calloused and used to killing, yet achingly gentle against my skin.

My shoulders hit the doors of the banquet hall as Vølund leant in, his face inches from mine. I had kissed him before, but not like this. What would it be like to close the distance between us? To take the leap from a polite, political arrangement to something more?

Vølund smiled, his muscular arms pulling me to him—

Footsteps. They rang loudly against the cobblestones, and as the clan leader turned, I looked past him to see—

'Oh, sorry,' Cassius drawled, not sounding sorry at all. 'Am I interrupting something?'

'You are, actually.' Vølund's voice was measured, but there was a hint of steel in it.

My lips twitched. Vølund wasn't one of Cassius's courtiers from Ravalia; wasn't the type to be intimidated or mince words. Though Cassius's expression was one of bland disinterest, I could see the calculating way he studied the clan leader, as though he was sizing up an opponent.

Vølund considered us both for a moment. I waited for him to dismiss Cassius, but then I realised he wouldn't. What had he said about his clansmen? That he didn't want to impose his will on them. And he wouldn't impose his will on me, either.

'I should return to the celebrations,' Vølund said with a wry smile. 'Kasmira, you know where to find me.'

The doors groaned open, affording me a flash of light and noise and the heady smells of cooked meat and spiced wine. Then they slid shut again, leaving me in quiet darkness.

'I didn't realise that you and Vølund were so close,' Cassius remarked, the words lightly mocking.

'That's what happens,' I said, turning to face him, 'when an engagement is based on mutual trust and respect.'

'And here I thought that he planned to hand you over to Roran for execution. He makes me seem positively merciful in comparison.'

I didn't deign that worthy of a response. Not after watching General and Lady Tiran lose their heads. But was I behaving any differently to Cassius? I had thought he was a monster for the lives he'd taken, yet my plans would cost lives too. Chief amongst them—

'Tell me, Mira. Are you as *close* with Vølund as you were with me?'

Cassius moved closer, his footsteps – that had previously been so loud and jarring – now completely silent. Cat-like. 'You blushed so sweetly. So *innocently*. Would Vølund still believe you're so innocent if he knew how you seduced me during the First Trial? Or how completely you surrendered yourself to me the night of my masquerade ball?'

'I didn't *surrender* myself to you—'

'I could have had you that night, and we both know it.' His hand traced its way up my bare leg, exposed through the slit of my dress. Slow, deliberate, making a point. Reminding me of how he had touched me that night, of how I had *wanted* him to—

My hand enclosed over his, stopping it on my upper thigh. I was breathing faster than I should have been, and I was furious with myself. But mostly, I was furious with him.

Somehow, we were still playing that game. That ill-fated, deadly game I had started during the first Trial.

'You can't stand it, can you?' I said coldly. '*Losing.*'

'I haven't lost anything. But you've lost your mind, Mira, if you think that Vølund will be enough for you.'

'What's the matter, Cassius?' I taunted. 'Jealous?'

His grip tightened on my leg, forcing me up against one of the colonnades, his muscular thigh settling between mine. Trapping me between the hard lines of his body and the stone.

The heat of him seared into me, and this was so different from Vølund's careful advances – not so much a flicker of desire, but a heady pulse, an ache that reverberated through my entire body. It made no sense. Absolutely *none*, that he would affect me this way.

Cassius held me there, his hand still against my skin but not wandering any further south. His voice was calm, contemplative, as he said, 'Tell me what you promised Vølund to change his mind.'

'Maybe my charms are just that good.'

'Believe me, Mira, I have a great appreciation for your *charms*.' A wicked smile curved his mouth. 'But Vølund isn't the sort to place personal desire above political advantage. The promise of marrying you wouldn't be enough to dissuade him from taking Roran's offer.'

'Not even if it saved his sister from being chained to a psychopath?'

'Not even then.' His breath ghosted across my throat as he whispered in my ear, 'Why else would I have advised that you kill Nari? Contrary to what you seem to think, murder isn't my opening gambit.'

I narrowed my eyes, unconvinced. Cassius might not do the killing himself, but he was talented at manipulating situations – usually in ways that conveniently ended with his enemies dead.

But he was right about Vølund. Marrying me wouldn't have been enough. Not without the promise of ruling an empire one day.

'This isn't the Ravalian Court, Cassius,' I said firmly, staring up into his dark gaze. 'You don't have to be so distrustful all the time.'

It was impossible to tell what Cassius thought of my words. He seemed content to let the silence linger – a tactic I'd seen him use in the past, when he wanted to tempt someone into confessing something damning.

Was it possible that he knew? That he'd *guessed* what I offered Vølund in exchange for this alliance?

'Old habits die hard, I suppose,' Cassius said pleasantly, and I felt the tension drain from my shoulders. 'If you tell me there's nothing else, I'll let it go.'

What had he said once? *If you want to survive in this Court, you're going to have to hide your emotions.*

'No,' I lied, my voice impressively steady. 'There's nothing else.'

I had finally learnt his lesson.

Yet Cassius's grip tightened on my thigh, his left hand rising to toy with my hair. Before I could pull away, he claimed my mouth.

Passion exploded between us as our lips met, making me gasp. Cassius had always reminded me of contradictions – controlled on the surface, but with explosive potential underneath.

There was something demanding and almost angry about the way he kissed me, his hands tangling in my hair, his body pressing against mine. I was so focused on his lips and the feeling of his body that I forgot all about his hand. His hand, pushing my undergarments aside and—

All words and thoughts and common sense left me. I arched against him, gripping the lapels of his tunic as a satisfied sound of approval left his lips.

That sound was enough to return some of my sanity. To remind me exactly who I was allowing to touch me like this, in full view of anyone who left the banquet hall, where my betrothed was waiting.

Tomorrow I would be *married*. I clung to that thought, placing my palm against Cassius's chest and preparing to push him off me—

But his mouth was insistent and sinful and entirely too talented. A perfect match to his fingers as he thrust two into me with delicious force, making my hips move against him and drawing a gasp from my throat.

Ruinous. The way he touched me was ruinous, and as my eyes locked with those wicked midnight-blue ones, I realised that was the point. He wanted to ruin me. To watch me fall apart beneath his fingers.

'You think you need Vølund to rule this country,' he said, voice velvety soft and far too intimate, 'but you don't. You already have me.'

'I don't *have* you,' I bit back, ignoring my quickening breaths. 'I never did. The only reason you're toying with me is because of the power I might give you. The moment I'm not useful, you'll turn on me.'

'Are you sure of that, Mira?' Cassius asked. 'Sure enough to chain yourself to some Kalurian brute?'

'Vølund offers my country stability. *And* he offers me protection from Roran.'

'I could protect you from Roran,' Cassius murmured, this time against my mouth. 'He would never get near you. I would kill him first.'

A shiver darted down my spine at his words – and the deadly promise within them.

I should have pulled away then. No – I should have run for my life. But my body betrayed me, leaning into Cassius even as I willed myself to stop this *now*. To do whatever it took to banish that self-satisfied smile from his face—

His thumb circled the most intimate part of me, an almost nonchalant gesture, like one of his throwaway witty lines. A feather-soft laugh left his lips as my hands tightened around his arms, fighting back the jagged moan building in my throat.

Too much. Having Cassius touching me like this was *too much*, and I knew I was a fool for ever believing I could dally with a prince who was darkness itself.

'Surrender,' he told me, those calculating eyes intent on me. Delighting in the sight of my trembling body, the power he had over me. 'Surrender to me, Mira.' Soft and persuasive.

Like what I imagined a demon's voice would sound like. *Surrender and let me take your soul.*

My mouth opened, forming the words: No. *Never.*

I thought I saw Cassius smile. But it was difficult to be sure it wasn't a hallucination as his fingers thrust into me a final time, right as his thumb found the perfect spot. Pleasure – aching, *blissful* pleasure – raced through my veins.

A kind of haziness settled over me as I collapsed against Cassius's chest, his fingers ghosting along my spine. A paralysing, drugging touch that made me wonder if I was dreaming. It was the look of masculine satisfaction on his face that convinced me I wasn't. That this was real, and I had just allowed him to—

'Oh, don't look so upset.' Cassius's tone was nonchalant once more. As if what we had just done meant nothing to him.

Except there was a definite curve to his full lips, and his hold on me was too tight to be anything other than possessive.

I did what I should have done in the beginning: I pushed him firmly away. Cassius didn't resist, his gaze raking over me as I tried to regain my composure. Contemplative, and . . . something else. Something that matched the tightness of his hold, the gleam in his eyes as he had told me to surrender.

'Why are you *smiling*?' I demanded.

'Because you're still mine, Mira.' His voice was low and dark and filled with sensuous promise. 'I wanted to make sure – but now I know for certain.'

He was still smiling as he turned and strode into the darkness, leaving me staring after him with mounting apprehension – because Cassius had smiled at me like he knew something I didn't.

He had smiled at me like he'd *won.*

CHAPTER FIFTEEN

Scarlett

Unlike the thousands of proud tents belonging to my army, the tribe's encampment was small – little more than twenty tents, the rest razed to ash on General Harte's order.

I hadn't agreed with his decision, but I hadn't argued against it. The Red Desert tribes were known allies of the Zigilians, and they had a reputation as fierce fighters. So we had dealt with them before they could pose a threat.

I glanced at the mass grave dug to the left of the camp, then back at the hollow-cheeked people who emerged from their tents. By the looks of it, my forces had been thorough. And I doubted that the remaining tribespeople – mostly healers, children and elders – would be eager to help us. A thought that was confirmed when a few dozen surviving warriors encircled us with raised swords and spears.

'*Do something*,' Lillian hissed from behind me.

The warriors were painted for war, instantly setting me on edge. As my vulnerability flared, so did pride and anger – but threatening them would achieve nothing.

I held up my hands in a gesture of submission. 'We come in peace.'

The warriors didn't respond except to drag Aric and Lillian off the horse, speaking in a language I didn't recognise – an unsettling development, considering I'd studied the native languages of Etheria and Zigilia. But since most of the Western Lands communicated in the common tongue, there must be *someone* who could understand it.

'Don't touch me,' I snapped, when one of the warriors reached upwards. I slid from the horse with as much dignity as I could muster, but as soon as my feet hit the ground they were on me, removing my dagger and the sword strapped to my hip. I strode forward, ignoring the weapons levelled in my direction.

'He's hurt,' I said, pointing to Aric. 'Do you have a healer who can help him? Where is your leader?'

The warriors merely tugged Aric from Lillian's arms. Two of them began to carry him into the encampment.

'If Aric dies,' Lillian said quietly to me, 'I'll never forgive you.'

I nodded curtly back, but it was too late to wish we had stayed in the Ravalian camp. After hours of riding through the desert, we had reached a critical point: our meagre provisions were severely depleted, we were exhausted, and our skin was burned and chapped from sun exposure and dehydration. It wasn't just Aric's survival that depended on these people.

Escorted at spear point, we followed the warriors inside the largest tent. I had been hopeful that Severin's name might still carry some weight here, and that perhaps we could come to amicable terms.

But as I passed the ragged, unsmiling people of the Red Dunes, with their hard faces and even harder eyes, I began to worry that they wouldn't bother with politics at all – and would simply cut our throats.

Severin.

The tribe's leader bore a striking resemblance to him. My traitorous heart stuttered as I took in the young man's red vest, dark skin, ebony hair, and bared, muscular arms. But his face was squarer than Severin's, and the keen eyes he fixed on me weren't piercing, mismatched shades of black and grey, but an ordinary hazel.

Though he was far from ordinary. Black tattoos decorated his cheeks: a palm with an open eye in its centre.

I went still. Those weren't the symbols of his tribe.

Those were the symbols of a *seer*. Sacred symbols that Zandri had dishonoured when she had used them in the Order of Artisans. And she hadn't merely stolen their symbols. No – she had stolen seers, too, hunting them down and offering them two choices: serve her or die.

This was going to be even harder than I'd thought.

Aric was laid out in front of the seer. A woman crouched nearby, bowls of herbs spread around her. A healer, no doubt. So the warriors had understood me after all.

I still tensed when she reached for Aric's bare chest, smearing a paste across his skin. When I made an involuntary movement forward, I heard the rasp of a sword unsheathing behind me.

'Hold, Korin.' It was the seer who spoke, his gaze fixed on the warrior I felt at my back. Satisfied that I wasn't about to be cut down, he refocused his attention on me. 'Your companion will not be harmed. Lilah is merely treating his symptoms, trying to dispel his fever. She will do nothing more until I give the word.'

A threat – or an offer. I couldn't tell which.

'I'm surprised to find a seer here,' I said cautiously.

'I'm sure you are.' His voice – Gods, it was deep and melodic, and it hit me like a punch to the gut. But Severin's voice had never been quite so cutting. 'I was in Damar for a while, trying to resolve the situation without bloodshed. By the time I Saw the attack on the Red Dunes, I was too late to stop the worst of it.'

All magic had its limitations, and this was one I was familiar with. Artisans – or seers – could only See a future outcome when someone decided to act. Unfortunately for the people of the Red Dunes, General Harte had made his decision quickly and executed it in a matter of hours.

'I didn't order the attack on your people.'

The seer tilted his head, studying me. 'Yet you didn't stop it.'

'Aric tried to.' I nodded at his motionless form, and the seer followed my gaze. 'He argued with the generals, even though he knew it was hopeless. If I hadn't intervened, he would have been demoted – or worse. That's how strongly he values human life.'

'And what of you?' the seer asked softly. 'What do *you* value?'

I forced myself to consider the question. The answer that sprang to mind wasn't the one I had been expecting.

'Freedom.' Realising how that sounded, I added, 'For myself – and for others.'

The warriors stirred sceptically at my back, but the seer considered my words in silence.

Taking his silence as an invitation to continue, I said, 'Zigilia is rebelling because of the absolute control imposed by my father. But I am not my father. I am willing to negotiate fairer terms, including lower taxes and the appointment of a Zigilian Provincial Governor, rather than a Ravalian one. If the insurgency had been willing to meet with me, all of this bloodshed could have been avoided.'

'For Zigilia to be free, Ravalia must first relinquish control. Any Provincial Governor you installed would act in the interests of the Ravalian Empire.'

'Zigilia is part of the Ravalian Empire,' I said, my voice sharp. 'I cannot change that, nor do I believe it *should* change. But I am willing to allow Zigilia many of the freedoms my father stripped from her.' I paused, choosing my next words carefully. 'My father's mistake was prioritising Ravalia's prosperity over countries like Zigilia, but we are all part of the one empire. I intend to honour that. And once Zigilia reaps the benefits of being part of the Ravalian Empire, I believe its people will consider some fair oversight an acceptable trade.'

'Seers used to rule Zigilia,' he said. 'Under your father's occupation, we were rounded up and forced to serve in the Order of Artisans instead. Any child born with the gift was either forced to report to the Ravalian Warriors – or flee to avoid detection, risking their life and the lives of anyone who aided them.'

Clearly, the man in front of me had chosen the latter. It was impressive that he had survived this long.

'I have no involvement in that practice,' I told him. 'My father's cruelties aren't mine.'

'They are if you do nothing to correct them.' The seer's voice was mild, but the implication of his words was not.

'I don't have the power to make those kinds of changes,' I said coolly. 'I'm not the empress.'

'But you could be.'

I watched the seer closely. I had seen a similar expression before – on Severin. Right after he had looked into the future.

'Is that a prediction?'

The man's smile held a calculating edge. Too late, I realised that my question had exposed a weakness. A weakness he could exploit.

But he didn't press his advantage except to say, 'Leave us.'

The warriors filed out, escorting Lillian along with them. She shot me a nervous glance as she left the tent, but I didn't try to intervene. I had no authority here, and nothing good would come from trying to force the issue.

When we were alone, the seer approached Aric. His eyes closed as he brought two fingers to Aric's feverish brow.

'Is it poison?' I asked anxiously, crossing the tent. The furs were soft against my knees as I knelt on Aric's other side.

'Of a sort,' came his distracted reply.

Do all seers speak in useless riddles?

Tempering my impatience, I said, 'Can you help him or not?'

'It's not my help he needs.' When the seer finally looked at me, his expression was hard to read. 'Did you truly believe you could invite death into you without a cost?'

'Are you saying . . .' I stared down at Aric's pallid skin, my chest tightening as I listened to his rapid, shallow breathing. 'Are you saying that *I* did this?'

'Magic comes with consequences,' he replied. 'To yourself – and to those closest to you. Every time you embrace death, your powers become stronger. But death is toxic to the living.'

I released my grip on Aric's arm, staring down at my hands. *I* had caused this. With my hands, my lips, my *touch*—

'You're no longer poisonous,' the seer said, his voice gentle. 'Your touch won't hurt him now. But if you want to save Aric, you will have to invite the death magic back into your body.'

I didn't hesitate. Reaching for Aric, I sliced a thin cut across his palm.

The moment the blood welled, my remaining doubts disappeared. The seer had told the truth.

I stared down at the black blood, wishing I could feel horrified at what I had done. But as the veins wound up my arms, all I felt was numb.

Colour slowly returned to Aric's cheeks. The colder and more distant I became, the healthier he seemed, until his sleep was no longer troubled but peaceful. I watched the rhythmic rise and fall of his chest, knowing that he was well again. Yet the knowledge didn't carry the relief it should have.

'Your death magic won't hurt you physically,' the seer said. 'But it skews your perceptions. After all, what does death want? What does a destructive power like this crave?'

More death. More destruction. I watched the black veins snake across my skin. Then I glanced up – into the seer's steady gaze.

He was a threat to me. A single touch, a single brush of my finger, and he would never be a threat to me again.

We watched each other in silence, only Aric's body separating us. And I knew that my eyes were wholly black.

How many people could I kill with this power? It occurred to me that perhaps I hadn't needed to siphon so much death into Cade. Perhaps I had only needed to use a fraction. In which case, I could murder this seer *and* the warriors guarding Lillian—

Fast as a viper, I grasped his hand with mine. Blackness surged, wrapping around our joined hands like inky ribbons.

The seer didn't even flinch. 'You said that you came in peace.'

I stared at the young man's ebony hair and strong face, swallowing past a sudden lump in my throat. He reminded me so much of Severin.

Suddenly, all I wanted was to make him pay. To destroy the man in front of me – just like I had destroyed the greenhouse back in Ravalia, smashing the glass and tearing down the plants with bloodied hands.

How dare *you leave me.* The thoughts surfaced in a familiar haze of rage and hurt. *How dare you turn your back on me as though I meant* nothing.

'I've Seen you kill me,' the seer continued steadily. 'Only the killing doesn't end with me. Your death magic spreads through the tribes like a contagion. It doesn't spare the children or the elderly, and it doesn't spare the two friends you came here with.'

'Lies,' I breathed, but I didn't release my control over the magic. 'You would say anything to save yourself.'

'It's the truth.' Something in his gaze made me believe him. A bottomless grief I had only seen in the eyes of people who had known true loss, and yet there was strength there too. The strength of a survivor and a leader. 'Your actions break you,' he told me. 'You give in to the magic – you decimate the Western Lands, kill Kasmira and your brothers and claim your father's empire. But your mind and body become as poisonous as the death you wield.'

I forced myself to look into his face – into that bottomless well of loss. And at last I felt the true horror of what he described.

I released him. The black veins swarmed back through my body like pinpricks of ice. But my hands remained cold and numb.

'Why didn't you try to stop me?' I asked through clenched teeth.

His voice was soft but not gentle. 'You needed to stop yourself.'

I climbed to my feet, trying to hide how shaken I was. I hadn't allowed my death magic to move into the seer, but it had taken all of my very tenuous control. If that control slipped, even for a second, and my skin brushed against Lillian's, or Aric's—

I stopped the thought before it could fully form. I *would* control it, and that was all that mattered.

'I don't understand,' I said at last, turning back to the seer. 'If you knew all this, why didn't you order your warriors to kill us when we first arrived? Why bother to meet with me in the first place?'

'Because of a promise I made our mutual friend.' He smiled faintly, waiting for me to put it together.

'Severin,' I said through bloodless lips.

The seer inclined his head. 'Severin helped me stay free from the Ravalian Court – as he did for others. Zandri sent him to track any seers that had been hidden from the Orders, and Severin found them and hid them when he could, even knowing that he would be punished for his failure.'

'That sounds like something he would do.' Tears welled in my eyes, but I refused to let them fall. 'What else did he say to you? *Where is he?*'

I advanced on the seer, but his expression remained unaffected. Not even a flicker of fear shadowed his handsome face. 'Close your eyes,' he instructed, 'and I'll show you.'

The moment I did, a vision rose up, crystal clear and relentless and terrible. Severin, silhouetted by the glowing lights of a city far below. Severin, so beautiful that the sight of him hurt, like trying to inhale with a punctured lung.

Time seemed to slow as I watched him fall from the Ravalian

battlements, his clothes and hair buffeted by a vicious wind, his arms outstretched – as though he was reaching for me.

And even though this was a vision, I could have sworn that his eyes stared straight into mine.

With his last breath, he smiled. A small, sad smile—

The vision disintegrated with a sickening crunch. The crunch of breaking bone and shattering limbs.

I opened my eyes, but even as I returned to reality, I knew a part of me had been forever left behind on those battlements. And this – *this* was the reason I had never wanted to fall in love. Because this pain would destroy me. It would destroy anyone.

But I had to ask. I had to force myself to say the words, to finish this, to make the pain complete.

'How?' I demanded. 'How did he die?'

The moment I said the words, I wished I could take them back. Some truths were too terrible to face.

Some truths were enough to shatter people in two.

Don't say it, I wanted to tell him. *Don't.*

But I couldn't make my lips move. I couldn't even breathe.

'Zandri,' he told me—

And I shattered.

CHAPTER SIXTEEN

Scarlett

My return to the Ravalian encampment was a victorious one.

I arrived ahead of a host of tribal warriors, with their leader, Malek, riding at my left and Aric at my right. To my army, it seemed like I had ventured bravely into the desert with the intent of winning the Red Dune warriors to our side. But when I lay alone in the darkness, there was no hiding from the truth: Severin was gone.

And he had taken part of me with him.

Using my illusions, I slipped past the guards and walked unseen through the camp – and beyond it.

The bodies from the latest skirmish littered the stretch of desert between our encampment and Damar's high walls. I had ordered them left there. Tomorrow, after I had signed the peace agreement with Malek, I would contact the Zigilian insurgency and relay our terms for surrender. Then they would be allowed to collect their dead, as they should have been from the beginning.

I hoped Severin would have been pleased with my plan. I hoped he would have understood that I was trying to be better than my parents. That I was trying to honour his memory.

I walked aimlessly for hours, weaving my way between the bodies, until one caught my eye.

I *recognised* this man.

It took me a moment to place him, to remember that Avril had provided me with sketches of the high-up members of the Zigilian insurgency. The rebel leader, Drakos, had three younger brothers – and the corpse in front of me bore a striking resemblance to them, with the same deep brown skin and heavy-lidded eyes. I wasn't sure which brother was lying in the dirt in front of me, but it hardly mattered. I would order the body brought back to camp, where Avril could identify it for me.

Except my legs refused to move. I couldn't look away from the young man's blood-splattered skin, imagining Severin in his place – his beautiful face caved in by the impact of his fall. Barely recognisable even to me.

I had known, hadn't I? Deep down, I had always known that Severin was too good, too kind to survive the Ravalian Court.

To survive *Zandri*.

The worst part was the knowledge of *when* he had died. In the seer's vision, Severin had been wearing the same clothes he had worn to Mira and Cassius's farce of a wedding, when I had dismissed him in favour of resurrecting Lillian. I hadn't even given a thought to Severin that night, too elated with my success, with the knowledge that I was one step closer to the Ravalian throne. Then Zandri had summoned me to the catacombs, and I had felt so certain in our plans, so sure that everything was coming together exactly as it should—

And all along, Zandri had known that Severin was dead. Had probably ordered one of her warriors to bury him in an unmarked grave.

A mirthless laugh bubbled from my lips. No wonder my search parties hadn't found him.

No wonder there had been no sign, no *trace*—

I turned away from the corpse in front of me. For the first time since I'd killed my father, I wished I hadn't done it. That I had listened to Severin's warnings and made a different choice.

I could have run away with Severin. I had access to my mother's cavern of blood rubies; I could have stolen his and fled to the Western Lands with him, or perhaps even left the Ravalian continent altogether. We could have started over somewhere new, free from the dangers and temptations of the Ravalian Court.

Instead, I had chosen politics and magic and power. Instead, I had condemned the man I loved to die at my mother's hand.

Instead, I thought as I walked through the field of corpses, black tendrils snaking through my veins, I had made all the wrong choices.

And now was I paying for them.

Nightmares plagued my sleep, leaving me with dark circles beneath my eyes. Aella dutifully concealed them each morning as she was doing now, never asking any questions.

She braided my hair and arranged it on top of my head like a crown, as I had once seen Mira do. Black veins surged at her touch, but I held them back with a thought, and the illusion over my skin didn't so much as falter.

'I'll take over from here, Aella,' Lillian said, softly but firmly. When my attendant had left, she met my gaze in the mirror. 'Will it be armour today? Or would you prefer a dress?'

'A dress,' I replied. 'We are supposed to be signing a peace agreement; armour might set the wrong tone. Though I'll wear my riding boots and a dagger. Just in case.'

Lillian nodded and walked back through the tent, collecting the items I'd asked for. I wondered if she could sense the gratitude squeezing my chest. If she could, she didn't remark on it.

Once I was physically and mentally prepared, I entered the crimson pavilion. Aric and his lieutenants were already sitting at the long wooden table, along with Malek and the Red Dune warriors who had accompanied him. With their spiked helmets on, it was impossible to tell what they thought about this meeting – or the peace agreement laid out in front of the seer.

I had formed the plan four days ago, when were at the Red Dune encampment. A way of ending this war with Zigilia without further bloodshed, and proving that the Ravalian Empire would be different under my rule.

It wasn't exactly the decisive victory I had wanted, but it was a compromise that I hoped both sides could accept.

Malek paused, his quill in hand. 'I have one last condition.'

It was hard not to feel frustrated, given the many hours we had negotiated and re-negotiated terms. But I thought of the way my people had massacred his, reminding myself that it wasn't easy to put aside old hostilities. Trust wasn't something that came naturally to me, either.

'I'm listening.'

'You mentioned that some of your Masks will remain behind to help oversee the transition. I would like Avril to be amongst them.'

I drummed my fingers against the table, considering his request. As far as I was aware, Malek had barely spoken to Avril – but she *was* Zigilian; I supposed Malek felt that gave them some common ground. And since Zandri had intended for Avril to become the next Provincial Governor, I doubted she would be missed in Ravalia.

'That seems fair.' My gaze slid to the Mask operative. 'Unless you have any objections?'

Avril shook her head, her mouth curving at the corners.

'Good,' I said, leaning forward in my seat at the head of the table. 'Do you have any further concerns about the terms?'

'I'm not concerned about the terms.' Malek's hazel eyes were steady on mine. 'I'm concerned about the collateral damage.'

'You said it yourself: seers used to rule your country. It was Ravalians who ripped away that tradition, and now we have the opportunity to restore it.' A few of Aric's lieutenants shifted uneasily in their seats. I ignored them. 'I can't negotiate with the current insurgency, which means more months of blood and death. But I *can* negotiate with you. And once this is signed, we can appeal to the ordinary people. They don't want this war to continue any more than we do. I suspect they will overthrow the insurgency themselves.'

'It's still a risk,' Malek said at last.

Fleetingly, I wondered what diverging futures he might have Seen – and how many of those futures led to peace. His hesitation made me think that there was at least an equal chance of this ending in more chaos and bloodshed. But the fact that he was sitting here at all . . .

'Everything is a risk,' I said steadily. 'But think of the benefits. Zigilia, the tribes of the Red Dunes . . . you've never had an ally like me before. I can help you. I am in a position to make a real difference – and so are you. All you have to do is sign.'

And he did.

I let out a breath, relaxing slightly as Aella brought the parchment to me. I picked up my quill—

Black-garbed Warriors poured into the pavilion. Malek's warriors sprang into position around their leader, drawing their swords and spears.

'What is the meaning of this?' I asked Aric, who was speaking with the Ravalian Warriors in a low voice.

I knew I wasn't going to like the answer even before he said, 'The political situation has changed. We've received instructions direct from Ravalia – the insurgents were unwilling to negotiate with you, but it seems they were willing to deal with your mother. Zandri has promised to recognise the rebel leader as the new ruler of Zigilia.'

Anger bubbled up, and my death magic rose with it. I pushed it back down, rubbing my temples.

'And what does *he* want?'

'In no uncertain terms,' Aric replied, 'Drakos has instructed us to discontinue all contact with the tribes and hand them over to him. He has also agreed with Zandri's order that Malek be sent to Ravalia, where he will serve in the Order of Artisans.'

Seconds. I had been *seconds* away from signing that damn treaty—

I turned on Avril with narrowed eyes. 'How did you let this *happen*?' I snapped. 'Drakos reached out to Zandri because he *knew* we were planning to install Malek in his place. It's the only reason he would make this deal.'

Avril didn't react to my anger. 'My Mask operatives have been more focused on external threats than internal ones. They do what they can, but as you know, the occasional spy can slip through the cracks.'

'That's not good enough.' Perhaps I was being unreasonable, but we had been so *close*. 'This should never have happened. I don't care what my mother says – Drakos has ignored me for months. I refuse to stand back and watch a real alliance dissolve around me.'

'Zandri has already made a deal with Drakos,' Avril reminded me. 'She will expect you to honour it.'

'It isn't Zandri's call to make. It's *mine*.'

'Scarlett,' Aric murmured at my side, 'you've only just united your army. Going against Zandri's public orders may not be wise. Particularly as we now have the opportunity to end this war.'

'By handing over our allies,' I said coolly, glancing in Malek's direction. His warriors encircled him, a solid wall of muscle, but they had no hope of standing against my army. If I gave the order, he and his people could be handed over to the insurgency in a matter of hours.

I didn't need to be a seer to know what would happen to Malek then. If he was lucky, he would spend his days telling futures for the Ravalian Court. If he wasn't, Zandri would take a liking to him, sending him on mission after mission, as she had done to Severin. He had never spoken about them afterwards, but I had seen the toll they took on him – and sometimes I had seen dried blood on his clothes.

The thought of Malek following in Severin's footsteps was sickening. If I allowed this to happen, it would invalidate everything Severin had done to keep him out of Zandri's clutches.

'No,' I said firmly. 'I'm not doing it. This was *my* plan – *my* alliance. The fact that Drakos went to Zandri only proves that my plan is sound.'

'Scarlett—'

'He's *afraid*, Aric. For the first time in months, we have something that he desperately wants.'

'Yes,' Aric agreed. 'And I think we should consider giving it to him.'

I walked past Aric to the front of the pavilion. Below the steps, a crowd of Warriors had gathered, reminding me of when I had dismissed General Harte. For too long, others had dictated the direction of this war.

Now it was my turn.

Avril looked at me, her expression carefully unreadable – but I knew that she approved. Even if she thought I was a fool for going against my mother. 'What will I tell Zandri?'

Tell her that I know what she did, I thought, twirling the quill in my fingers. *Tell her that she can go to hell.*

But I couldn't confront her about Severin's murder. Not here, not like this. The only way I would win a war against Zandri was if she never realised there was a war at all.

'Tell her . . .' I paused. 'Tell her that it's handled. And that I look forward to explaining my reasons upon my victorious return.'

Avril raised an eyebrow, but nodded. 'Your funeral,' she muttered as she walked away.

Her words didn't bother me. Not as I thought of Drakos's brother lying in the dirt, a spear through his chest. I had known that discovery would prove important. I just hadn't known *how* important.

'I'm assuming you have a plan,' Aric said from behind me.

'Of course I do,' I said, turning to face him with a razor-sharp smile. 'All along my army has wanted a decisive military victory. I intend to give them one.'

CHAPTER SEVENTEEN

Mira

I sliced my palm with the blade, watching as the high priestess leant in to capture every precious drop.

Tonight's ceremony was more important than most, and Velanthe's ancient blessing raised the delicate hairs on the nape of my neck. The language she spoke in was strange – unsettling and powerful.

I felt dizzy as I bled into the chalice – though I wasn't sure if it was from the blood loss or the knowledge that soon I would be a married woman. Tomorrow Vølund and I would complete the Kalurian hand-fasting ceremony on the balcony attached to this very hall, in full view of our people.

Velanthe reached for my bare arm, steadying me as priestesses passed around the chalice, which gleamed a deep gold in the firelight. It was still disconcerting to see them drink from it as though my blood was a sweet wine. All the priestesses were young and beautiful, and their white, fur-lined cloaks gave the impression of innocence – an illusion that was dispelled as one smiled at me, my blood a red film across her lips.

For a second, I could have sworn her smile stretched too wide, filled with tiny, pointed teeth. Then my vision cleared, and it was just Revna, her long, shiny raven hair gleaming as she handed the chalice to the next priestess.

No one tried to stop me as I approached the life-sized statue in the centre of the Inner Sanctum, my fingers hovering an inch from the black stone. I had once spent hours praying before this very statue. Hoping – *begging* – the Sorceress to hear me. To answer my prayers.

She never had.

Given no one had seen or spoken to the Sorceress in centuries, I shouldn't have been surprised. Wherever Selussa was – if she even still existed – she was clearly far beyond my reach.

But I couldn't help wondering if she hadn't answered me for different reasons. If she had turned her back on me the moment I entered the Ravalian Trials. Or the moment I had killed Governor Halvor.

'I am certain the Sorceress is watching you, Kasmira,' Velanthe said quietly from behind me. 'And I know she would be pleased.'

It was a nice thought. I tried to believe it.

'I think my father would have approved,' I said at last. 'Of Vølund.'

Velanthe rested her hand on my shoulder. 'He is a good choice. Steadfast and capable. He will make a wonderful king consort.'

And yet I was no longer thinking of Vølund or my father. I was thinking of how I had said much the same thing to Cassius: how Vølund offered my country stability. How he offered me protection from Roran.

I could protect you from Roran. Cassius's words rang in my mind, filled with ruthless certainty. *He would never get near you. I would kill him first.*

'You're making the right choice, Kasmira,' Velanthe murmured. 'For your country – and for yourself.'

I forced a smile, but it didn't really matter if Vølund was the right choice.

He was my *only* choice.

For the next few hours, I soaked in the bubbling hot springs below the domed Temple – a volcanic cavern that cocooned me from the chaotic world above.

What followed was anything but relaxing, an endless parade of serv-ants – attendants, priestesses and seamstresses – all intent on preparing me for tomorrow's handfasting ceremony.

It was a relief to finally shut the door to my chambers. Crossing through to my bedroom, I sank down onto the plush mattress. The moment I closed my eyes, though, I inhaled the tell-tale scent of rose oil. 'Please don't tell me there's *another* blessing to be performed.'

The bed dipped as Odessa sat next to me. I didn't need to open my eyes to imagine the way she perched primly on the edge, her sandal-clad feet crossed demurely at the ankles.

'No, Mira.' There was a hint of laughter in her voice. 'You can relax. I'm here on a social visit.'

But when I cracked open one eye, I noticed the way Odessa stared at the wall. As if she was staring *through* it – into the chambers next to mine, that now belonged to Cassius. A decision I had made to keep an eye on him, and one I had quickly come to regret.

My cheeks heated with shame as I recalled our encounter the other night. How easily I had allowed him to seduce me, to pull me back into his orbit, all the while *knowing* that was what he did. How many people had he lured in with his beautiful facade, only to discard when they were no longer of use?

'He didn't waste any time,' Odessa remarked.

I went still, thinking she was referring to me, that she had *seen*—

But then I heard it. Soft, feminine laughter.

'That poor priestess,' Odessa said, sympathy softening her face. 'She's bedded a viper, and she has no idea.'

I ignored the sick lurch of my stomach, turning decisively away from the wall. Cassius had never been celibate – far from it. Of course other women would seek him out, and of course he would welcome their attention. Hadn't I known that Cassius's advances towards me were just another manipulation?

'I doubt she's *bedded* him,' I said, fighting to keep my voice level. 'Don't priestesses have strict rules about those sorts of things?'

'Not Kalurian priestesses. They're of the opposite opinion – most men and women here value experience over virtue. In fact . . .' The suggestive way she looked at me was wholly Odessa. No trace of the Temple acolyte to be seen. 'I'm surprised Vølund hasn't tried to tempt you into bed yet. You certainly seemed cosy enough at that tree-top village.'

'You were there?' I asked, wondering if I should be annoyed.

'Oh yes,' Odessa said, without any trace of shame. 'I've been shadowing you on all your excursions with the clan leader. So has Jadis. Why else do you think Velanthe would allow you to wander around without guards?'

'I'm perfectly capable of defending myself—'

'I know you are. But even a warrior can be overwhelmed by numbers or taken by surprise.'

I said nothing, conceding the point. Unfortunately, it was no longer the priestess's soft laughter that punctuated the silence.

I crossed to the oval windows and flung them open, trying to distract myself from the sound of her breathy moans. It occurred to me that Cassius could have done this deliberately – his way of proving a point and getting under my skin.

But that was a very self-centred thought. Cassius didn't owe me anything, and his decision to take a lover probably had nothing whatso-ever to do with me. Yet I resisted the urge to storm out of my chambers, knowing that if this *was* part of a game, leaving would be as good as conceding this round to Cassius.

Better to stay and pretend that I couldn't care less.

And I don't, I thought viciously. *I most definitely* do not care. *I had the opportunity to marry Cassius back in Ravalia and I fought like hell to be free of him—*

Odessa came to stand at my side. 'You think that you can control Cassius,' she warned, 'but you can't. The only way is to use your magic on him, or lock him back in the dungeons.'

I wondered if Odessa would feel the same way if she knew what my magic had done to her.

'Doesn't Temple doctrine say that everyone deserves a second chance? I've made plenty of mistakes of my own; Gods, I killed the Kalurian *Governor*, but the Kalurian people seem willing to forgive me.'

Odessa shook her head, sending her white-blonde hair fluttering. 'It's not the same.'

'Isn't it? I haven't been to many Temple services, Odessa, but I don't think we get to pick and choose who is and isn't worthy of forgiveness.'

'*You* can.'

I blinked at her. 'Pardon?'

'Don't you see, Mira?' A strange intensity lit Odessa's face as she leant forward, clasping my hands. 'I doubt Cassius has any intention of trying to change, but you – you can *make* him.'

I slid my hands out of her grip. 'By taking away his choice, you mean.'

Odessa stood without answering. For a moment, I thought she was going to walk out – but then she reached for the Sorceress's grimoire. It was lying open on the writing desk in front of the windows, and I watched her trace the opening sentence with a reverent finger.

Do you know what happens when a god loves you?

Even now, that sentence gave me a chill. Not the question, exactly, or its implication – but the elegant, looping black cursive of my ancestor.

That handwriting was proof – real, tangible proof – that the Sorceress had really lived. That she had walked the earth, just like in my mother's stories and the murals covering every inch of the Temple's walls.

They do terrible things to you, the grimoire continued. *Curse you with eternal life. Existence without consequence.*

'I used to think the Ravalian Court was the entire world,' Odessa said pensively. 'But when I came here, I realised that the world was so much bigger than I believed. If beings like the Sorceress can exist, Mira, then anything is possible.' Her eyes shone with sincerity. '*Anything.*'

Maybe her enthusiasm should have been contagious, but all I felt was exhaustion.

'I know you think my magic is a miracle. But—'

'You've read this grimoire,' Odessa said, sounding impatient now. 'You know everything that the Sorceress endured – everything she *survived*. She should be an inspiration to you, as she is to the rest of us. I don't understand why you shy away from the Temple's teachings.'

'I'm frightened of this power,' I confessed in a low voice. 'If anyone can understand that, it should be you.'

'The Orders aren't fundamentally evil, Mira. Nor is the power Zandri used to create them. She just shaped them in her image.'

I agreed with Odessa about one thing: Zandri was evil enough to taint the Sorceress's magic and create something perverted with it. The trouble was, how could I be certain that the Sorceress's magic wasn't tainted to begin with?

Odessa turned towards the doorway. But then she hesitated. 'This alliance is *everything*,' she said, fixing me with beseeching amber eyes. 'If you're not going to use magic on Cassius, then at least lock him back in his cell. I've seen the way he looks at you – and at Vølund. You're playing with fire.'

I didn't disagree. But rather than thinking about the terrible choices he'd made in the past, I found myself remembering his words in the dungeons. The sincerity of them.

I'm not the monster you think I am, Mira. Or at least, I don't want to be.

'I know he'll use this situation to his advantage. I'm prepared for that. When he starts scheming—'

'Mira,' Odessa interrupted, 'he already *has*.'

She shook her head sadly and left without another word. Leaving me alone with nothing but the memory of her disappointment.

And the continued sound of Cassius taking his pleasure with another.

CHAPTER EIGHTEEN

Mira

How strange it was to realise I would soon be a married woman. Even stranger to realise I wasn't dreading it.

'It's nearly finished,' Velanthe said as she tattooed my forehead. Her eyes were highlighted by crimson ink, reminding me uncomfortably of blood. 'You have done well, Kasmira.'

I kept still with an effort, though the pain never seemed to lessen. My skin felt like it was on fire.

'Why didn't you tell me the real reason the clans distrust the Temple?' I asked.

Velanthe's expression shuttered. 'Vølund told you.'

'*You* should have told me.' I was surprised by how much it stung. I had come to rely on Velanthe's advice. The fact that she had kept information from me—

'You're right. I should have.' Though her fingers didn't pause in their work, I sensed the mood shift. 'I'm ashamed of what the Temple did, Kasmira. I'm even more ashamed of the role I played in it.'

And there it was: the confirmation I had been dreading.

I stood abruptly, needing to put some distance between us. 'Did you kill them? My grandparents?'

'Not directly, but I might as well have,' she said. 'I was a young, ambitious priestess when I met Zandri. She convinced me to teach her blood magic – not that she had to try very hard. I believed I was serving my future queen by fulfilling her wishes. Then her mother found out, and destroyed centuries of matriarchal tradition by making Arioch her heir instead. When the Temple gathered to decide where their duty lay – with the queen they had pledged to, or the daughter who had been robbed of her birthright – I spoke on Zandri's behalf. I convinced the high priestess that it was a miscarriage of justice not to act against such an edict.'

Velanthe's lips pressed into a thin line. 'I expected that the Temple would publicly align themselves with Zandri – put public pressure on the crown. But after the high priestess met with Zandri in private . . . she ordered us to take up arms. I left when I understood the extent of her plans, when I realised what Zandri had used blood magic to achieve. I took as many priestesses with me as I could, and fled to the Wilds. But even though I didn't take part . . . the massacre is still my fault. I'm responsible for the bloodshed Zandri caused that day, and every day since.'

The heaviness in Velanthe's face, in her shoulders . . . how long had she been carrying the weight of those lives? What must it have been like for her – to feel responsible for the deaths not just of the queen and her consort, but of the high priestess, who she had clearly looked up to?

'You couldn't have known.' My voice was gentle. 'Zandri is skilled at manipulation.'

And so is her daughter, I thought.

Velanthe didn't meet my gaze immediately. When she did, her dark eyes were shadowed. 'It's the reason I'm pushing you so hard, Kasmira,' she said, resuming her tattooing as I sank back into the chair. 'The reason I'm so determined that you wield blood magic. One day, Zandri will turn her attention to Kalure, and when she does . . . you need to be prepared.'

That was a terrifying thought. Bad enough that I had Roran and Scarlett to contend with.

But *Zandri* . . .

'All done,' Velanthe announced, stepping back and surveying me. I couldn't see what the tattooed crown looked like, but I could imagine it based on her drawings: delicate, interlocking patterns that reminded me of links in a chain.

She swept past me before I could respond, her robes rustling. I hesitated before following her out onto the balcony, where Vølund was already waiting – the black crown across his forehead a perfect twin to mine. A permanent reminder of our new position as king and queen, and one that couldn't be taken away from either of us.

I stopped dead as I reached the balustrade. It seemed like every Kalurian warrior had journeyed here, lining the clearing from the Temple to the forest. There were even priestesses gathered outside, clearly visible in their silver robes.

'There's . . . there's an *army* out there.'

'Yes.' Vølund was smiling. 'They're here to pay fealty to you. To *us*.'

While they looked on, Velanthe tied our hands together with strips of black cloth: a symbol of our union. Our pledges to each other were short but heartfelt. Declarations – not of love, but of duty and protection.

'As your hands are bound together by this cord,' Velanthe declared, 'so too shall your lives be bound as one. Let no man, woman or deity tear apart what has been joined together this day.'

A rhythmic thudding met my ears – the army pounding their shields against the ground. The tempo picked up, a roar swelling through the crowd as we lifted our entwined hands.

Joined together in marriage. Just like that.

'What is it?' Vølund asked softly in my ear.

The afternoon sun lit up his hair and set his green eyes sparkling. It would be no chore to be married to this man, and as I stared out over the gathering, I knew I should have been pleased. This was what I had wanted – what I *needed*, if I was going to stand against Roran. But—

'I'm thinking about the cost.'

Neither of us had spoken about the ruthless practicalities underpinning our alliance. But they soured every shared smile, every careful brush of Vølund's hand against mine.

'There is always a cost,' Vølund reminded me. 'Sometimes, in order to make a body healthy again, a limb must be severed. So it is with the Ravalian Court.'

An apt metaphor, I supposed, but it didn't make me feel any better.

'What is it that bothers you so?' Vølund murmured, tracing my cheek with his finger.

'Killing on a battlefield is one thing. This feels . . . calculated. Cruel.'

'By killing three people, you will save untold thousands,' he said.

'You already know that Roran has to die to win this war. You've made your peace with that. All you need is to make your peace with this. Can you do that? Can you do what is necessary to secure the Ravalian Empire?'

When I looked at him, Vølund's face was alive with determination. With passion.

I let that passion seep into me. Let myself pretend, if only for a moment, that this was as simple as a man and woman committing to one another.

'Yes,' I told him, with as much certainty as I could muster. 'I can do that.'

Vølund took me in his arms and kissed me. When we finally broke away, the crowd was screaming and I was breathing hard.

'Until tonight,' he said, the words filled with sensuous promise.

'Until tonight,' I echoed, and tried my best to smile.

I crossed back into the courtyard, feeling curiously adrift. The priestesses were preparing for the upcoming handfast celebration; everything was a hive of activity, like an overturned hornet's nest. I liked the Temple better like this. It reminded me less of a mausoleum.

But without Vølund's steadying presence, all the doubts I'd been ignoring threatened to overwhelm me. As if by instinct, my gaze rose to a set of windows high above the courtyard – where Cassius stood watching.

We hadn't been friends in the past – had barely been allies. Still, he had helped me with Roran. And he had been the closest thing to a confidant I'd had in the Ravalian Court. But he was the one who had always counselled me to be ruthless – to do whatever it took to survive.

I turned decisively away from the window, but even as I walked away, I could feel him watching me.

My marriage to Vølund would give me everything I wanted: an army, a crown, and an empire.

And all it would cost was Cassius and Scarlett's lives.

I strolled through the gardens that flanked the Temple complex, smiling at the sight of ordinary citizens enjoying the celebrations. Children laughed as they ran through the hedge maze, and I passed more than one couple locked in a passionate embrace.

There was a definite bite in the air, the priestesses bundled in furs. I had acclimatised to the colder weather, but I was grateful for the ermine trim of my dress – and for the bonfires blazing up ahead.

I glimpsed Velanthe, Odessa and Jadis huddled around the closest one. I smiled as I noticed Odessa and Jadis sitting together, their hands brushing. I hoped this meant that they had sorted out their differences; they had both lost so much, and they deserved to find happiness. Elian was nowhere in sight, but he'd fashioned himself as something of a spy here in Kalure, blending in so well that sometimes I didn't even recognise when he was around.

Then my eyes fell on Vølund. My husband.

He was surrounded by Kalurian clansmen, all clapping him on the back and smiling. Looking on from a distance, marriage felt lonelier than I'd thought it would – perhaps because I had been torturing myself with memories of Aric. Lillian had once confided that she'd envisioned us marrying in the mountain meadow where we'd trained on Aldara. That had been her dearest dream: for me to become her sister in truth.

But that dream was dead, Lillian along with it. Thanks to Scarlett.

I wanted to kill her for it – and I would happily end Roran if I had the chance. So really, it was only Cassius's death that gave me pause. But I'd come up with an answer to that: I would lock him back in the dungeons, and once Roran and Scarlett were dealt with, use blood magic to neutralise the threat Cassius posed. Not a perfect solution, but one I could live with.

I didn't bother with the chairs or divans the priestesses had arranged. Tonight was supposed to be about me, and what I wanted was to sit on the grass and look up at the stars with my husband – while drinking enough wine to numb my remaining doubts.

Unbidden, I caught sight of Cassius, his golden-blond hair and white furs like a beacon in the darkness. As usual, he wasn't bothering to practise restraint; his appearance was slightly dishevelled, and a goblet lay discarded at his side. My eyes narrowed when I noticed the woman he was speaking with, his arm casually draped over her slender shoulder.

'I thought . . .'

'You thought what, my love?' Vølund asked, following my gaze to Cassius. His expression darkened, probably misinterpreting my confusion for jealousy. He couldn't have been more wrong.

'He was with a woman last night. I heard them through the walls of my chambers.' Realising this explanation was not helping my case, I hurried on, 'I thought she was one of the priestesses. It seems I was mistaken.'

Astrid left Cassius and returned to pour us wine, keeping her head bowed respectfully. I supposed Vølund's attendant was beautiful, with her wavy chestnut hair and innocent face. I just hadn't expected Cassius to go for a Kalurian – but really, since when was I an expert on the kinds of women he liked?

Gods, maybe I *was* jealous.

'Perhaps you should slow down,' Vølund advised after I finished my second goblet.

I was content to take his advice. Everything had taken on a pleasant haze. Even the thought of the consummation no longer felt quite as daunting.

I leant back against Vølund's chest. His arms tightened around me, and even though I didn't love him, I realised I felt safe in his arms. Maybe that was because of everything this alliance signified – but I suspected it was also because of the kind of person he was. Solid. Caring. Fierce.

I wondered if there was more to him. Perhaps it was the wine, but I was curious to find out.

'Come with me,' I said with a flirtatious smile, pulling Vølund to his feet.

People turned to stare as we made our way back through the gathering. Cassius was one of them, though I avoided his intense gaze, focusing on the warmth of Vølund's body against mine, the feeling of his pulse beating beneath my hand. It was faster than usual, as if he liked the idea of leaving our own celebrations behind.

Once we were inside the hedge maze, the hum of voices faded to silence. I might have called it peaceful, but there was a kind of energy here – just as there was in the Wilds. It called to me, and as it did, a breeze raced through the maze. Scattering the leaves on the path.

'You should surprise me more often,' Vølund murmured. And then he claimed my mouth.

This kiss was less polite than his others, and more demanding. But I liked it.

Both Vølund and I had warrior instincts. I embraced the push-pull that I'd felt during our sparring sessions, pressing him against the hedge. His hands ran over my body, his touch explorative and somehow reverent.

Vølund's hands threaded through my hair. I closed my eyes, surrendering to sensation, uncaring that the priestess's careful work was being undone. When we returned to the celebrations, everyone would know what we had been doing. But what was wrong with that? We were married. And even if we weren't, Kalurians apparently valued experience over virtue . . .

I was thinking too much. I tried to refocus, to lose myself in Vølund's touch, in the hardness of his muscular chest against mine.

Yes, that was better. But when I closed my eyes once more, it wasn't Vølund I was imagining.

My mind was cruel to conjure Aric's face. His intent gaze. How he had taken his time, never releasing eye contact, until he had been as overwhelmed as I was. We'd lain in each other's arms afterwards, and it had felt like the beginning of something. Something wonderful.

Vølund was kissing my neck. His lips left a burning trail, and a breathy sigh escaped me.

That sigh reminded me of Astrid. Of Cassius.

And suddenly I was thinking of him instead. Imagining how it might feel with Cassius in Vølund's place, unpredictable instead of steady, dark instead of light, his lips calculated and commanding and utterly forbidden—

I was just about to push Vølund off me, to tell him it was no use, when his body stiffened.

And then he stumbled.

My first thought was that I had done this to him. That my chaotic emotions had triggered my magic and that magic had targeted my husband. Why else would blood be pouring from his eyes?

Then Vølund gasped out a word that made more sense. '*Poison.*'

'I'll get help,' I told him frantically. 'You're going to be fine. Velanthe will find a way to fix this.'

She has to.

I thought I heard Vølund murmur something. It sounded like *Stay*.

But I was already running back through the maze. I cried out in frustration as my path ended in a dead end, forcing me to retrace my steps. Desperation made me clumsy. I tripped and stumbled but righted myself and kept moving, each step taking me closer to the entrance.

And then I was hurtling towards the bonfires, and I must have looked a fright because people were murmuring and pointing—

'Vølund,' I shouted – but it came out more like a whisper. 'Vølund has been poisoned. He needs help . . .'

Light-headedness made me sway. I tried to blink, but it was as if a red film had covered my vision. I raised my fingers to my cheeks. They came away wet with tears.

No – not tears. *Blood.*

Cassius caught me as I fell. And then the world was tilting – he was lifting me, carrying me in his arms. I tried to protest, but nothing left my lips except a groan.

'Get Vølund,' Velanthe's voice barked from behind me. 'Bring him to the Temple.'

Then she lowered her voice, speaking with the other priestesses. I caught snatches of their conversation.

'—the same poison that killed King Arioch—'

'—Zandri's own recipe—'

'—might have an antidote—'

'—Temple stores—'

I let out a pained gasp. 'Cold,' I said, or thought I did. 'I feel so cold.'

Cassius's grip tightened. 'I know, Mira.' He moved faster – was he running? – and the impact should have been jarring, but I felt separate from my own body. Except for the cold. It was spreading – like sickness through my veins.

Like poison.

My eyes fluttered shut. When they reopened, my teeth were chattering, and I was surrounded by dark stone. A pair of red eyes blurred in front of me, and I shook my head, trying to clear my vision. Why weren't they midnight blue?

'You look like a demon,' I whispered.

'Shh.' Cassius caught my outstretched hand. I barely felt it. 'Don't try to talk.' Less gently, he turned to shout at the priestesses, 'Have you found it yet? She's delirious.'

A priestess hurried over, holding up a vial of clear liquid. 'There's only enough for one dose.'

Dimly I heard Velanthe shout an order from across the room. 'The queen! *Save the queen!*'

My eyes dropped to the vial in the priestess's hand. My delirious brain could barely comprehend what was happening, but I clung to clarity long enough to think of Vølund dying. To remember the promises I had made to him and the way he had begged me to stay.

'Give it to him,' I gasped. My final order. 'Give it to Vølund.'

The priestess hesitated, her hand trembling. 'Y-your Majesty . . .?'

My voice was so faint it was barely audible. But I managed three last words: 'Obey your queen.'

I watched her hover over Vølund's still form beside me, the antidote in her hand. All the priestess needed to do was open his mouth—

Cassius snatched the vial from her. 'Wrong choice,' he said, and forced the liquid down my throat.

CHAPTER NINETEEN

Scarlett

The strain was immense.

It pulled at my magic, my insides, my mind. And I knew I couldn't maintain this much longer.

'Answer the question,' I told Anton, my power like a vice.

The muscles in his throat tightened as he fought to swallow, but even as he did, I knew he wasn't getting enough oxygen. My magic wouldn't allow it.

'Every four hours,' he gritted out. 'The guard rotates every four hours.'

'Good.' I softened my invisible hold. 'That wasn't so hard, was it?'

I glanced at Avril. She had been leading this interrogation, finding out the necessary information for me to take Anton's place and infiltrate the Zigilian palace. She murmured something to the masked woman at her side, who promptly left the tent. Then Avril nodded at me.

I allowed myself a tiny sigh of relief. I couldn't risk tiring myself out further – not when this entire war hinged on my performance tomorrow.

My gaze locked with Anton's. Despite the colour in his cheeks, he still resembled a corpse more than a living person – mainly thanks to the gaping wound in his chest and the blood caking his clothes and skin.

He looked at me with so much impotent hatred that even I felt a trace of pity for him. But really, what had I done that was so terrible? He was already dead.

I didn't even need to reach for the dagger strapped to my side. It was my magic that allowed his heart to beat, and my will that maintained the tether between us. I focused on that tether now, imagining a thread of darkness connecting us together. A thread that I could sever—

Anton lunged for me. He didn't have a weapon, but he didn't seem to care, his arms outstretched as though he would crush the air from my lungs. He moved quickly, desperation making him unnaturally fast.

But I was faster.

I shielded my face against the searing sun, squinting across the rolling expanse of desert.

The Zigilian insurgents waited in the middle of no-man's-land, the warriors wearing spiked helmets. Only Drakos's face was visible, ruggedly handsome with a strong jaw and dark brown stubble that matched his close-cropped hair. Heavy body armour emphasised his hulking build.

I rode closer, leading my small procession. Flanking me at a respectful distance were Aric and Avril. Behind them were the Red Dune warriors and Malek, whose gaze I could feel boring into the back of my head.

I hadn't told him my plans; he would have Seen my decision the moment I made it. Though I hoped he had given his warriors some forewarning. Otherwise, they would believe that I was willingly handing them over to Drakos.

'Brother,' Drakos called, his wide mouth cracking into a smile. 'What a momentous day this is!'

Yes, I thought with a twist of my lip. *It is.*

When I was close enough, I grasped Drakos's arm with my own. A traditional Zigilian greeting.

Dark eyes swept over my face and body, lingering on the blood staining Anton's armour. 'Did they harm you?'

'I was wounded in combat,' I replied, in the steady tone I had practised, 'but their healers treated me in time. Along with Khalid and Arjun,' I said, referring to the two fighters Aric and Avril appeared to be.

A shadow of emotion passed over Drakos's rugged face as he looked at me. 'I truly believed you were dead. And then, when I heard you were alive . . . I was certain the Ravalian bitch would try to ransom you. To barter for better terms.' He barked out a disparaging laugh. 'Not much of a strategist, is she? Shouldn't have dismissed all her senior generals.'

With one last glower at Lillian – who stood at the forefront of my distant army, disguised as me – Drakos urged his horse into a canter. I said nothing as I followed, with a fleeting glance at Malek and the Red Dune warriors, who were surrounded by Drakos's loyal contingent of fighters.

The possibility of using Anton as leverage had occurred to me, since it was common knowledge that Drakos was close to his brothers. But masquerading as someone he loved suited my purposes far better, and was infinitely more satisfying.

My heart quickened as the gates came into view: solid timber, reinforced with iron. How many months I had spent staring at those gates, praying for a way past them?

I had to force myself not to react as they opened and we rode through. Into the fortified city of Damar.

I raised my hand to the cries of Anton's name, taking note of the Zigilians who thronged the palm-lined street. The horses' hooves kicked up dust as we passed between mud-brick buildings and bustling bazaars.

'Drakos!' they screamed. And then, less often but just as enthusiastically, 'Anton! *Anton!*'

Their enthusiasm could prove problematic. But I noticed the way the crowd stared at Malek, too – taking in the tattoos on his cheeks. I caught a few murmurs of, 'Seer,' said quietly but with reverence.

A promising sign. Once Drakos was dealt with, there was no reason their devotion couldn't be redirected to Malek.

We dismounted and entered the Zigilian palace. Unlike the temples and monuments of the Western Lands, my father had left the palace mostly intact – either out of appreciation for the architecture, or pragmatism, considering the cost of rebuilding. I had only been inside once before. I could remember marvelling at the soaring ceilings, elegant archways and earthy colour palette, staring down at my sandalled feet as I walked over the elaborate terracotta tiles.

Today, I was careful not to look around me. If Anton was anything like Drakos, he was so familiar with his surroundings that he wouldn't give them a second glance.

I wondered what had happened to the Provincial Governor who used to live here. I had a vague memory of meeting him – along with his son and daughter, a few years younger than I was at the time. My father had spoken with the governor in one of the many courtyard gardens, while I had played amongst the greenery with the other children. I doubted they were still alive. Coups didn't discriminate between the young and old, any more than war did.

Drakos brought us into the generous banquet hall, where his two other brothers were already waiting, along with a few white-robed Zigilian advisers. He greeted them all informally, kissing their cheeks. Victory had made him jovial.

'Come, Anton,' he called to me. 'Join us in our celebrations.' I walked over to him as his eyes cut to the warriors – Zigilian and Red Dune alike. 'Leave us,' he instructed.

This wasn't a surprise, but I still tensed as Aric left the hall. I could maintain my illusion only so long as he was reasonably close – as I had warned him. He would have to rely on his ingenuity for the next part of our plan.

As for Avril . . . well, everything depended on her remaining close.

'Wait,' Drakos called, his voice echoing through the pillared expanse. My throat went dry, thinking that he had noticed me shift the illusion on Avril, transforming her into a palace servant. 'You – the seer. You can stay.'

I resisted the urge to glance at Malek. I had expected him to be contained along with the other tribespeople, and I wasn't sure how to take this change in plan.

But Drakos was smiling broadly as he claimed the seat at the head of the table. 'I hope there are no hard feelings, friend,' he said lightly to Malek. 'Returning you to Ravalia was a condition Zandri refused to budge on. The least I can do is give you a proper send-off.'

Servants lined the sandstone walls. The moment I took the empty seat at Drakos's right – a position of honour – they began serving food and wine. I deliberately avoided looking at Avril as she moved along the table.

'I understand completely.' Malek was seated further down, next to Drakos's advisers, but his voice carried easily enough.

'Glad you've seen it my way,' Drakos remarked, idly swirling his glass. 'No reason we should be enemies – we are both Zigilian, after all.'

And what of the warriors from the Red Dunes? What are you going to do with them?

I casually took a bite of the salad in front of me. I already knew the answer, of course – as did Malek. I wondered whether that was the reason he ignored the food in front of him. I didn't have much of an appetite either, but Anton would have devoured the rich date wine and vibrant tropical fruits.

Conversation flowed as easily as the wine Avril poured. Everything had already been through multiple tasters; it didn't even occur to Drakos to be cautious. I watched him laugh with his brothers, only participating when it was required of me. No one seemed to notice my distance; perhaps Anton had always been a little aloof.

When it was time for the next course, the servants left. Avril disappeared along with them.

The poison took effect quickly.

With cool detachment, I watched Drakos's brothers and advisers stiffen. Their hands rose to their throats as they coughed – great, hacking coughs that sprayed blood and spittle onto the white tablecloth.

And then the tablecloth was dragged to the ground as one of the advisers fell, twitching, to the floor. Drakos started forward, only to pause, torn between his two dying brothers. He called for help, but there was no one to hear him. No one to answer his pleas.

'Anton!' he shouted, kneeling over one brother. 'Anton, run – find a healer—'

I went to Drakos's side, holding a finger to his brother's throat. There was no pulse.

Drakos looked up at me. I didn't know what he saw in my expression, but it was enough for horrified realisation to contort his face.

I released the illusion. I had no need for it anymore.

'*You.*' The word sounded strangled.

'Me,' I agreed, slowly standing and surveying the destruction. Wine cups had spilled, and broken plates and food littered the floor around the bodies. Malek was the only person still seated, his shoulders stiff, his expression stoic.

I refocused on Drakos, unrolling the piece of parchment I had brought with me. I even extended a quill.

'The poison I chose for you is slower acting,' I said, crouching at his side, 'but it's no less lethal. However, there is an antidote.' I rotated a glass vial in my fingers. 'I'm willing to give it to you. All you have to do is sign this document, transferring your power to Malek.'

Drakos was silent for a long time, his face and being anguished. He glanced down at the body of his brother.

'You need to decide quickly,' I told him. 'If you wait too long, the antidote won't help.'

'Fine.' Drakos snatched the quill and signed his name. 'The seer can be your new puppet leader.'

I glanced at Malek. He had to know what was coming, but if he felt any surprise or horror, it didn't show. His gaze was steady and measuring, like Severin's would have been.

I looked away.

'There isn't an antidote, is there?' Drakos asked, his muscles spasming. The final stage of the poison.

'There is,' I said, watching his body contort. 'I just don't have it.'

Perhaps it was for the best that Severin wasn't alive to see this, I thought as Drakos bent in a painful arch – and then went still. His brown eyes stared up at me, glassy and unseeing.

I closed them and stood, heedless of the blood smearing my fingertips.

Severin had always dreamt of peace, and it was a beautiful dream. But this world didn't belong to the dreamers.

It belongs to the monsters.

CHAPTER TWENTY

Scarlett

I remained in Damar long enough to ensure order. It was a smooth transition: from the moment Aric had opened the gates and let my army inside, the Zigilians had understood that resistance was futile.

It helped that Drakos and his closest supporters were dead. I could have locked them up or had them publicly executed – but it had been simplest to dispense with them quietly and quickly, allowing Malek to step into Drakos's position. As replacements went, he had been a popular choice – and not just because he was a seer. Malek's aptitude for politics and diplomacy almost equalled Avril's.

Thinking of Avril was bittersweet. As per Malek's request, I had ordered that she remain behind, along with some other Ravalian advisers. Despite the peace agreement Malek and I had signed, it was necessary to have some close Ravalian oversight for a while – and I trusted Avril to coordinate the Masks in Damar, who had the daunting responsibility of keeping Malek alive and in power.

But I still would have preferred to keep her with me. I had come to like her – much like I had come to like Aric and Lillian.

Trumpets sounded as our boat approached the main dock. Most of the Ravalian fleet had accompanied Roran to Kalure, but I admired the vessels we passed, their golden sails billowing in the breeze.

The Azure Sea was calm and sparkling today; there was no trace of the afternoon storms that usually struck around this time. Above us, the sky was bright, the sun shining.

I couldn't have imagined a better day for my victorious return.

Thousands of people had gathered to welcome home their princess:

so many that the crowds extended from the docks all the way up the sloping Imperial Road. I followed the trail of people with my eyes, taking in the familiar obsidian dome of the fighting arena and the ruby turrets of the Crimson Palace.

Somewhere in the palace, my mother was watching the spectacle. I wondered if she was pleased by the turnout.

If she was finally proud of me.

Then I remembered that I no longer cared what Zandri thought about me. And that I had disobeyed her direct instructions in order to install Malek in Drakos's place.

This could be a very dangerous homecoming.

My hand tightened around the rail, and I focused on the steadying warmth of Aric's body next to mine.

'You look stunning,' he said, probably noticing my reaction and assuming that I was nervous. He was right – but it wasn't the crowds I was nervous to face. 'Every inch the conquering queen.'

Empress, I almost corrected him. Instead, I bestowed him with a smile, accepting his compliment in the spirit it was intended.

'This victory is as much yours as it is mine,' I told him. 'I would like to have you by my side. The people should honour their general.'

'Of course, Your Highness.' At my sharp glance, his expression softened. 'Scarlett.'

We were now so close to the wharf that I could hear the people shouting my name, but I only had eyes for Aric. Dressed in polished black armour, he looked handsome and fierce, the sunlight playing over his tanned face and strong jaw. But his eyes were distant.

'You haven't come to my bedchamber for over a week,' I whispered. 'Ever since we took Damar.'

'Lillian suggested that I give you space,' Aric said, staring out over the water. 'She told me about what happened to your lover.'

'And here I thought you were avoiding me,' I murmured, 'because of what I did to Drakos and his supporters.'

'I understand why you did it. There were other options, but they all came with their own set of consequences.' Aric glanced back at me, but despite his words, I saw the truth reflected in his eyes.

How far could I push him before his morals demanded he push back?

But then we were docking, and the crowd was screaming, and for a brief moment, the old warmth returned to his face. I hadn't realised how much I had missed it until then: the ease between us. His steadfast support.

Taking his offered arm, I stepped out onto the wharf.

I strode ahead, leaving Aric to follow at a slight distance. My Warriors formed a guard behind me, but it was for show rather than protection. My mother was no fool. Black-garbed Warriors were already in position, keeping the crowd back and maintaining order. Somewhere, blending in with the ordinary people, Zandri's Masks would be ensuring this parade went smoothly. I glanced at the distant rooftops, suspecting that Masks were strategically placed to assassinate any would-be assailants.

A gilded carriage was waiting to take me to the palace. Riding in it was the intelligent choice – the safe choice. But my pride outweighed my caution. I wanted my people to see their future empress.

'Unhitch the horses,' I said to the driver.

He blinked at me. 'Your Highness, your mother—'

'Does not give the orders here. *I* do.'

I watched impatiently as the two Zigilian stallions were stripped of their harnesses. Then I swung onto the lead horse, and offered the reins of the second to Aric. He mounted in silence, his expression unreadable – but he surveyed the crowd and surrounding buildings with military focus.

Flower petals rained down from the rooftops as I pranced through the streets. All were red, the traditional colour for a victory parade. They drifted down onto my head and shoulders, vivid against the black of my horse's mane.

'Your Highness! Your Highness, welcome home!'

'We love you, Princess Scarlett!'

Like I had in Damar, I raised my hand in response to the shouts and cheers. It was infinitely more satisfying to be celebrated for who I really was rather than hiding behind an illusion.

This, I thought as I rode past the people screaming my name. *This is what true power feels like.*

We continued around the arena and through the Higher Districts, where there were markedly fewer Warriors. A commotion disturbed the soldiers ahead, and my stallion reared up unexpectedly. My heart leapt into my mouth, knowing that it had finally happened – one of Roran's agents was trying to kill me.

But when I calmed my horse, pulling back on the reins, I saw that a group of children had rushed out onto the road. Their mother darted after them and quickly tugged them back into line, bowing her head under the weight of my stare. I noticed that she was trembling.

'What did she think I was going to do to her?' I asked with irritation as we continued on. 'Have her executed? Whip her children?'

Aric cast me a sideways glance. 'No one would stop you.'

'Because that's exactly what I want to do after returning from months of war: order more bloodshed.' Sarcasm was thick in my voice. 'Even my father wasn't *that* callous. Roran, maybe . . .'

'The people don't know you yet,' Aric said. 'Once they do, their wariness will fade.'

My temper flared. 'They've had years to get to know me. It's their own fault they never thought a princess was worth much.'

I urged my horse into a canter, my hair flowing out behind me like a crimson banner. Heedless of appearances, I left my Warriors far behind as I rode through the imposing imperial gates and into the manicured gardens.

I dismounted in front of the palace, handing the reins to the first servant to reach me. He bowed so deeply that it looked uncomfortable, his golden livery a brassy yellow in the hot sun.

'I'll wait for the other Warriors to arrive,' Aric told me, still on horseback. 'This is your moment.'

I nodded distractedly. Murmurs drew my attention to the nobles gathered on the palace steps; men and women I had known since childhood, who had never given a damn whether I lived or died. They curtsied and bowed at my approach, the women with preening, false smiles on their perfectly made-up faces.

I hated them all on sight. But I smiled back, allowing a hint of teeth to show.

Then their ranks parted.

Amongst the colour and finery of the nobles, Zandri was a pillar of darkness. She wore her favourite fitted black combat outfit, her shoulders decorated with feathers that gave the impression of wings. Her dark hair was cut as short as I remembered it, doing nothing to soften her sharp cheekbones and red lips, thin as a knife's gash. Even in her severity, there was a striking kind of magnetism about her. A power and presence the nobles couldn't hope to match.

'Mother.' I rarely called her that, but the word escaped my lips almost without permission.

'Daughter.' Zandri's dark eyes were impossible to read. 'A decisive victory.'

Even though I outranked her, Zandri made no attempt to descend the steps – waiting for me to come to her. She tilted her head as she watched me, a small smile playing across her mouth. Curious to see what I would do next.

I closed the distance slowly, my steps measured. I didn't spare a single glance for my audience, keeping my attention on Zandri. She was the only one who mattered.

I wanted to hate her. I *should* hate her – for what she had done to Severin, for her lies, even for the way she had diminished my success with this little game. I felt the nobles watching us intently, and I knew Zandri's power play wasn't lost on them.

But I also knew that Zandri wouldn't seriously damage my political standing. She needed me.

And I needed *her*.

The thought caused anger to rise, colder than ice. Harder than steel. But I hid it behind a dutiful smile as I leant in and kissed her cool cheek.

'Don't think you've bought their favour with this victory,' Zandri said quietly, her narrow-eyed stare flicking over the gathered nobles. 'They're as fickle as sheep, and about as useful.' Her eyes cut to me. 'You should have followed my order.'

I had expected this – Zandri's frustration that I had turned her victory into mine. That I had disobeyed her, and she had lost face in the process.

'I thought mothers were supposed to celebrate their daughters' successes,' I murmured. 'I thought you would be pleased. I'm finally acting like the empress you taught me to be.'

'If that were true, you wouldn't have gone to the Western Lands in the first place. We both know what motivated that decision, and it had nothing to do with proving yourself to your subjects. You've been reckless ever since the Artisan's death.'

The Artisan – as if Severin had been nothing to Zandri. As if she hadn't sent him on countless missions and relied on his predictions. And yet, I shouldn't have expected anything else. Severin might have been one of my mother's favourite tools, but all tools could be replaced.

'I saw what you did to the greenhouse,' Zandri continued. 'The plants, flowers and glass torn down in your blind rage . . . It was unnecessary. The cost of restoring it will be immense.'

'Then leave it.' My voice was sharp. 'No one else cared to visit it anyway. The court found the poisonous plants unnerving.'

Zandri didn't respond. She turned on her heel and I followed, our steps strangely synchronised as we entered the palace.

As she filled me in on Ravalian politics, I was careful to look attentive. To express concern and gratitude in all the right places and ask all the right questions. And the wariness in Zandri's eyes slowly began to fade.

She wouldn't forget my decision to disobey her, but perhaps in time she would dismiss it as a childish attempt to gain power. I doubted she suspected my true intentions: to honour Severin's memory and transition away from the old Ravalian Empire to something new.

'I have organised a fighting match in your honour,' Zandri said as we ascended the grand staircase. 'It will be the first of many public appearances, so it's important that you make an impression.'

I nodded in assent. I hadn't expected anything less.

We reached the landing, but when I started to turn, Zandri stopped me. 'I have a present for you,' she said, continuing straight ahead – to a set of gold-plated doors guarded by two female Masks. My eyes dropped to the filigree doorknobs, shaped like roaring lions.

The Masks brought their arms to their chests at our approach – a Ravalian gesture of respect and fealty. And then they opened the doors.

The doors to my father's chambers.

I stepped inside in a daze. I had only been invited to Emperor Kalias's private chambers a handful of times, but everything was as

I remembered: the imposing obsidian floors, soaring marble columns and carved furniture upholstered in rich, dark shades.

Crossing the spacious parlour, I approached the floor-to-ceiling glass beyond. My chambers had overlooked the gardens, but Emperor Kalias had a direct view over the arena and sprawling city beyond. It was surreal to gaze out of those windows as he once would have done.

'I understand if you prefer to return to your own chambers,' Zandri said, and for the first time, she sounded slightly uncertain. 'Or if you would like the servants to redecorate—'

'Why would I do that?' I asked, finally turning to face my mother. 'What would be the point of ruling the Ravalian Court – of controlling every inch of this palace, including these chambers – if I redesigned it so that it was unrecognisable?' Slowly, I started to smile. 'This is the best gift you could have given me. And it's so much better to leave it exactly as it is, knowing that it's all mine now, and Emperor Kalias is dead and rotting in the ground.'

And as my eyes locked with Zandri's, something passed between us—

A shared understanding.

If a dark one.

Standing before the full-length mirror, I tilted my head to admire the gown: red and black, with a fitted bodice and slitted skirt. A golden snake slithered its way down the otherwise open back, held in place by matching chains.

Aella swept my hair off my face with two scorpion hair pieces. I allowed her to replace my earrings with rubies that dripped down like blood, but when she reached for my necklace, I slapped her hand away.

'Leave it,' I said, reaching protectively for Severin's necklace. The aquamarine pendant didn't go with the rest of my outfit, but I didn't care. I hadn't taken it off since he'd given it to me.

Aella cast her doe-like eyes down to the floor, and I regretted my harshness. There was something so delicate about her: a childlike fragility that didn't suit the cut-throat Ravalian Court. With the way she so rarely spoke or looked me in the face, it was easy to forget that she had a personality of her own.

No doubt Zandri thought the same about her servants. That realisation didn't sit well with me.

'You've done wonderfully,' I told Aella, softening my voice. 'Take the rest of the evening to enjoy the celebrations.'

When she left, I turned my attention to Zandri. My mother was standing at the window, where she had a view of the firelit arena. As night fell, it seemed to pulse like a ruby heart.

I wasn't eager to attend the gathering in the banquet hall, where the nobles would already be eating and dancing. But tonight's fighting matches – those filled me with bloodthirsty anticipation. How long had I waited for this moment? For my achievements to finally be recognised by the Court?

Zandri's thoughts echoed mine. 'I am so proud of you, Scarlett. You're becoming everything I always hoped you would be.'

Two sentences. That was all it took – two simple sentences to convey what I had spent my life longing to hear.

If I was honest with myself – truly honest – I had betrayed Mira for *this*. Not just because she was a threat to me or my future plans, but because I had wanted to finally prove myself to my mother.

But now . . . now, I found myself thinking of how Zandri had risked my life in the pursuit of power. And the role she had played in Severin's death.

His *murder*.

I sank into my father's favourite wing-backed chair, tapping my fingernails against the armrest. I had everything I had bled and sacrificed for. *Everything*, and yet—

'What did you do with his body?'

Zandri's shoulders stiffened. Just the slightest movement – but it told me everything I needed to know.

I smiled mirthlessly, something in my chest caving in. I hadn't doubted the seer's vision, but a part of me had still hoped that Zandri hadn't been involved.

'His body was burned,' she said at last. 'There's nothing left of him to resurrect, if that's what you're thinking. Even if there was, I warned you once before: the Sorceress herself couldn't resurrect someone who had been dead too long.'

I had already suspected as much. Had never allowed myself to hope otherwise.

'You killed him, didn't you?' My voice sounded dead even to me. Fitting, since a part of me had died with Severin. A softer, kinder part that Zandri wouldn't have believed existed.

'He left you, Scarlett.' Zandri slowly turned to face me, her expression inscrutable. 'He chose to die because he couldn't stand to see the person you had become.'

'No.' I stood abruptly. 'That's a lie. I saw the vision of him dying, and the seer said—'

'Did you *see* me kill him?'

'I didn't see you try to save him.'

'*Save* him.' She barked out a harsh laugh. 'And why would I do that? He was *weak*, Scarlett. Not like you.' Zandri moved closer, her dark eyes boring into mine. 'Not like us. If you expected me to intervene for him, then I have truly failed you as a mother – and you have misunderstood every lesson I have ever taught you.'

I shook my head. 'This is what you do – you twist things around. But I *know* – I *knew* Severin. And he wouldn't have done this. He wouldn't have . . .' I couldn't say the words. Could barely even think them.

'People are generally disappointing.' A hint of what looked like genuine sympathy softened Zandri's hard face. 'Severin clearly wasn't who you thought he was. But you should have known better than to expect genuine devotion from a slave.'

'He was so much more than that – and he was far stronger than you give him credit for.' I raised my chin, facing her with all the defiance left in me. 'This was *your* doing, not his. You corrupt everything you touch. Even someone as pure as Severin.'

Those dark eyes blinked, as if to say, *Pure? Severin?* 'Do you even know what I used him for?'

'I don't care what missions you sent him on. He never had any choice but to—'

'Oh, he had a choice. They all do – and they *choose* to live, even if it means killing others to advance the empire's interests. As noble as you believe Severin to be, he was no different from the others. Perfectly content to kill whoever I told him to, to predict the outcomes of battles to ensure Ravalian victory, to report on rebellions before they happened. He was nothing more than a murderer. A traitor to his own people.'

I stared at Zandri, finally understanding exactly how she saw the Orders and the people under her command – not as people at all, but as weapons to be used and then discarded, without regret or hesitation. And Severin . . . Severin had been no different in the end.

'You used Severin's blood ruby, didn't you?' I said, because it was the only thing that made sense. 'You ordered him to throw himself off the battlements, because—' My voice broke. I swallowed and tried again. 'Because you knew that I loved him.'

Zandri didn't laugh this time, but her incredulous expression was almost worse. 'Oh, Scarlett.' The pity in her voice was cutting. 'You didn't *love* him. You're not capable of that. Not true, unconditional love.'

I backed away from her. 'You're wrong.'

'Severin knew it too,' she continued ruthlessly. 'In the end, he saw exactly what you are – and he couldn't stand it. He chose to die rather than be with you. What does that say about him? What does that say about *you*?'

You think me selfish, I had said to Severin once. And his slow, cautious reply: *I think that you can be relentless when it comes to what you want.*

I closed my eyes, and this time my memories of Severin were darker. No longer sweet and passionate, a shared love between equals, but – a princess and a slave. A slave who had dared to believe he saw something kind in me, only to realise that he had been mistaken.

There's always another way, Scar. Always.

I could still hear the love and desperation in his voice. Could taste it in his final kiss on the battlements, when he had kissed me like it was the last time.

Because he'd known then, hadn't he? He'd *decided* that he was going to die. To leave me cold and alone, because of course someone as honourable and decent and wonderful as Severin could never have loved someone like *me*.

Maybe Zandri saw the devastation on my face, the emotion I was too slow to hide. Maybe, for a brief moment, she saw her daughter and not a future empress. Her expression softened into one I recognised, one she reserved for wounded and emotionally traumatised agents who required careful handling.

'Severin couldn't accept you for who you are,' she murmured. 'But I accept you, Scarlett. I see every part of you, even those parts you try to keep hidden. And what I see is *magnificent*.'

I looked up into my mother's dark stare, burning with conviction. With truth.

How easy it would be to seek comfort in that conviction. To let myself drown in it.

'They all turn against you in the end, don't they?' Zandri said, the sympathy in her voice making something inside me ache. 'But I never have. And I never will.'

Flashes of memory unfolded before my eyes. Zandri teaching me magic. Zandri leaving hidden weapons in my chambers. Zandri ordering her Masks to look out for me when she couldn't.

And I realised she was right. Zandri was the only person who accepted me, even if it hurt to admit it.

Zandri was the only person who knew me at all.

'There were so many things that your brothers did to you,' she said after a long pause, those onyx eyes intent on mine. 'So many small cruelties that I had to watch, knowing that I couldn't protect you from them. I'm sorry for that. More than you know.' Zandri took a hesitant step towards me. 'But I do love you, Scarlett. Whatever part of me that is still capable of love will always love you.'

There was nothing Zandri could say to rewrite the past. The things she had done, the choices she had made . . . they couldn't be forgotten or entirely forgiven. No matter how many empires we tore down together.

But I believed her. After all this time, I finally believed that Zandri loved me. And that knowledge made all the difference.

I placed my hand over hers. It was the only thing I could think to do. The only way I knew to show how I felt.

Eventually, there would be a reckoning. There would have to be, because I didn't intend to rule as my mother's puppet. But the Ravalian throne was mine. It was my inheritance.

And Zandri could help me win it. Together, we could achieve anything.

The tender moment lingered for another handful of seconds. Then Zandri pulled her hand from mine.

'Enough sentimentality. We've kept the Court waiting long enough; any longer, and they will begin to wonder if you're afraid to face them. Which is the last thing we want.' Zandri turned on her heel, only to glance back over her shoulder. 'And get rid of that necklace. There's no point clinging to reminders of the past.'

I straightened my shoulders and followed Zandri from my father's chambers.

But I left Severin's necklace on.

CHAPTER TWENTY-ONE

Mira

I saw the procession before I even saw the beach.

The long line of white-robed priestesses and armoured warriors parted as I rode into view, bowing their heads and touching their fingers to their foreheads. Their deference reminded me painfully of my handfasting ceremony with Vølund, when these same men and women had stood before us and celebrated our union.

On the shore in front of their ship stood the clan heads, two open caskets before them. Velanthe was at Nari's side, murmuring something I couldn't hear. Cassius remained at a slight, respectful distance, along with a dozen priestesses and a contingent of Kalurian warriors.

Everyone turned at my arrival, watching me and my companions dismount in sombre silence. The only sound was the water lapping against the sand.

An icy breeze ghosted across my exposed skin, making me even colder, despite the furs covering my shoulders. The cold had been my constant companion these past forty-eight hours – the last, lingering consequence of the poison I had survived.

'Are you sure you're well enough for this?' Jadis asked as she swung down from the saddle. 'No one would fault you if—'

'I've already missed the funeral rites,' I said firmly. 'I won't miss his send-off.'

A queen couldn't afford to be seen as weak – not even amongst her allies. So I crossed the beach unassisted, flanked by Jadis and Elian. The light of their fire torches illuminated the rocky path in front of me.

Nari reached me first. From what I'd heard, she had been

impressively stoic throughout the rites conducted in the Temple, but her cheeks glinted with the evidence of tears.

'You're just in time,' she said. 'Thoren and Ulrik are about to release their bodies.'

I followed her to the shoreline, ignoring the stares lingering on me. My stomach dropped as I saw the two wooden rafts, decorated with flowers. Laid out on those planks were the bodies of Vølund – and Astrid.

I had always known a Mask killed my father. An operative Zandri had recruited – with the goal of assassinating my mother as well. It seemed that Astrid had been the sleeper Mask's unwitting vessel, responsible for pouring the poisoned wine. Had she lived, perhaps she could have exposed the assassin's identity. But she hadn't, and I was terrified that the chance for answers had died along with her.

'Vølund looks . . .' I couldn't finish the sentence.

Nari's voice was quiet. 'I know.'

Velanthe and the priestesses had done well. There was no trace of the ravages of the poison that had killed Vølund; he looked at peace, with his eyes closed and his arms folded respectfully. He even had a faint bloom of colour on his cheeks, as if he was merely asleep.

I knelt on the sand. I didn't touch Vølund's hand – didn't want to risk feeling his cold skin and absent pulse. But I couldn't stop myself from leaning down to kiss his lips. Just the lightest brush of my mouth.

'Thank you,' I whispered. 'For everything, but mostly for making me feel less alone.'

I rose to my feet without touching Astrid. I didn't feel that I deserved that right, not having interacted much with her in life. But I mourned her death just the same. She had been so young; it was cruel that she hadn't had more time.

Thoren and Ulrik carried the wooden rafts out to sea. When they were deep enough, they pushed them into the dark water – sending Vølund and Astrid on their symbolic final journey to the afterlife.

'He died here,' Nari murmured next to me. 'It is only right that he is mourned here . . . But the sea will carry him home.'

A Kalurian archer stepped forward. After lighting his arrow on fire, he reached for his bow.

Before I could think better of it, I said, 'Let me.'

I took the bow and arrow from him. After a glance at Nari – who nodded her assent – I notched the arrow, training my eyes on the raft carrying my husband. I understood why an archer had been chosen to make this shot: already it had travelled far from the shore, and the slight breeze made aiming difficult. But when I closed my eyes, that familiar, instinctual pull answered.

Instead of merely feeling connected to my target, I felt connected to everything: the ocean in front of me, the people gathered at my back, even the fire blazing on my arrow. When I released it, it struck true.

Fire engulfed Vølund in its warm embrace. Though the two rafts had diverged, it somehow jumped to Astrid as well, resulting in a few startled murmurs from the audience.

I watched the bodies burn across the dark water, but something about the sight felt wrong. Too slow, too gentle, for the vengeance and rage that ignited in my chest.

People exclaimed in shock as the fire erupted in a blaze of heat. Two twin pillars, grasping for the starlit sky.

'We will see him avenged,' I vowed. 'I swear it, Nari. I will find the person responsible for this – and I will make them pay.'

But when Nari looked at me . . . there was none of the sadness or gratitude I had expected.

'I already know who is responsible,' she said, and there was unbridled anger in every line of her face.

'You know who Zandri's sleeper Mask is?'

Nari's laugh was devoid of humour. 'This was never about Zandri. I don't even believe it was about politics. It was about *you*.'

I stepped back from her, my eyes flicking to the Kalurian clansmen – to the *armed* Kalurian clansmen. Their numbers hadn't seemed threatening before, but now, with their swords and axes gleaming in the firelight . . .

'I didn't harm Vølund. I would *never*—'

'I am inclined to believe you were as much a victim of this as my brother was. But your Ravalian prince is another matter.'

Slowly I turned to face Cassius. His midnight-blue eyes were unreadable, a perfect match to his expressionless face.

'Do you have any proof?' I asked, directing my words to Nari but never shifting my gaze from Cassius.

'He was seen inside the Temple, where the poisons were stocked. He bedded Astrid before she poured the poisoned wine. And I have spent enough time around him to see the way he watches you.' Nari's voice hardened as she said, 'If that wasn't enough, he disobeyed your direct order to give the antidote to Vølund. As a result, your husband – our leader – is dead. If you want to maintain this alliance, Kasmira, I demand retribution.'

'From what you've told me,' I said slowly, facing Nari once more, 'the only concrete evidence you have is Cassius's decision to save my life. Surely that is forgivable.'

'Not to me.' Nari's face was hard. Uncompromising. 'I will accept nothing less than his death. His death, in recompense for my brother's.'

Velanthe's dark eyes met mine. The high priestess didn't speak, but the slight dip of her head said enough.

Whether it was fair or not, in the eyes of the clans, this was the only reasonable choice. And suddenly, I was back on that icy mountain plateau, trying to choose between Nari and Darius's lives.

I had sworn never to make that mistake again. Never to put one life ahead of the lives of my people, and my duty as queen. In order to protect my position, in order to defeat Roran, I had to do this.

Cassius didn't try to stop me as I reached for his face, running a finger down the contours of his cheek. Sharp – his cheekbones were so sharp. Just as sharp as the rest of him.

Only it was easy to forget that, wasn't it? Easy to be lured in by that beautiful, careless facade. A facade he cultivated for precisely that purpose.

All it took was a little bit more pressure and my nails were sinking into his flesh, causing a thin red line to well. How strange it was to realise that he *could* bleed. That he was every bit as human as I was, even if his veins were filled with ice.

A single thought had Cassius's blood slowing. He collapsed to his knees, his eyes widening – not in fear or surprise, but in something darker. As if my actions made complete sense to him.

It seemed I had my answer.

'I lied to you,' I admitted, my voice quiet – too quiet for Nari and the others to overhear. 'But you've known that all along, haven't you? You knew exactly what I promised Vølund in exchange for an alliance.'

Cassius didn't deny it. The moonlight slashed his face in half, and I finally saw the anger he had been concealing.

'Yes,' he replied, equally softly. 'I knew. I knew that for your alliance to have worked, you would have had to kill not only Roran, but his entire family. *My* entire family.' He stared up at me, his blue eyes flashing. 'You decided that Scarlett and I were acceptable losses.'

I thought of the red tears running down Vølund's face, and my heart hardened. What had Cassius said once?

Both Scarlett and Zandri are known for their ruthlessness – and your priestesses stock poisons in the Temple. Some are even Ravalian in origin.

Gods, if only I had pieced it together earlier. I could have saved Vølund's life – and Astrid's.

I stared into Cassius's resolute face. I had no doubt that he'd always intended for me to survive; he must have chosen the poison knowing that Velanthe had an antidote, and poisoned me so I wouldn't be implicated in the assassination attempt. Perhaps, in his own mind, he had acted in some kind of twisted self-defence, killing Vølund before the clan leader could kill *him*.

But even if I could forgive him for that, there was still Astrid to consider – an innocent woman who had died merely to ensure her silence.

I reached for the dagger strapped to my side. Everyone was watching me, my surroundings so silent I could hear the whisper of the wind and the gentle lapping of the water against the rocky shore.

Two of Nari's warriors drew closer, on either side of me. I couldn't tell if their placement was meant as a threat – or protection, in case Cassius were to escape the influence of my blood magic and attack me.

'I was wrong to release you from the dungeons,' I told Cassius in a carrying voice. 'I should have known that it would come to this.'

'I was the one who was wrong,' he murmured, something indefinable shadowing his midnight-blue gaze. 'When I said that I couldn't imagine you being as ruthless as me or Roran. I was wrong.'

His words stung – exactly like they were supposed to. It would be easy to finish it. A quick slice across his throat, and Cassius would be gone. It was what I should have done weeks ago.

Months ago.

I closed my eyes, fighting for control. I was furious, suddenly – furious with Nari and the clans, furious with Cassius and the tattooed crown on my forehead that meant nothing at all. Red seeped into my vision, and with it came something dark and monstrous. A sense of certainty I had never felt before.

When I reopened my eyes, I knew that Cassius would see nothing human in my face.

Nothing remotely merciful.

But he didn't flinch as my grip tightened on the dagger. Didn't so much as shift his gaze from mine. And then . . . a faint smile curved his lips. Like we were sharing a secret.

I acted in a lightning-fast movement – two quick slashes, right then left. Blood sprayed over me and Cassius like a fountain, coating us both in crimson as the two clan warriors fell. When I swallowed, I tasted something hot and metallic.

'Restrain the others,' I ordered the priestesses and my warriors. 'No one escapes.'

I didn't turn to see if my order had been obeyed – didn't need to. Velanthe was nothing if not loyal.

'You're making a mistake.' Nari's skin was sickly pale as she stared down at the two men bleeding out on the beach, then back at me – and Cassius, standing at my side. I had the sense he was still smiling. Amused by the direction this had taken.

'You're the one who made a mistake,' I said evenly, strolling towards her. 'I am a queen, and I am done taking orders. Cassius is *my* subject, not yours. It is my decision what to do with him.'

One of Nari's warriors moved to block my path, but I didn't pause. As blood spilled around me, my power strengthened. At my glance, the blood began to rise and expand, snaking through the air with exhilarating speed before forming into a spear and—

The warrior crumpled instantly as the red spear pierced right through him, only to dissolve once more, mixing with his own blood.

So much blood that it drew me closer, its pulsing energy begging me to reach out and *use* it.

A sudden sense of connection rose up in me, and when I glanced down at my hands, they were glowing with an eerie reddish light. I let the dagger fall as I advanced on Nari, filled with the certainty that I no longer needed the weapon.

'Stay back, demon.' Nari raised her sword, but her hands were trembling. 'Even if you kill me, you will not win. The Kalurian clans will rise up against you.'

'Will they?' I asked mildly, taking in the scene around me. Most of the clansmen were still fighting, responsible for the bodies of priestesses and a few of my warriors lying motionless on the ground. *And that is unacceptable.*

I had feared my power for so long. Had resisted using it, resisted finding out what I was truly capable of. But I didn't need to resist it or control it any longer. I needed to *unleash* it.

A hand took hold of my arm, and the flicker of emotion that crossed Cassius's face as I met his gaze . . . Gods, what must I look like, if even *Cassius* seemed unnerved?

'Mira.' His voice was cautioning. 'Are you sure you want to do this? You'll have to kill them all.'

'No,' I told him. 'I won't.'

Letting go of my power felt like unleashing a natural disaster. It was an explosion, a tidal wave, extending from me and sweeping up everyone in its path until I was connected to every single one of them, their hearts and minds and souls mine for the taking.

A reddish haze overcame my vision as I focused on maintaining the tether, straining against the limits of my endurance and the pain screaming through my body as I forced one crucial, all-encompassing command into their minds:

I am your queen.
And you will obey me.

CHAPTER TWENTY-TWO

Mira

The tide of blood pulled at me.

Its thick warmth was like a cocoon around my body, except no matter how much I thrashed, I couldn't seem to get free—

'It's alright,' a voice murmured in my ear.

But when I tried to inhale, warm liquid flooded into my mouth. Blood. I was choking on it – I couldn't *breathe*—

'For Gods' sake, Mira!' Smooth hands took hold of me, and I was dimly aware of leaning back against the hard muscles of a man's chest. 'You're fine – you're safe. Just take a breath!'

This time I inhaled air. Hot, unexpectedly humid air, with a faint edge to it – sulphur?

My eyes shot open. I wasn't submerged in blood – I was floating. Floating in the hot springs beneath the Temple, priestesses lining the cavern walls around me, vague outlines in the flickering light of the sconces.

And the body I was pressed up against, his arms holding me carefully above water . . .

'That's better,' Cassius said, his midnight-blue eyes intent on mine. He stroked a strand of damp hair back from my face. 'Just concentrate on me. Ignore everything else.'

But it was impossible to ignore the sounds. They echoed through the cavern – not quite as loud and shrill as screams, but not as soft as gasps. I'd never heard anything quite like them before.

'W-what—?'

'Don't try to talk,' Cassius soothed, but the fact that he was being so *nice* only made me tenser.

Then I realised – the sounds had stopped when I'd spoken. Were they – had *I* been making those noises?

'That she's conscious is a good sign,' one of the priestesses – *Velanthe* – murmured, directing her words to Cassius. 'Physically, she should be fine. It's the mental consequences we need to assess.'

Cassius's grip tightened slightly before he softened his hold. When I shifted, I saw that his back was against the stone wall. How long had he been holding me like this? And more importantly, *why*?

'The high priestess,' Cassius drawled, 'believes the hot springs possess healing powers.'

He didn't sound entirely convinced of this, but the fact that he had gone along with it . . .

I cast my mind back, desperate to remember what had happened. Desperate to understand exactly how injured I had been. But no – Velanthe hadn't been concerned about my physical condition. Just my mental one.

Icy fear raced through my veins and I shivered, despite the steam coming off the water. Yes, I remembered now. Nari's ultimatum. Using blood magic to kill her warriors. Then that final, desperate push to secure the alliance, even though my whole body had been screaming at me to stop. *I am your queen.*

I pulled away from Cassius and stood, conscious of the way the water barely covered my bare breasts. I folded my arms across my chest as I looked up at the high priestess. 'Did it work?'

A faint, reassuring smile. 'Nari and the clan heads are loyal to you. They know that Cassius was responsible for Vølund's death, but thanks to your blood magic, they have accepted your judgement as their queen. All three voted to make you clan leader.'

Because I took away their choice. That knowledge settled into me like a leaden weight, and I remembered Vølund telling me how he refused to impose his will on the people under his command.

How I had admired him for that. How deeply I had wanted to be a similar kind of ruler – a true leader, who inspired loyalty and respect in her subjects. Now, less than two days after his death, I was already defiling his legacy. Claiming a title I hadn't earned and didn't deserve.

A slight pucker appeared between Velanthe's brows. Concern – because I had taken too long to respond to what she considered welcome news. No doubt she was assessing my mental stability even now.

'That's a relief,' I told her, but the words lacked conviction. 'At least one crisis has been averted.'

'Not exactly,' Cassius said, and I didn't miss the glance he exchanged with the high priestess. 'It's not official yet. It won't be, not until the Council of Ancients give you their blessing.'

'We discussed this.' Velanthe's voice was cool. 'The Council of Ancients despises Kasmira—'

'They despise the Temple,' Cassius interrupted. 'There's a difference.'

Velanthe stared at Cassius for a long moment, her dark eyes as hard as river stones. Then her attention returned to me. 'The Council of Ancients will not meet with you unless they wish to. If you seek them out uninvited, it's unlikely you will survive the encounter.'

'Then I'll lose the clans,' I said, the realisation filling me with heavy finality. 'It doesn't matter what Nari and the clan heads tell their warriors; certain traditions are too entrenched. They will stand against me, refuse to accept my leadership.'

'Not if you influence them with blood magic. You've already proven what you can accomplish with your powers; you only need to use them on a larger scale. If you can convince the clans to overturn their traditions, they will follow you regardless of the Council of Ancients.'

'That would involve Mira influencing thousands of warriors,' Cassius broke in, his jaw clenching. '*Look* at her,' he ordered Velanthe, stabbing a finger at me. 'Do you think she has the strength to do that? She nearly died a few hours ago, and that was after influencing, what – fifty clansmen? Forty?'

'The more Kasmira practises,' Velanthe countered, 'the stronger she will become. In time, she will be capable of feats beyond your imagining. Her blood magic could allow her to turn the tide of this war—'

'Wars shouldn't be dependent on one person.' There was something almost angry about the way Cassius looked at the high priestess.

A sentiment that Velanthe clearly shared, given her thin lips and the lack of her usual serene expression.

A headache built in my temple. 'Can you give us a moment alone?'

Velanthe's eyes lingered on Cassius. But she nodded and turned on her heel, the other priestesses hurriedly following her out.

I reluctantly returned to my attention to Cassius, who was leaning against the lip of the hot springs with irritating nonchalance. As if he hadn't been in the midst of a heated argument minutes earlier.

'You deliberately antagonised her,' I accused.

Cassius merely shrugged. 'She's used to you taking her advice without question. That's dangerous in politics. You can have favoured counsellors, but the moment you start relying on only one person, you make yourself vulnerable. And Velanthe has gone to great lengths to ensure she's the only person you can turn to.'

'I trust Velanthe implicitly,' I said, stung by the implication.

Cassius moved through the water towards me, smooth, liquid and compelling. His golden-blond hair glistened, water droplets sparkling. A few rolled invitingly down the hard planes of his muscular chest. 'And yet,' he said, 'you sent her away in order to speak to *me*. Because you know a queen needs more than one adviser – and like it or not, I'm far more useful than your precious high priestess.'

He was close – so close that he towered over me, a shadowy figure even in the firelight. I went still as his finger brushed my upper lip, only understanding when he held it up to me.

I stared at the ruby liquid. When I touched my face, my fingers came away wet with blood.

'Someone,' Cassius said softly, 'needs to look out for your interests. As strong and fierce and compassionate as you are, Mira, you have a blind spot where court politics are concerned. You don't understand how selfish and cut-throat people can be.'

'What does a nosebleed prove?' I asked, drawing back from him. 'Velanthe said that I would get stronger with practice—'

'Forget what Velanthe believes. Whatever loyalty and affection you feel for her, her greatest desire is to win this battle against Roran. Have you ever considered that victory might mean more to her than your life?'

'No.' I took another step back from Cassius. 'I'm her queen. She is sworn to protect me.'

'She has also been ruling over the Temple for decades, *without* a queen to answer to. Do you remember what I told you once?'

'It's difficult to relinquish power once you have it,' I murmured.

A sharp nod. 'No one is immune from that particular pitfall. Not even a high priestess.'

I didn't want to believe that. Didn't *want* to, but the charged intensity behind his stare made it difficult to doubt him.

The water lapped at his lower abdomen, and I realised that Cassius had jumped into the hot springs half-clothed. A glance over my shoulder showed me a pile of my clothing, tattered in a way that suggested he had ripped them off me.

Something tightened in my chest. 'You helped save my life.'

'You saved mine.' Cassius's full lips turned up at the corners, reminding me of the way he had smiled just before I turned my blood magic on Nari's warriors. Like we were sharing a secret.

'Did you think that was wise?' I asked. 'That you could nurse me back to health, and I would forget that you killed my *husband?*'

'Fiancé,' Cassius corrected. 'Unless you had time to consummate the marriage in the hedge maze.'

'Stop it.' I narrowed my eyes at him. 'Stop making light of this. No matter how you try to justify it, you still murdered two people. And you can tell me your life was at stake, but I had other plans for you, and anyway, while Roran was alive—'

'I'd be safe?' Cassius finished with a mirthless laugh. 'Did you ask Vølund what he thought about that?'

I said nothing.

'Do you know what the hardest part was, when you chose to lie to my face? It was that you almost convinced me to trust you. I wanted to – I wanted to believe that my instincts were wrong. But I couldn't lie to myself hard enough.' Midnight-blue eyes met mine. They were almost black in the shadows, and far from inviting. 'You've learnt more from me than I think you realise.'

'Maybe I have,' I said dully, thinking of the clansmen I had killed. 'But *you* have learnt nothing at all.'

I closed my eyes, attuning myself to the beat of Cassius's heart. Steeling myself for what had to happen next.

'I promised Nari that I would avenge Vølund's death,' I told him. 'Which leaves me with only one option.'

'Making me disappear,' Cassius said without inflection.

Of course *murder* was the first conclusion he came to. An unstable laugh bubbled from my mouth, and as my concentration faltered, Cassius seized his chance – reversing our positions and pushing me against the stone lip of the spring. Before I could re-establish my control, he wrapped his hands around my throat.

Not pressing down – not yet. But his grip was tight enough to show that he could, and I wasn't sure if I would be able to stop him in time.

I could still sense his blood, and the pounding of his heart. I could slow it – or stop it altogether.

But all it would take was the slightest increase of pressure, and he could take me down along with him.

'Part of me is impressed,' he said against my ear. 'When I first met you, I knew you had *potential*. But I warned you not to play games with me, Mira.' His voice lowered, turning frighteningly intimate. 'Do you remember what I told you?'

'They usually have deadly endings,' I whispered, my heart pounding so hard that I felt light-headed.

Something was about to happen. I could tell by the passion burning in his voice; a mixture of fury and desire. He was either going to kiss me or try to kill me, only I had no idea *which*—

He released me.

I stumbled before I steadied myself against the stone, staring over my shoulder at him in disbelief.

Cassius watched me steadily. 'I think a part of you is relieved he's dead. Now you don't have to chain yourself to someone else to rule your own country.'

I turned on him, my entire body shaking with rage. 'Don't you dare! I didn't ask for this – I *never* would have asked you to—'

'You didn't have to,' Cassius said calmly. 'Isn't that why you visited the dungeons in the first place? Because you knew you needed me to help you make decisions you found unpalatable?'

'You're delusional,' I said tightly.

'Am I?' he asked. 'What am I to you, Mira, except your pet monster? Isn't that why you spared me – because you knew I could be *useful* to you?'

'I never thought of you like that. I'm not one of your twisted, power-hungry family members.'

'I might have believed you, if you hadn't threatened my life.' This time, when Cassius's eyes met mine, I saw the anger blazing within them.

'I wasn't going to – I'm *not* going to kill you,' I said, my rage spiking even further, infuriated by my use of the past tense. Already, he was twisting things around. Sowing doubt.

'Then what *were* you going to do?' Cassius asked, his tone indulgent.

'It occurred to me, after our talk in the dungeons, that maybe you hadn't been born this way. That perhaps you're a product of a cruel upbringing and a brutal father. And that perhaps . . .' I paused, taking a deep breath. 'Perhaps I could forgive you. Or make you worthy of forgiveness.'

'You were going to use blood magic – to change me.' Cassius's expression shuttered completely.

'It's what I should have done in the beginning.'

'When you visited me in the dungeons,' he said slowly. His eyes narrowed. 'That bottle of wine . . .'

'It had some of my blood in it,' I finished.

'But you took it with you.' Inexplicably, Cassius started to smile. 'You changed your mind.'

'I did,' I agreed, taking another step towards him. 'I won't this time.'

Cassius's body suddenly seemed coiled and dangerous – a snake debating whether to strike. But he said evenly, 'It isn't true loyalty if it's coerced.'

'And what would you know about true loyalty? Everything you do is about coercion – ensuring that other people are in your power. I don't think a single person in the Ravalian Court served you willingly. You always had something held over them.'

'I was wrong. I realised it after I betrayed your trust.' There was something dangerously sincere about the way he was looking at me. 'Until you, every interaction in my life was transactional. Adoration, loyalty – none of it was real. But *you*, Mira . . . you were real. You would do anything for the people who truly matter to you, and I wanted to be one of those people. I still do.'

'Don't,' I said, turning away. 'Don't pretend to care.'

'But what if I do?' he murmured, his hand rising to brush my cheek. 'What if I do care, Mira?'

Just that single touch and my body went still, as though his fingers were a paralytic. I felt like I was breathing hard and somehow not at all, my focus narrowing to the slow, deliberate strokes of his fingers as they traced the line of my jaw and down my throat, lingering on the base of my neck.

This is how a mouse must feel, I thought dizzily, *when it's caught in the jaws of a snake.*

'What if I proved it to you?' Cassius continued, his lips at my ear. The hardness of his body pressed against my back, and suddenly his left hand was splayed across my abdomen, keeping me pressed against him.

'I wouldn't believe it,' I said, even as my body betrayed me – leaning into him rather than pulling away.

I felt Cassius's amused exhale against my skin. 'I think you're afraid you *will* believe it,' he murmured, 'because that would mean trusting me. And the thought of trusting me terrifies you. But tell me, Mira: which of us has more reason to distrust the other?'

I glanced down at his right hand, which lingered on the side of my neck – just above my pulse.

All it would take was a slight shift of his hand, and he could cut off my air. He could end my life and never have to worry about me using blood magic on him again.

He left his hand right where it was. Allowing my heartbeat to reverberate through us both.

I turned and those dark blue eyes met mine. I had the sense that he saw more than I wanted him to, but he merely smiled that casual, disarming smile of his, as if things hadn't changed between us. As if he couldn't feel the way my heart picked up speed, pounding so hard that I felt slightly dizzy.

'I know I have a great deal to prove – to you, and to myself. But when this war is over, and Kalure is truly yours, I want us to be together, Mira. I want us to at least *try*.'

That snapped me out of my trance, and I pushed him away. He didn't try to stop me.

'What makes you think I'll even consider that?'

I couldn't see Cassius's face as he climbed out of the water, but I could hear the smile in his voice.

'You already are.'

CHAPTER TWENTY-THREE

Scarlett

I strode through the banquet hall, delighting in the way the nobles parted for me like they had once parted for my father and brothers. They were all staring – whispering, too – but I welcomed the attention.

It felt exhilarating to be *seen*. Not as a toothless, ceremonial princess – but as a military commander, deserving of respect. *And fear.*

For once, I made no attempt to avoid Empress Ivalene's former ladies, instantly recognisable by their fine gowns and insipid smiles. I walked right over and waited for them to fall into curtsies. Lady Verne, my old etiquette teacher, was the first to straighten. The first to dare to meet my gaze.

'I'm surprised to see you in attendance tonight,' I said conversationally, plucking a goblet of wine from a nearby refreshment table. 'I thought you would be too busy packing.'

Her eyebrows rose high on her forehead. 'Packing, Your Highness?'

'Oh, I assumed Zandri would have told you.' I swirled my goblet, not bothering to look at the other ladies as I said, 'I've decided to exile Ivalene to the Red Dunes – along with her former ladies. Which I suppose means all of you.'

Lady Verne's face whitened to the shade of curdled milk. 'T-to the Red Dunes, Your Highness?'

'I needed to choose somewhere isolated. I can't have her causing problems in my court. After all, she helped Cassius *murder* Emperor Kalias.' At least, that was the story Zandri had instructed her Masks to circulate, so she had an excuse to lock Ivalene up in the first place. 'Who knows what lengths she will descend to if left unchecked?'

Beneath her carefully polite mask, I knew that Lady Verne was cursing my name. But the knowledge of what my mother had done to Cassius's loyal supporters no doubt stilled her tongue. Being shipped off to a remote corner of the Western Lands was a better alternative than being sentenced to the dungeons – or fighting for her life in the arena.

'Your Highness,' a matronly woman interjected, 'what does Prince Roran have to say about this? Surely such a crucial decision can wait until after he is crowned.'

Though her words were respectful, she watched me with a sharp gaze. The other ladies stiffened as they waited for my response.

After setting my goblet back on the banquet table, I said, 'Should my brother survive his campaign in Kalure and become emperor, he can overturn my decision. Until then, Ivalene will have to embrace her new life in the desert. With such devoted ladies by her side, I'm sure the transition will be a smooth one.'

'Yes, Your Highness,' Lady Verne said with a stiff curtsy. The others murmured their assent.

'I wish you all a safe journey,' I told them. 'Remember to pack your coolest clothes – the heat is at a record high this year.'

I turned on my heel with a thin smile. Laughing without a word.

'How long?' one of the ladies burst out. I glanced over my shoulder, noting that it was a younger woman who spoke. I didn't recognise her; she must have been a recent appointment to Empress Ivalene's ladies. 'How long do you intend to banish us? Surely not forever.'

'Of course not,' I said, and the woman looked relieved. 'Only until Roran is officially crowned and orders you back to court – or until your mistress dies. Whichever comes first.'

I wondered how long it would be until they grew tired of all that heat and isolation and their demanding mistress. Surely at least one of these ladies had a hint of steel buried beneath their manners and their pedigree – enough to abandon Ivalene in the desert or slip some poison into her glass.

I felt no guilt at the possibility. Ivalene would have killed me a hundred times over if she could have; as it was, she had given Roran free rein to terrorise me as a child, not caring that he also turned his cruelty on Cassius. It seemed only fitting that I pay her back for everything we had endured.

Striding away, I made a beeline for the dais – where Zandri was entertaining a few of the more useful nobles. But before I could reach her, Aric stepped into my path.

'You're in a good mood,' he observed, his dark eyes twinkling.

'I'll be in an even better one when we leave for the arena,' I said, smiling up at him from beneath my lashes. 'Care to escort me?'

'Won't your admirers mind?'

I raised a brow, not understanding at first. When I did, I had to suppress the urge to laugh.

'They're not looking at me,' I told him. A steady stream of noblemen had vied for my attention earlier, but I'd long since dismissed them, and our current audience was made up of mostly women. 'They're looking at *you* – the youngest and most handsome general in the last few decades.'

'Only the last few decades?' Aric's smirk was positively wicked.

I looked him brazenly up and down. He really should wear courtly clothes more often; with his broad shoulders and athletic build, he was easily one of the most handsome men in attendance.

'The youngest and most handsome general in Ravalian history,' I amended, linking my arm through his. 'No wonder so many women are scowling at me. But they can't have you. You're all mine.'

Aric didn't object to that, though he might have if he'd seen the disapproval in Zandri's lingering stare. I pretended not to notice. Tonight was for me. Tonight, I made the rules.

But as I left the hall with Aric, I could have sworn I heard Zandri's voice follow me out.

Didn't you learn your lesson with Severin? her insidious voice whispered. *Aric will never love you. No one will.*

No one, except me.

I reclined in the box seat that had been reserved for Emperor Kalias, which afforded me the best possible view of the fighting matches.

Zandri and Aric were in positions of honour at my side. Lillian would have been welcome too, but she had opted not to attend. Instead, a few of Aric's lieutenants lined the nearby seats, and some of Zandri's most treasured Masks.

I had to hand it to my mother: she had outdone herself. The fighters were all evenly matched, and there was a steady stream of them – members of Cassius's so-called court pitted against each other.

It was just a pity Roran wasn't here to see this. But he would know soon enough.

I hoped his spies told him that I had claimed the seat belonging to the rightful ruler of Ravalia. And that my opening speech had been so well received that the crowd had cheered for a full three minutes.

Zandri grew bored as the matches continued, her attention drifting. In contrast, Aric seemed to grow steadily tenser.

I tried not to hold his reaction against him. Aric was Ravalian, but he'd grown up away from the capital and our more bloodthirsty traditions. Still, as my senior general, he should set an example for the others.

Nearby, his lieutenants were getting into the spirit of the evening: I heard the clinking of coins pass between them as they betted on the outcome. But even they frowned as one of the prisoners hurled his sword – not at his opponent, but at the sand.

This happened occasionally. Even with their freedom as an incentive, not all prisoners wished to fight.

And these two . . . well, in another life they might have been friends. I wondered if they regretted throwing their lot in with Cassius now.

The Warriors encircling the arena looked at me, awaiting my order. A single nod was all it would take, and this man would be killed or dragged back to the cells, his opponent matched with a different prisoner.

I held up a hand instead, content to watch this play out. Self-preservation was a powerful motivator.

The two men were similar in height and build. Their main differences were their hair colours – and their enthusiasm. The blond man swung at his disarmed opponent, forcing him to retreat until his back was against the arena wall. I leant forward, not wanting to miss a second.

What a delightful punishment *this* was. Far better than execution, or allowing them to languish in the dungeons.

The blond man landed another hit – this time with his fist rather than his sword. He was drawing this out for the benefit of the crowd, as his opponent should have been doing.

'You can stop this,' Aric said quietly next to me. 'If he doesn't want to fight—'

'It doesn't matter if he wants to,' I replied, watching the dark-haired man intently. 'He will.'

The crowd was shouting, yelling at the blond to finish it. But he knew this was a show, and he knew that the audience wouldn't free him unless they were suitably entertained.

His punches kept coming.

The dark-haired man was bruised and bloodied, but with every strike, his body became tenser – a cobra coiled to spring. And sure enough, when the blond drew back his fist for the next punch, the dark-haired man grabbed his hand and *twisted*.

What happened next was entirely predictable, but it still succeeded in taking the crowd by surprise. Shocked cries erupted as the dark-haired man disarmed his opponent and ran him through.

I watched him stumble backwards as the blond crumpled to the ground, the sword still in his stomach. The crowd's shouts gave way to silence. But their silence was just another death sentence.

His mistake was not making it a show. If he had drawn it out, I might have been merciful. As it was . . .

'Take him back to the dungeons,' I instructed the Warriors in a carrying voice. 'He fights again tomorrow.'

The hatred in the man's face sapped any enjoyment from the proceedings. I leant back in my seat with a sigh.

'You did well,' Zandri murmured, but I wasn't looking at my mother. I was looking at Aric.

Though he met my gaze, it would have been kinder if he hadn't. I saw the opposite sentiment reflected in his eyes.

I can't overturn centuries of tradition in one night, I wanted to tell him. *That's just not how it works.*

But Aric was already refocusing on the arena, watching my Warriors drag the body across the sand. Too quietly for Zandri to hear, he murmured without looking at me, 'During the parade, you said that you didn't want your subjects to fear you. Decisions like this ensure that they do.'

Zandri would say that it was better to be feared by my subjects. That their fear was another kind of protection. But I thought of the trembling woman during the parade, and I wasn't so sure.

Trumpets rang through the stands – a sound that heralded a royal arrival. For a brief, delirious second, I thought that Emperor Kalias was approaching. Then I saw the black armour, and shock flooded into me like ice.

Zandri stood in a fluid movement, shielding me bodily from view. Despite our disagreement, Aric did the same.

'I didn't think he would come here,' I said, reaching for the dagger strapped to my thigh.

Neither Zandri nor Aric replied. They were so tense that I half expected fighting to break out in the stands. But my Warriors let the small procession pass, tens of thousands of eyes following the imposing figure in black armour. A helmet concealed his face – but I was certain this was Roran.

Who else would come into the heart of Ravalian territory unannounced? Who else would *dare*?

When the procession was close, I brushed past Zandri and Aric. I wouldn't allow Roran to see me cowed.

But it wasn't Roran I saw when the Warrior removed his helmet.

'General Harte,' I said, almost too incensed to speak. 'What an unexpected surprise. I presume you've come to offer yourself up for tonight's finale? Watching a disgraced former general fight to the death would be suitably dramatic.'

'A disgraced former general?' He spat on the obsidian at my feet. 'I returned to Kalure to fight for my true sovereign, Prince Roran Valerian. Last I checked, he was next in line to rule the Ravalian Empire. Not you.'

Aric raised his sword until it was pointed at General Harte's chest. The general sneered at the dagger strapped to Aric's hip – the dagger I had taken from *him*.

'You disobeyed a direct order from your princess,' I reminded him coldly, taking a threatening step closer. 'Give me one reason why I shouldn't order your execution right now.'

'You don't deserve to rule,' General Harte said disgustedly. 'Dismissing and humiliating all your senior generals, all so you can elevate your lover to a position he hasn't earned and doesn't deserve.' He glowered at Aric, then back at me. 'It's a wonder that Roran is willing to show you any mercy.'

'I don't need Roran's mercy, and I didn't ask for it. If you think that his protection makes you safe—'

'Killing me,' General Harte interrupted, 'would be tantamount to declaring war. *You* might be impulsive enough to overlook the consequences, but I doubt your mother is so foolhardy.'

As if to highlight his point, Zandri shook her head at me. A minuscule gesture, but General Harte caught it. He smiled – a smug smile I wanted to carve off his face with my knife.

'Your brother,' he continued, 'congratulates you on your military victory in the Western Lands, and orders that you join him in Kalure. He also requests that you bring additional Warriors and ships to assist in the war against Kasmira Volaris.'

'Roran's war has nothing to do with me—'

'It's a war that your father started,' General Harte cut in. 'You're duty-bound to honour Emperor Kalias's last standing orders. And now that the clans have allied with the Volaris girl, your brother requires your assistance. Or are you refusing a direct order from your future emperor?'

My teeth ground together as General Harte's eyes glittered with dark satisfaction.

I glanced at Zandri, whose expression was unreadable. I knew what she would tell me if she could: committing publicly wasn't wise. The safer option was to wait and consider my options.

But it was always going to come to this.

For the Ravalian throne to be mine, Roran would have to die. And killing him would be much easier in person.

Before anyone could stop me, I said, 'I'll be there. Tell Roran that I'm looking forward to it.'

Without waiting to be dismissed, General Harte strode away.

He had an unfortunate habit of turning his back on me, but soon enough, I would have the opportunity to bury a blade in it.

Conscious of everyone's eyes on me, I reclined in my chair and raised a hand to recommence the fighting matches.

As the next two fighters were led out, I raised my glass in a wordless toast to my brother. Roran wasn't even in the country, and yet somehow, he had still managed to ruin the celebrations.

But that was alright, because I intended to ruin *him.*

CHAPTER TWENTY-FOUR

Scarlett

Wind whipped my hair back from my face as I climbed to the battlements.

It was the one place that I knew I could be alone. The one place that I could properly mourn Severin.

He was everywhere here. Inescapable.

I wondered what he would think of my decision to sail to Kalure tomorrow. Would he think that I had made a fatal mistake? Perhaps. Zandri certainly seemed to think so.

But it wouldn't have felt so overwhelming if I still had Severin with me. Instead, I had Aric – and Lillian. The two people who should hate me most, who would eventually have to choose between their loyalty to me and their loyalty to Mira.

Life certainly had a sense of humour. But I couldn't tell whether the joke was with me or on me.

I supposed I would find out soon enough.

I slumped against the parapet and raised my knees to my chest. Alone except for the death magic inside me. I watched the dark veins crisscrossing my skin, filling me with ice. The ice that only Severin had dispelled.

I missed his warmth. I missed his tenderness, his inner strength, the passion he had reserved just for me.

My gaze shifted towards the distant city of Ravalis, where my people slept peacefully, utterly untouched by their princess's suffering.

Death rose up in me, eager to be unleashed. To consume, to *punish*—

I shuddered at the sensation. If Malek was to be believed, this power was warping my mind. What a terrible irony it would be if I claimed the Ravalian throne only to destroy my subjects and all the countries under my command.

Was *this* what Severin had seen in me – a darkness so terrible he hadn't been able to look at me the same way ever again? A darkness that could surpass even my father? My mother?

Tears blurred my eyes, but I refused to let them fall. I didn't want to feel this grief anymore.

As if responding to my wishes, the death magic travelled up higher – until I felt its coldness wrap around my heart.

I could have willed it back. Instead, I closed my eyes and allowed the darkness to take me.

At some point, I must have fallen asleep. I knew I was dreaming, because what I was seeing couldn't possibly be real.

My breath hitched as Severin gazed up at me from his knees. His smile was soft and sad – the same sad smile that he had worn in the seer's vision.

A bejewelled hand wrapped around his throat.

'No!' I screamed at the figure standing behind him. 'Stop it! You're *killing* him!'

Zandri didn't stop. Her malicious smile widened as Severin's gasps grew weaker and weaker.

Then they stopped altogether.

Somewhere in front of the dais in the throne room, the court laughed and tittered. Like this was an entertaining show.

'Get up,' Zandri said coldly as my legs gave out underneath me. 'I taught you to be stronger than this.'

But when I glanced up, it was no longer Zandri standing over Severin's body. It was the version of myself that I had seen on the lake in Kalure, inhumanly perfect and inhumanly cold. My father's bone crown gleamed on top of her head. And when she finally looked up and met my gaze—

Her eyes were as black as tar.

'Isn't this what you wanted?' she asked me, stepping over Severin without a glance. The train of her dress left a trail of blood in its wake.

'It should be. You won't be empress for long if you show weakness. Or do you think *they'll* save you?'

I followed her stare to the watching crowd. Mira, Roran, Cassius – they were at the front, their black eyes burning with vengeance as they watched me, their corpse-pale skin riddled with dark veins. And beyond them . . . I recognised my father. Drakos and his brothers. The stableboy I had killed, the vendor I had poisoned—

A sea of corpses. *My* corpses.

Each of them ravenous and furious and terrifying. Far more terrifying in death than they had been in life.

'They only answer to *me*,' my doppelgänger laughed, and threw me backwards.

I teetered on the edge of the dais, staring down into the hundreds of merciless faces.

I opened my mouth to scream—

Lillian grasped my hand. Her grip was unnaturally strong; I gasped as I saw exposed bone in the place of skin. When I looked up at her, Lillian's skin was rotted, her eyes empty holes in a skeletal face.

'I didn't mean for you to die,' I said desperately, staring pleadingly up at my friend.

'But I did.' Lillian's expression softened, until her features were heartbreakingly sad. 'You should have let me stay dead,' she whispered—

And let me fall.

'You look terrible,' Zandri said in greeting as she swept into my chambers.

'I didn't get much sleep,' I replied, lacing up my boots. 'I've had a lot on my mind.'

'I should say so.' My mother's voice was sharp. She hadn't spoken to me – not one word – since I'd accepted General Harte's ultimatum. She'd barely even looked at me. 'It will be a miracle if you survive this. Roran is no fool; the smartest play is to dispose of you quickly. I've spelled a contingent of loyal Warriors to sail with you to Kalure, but even they may not be enough.'

'They will be,' I said, with a certainty I didn't feel.

Aella's fingers deftly braided my hair, correctly assuming that I would want it out of the way. I watched her darken my eyes and lips with cosmetics, her attention never straying from her task. It was bad enough that Lillian would have to accompany me, but she had to remain reasonably close in order to stay breathing. Aella had no such restrictions.

'You don't have to come to Kalure,' I said suddenly, and Aella's hands stilled in their work. 'If you prefer, you can remain here—'

'Don't be ridiculous,' Zandri interrupted. 'I want her with you. A loyal servant could prove useful.' Under her breath, she muttered, 'Sorceress knows you haven't given me much else to work with.'

If Aella took offence at that remark, she didn't show it. Just dusted some red eyeshadow across my lids.

'Despite what you clearly believe,' I said, glaring at my mother in the mirror, 'I didn't accept Roran's invitation so that he could kill me. I accepted it so that I could kill *him*.'

'Then you're a fool.' The blackness in Zandri's eyes was more prominent than usual, probably a result of whatever magic she had performed on those Warriors. Combined with the blood splatter on her cheek, she was downright unnerving as she advanced on me. 'You should have stayed in Ravalia, and allowed Mira and Roran to finish each other off.'

'You're forgetting about my death magic. All I need is to get close to Roran, and I can end this war with one touch.'

'And if he decides to kill you from a distance?'

'That's more Cassius's style,' I said after a pause. 'Roran is furious with me for my victory in the Western Lands – I think he'll want to look into my eyes as I die. To savour the moment.'

Zandri crossed her arms. 'It's still a gamble.'

'It's the only chance we have.' I stepped away from the mirror, conscious of dawn brightening the horizon. 'Now that I've accepted Roran's terms, there's no going back. If I did, I would lose the support of the Ravalian people. I would lose the *throne*.'

I knew all of this had already occurred to Zandri, but she seemed content to let me say it. She reached over and took my hand in hers. I flinched in surprise as she pressed something into my palm.

'Aric's blood ruby,' she told me. 'Just in case.'

I stared down at the pulsing jewel, feeling its warmth travel through my skin. I didn't need to ask why Zandri had given it to me. She must have had the same concerns I did about Aric's loyalty – and whether it would hold up when he was finally reunited with Mira.

I rolled the blood ruby in my palm. If I had to, I could use it to ensure Aric's obedience. But he'd given me his loyalty freely these past few months, and it felt wrong to contemplate taking it by force.

I still pocketed the blood ruby.

'What about Mira?' I asked. 'You have hers too, don't you?'

'You let me worry about Mira,' Zandri said with a secretive smile. 'I have a plan to deal with her. And the Temple.'

I wanted to ask her what that plan was, but perhaps it was better if I didn't know. I had one focus right now, and that was Roran.

I followed Zandri to the oval windows, staring in the direction of the docks – where a ship would already be crewed and waiting. When I glanced back at my mother, her dark eyes were no longer hard and cutting, but filled with unexpected softness.

'Go, Scarlett,' she told me, kissing my brow. 'Kill your brother. Take Mira's throne for your own. Win back everything that was stolen from us. And become the empress I always knew you could be.'

I rolled Aric's blood ruby in my palm as the harbour of Taiga came into view: a calm expanse of glacial blue water with craggy cliffs on either side. Roran's fleet was moored in the natural harbour, the elegant vessels bobbing gently in the briny breeze. His black-garbed Warriors lined the wooden docks, an impressive show of force.

But they were nothing compared to the morbid display that stretched from the docks to the Kalurian palace.

Roran never was one for subtlety, I thought as we disembarked.

'Don't react,' I warned Lillian, feeling her tense beside me. 'Just focus on a point ahead of you.'

Aric remained close at my side, his hand on the hilt of his sword. 'I thought I'd seen horrors in the Western Lands,' he murmured, 'but *this . . .*'

I allowed my gaze to drift up to the posts lining either side of the path – and the bodies nailed to them.

'I know,' I said. Even *I* felt sick, and I'd grown up with Roran.

The procession was a grim one. Only Roran's Warriors showed any enthusiasm; the Kalurian people watched us approach, silent and unsmiling. I wondered if Roran had forced them to attend. Perhaps he had even ordered them dragged from their homes.

If I wasn't here to confront Roran, I might have admired my surroundings: the snow-capped mountains silhouetted behind the palace's high walls; the icy lake to the west, partially obscured by snowy pines, and the reflective ice sheets that stretched to the north, where the Kalurian settlement of Frør was located. But my senses were alert, screaming at me. Touch, smell, taste, hearing – everything was heightened to an almost painful degree.

I didn't know how Roran planned to murder me, only that he did. And making my way through streets packed with unfriendly Kalurians seemed like the perfect opportunity to plant an assassin. Even with my own Warriors positioned around me, all loyal and hand-picked by Zandri, a strategically placed arrow could still cut me down.

But I had to trust my instincts. And my instincts told me that Roran wanted to face me one last time, to dangle my impending death in front of me.

'This is our best chance,' I whispered to Aric, knowing that he needed to hear it. 'To end this war – and to avenge Kain.'

Aric stiffened at the sound of his brother's name. We hadn't spoken about Kain in months – but I knew that Aric hadn't forgotten Roran's role in his death. Or his vow to avenge him.

He nodded, his jaw hard with tension. Behind him, Aella's brown eyes met mine – but it was too late to regret my decision to bring her along. Her life was in my hands now, just as surely as Lillian's was.

My heart quickened as we approached the fortified city of Taiga. Roran's Warriors opened the gates, affording me a glimpse of grey stone buildings and narrow alleyways where the pitched roofs almost touched, providing some much-needed shelter from the elements. But it was the Kalurian palace that demanded my attention: a hulking fortress, built by my father in the image of our ancestral kings.

Roran stood at the top of the palace steps, an emperor surveying his kingdom. High-ranking Warriors flanked him, including the grim-faced

General Harte. I wondered whether one of them had already been instructed to take my life.

I didn't intend to give them the chance.

Dressed in Ravalian colours – red and gold – Roran stood out against the grey stone backdrop of the palace. I was dressed similarly, in a red battle dress with golden armour, and I knew that Roran was taking note of this. Calculating whether my choice was a show of solidarity, or an attempt at competition.

'Sister,' Roran said, the word filled with false warmth.

'Brother.' I wondered whether he could sense the death looming behind my smile.

I sank to one knee.

Roran watched me with an unreadable expression. Behind him, his Warriors looked on with a mixture of wariness and curiosity. But I noticed a few considering glances too. By now, they would have heard of my victory in the Western Lands.

Come on, I willed my brother. *Take the bait.*

Sure enough, Roran slowly descended the palace steps. He extended his arm, too, as if he might invite me to kiss the gaudy ring on his middle finger.

Anticipation rose, and my death magic rose with it. A single brush of his skin was all it would take—

Roran paused. His green eyes went past me – to something or someone I couldn't see.

He withdrew his arm in a sharp, violent movement. His Warriors sprang into action immediately, forming an impenetrable guard in front of their prince. Though Roran was only three steps above me, there was no way I could reach him now. His Warriors were too well shielded by their black armour.

More than anything, I wanted to turn my head and discover what had caused Roran's uncharacteristic hesitation. But I couldn't afford to take my eyes off him. Not even for a second.

'Get off your knees,' Roran instructed over the heads of his Warriors. His cruel mouth twisted in distaste as he said, 'I have no interest in theatrical displays of loyalty. Or is this your attempt at begging for your life?'

'Would it make any difference?'

Roran pretended to think. 'No. Though I could be convinced to hasten your death.'

He motioned to his Warriors, who encircled me in a wall of black. I resisted the urge to reach for my hidden knives as General Harte took Aric's place at my back, his sword and dagger already drawn.

'Shall we?' Roran asked with sickening politeness, turning towards the Kalurian palace.

With no other choice, I reluctantly followed, General Harte's dagger pressing into my back every step of the way.

CHAPTER TWENTY-FIVE

Scarlett

The inside of the palace was no less foreboding, its sparseness intimidating in a way that the luxuries of the Ravalian Court never could be. And around every corner were Warriors. Black-garbed men and women standing guard, swords and spears ready at their sides.

General Harte didn't spare them a glance. He escorted us through a servant entrance towards the stables, and my stomach sank as I saw the austere courtyard – and the steel gates. But there was nothing I could do as the Warriors pushed me inside.

The gate slammed shut – separating me from my companions. General Harte's Warriors took hold of Lillian's and Aella's arms, while the general himself dragged Aric from view.

I wrapped my hands around the steel gate. Black veins crawled down my arms – but my death magic didn't travel into the gates like it travelled into flesh.

I released my grip with a frustrated hiss, glaring at my surroundings. I was in a holding area next to the main stables, solid stone walls blocking me at every turn. When I glanced up at the battlements, I saw a dozen archers with their bows drawn. Roran wasn't taking any chances.

'You've finally stopped underestimating me,' I said a few minutes later, when the steel gate opened once more.

Roran stepped inside. Every inch of his skin was covered by armour, barring his face, and he was accompanied by a retinue of Warriors. But his expression was amused as he regarded me.

'Our father never saw you as a threat, and look how *that* turned out for him.' He smiled at my surprise. 'Yes, Scarlett. I know that you were responsible for his death. I have sources of my own – or did you truly believe I would rely on Zandri for information?'

'But you can't possibly know that,' I said, more to myself than him. 'Only Zandri and her Masks—'

My voice cut off as a masked woman stalked into the courtyard. In fitted black fighting feathers, with long, pin-straight copper hair that fell almost to her waist, she was quite striking – and she was clearly one of my mother's Masks.

But while Roran might be foolish enough to believe that this woman was loyal to him, I wasn't convinced. All Masks were taught how to manipulate their enemies – and my mother had ways of ensuring their obedience.

The Mask strode brazenly up to Roran's side. I caught a whiff of her perfume: linden blossom and sage.

It was vaguely familiar, but I couldn't recall where I'd smelt it before.

'You ought to look more worried, Sister,' Roran drawled, opening his palm to reveal a blood ruby. 'I may not have magic of my own, but Emperor Kalias trusted me with all his secrets – and your mother's.'

I stared Roran down with loathing. 'So she's to be my executioner, then? I suppose it gives you some kind of perverse satisfaction, forcing a Mask to kill Zandri's daughter.'

'You're wrong on both counts,' Roran said, passing the blood ruby to the masked woman and smiling at my shock. 'As you can see, I'm not forcing her to do anything. And she's just convinced me to spare your life.'

I glanced from the Mask to Roran and back again. 'If this is some kind of game—'

'It's not a game,' Roran interrupted smoothly. 'It's an offer. And my terms are simple: a life for a life. In this case, Mira's life for your own.'

I studied his face – and then I laughed, though the sound contained no humour. 'You can't be serious.'

'It should be easy enough,' he continued, as if I hadn't spoken. 'Aella told me all about your magic – and how it's transmitted through touch. What better way to kill one monstrosity than by using another?'

But I was no longer listening. I had stopped listening at the sound of my attendant's name.

Now that Roran had said it, it seemed obvious. The woman's slight stature, her perfume—

Aella had seemed so small to me before. So delicate. But there was nothing small or delicate about her now.

'Don't feel too bad about it, Scarlett,' Aella said, picking at her nails. Her voice was still soft – but now it carried a razor-sharp edge. 'No one ever notices their servants. It's the whole reason Zandri assigned me to you in the first place; so that I could watch over you and report back to her without anyone knowing. Including *you*.'

'But if you were following Zandri's orders—'

'I stopped taking orders from Zandri a long time ago.' Through the mask, Aella's eyes were as cold and hard as stones. 'Getting close to you suited my purposes, that's all. And Roran's.'

I looked away from Aella and refocused on my brother. 'You would trust me? To kill Mira?'

'Not without insurance. I'm sure you're aware of the deal Emperor Kalias and Zandri signed in blood,' Roran said conversationally, 'which prevented either of them from physically harming the other. As a descendant of the Sorceress, your blood contains the same magical power to hold us to our promises.' He paused, his eyes glittering. 'I'm prepared to give you – oh, let's say a month – to kill Kasmira Volaris, and in exchange, I will allow you to live. If you fail – well, I've heard it's a horrific way to die, choking on your own blood.'

I had heard the same. According to my mother, once a deal was signed in blood, there was no voiding it. And I knew that she had tried.

'Your survival should be enough motivation on its own,' Roran continued, 'but if you do a good job, who knows? I might allow you to serve me in the Order of Masks. I'm sure your gift for assassination would prove useful.'

I looked up at him blankly. The last thing I wanted was to live out my mother's existence: serving an emperor that I couldn't kill, and plotting his downfall for decades. But what other choice was there? At least this bought me some time – at the expense of Mira's life.

But that was a trade I was willing to make.

'Fine,' I said through gritted teeth. 'But I want Aric and Lillian included. They live – or the deal is off.'

'Of course,' Roran said, too easily and too pleasantly. 'Aella, why don't you bring them back in? There's one last piece of business to conclude.'

I stepped towards Roran, heedless of the arrows trained on me. Roran held up a hand – instructing them to hold their fire.

'If you could have ended me, you would have done it by now,' he said dismissively – but his gaze sharpened as he watched my death magic rise, the dark veins twisting across my bare arms.

I had hoped to see fear in his eyes. Instead, I saw hunger.

That hunger shifted as Aella and General Harte returned with Lillian and Aric. It darkened into something vengeful and terrible. Foreboding gripped me as I glanced between Aric and Roran. A year had passed since Aric had humiliated Roran during the Choosing Ceremony, but I knew Roran hadn't forgotten.

'You resemble your brother,' Roran said conversationally, approaching Aric. 'Kain, wasn't it?'

Aric jerked against General Harte's iron hold. 'You don't have the right to say his name.'

The general kicked at Aric's legs, sending him to his knees. Roran moved closer, taking Aric's jaw in his gloved hands. Forcing him to look up into his pitiless face.

'Your brother died well,' he said. 'Too well for a traitor. Had it been up to me, I would have made sure your entire family suffered for his folly. How fortunate that fate has seen fit to rectify that mistake.'

I tensed as the gate groaned open, but didn't dare shift my gaze from Roran as he approached Lillian.

'Don't *touch* her—'

General Harte backhanded Aric across the face. He spat blood onto the ground and fell forward, onto all fours. When the general reached for him, Aric reacted – elbowing him in the stomach and lunging for his sister.

'Behave,' Roran said calmly, shifting so that he stood behind Lillian, one hand on the base of her throat and the other resting on the back of her neck – in the perfect position to snap it. She said nothing – did nothing – but the rapid rise and fall of her chest betrayed her.

And then I heard it. The low, rumbling growl.

Lillian's face went pale as the hound approached, its snout wet with blood, its hulking body covered with spiked armour. *Black* armour, similar to what Ravalian Warriors wore.

'Call it off,' I said coldly to Roran, trying not to imagine those jaws ripping Lillian to shreds. Not even my death magic would be able to resurrect her then. 'You've made your point.'

He merely smiled. 'My spies tell me that the Volaris bitch intends to become clan leader. To do that, she will have to leave the safety of the Temple and seek out the Council of Ancients. You will take a small force and assassinate her – ideally before she reaches the council, but if she makes it there first, you will convince the council to deny her request. If you undermine me in any way, if even a *rumour* of a kind word between you and Kasmira reaches me, I will give Titus the attack word. It would be a shame to see such a pretty girl ripped to shreds.' Roran released Lillian abruptly. She stumbled to the side, tripping on her skirts as she tried to put some distance between herself and Titus.

'As for you . . .' Roran returned his attention to Aric, whose gaze was on Lillian and the circling hound, its every movement filled with barely leashed aggression. 'I'd like you to give Kasmira a message for me.'

'You can't kill him,' I said quickly. 'Aric is part of our deal; I need him alive—'

'Who said anything about killing him?' Roran twirled a dagger in his palm – *Aric's* dagger.

He nodded to General Harte, whose grip tightened on Aric, holding him immobile. And then Roran sliced the dagger down Aric's cheek in a jagged line.

Lillian screamed, clawing for her brother. Roran's Warriors held her tight as blood ran down Aric's face in rivulets.

Aric didn't cry out. Didn't so much as stumble as he lifted his searing gaze to Roran's.

'There,' my brother said, smiling as he walked past me. 'Still perfectly functional. Just not quite as *handsome*.'

CHAPTER TWENTY-SIX

Mira

Mottled green light and dense trees flashed past as we rode. Sometimes I caught a glimpse of the purplish outlines of a mountain range through the canopies. It was thrilling to realise that I was truly in the Wilds now – the unexplored, mysterious reaches far beyond the clan settlements.

I had always wondered why Emperor Kalias had wanted Kalure so badly. I had assumed it was because of the natural magic that was so common here, but it occurred to me that perhaps the Wilds concealed hidden treasures of their own.

'You seem lighter out here,' Cassius observed, and I wondered how long he had been watching me.

'So do you,' I said, and I was startled to realise it was true.

Cassius usually reminded me of a creature of the court: tall and athletically lean, with tailored clothing and the kind of sigh-worthy features that allowed him to charm anyone he found useful. But outside the confines of the Ravalian Court or the Temple, there was something softer about him. Something more real.

I studied his hair – longer and adorned with a few stray leaves – and the freckles dusting his pale skin. They were subtle changes, but they made it easier to think of him as a young man rather than a scheming prince. Maybe too easy.

I thought of what he had told me in the Temple hot springs. The sincerity in his face as he had said it. *When this war is over, and Kalure is truly yours, I want us to be together, Mira. I want us to at least* try.

I looked away from Cassius very quickly, and I set a punishing pace after that – though no one complained. Jadis and Odessa kept pace with me easily, the dirt road wide enough for us to ride comfortably next to each other. Twenty clansmen followed at a slight distance, guarding the cart piled high with our provisions.

All three thousand clan warriors had gathered to witness my send-off at the Temple, bowing deeply as I passed through their ranks. Such a different response to a few weeks earlier, when they had surrounded the sandstone walls, refusing to let anyone leave. Refusing to take a single order from their queen.

But any satisfaction I might have felt was cold and dead in my veins. Tainted by Vølund's murder.

And the memory of the warmth on Nari's face.

That undeserved warmth was the reason I had ordered her to stay behind. Not to protect the Temple as I had claimed, but because it was too difficult to be around her, knowing that every pleasant inter-action, every obeyed order, was a lie. She hadn't mentioned Cassius once.

'Ruling is all about making hard choices,' Odessa said softly to me, reading my thoughts far too well.

I forced a smile, wondering if she realised how similar she sounded to Cassius. To Velanthe.

I hadn't told anyone the high priestess's parting advice. I doubted Cassius would be pleased that she had asked me to use blood magic on the Council of Ancients – not just because of the consequences if I failed, but also because of the strain it would take on my health. I sometimes caught him casting me careful glances, and he didn't know about the nosebleeds I was still having.

We turned the corner and I abruptly reined in my horse, conscious of my companions doing the same. Silence descended, interrupted only by the chirp of distant birds and the impatient pawing and snorting of the horses . . .

And something else. A strange, hollow sound that drew me closer.

'Is that – are those *bones*?'

I didn't glance over my shoulder at Odessa. Didn't look away from the white shards tied to the branches above me – like morbid wind chimes.

'It's a warning.' Thoren's deep voice made me turn. The clan head was studying the bones with uncharacteristic wariness. 'We should take a different route.'

'Velanthe's instructions were clear,' I reminded him. 'This is the path that leads to the Council of Ancients. If we take a different one, we risk losing our way. And we can't afford any delays.'

Cassius drew his large black stallion up alongside my smaller grey mare, regarding the bones – and Thoren – with an assessing gaze. 'What aren't you telling us?'

'Strange rumours surround the deepest parts of the Wilds,' Thoren said shortly, looking only at me. 'Tales of magic and dark rituals and missing people. Before Vølund became clan leader, his predecessor decided to expand our reach and build a settlement in these forests. Not a single man or woman returned.'

His words echoed what I had once heard about Emperor Kalias's forces. He had sent an entire regiment into the deepest parts of the Wilds, and not even those hardened Warriors had made it back. What had my mother said to me once? *Some places, and magic, are too powerful to be conquered or controlled.*

But I wasn't here to conquer or control anyone. I was here to protect these forests and the people within them from Roran. To do whatever it took to save my country.

'Vølund met with the Council of Ancients,' I pointed out. 'He survived the journey.'

'Vølund was invited to come here, and a representative from the council escorted him safely to their meeting place. Without such an understanding . . .' Thoren didn't need to finish the sentence.

I glanced at the bones again. If I disregarded this warning, would I get everyone with me killed?

Yet the fate of Kalure depended on my success. I *had* to find the Council of Ancients, no matter the cost to myself or the people around me.

'Stay close,' I instructed my companions as I passed beneath the bones. They clinked eerily, a sound that seemed to echo through the forest – suggesting that there were plenty more ahead of us. To Thoren, I said, 'Tell the clansmen to close ranks and expect an attack.'

I heard the sound of retreating hoofbeats, then the unmistakable hiss of steel sliding free as Thoren recounted my orders to the clansmen. Jadis took Thoren's place with a nod at me. Her grip tightened on her crossbow, as if to say, *I'm ready for anything.*

I squeezed my legs and my horse responded immediately, shifting into a brisk walk – almost as if it was eager to leave this place behind. That made two of us, though I doubted our destination would be any better.

'I don't understand Kalure,' Cassius muttered from my other side. 'If a Ravalian ruler was travelling through their kingdom, they could expect to be greeted with hospitality and obedience. Not—' he waved a hand at the dark, uninviting path in front of us— 'whatever *this* is.'

'You sound concerned, Cassius,' I drawled. 'Don't worry; I'll protect you.'

I urged my horse into a trot, my hair streaming out behind me. The sound of Odessa's laughter chased me into the bone forest.

By sunset, every inch of my body felt sore, and my stomach was cramping with hunger. Though it was far more temperate on this side of the Archasian mountains, the rain was icy; it dripped through the leaves and slid down the back of my neck, leaving an uncomfortable chill in its wake.

'We should set up camp soon,' Cassius said, his eyes wary as he looked at the skulls dangling from trees.

Thoren sent two scouts ahead – to search for a sheltered clearing large enough to accommodate us and far enough from the road to be hidden. The longer their absence, the more insistent my feeling of unease became.

Flickers of movement danced in my peripheral vision, making my hand tighten around the sword strapped to my waist. But whenever I turned to look, all I saw were the shadowy shapes of retreating animals and the glowing eyes of sharp-beaked birds watching us from nearby branches.

I am the most frightening thing in these trees, I told myself. I wasn't sure I believed it.

Thoren finally came back into view and led us into a clearing filled with white wildflowers that resembled snow. I immediately saw what had delayed him; his scouts were checking a series of wooden huts that sprawled across the clearing and extended into the treeline. And above those huts . . .

It was like being back at the treetop village near the Temple. The same style of dwellings were built into the trees, artfully connected by wooden bridges and platforms, the light of the sunset filtering down and casting them in a reddish haze.

Yet there were no faces peering curiously or warily out from those homes. No whispers or distant hum of conversation.

I rode over to where Thoren had already dismounted, conversing in a low voice with his scouts.

'What happened to the people?' I asked the clan head. 'Are there any signs of a struggle?'

'None,' Thoren replied. 'It's possible they moved on.'

I studied the village around me. It was eerily intact, raising the obvious question: why would they leave? Was it possible they had discovered our presence and fled? But if they had—

Thoren must have had the same thought. He bent down to examine the soil, searching for footprints.

'Animal tracks,' he said, looking up at me. 'Fresh ones.'

'Some of those tracks are quite large,' Cassius observed, his horse snorting as he reined in next to me. 'Do you think it's safe to camp here?'

The clan head shrugged his massive shoulders. 'I don't see why not. We can start a fire – that should deter any wolves or other predators, and if it doesn't, our weapons can do the rest. I will position my warriors in a perimeter, and those treetop dwellings will be a good vantage point for the night watch.'

'Fine,' I said, when it became clear Thoren was waiting for my agreement.

Once he strode off to take care of those practicalities, I gratefully slid off my horse – only to realise too late that all the strength seemed to have left my limbs.

Steady hands took hold of me before I could fall in an ungraceful heap, one hand around my waist and the other settling against my lower back. The warmth of Cassius's touch burned through my sodden clothes and into my skin.

I expected him to make some sort of sardonic comment, but he merely said, 'My legs collapsed the first time too. Unfortunately for me, I had a much larger audience – Roran, my father, and all the Warriors under his command.'

I stared up at him in open surprise. It was still so unexpected when he shared something personal. 'How old were you at the time?'

'Seven.' Cassius smiled faintly at my shock.

'Your father had you accompany him on military campaigns when you were *seven*?'

'He considered it educational.' Cassius released me, but didn't step away. Too quietly for the others to hear, he said, 'You did well today. Most inexperienced riders can't stay in the saddle nearly as long.'

I nodded, though that was little comfort right now. Not when I had days of riding ahead of me. I forced myself to take a stiff step, and then another. Every muscle screamed in protest.

Cassius cast me an amused glance. 'Don't worry; it gets easier.' He took the reins of both horses.

'Where are you going?' I called after him as he strode amongst the wildflowers.

He shot me one of his signature, devious half-smiles. 'Come with me and find out.'

Irritation warred with intrigue. Intrigue won.

I wove my way through the clearing, which was quickly transforming into a makeshift camp: Jadis and Odessa helping to unload provisions, while warriors collected firewood, tended to the horses and disappeared into the forest with spears drawn.

'I should help them,' I said, starting to slow. 'I can set up snares and—'

'One advantage of being a ruler, Mira,' Cassius interrupted, 'is the opportunity to delegate. Let the warriors tend to domestic matters and focus on yourself. I assure you, they are familiar with hunting game.'

'Just because a ruler can delegate doesn't mean they *should*,' I said as I caught up with Cassius.

'Consider this a better use of your time.'

I followed his gaze to where a deep stream wound its way through the trees, only the faintest sound of rushing water announcing its presence. I remembered Cassius telling me that he used to hunt and track, but I was still surprised that he had known it was here.

After allowing the horses to drink their fill, he tethered them nearby and approached the bank. A hint of reddish light filtered through the trees, almost the exact shade of the soil beneath my feet, interspersed with tall, yellow-green reeds.

'Seriously?' I said as Cassius stripped out of his tunic and reached for his leather breeches. '*That's* why you brought me here? To parade your body in front of me?'

I could hear the smile in his voice as he said, 'Not everything is about you, Mira. Believe it or not, I like to be clean.' He arched a golden brow at me. 'And no one is forcing you to watch.'

I turned decisively on my heel, putting my back to him. I could have sworn I heard him laugh.

Even though I couldn't see Cassius, I could picture him well enough. The image of him in those hot springs was burned into my mind: the proud set of his shoulders, the lean muscles of his arms and chest, the way his breeches had clung to—

'You can turn around now, Mira. You won't see anything that offends your delicate sensibilities.' Yes, there was definite amusement in his voice. 'Not that I think there's anything particularly delicate about you.'

Ignoring that last comment, I told him, 'Go back to camp. I'll return when I'm done.'

Cassius settled against a tree trunk, leaning back against it in his usual nonchalant way. 'Given our less than hospitable welcome, I don't think it's wise to leave you on your own. Besides, I've seen you naked before.'

I folded my arms across my chest. 'That was different.'

A curious tilt of his golden head. 'Why?'

'Because I was unconscious when you carried me into those hot springs,' I said shortly. Gods, he was *infuriating*. 'Turn around.'

When he did, I slid off my own tunic and leggings. The soft soil was soothing against my bare, aching feet as I approached the stream – but the water was utterly frigid. I let out a gasp of surprise.

'Want me to come in there and warm you up?'

'Has anyone told you,' I shot back without turning, 'that you have an uncanny ability to make light of absolutely *everything*?'

'Oh, I'm sorry,' Cassius's indolent voice drawled. 'Did you think that was a joke? I was being quite serious.'

I shook my head in annoyance, but I was smiling as I submerged myself in the water, letting it sweep the dirt from my skin. After combing my fingers through my hair, I stood and waded back across the slick pebbles—

Only to look up and find midnight-blue eyes watching me.

Cassius held up his hands in a pacifying gesture, but his mouth curved suspiciously at the edges. 'I never promised not to look.'

I let out an exasperated huff as I quickly dressed and stalked past him towards the horses. Even though it was still sunset, the trees were so thick here that it felt like late evening. Perhaps that had bothered the horses too. My mare neighed and pulled away from me when I tried to untie her, and Cassius's stallion rolled his eyes in distress.

I tried to soothe them, but nothing seemed to make a difference. And then they went silent.

The silence was complete. Absolute. Even the birds stopped their chirping.

I felt the delicate hairs rise on the back of my neck. Slowly and carefully, I glanced past the horses – towards the shadowy forest beyond.

Glowing eyes watched me through the trees. As my hand dropped to my sword, I caught a glimpse of four-legged beasts – their bodies protected by bony plating that resembled armour.

And I realised that I had been wrong. The Wilds didn't conceal hidden treasures.

They concealed monsters.

CHAPTER TWENTY-SEVEN

Mira

I turned and ran, the ground thudding as the beasts launched themselves through the trees. Cassius's eyes widened and he reached for his sword, but he quickly dropped his arm, having seen the same thing I had: the thick, bony armour protecting their hulking bodies.

'Shoot them!' I screamed, hoping that my warriors could hear me. 'Aim for their throats!'

Arrows whizzed through the air. But despite their size, the beasts were quick. A single leap took them further than a dozen of my strides, and the beasts behind me weren't the only ones. More rushed into the clearing ahead, forcing the clansmen to retreat to the tree line as they continued aiming arrows. A growl reverberated through the ground as one of their arrows connected with a beasts' neck – but it didn't penetrate the tough skin.

I watched the arrow fall to the ground in stunned disbelief.

'What are you doing?' Cassius hissed at me as I started to slow. 'We have to run—'

'There are more of them,' I told him, my eyes on the shadowy shapes emerging from the forest.

I risked a glance behind me. The beasts had paused in their pursuit, knowing we had nowhere to go. But one among their number pushed through their ranks – even larger than its companions.

The approaching beast regarded me with its golden eyes. Those eyes narrowed as they shifted to Cassius.

I watched it prowl closer, wondering if I could get in a lucky strike before it took me down. Cassius tensed, and I knew he was thinking along similar lines, but I didn't dare shift my gaze from the creature. When it was less than five metres away, it tilted its head. Considering me. Like it was—

Thinking.

I took a cautious step forward. The beast watched me steadily but made no move to attack, and somehow, I knew that it wouldn't unless I attacked first. Cassius hissed something that I ignored.

My heart pounded as it pressed its snout to my chest.

No – not to my chest. Impossible though it seemed, it was examining my *locket*. I lifted it up, so the beast could see the engraving in the gold. The wreathed crown.

'We mean you no harm,' I told the creature, ignoring how foolish it felt to converse with an animal. Yet I felt certain this was no ordinary animal. 'I am Kasmira Volaris, and these are my companions. We're searching for the Council of Ancients.'

The beast humphed in what I took as acknowledgement and rejoined its companions, who backed away to give it space.

The leader. I had spoken to their leader, and it had somehow understood me.

I blinked a few times to make sure I wasn't imagining this. But no – the beast was leading the others through the clearing towards me. I tensed, then forced myself to relax. Not to reach for my weapon.

'You seriously want to trust those things? Are you *insane?*'

I only glanced at Cassius for a second. But in the space of a blink, the leader's snout began to shorten and widen, its body and shadow seeming to stretch in height and condense inwards—

I stared at the man in front of me, his shoulder-length ebony braids the same shade as the beast's hide. And the armour he wore, the exact white of bone . . . The same bony armour that I had seen on him minutes earlier.

It was an effort to hold my ground. An effort not to look away from the man in front of me as his companions transformed, their forms writhing and undulating in my peripheral vision.

'I am known as Conall,' said the towering man in front of me. For the first time, I noticed the gold medallion he wore, engraved with the same symbol as my locket. 'Welcome to the Council of Ancients.'

I hadn't realised magic had a scent to it. But shifter magic possessed a tang – a natural scent that permeated the air around us, ancient and fresh and faintly reminiscent of pine.

That scent intensified as more shifters joined us, colourful birds swooping down from the treetops and transforming into women just as they reached the ground. Unlike the bone armour worn by the men, they wore sheer tops woven from vines and decorated with wildflowers. For skirts, they favoured the broad, yellow-green reeds I had noticed earlier near the stream.

As quickly as they transformed from animals into humans, the shifters' presence transformed the treetop village into a home. The shifters were already eating and drinking in front of the blazing fires, sharing skewers of roasted meat with my companions. A few children raced up to where I sat at the central fire, eyeing me with as much curiosity as I felt towards them.

'I've never met a queen before,' a tawny-haired girl said, tilting her head in a very bird-like way.

'That makes two of us,' I said warmly to the girl. 'I've never met a shifter before.'

She grinned at me in obvious delight, but then her tiny brow furrowed in confusion. 'You mean . . . you can't change? Not into anything?' At the shake of my head, she looked at me very seriously. 'I'm so sorry,' she said, pity thick in her voice. 'It must be terrible to be stuck in one form forever.'

'Vivica,' Conall reprimanded, but he was smiling. 'This is my daughter,' he said to me. 'Mine and Sionnach's.' He gestured to the tall, imposing woman at his side, who was watching Vivica with amusement. She wore an identical gold medallion to her husband, as did the five other council members ringing the fire.

'It's alright,' I told Vivica softly. 'It's impossible to miss something you've never done.'

Vivica nodded solemnly back at me. 'If you ever find that you do miss it, you should visit our temple. It's a ruin now, but my mother believes it still holds power, even after the priestesses—'

'*Vivica.*' This time, Conall's voice was sharp.

'Sorry.' Before Vivica left, she whispered in my ear, 'You can ask the Sorceress for favours, you know. She doesn't always answer us, but she's bound to answer *you.*'

I watched as she darted off to rejoin her friends, turning her words over in my mind and wondering what she had been about to say when Conall stopped her. No doubt something less than flattering about the Temple, which was hardly a surprise. I had come here prepared for wariness and distrust.

'You can speak freely,' I said, returning my attention to Conall and Sionnach, who seemed to be the only members of the council willing to address me directly. 'What did the priestesses do?'

Conall's mouth twisted. 'They tore down our temple.'

'People from across the Wilds used to come here to connect with the Sorceress,' Sionnach explained. 'But that was before the high priestess decreed there should only be one Temple, under her leadership.'

I frowned. Velanthe had never said anything about priestesses tearing down temples. No wonder there was a rift between the Temple and the Council of Ancients.

'I will fix this,' I promised, looking around the fire and holding each of the councillors' gazes. There were a mixture of ages and appearances, but each of them emanated strength and wisdom. From what Conall had told me, their roles had been handed down from mother to daughter and father to son for generations. 'You deserve to practise your faith as you choose.'

Their expressions were difficult to read, but I hoped they could see that I meant it – that I was willing to stand up to the Temple on their behalf. Maybe it would help lessen some of their animosity towards me.

'Are the priestesses the reason you placed bones in the trees?' Cassius asked, catching the end of our conversation as he approached the central fire. 'It was clearly a warning of some sort. And given the warmth of your hospitality, that warning was not intended for us.'

'Very perceptive,' Conall observed. 'Your spymaster?' he guessed, glancing at me.

My lips curved. 'Something like that.'

Sionnach moved aside to make room for Cassius, though I didn't miss the wary glance she cast at him. Our arms brushed as he took his place on my other side, accepting a pewter cup from Conall.

'There are factions amongst shifters,' Conall admitted after a pause. 'Most of us still worship the Sorceress and believe her descendants ought to rule.' A brief nod at me. 'But there are others who are less benign. They consider themselves agents of Fennec.'

I went still. I knew that name – had read it in the Sorceress's grimoire.

'You've heard of him,' Conall said, watching me. 'I presume you're familiar with the legend?'

I thought of everything I had read about the Sorceress's early life. How she had healed a fox, not knowing that it was really the beloved servant of a trickster god. How the god had courted her in the guise of a man, and won her, and then stolen her mortality so that he might possess her forever.

But the Sorceress had hated the god for taking away her choice, and spent her newfound eternity travelling the world and dismantling monuments to Fennec in every city she visited. She convinced his acolytes to worship her instead, delighting in the knowledge that with every prayer she stole, her ex-lover grew weaker – while she grew stronger.

'He was a god,' I said carefully. 'A trickster god.'

'A god that could take animal form, like those who served him.' Conall glanced at the other council members, and something seemed to pass between them. As they nodded, he said to me, 'Shifters are descended from Fennec. It's the reason we're able to transform – but trickster gods are notoriously mercurial, and they have little value for human life. The shifters who worship Fennec make blood sacrifices in his name. The bones are a warning that they will not find us easy prey.'

My blood ran cold. *Human sacrifice.* That was what Conall was referring to – the threat his people faced.

'Why haven't I heard about this?' I demanded, rising to my feet. 'If you had come to me or the Temple—'

Conall spat on the ground. 'The Temple would not assist us, nor would we welcome their assistance. Dealing with fellow shifters is our responsibility.' There were murmurs of agreement from the other councillors.

Conscious of the stares of the shifters and my nearby warriors, I retook my seat and accepted a round native fruit from Cassius. Succulent sweetness flooded into my mouth as I bit into it, buying myself time to think. Following Sionnach's lead, I washed it down with a slug from the waterskin.

'I respect your wishes,' I said, choosing my words carefully. 'But if you're willing to give me your blessing as clan leader, I can help you stand against all your enemies – not just the shifters and the Temple, but also Roran. If he wins this war, he will massacre your people, burn down your homes, and he won't stop until the Wilds are nothing but ash.'

'I'm afraid you're misinformed.' The firelight deepened Sionnach's brown hair to a reddish shade as she leant forward. 'It isn't our blessing that you need, Kasmira. It's the Sorceress's.'

'That's impossible.' My voice came out sounding flat. 'She's been missing for centuries.'

'Missing,' Sionnach agreed, 'but not dead. I can guide you through a ritual that will allow you to commune with her spirit, if she deems you worthy.' Her fingers gripped the medallion around her neck as she said, 'It is dangerous, however. Many of Vølund's predecessors died during the attempt. You must decide if becoming clan leader is worth risking your life.'

I didn't hesitate. 'It is.' I had come here knowing that death was a possibility, and I had made my peace with it.

'In that case, I will leave you to enjoy the celebrations. Tomorrow I will begin making preparations.' With a parting nod for me and the other council members, Sionnach took Conall's hand and rose.

As if it was a signal, shifters peeled away from the blazing central fires. Somewhere, the deep sound of drums reverberated through my bones, and the shifters began to dance with abandon, led by Sionnach. A group of women threw their heads back and twirled, raising their hands to the sky with wild ecstasy. It was only as men joined the fray that I understood this was more than a dance: it was a coupling ritual.

My face flushed as the drumbeats grew faster, more frenzied. Amidst the circle of dancers, Conall and Sionnach had discarded their clothes. There was no sign of any children now, and I heard a few sensuous sighs even over the drums. In the distance I saw Jadis and Odessa join the revelry, their hands intertwined.

As the rest of the council dispersed, I became intimately aware of Cassius's presence – and the considering glances of the shifters around us, men and women both.

'Come on,' Cassius said, rising with a faint smile at his admirers. 'Let's retire. Unless you'd prefer to join them?' The taunting edge to his voice stopped me from taking his hand.

'Maybe I would.' I cast a glance over the male shifters: all tall, well-built, and clearly interested in me. Judging by the way their attention slid to Cassius, they wouldn't mind including him as well.

Cassius arched a blond brow at me, as if to say, *I'm game if you are.* But his smile was filled with knowing amusement.

I took his hand.

As he guided me through the fray, I was reminded of his masquerade ball back at the Ravalian Court. We had passed half-clothed couples then, and Cassius had steered me past them, keeping his hand possessively on my lower back. Staking a claim in a way that stopped others from propositioning either of us.

And yet . . .

'Aren't you tempted?' I asked as we climbed the steps cut into the trees, holding onto the vines provided for balance. Candlelit lamps hung from branches, illuminating our path in a beautiful golden glow. It was a great sign of respect, I knew, for the council to have offered us two of their treetop dwellings.

'I cultivated a certain image in the Ravalian Court,' Cassius said at last. The high wooden platform creaked as I stepped onto it, joining him at the rope railing. 'It was a way of disguising the true purpose of the wild parties I threw – the influence and political favour they afforded me. Not that I didn't partake in the entertainments.' A smile that was all wicked intent graced his full lips. 'But after a while, it all became . . . monotonous. Predictable. At least until I met you.'

And there it was: the seductive, carefully planned line I had been waiting for. Because of course Cassius had chosen me over the shifters below. Why wouldn't he, when I was his ticket to power?

Yet if I allowed him to draw me in again, if he ever believed he truly *had* me . . .

I knew what would happen then. We would make another bargain, and more people would die. And one day, when I was no longer useful, I would die too. Because that was how Ravalian politics worked.

And Cassius was an expert at Ravalian politics.

'Always so distrustful,' Cassius murmured. Even the moon must have fallen for his charms, because somehow the silvery light softened the sharp angles of his face. 'For what it's worth, I regret the way I used you back in Ravalia. But making you my fiancée wasn't just about power.'

I hated how much his words affected me, how much I wanted to believe them. To believe in *him*.

Down below, the blazing fires and cavorting figures drew my attention. There was something so refreshing about Kalurians. Their honesty, their fierceness and honour. Their lack of pretence.

'I see it now,' Cassius said, and I realised he was studying them too. 'Why you want to protect these people. Their way of life.'

I glanced up at him. 'That's not what I expected you to say.'

He arched an eyebrow at me. 'What would you have expected?'

'That you would look at them and see a weapon.'

Cassius was silent for a long time. A crisp breeze raced through the treetops, making the lamps swing in a way that sometimes bathed his features in golden light and other times in shadow. 'I'm not my family, Mira.'

I said nothing after that, and neither did he. When I finally left for my tree house, I did so without a word. Accepting there was an attraction between us – that was one thing. But it was altogether different to consider that we might share something deeper. That he might actually be good for me – and me for him. Even the thought felt like something out of an ill-fated fairy tale.

But later that night, when I was shivering alone beneath a pile of furs, I felt the warmth of Cassius's body settle next to mine. And though I knew I should push him away, I didn't move an inch.

Slowly, almost tentatively, Cassius's hands made lazy circles across my back. A gentle, almost hypnotic touch—

That sent me off into a deep sleep.

CHAPTER TWENTY-EIGHT

Mira

I dreamt of battlefields and death. Charred remains of people and animals littered the ground around me, the screams of those still fighting filling the air as they crashed against a shadowy enemy force.

Their screams grew louder. So loud, so desperate, that I clapped my hands over my ears, trying to block out the horror, silently begging someone to make it stop—

A sharp, stinging sensation erupted across my cheek. My eyes flashed open, my mind a haze of shock and confusion as I struggled to make sense of why *Cassius* had struck me. Why he was grabbing hold of my shoulders and dragging me to my feet.

I struggled against him until I heard the shrill, piercing screams. Not part of a dream at all, but—

'Ravalian Warriors,' Cassius told me, every word harsh and clipped.

'How many are there?' I asked urgently as we reached the door. Because that was what survival would come down to: their numbers against our own.

'Too many,' was Cassius's grim reply. 'They're already—'

BOOM.

Something heavy slammed me to the ground, the impact sending stars exploding before my eyes. For a heartbeat, I could only lie there, dazed and winded. Then my vision cleared, and I realised I was pinned beneath the remains of the door.

I turned my head to see Cassius fighting a Ravalian in red and gold armour, whose two blades moved so fast they were a blur of silver. Cassius was engaging the Warrior with a sword in one hand and a dagger in the other, cutting and parrying and stabbing – compensating for his opponent's strength and speed by keeping him distracted. But that approach would only work for so long.

And it wouldn't work against two of them.

My eyes locked with the second Warrior as he stepped into the splintered doorway, looming over me like a spectre of death. Quickly freeing myself, I reached for my discarded sword and thrust it upwards, skewering the Warrior through the stomach as he lunged for me.

But I was too late to stop his warning shout. It echoed through the tree house and into the crisp night like a call to arms.

I could only hope that it went unanswered.

Hurrying towards Cassius, I saw that the Warrior he was fighting was larger than normal and far stronger. I grasped my mother's locket, needing the fiery magic contained within. But when my fingers enclosed around it—

It glowed red, flickered, and then went out.

Staring down at it in shock, I barely dodged in time as the Warrior disarmed Cassius and struck at me with his blade. I hurled myself to the side, his blade slicing off a lock of my hair.

And then his attention returned to Cassius.

'Your left!' I shouted. '*To your left!*'

Cassius heard me and turned – too late. The Warrior's sword sliced through the air as if in slow motion, seconds away from slicing through Cassius's neck.

No. I wasn't sure if I thought it or screamed it, but it was deafening in my mind. Fury tinted my vision red, and thorny red tendrils exploded out of my hands, snaking up the Warrior's body with impossible speed.

I willed them to tighten. To—

The Warrior's sword hit the ground along with what remained of his arm. An agonised groan left his mouth as blood sprayed in a gushing torrent. The tendrils fell on it immediately, like leeches sucking up his blood. Yet as they grew thicker and stronger—

Something hot and wet trickled down my neck. Another nosebleed, I assumed – until I saw Cassius's expression and the direction of his gaze. This blood was coming from my ears.

'Release the magic.' He took hold of my shoulders, drawing my focus to him – even as the sounds of fighting drew closer. 'You're bleeding from the brain, Mira. *Release the magic.*'

Another Warrior entered the tree house, her weapon already drawn. But my tendrils were waiting. They latched onto her hungrily, heedless of her screams. In moments, the Warrior's body was entirely gone from view, buried beneath a pulsing blood-red mass.

My vision darkened, my heart stuttering. A wave of exhaustion crashed over me as more blood dripped onto the floor. *My* blood.

The tendrils devoured that, too.

Without giving me the chance to realise what he intended, Cassius drew his sword and sliced through the tendrils – hacking them into pieces until their eerie red light was extinguished and they dissolved into a puddle of blackish blood.

'What have you *done?*' I demanded as Cassius pulled me from the tree house. 'I'm too weak to summon them again.'

'Good,' Cassius said shortly. 'Maintaining them was killing you. Using blood magic is clearly a death sentence.'

'The cost doesn't matter,' I snapped as screams rent the air around us. 'I'm the reason Roran is slaughtering these people. I have to stop him. I have to do *something.*'

Smoke clogged my lungs as flames consumed the wooden dwellings below. A glance over the side of the suspended bridge showed black-armoured Warriors advancing in four neat, uniform lines of fifty – an overwhelming force, yet if anyone could break their lines it would be the shifters. They were fighting in animal form, their roars loud enough to shake the branches around me. An aerie of eagles launched themselves into the air, their talons extended.

Cassius's grip tightened as I prepared to wrench my arm from his. 'You're of no use to anyone down there. Besides, they're bringing the fight to us.'

Panic settled into my bones as I saw the Warriors scaling the trees, their red and gold armour a stark contrast amongst the thick brown trunks. Making a split-second decision, Cassius and I raced across the bridge to a much larger platform between the various dwellings, where Thoren and his twenty clansmen were fighting to hold the line.

Cassius unsheathed his sword as he prepared for battle. I wanted to do the same, but what use would that be? Vølund had once told me that Queen Rúna destroyed an entire army with blood magic. And yes, it had cost my great-grandmother her life, but—

I reached desperately for my magic. There was so much blood here. Surely I could tap into it, use it to increase my power—

Cassius took one look at me and swore, reaching for me when I swayed on my feet. The effort of summoning those tendrils had been too much, and I felt weighed down by the knowledge that my magic was next to useless when it counted.

'Get in front of her,' Cassius shouted as he ran to meet the attacking Warriors. 'Protect your queen!'

Half a dozen clansmen immediately encircled me and Odessa – and Jadis, who was bleeding from a wound to her side.

'Take it,' she grimaced, passing me her dagger.

Gripping its hilt, I straightened my shoulders, preparing for the inevitable bloodshed when the Warriors made it onto the platform.

My berserkers surged to meet Roran's forces, Thoren leading the charge. He was incredible to watch in action, his movements almost as unnaturally fast as the Ravalian Warriors. I knew he had given himself completely over to the fight, as had the others – embracing a wild, adrenaline-filled state where they barely felt pain.

And yet, no matter how strong and fierce they were, they were being steadily worn down. Overcome by the multitude of injuries they sustained, by their enemy's superior numbers and unnatural, magically enhanced endurance. Tears blurred my vision as I sent my guards to boost their numbers, all the while knowing it was hopeless. Even Thoren was beginning to tire.

No matter how many Ravalians he killed, more kept coming. And with the shifters occupied below . . .

We're going to be overrun.

Just as I had the thought, their commander crossed the bridge. I realised he had been holding back for this very moment, waiting until my forces were diminished. His Warriors followed suit, striding onto the other bridges and facing the few clansmen who remained.

Cassius retreated to the platform where I waited with Jadis and Odessa, our backs to each other as we each kept our eyes on the bridge in front of us. I glanced around me for my other guards, but they were all gone. All dead on the bridges, except for Thoren and eight of his best warriors.

Four were still standing on the bridge in front of me: Thoren and three others. They met the Ravalian general as a united force, but it was immediately clear they were outmatched. If Thoren hadn't been fighting for so long already, if he hadn't lost so many of his companions, he might not have been drawn in by the feint. At the last second he recognised it for what it was and tried to shift his position.

But the Ravalian general didn't give him the chance. He disarmed Thoren and promptly ran him through.

A scream burst from my lips as Thoren fell from the platform. I thought I saw the general glance in my direction, but it was difficult to be sure with the helmet concealing his face. I noticed that he wore golden armour as opposed to the red and gold of the others, and he fought with such brutal grace that for a moment I thought I was facing Roran himself.

But there were no mocking taunts as he stalked towards me, cutting down the remaining warriors who tried to attack him and kicking them off the platform. He was all momentum, and I knew that I had to be too. I strode to meet him, heedless of Odessa's shout behind me.

Our swords met in a shower of sparks, my arms already straining at the effort of holding him off.

I broke away from him, knowing that I couldn't maintain that position for long. I whirled to the side and stabbed at his ribs, but he countered my attack almost lazily, resisting my attempts to gain ground. It was as if he could anticipate my every move.

I aimed thrust after thrust, until he forced my sword aside with an elegant flick of his wrist—

A *familiar* flick of his wrist.

The Ravalian general flung off his helmet. And I felt all the blood drain from my face.

'You've been practising,' Aric said, running his left hand through his sweaty dark hair. I noticed that he didn't lower his sword. 'But you're still too impulsive, Mira. That much hasn't changed.'

I stared at him mutely, unable to fully believe what I was seeing. Memories resurfaced, chaotic flashes of colour and emotion: the way he had held me together after my mother's death, the desperate way his lips crashed against mine in the arena, all the times he had laughed with me, trained me, helped me. And then came the memories of that precious night spent in his arms.

I could still see the tenderness in his gaze. Could still feel his body settling over mine, achingly gentle as he gave me time to adjust. The certainty I'd felt as our bodies had joined together: that I was exactly where I belonged.

A certainty that had crumbled when Aric had confronted me on that gangplank, looking at me with nothing human in his face.

It was that Aric who stood in front of me now. Not my childhood friend or lover, but someone utterly unrecognisable. Someone who looked at me and saw a monster responsible for his sister's death.

My eyes caught on the jagged wound running down the right side of Aric's face, the angry skin held together by stitches. I might have felt concerned for him, if the memory of Thoren falling off the platform hadn't been so fresh in my mind.

'You killed Kalurians.' My voice was choked. '*Innocent people*, Aric, who were only fighting to defend themselves. What did they ever do to you? Why would you be involved in something so cruel?'

Aric took the opportunity to appraise me too, but there was no softness on his face. He didn't answer my question.

'I promised there would be a reckoning when we met again,' he said in a low voice. 'It seems that reckoning is finally here.'

I took a step back from him. I didn't want to feel afraid of Aric, but I would feel much better with a sword in my hand. Mine lay discarded at his feet – impossible to reach before he did – but bodies were strewn across the wooden platform, and all of them had weapons. If I could reach one of them—

'You're fighting for *Roran* now?' I asked, stalling for time. 'Do you really hate me that much?'

'Not everything is about you.' Aric smiled faintly, but it didn't reach his eyes. 'I have my own plans.'

'And do those plans include letting me go?'

'That's up to *her*.' Aric nodded across the treetops, where the ranks of Ravalian Warriors parted.

My heart sank as Scarlett strode across the sky bridge, an imposing figure in black armour. Her red hair was braided on top of her head like a crown – in place of Emperor Kalias's bone crown, which she had worn the last time I'd seen her. I supposed even she was wary of openly antagonising Roran.

'So glad you survived, Mira. Pity about your fighters, though,' Scarlett said, not even glancing at the bodies. Her Warriors had cleared most of the dead from her path, though the wood was still slippery with blood.

Betrayal and anger resurfaced at the callousness of her words, at the memory of how brazenly she had turned against me in the Ravalian Court. And now she had come here, to kill my people, to taunt me with the knowledge that I was at her mercy—

'Mira, no!' Cassius shouted, but I was already moving. Already using the last vestiges of my blood magic to slow Aric's pulse and slip past him to—

'Give me one reason,' I hissed into Scarlett's ear, pressing my dagger to her neck. 'One reason why I shouldn't end your life right now.'

'Because if you do,' she breathed back, barely moving her lips, 'Lillian dies.'

I paused, the tip of my dagger digging into the column of Scarlett's throat. We were both breathing hard now. Blood dripped steadily from my nose into my mouth. 'But Aric said – he told me she was—'

'Dead?' Scarlett finished with a taunting smile. 'She was. It's only thanks to my magic that she's alive.'

'That's a lie.' My voice was so cold that it burned. 'Every word that leaves your lips is a lie.'

But when I looked at Aric, the connection between us surged – and suddenly I was seeing past his face and into the maelstrom of emotion beneath. He was conflicted, and furious, and achingly sad. But above all—

I flinched back from it. His betrayal. His *hurt*.

My hold over him snapped. Aric remained where he was, his eyes – usually a warm, golden brown – as cold and hard as river stones, his hand shifting to his sword. He studied the blood staining my lips, and I knew he suspected exactly what power I had used against him.

'Didn't you ever wonder,' Scarlett whispered as my hold tightened, 'why Aric serves me with such *devotion*? It's not purely out of hatred for you. It's because I saved his darling little sister. Your supposed best friend.'

End it. Every part of me screamed those words. Urged me to do it. But I couldn't seem to move.

'She died for you, you know.' Whether it was a trick of the light, for a second, I saw dark veins webbing across Scarlett's pale skin. 'She stepped in front of a swordsman to save your life. And now here you are, considering killing me – killing *her* – purely out of spite.' Too quietly for anyone else to hear, she murmured, 'You might not have killed Emperor Kalias, Mira, but you're just as selfish as Aric believes you are.'

'And *you*,' I hissed, 'don't know when to shut up.' I glanced down at my dagger, intending to press it in deeper, but a shocked gasp left my lips at the sight of the strange veins darkening my skin. Horrified realisation flooded into me like ice.

For an instant, I was back in Ravalia, staring at the soldier Scarlett had killed. The soldier who had tried to cut her poison out of his skin. It hadn't worked for him, and I knew it wouldn't work for me.

But I can still take Scarlett down with me.

My eyes locked with Aric's, whose gaze seared into me with punishing force. The condemnation in his face cut into me far deeper than any blade. He truly believed *I* was the villain here.

And the moment I killed Scarlett . . . I would prove him right. Would die with hatred and lies between us.

'You blame me for what happened to Emperor Kalias,' I said, looking only at Aric, 'but you're wrong. The person at that wedding *wasn't me.*'

'I *saw* you—'

'You saw what *she* wanted you to see. Has Scarlett ever mentioned her illusion magic to you?'

'Don't try to turn this around.' Aric's expression didn't so much as flicker, and I realised that he trusted Scarlett implicitly. 'There were two people involved in that assassination: you and Cassius. Whatever powers Scarlett might or might not possess, she couldn't have killed him alone.'

Watching from his knees across the platform, Cassius wasn't in a position to back me up. Not with Aric's Warriors towering over him, ready to deliver the killing blow.

'I know how it sounds,' I said to Aric. 'I really do, but you have to believe me—'

'Believe *you*?' Harsh and unforgiving. 'I've seen what you're capable of – how far you're willing to sink to achieve your goals. I tried to make excuses for you in the Ravalian Court, and all that brought me was death and heartbreak. I don't believe a word out of your mouth.'

Furious tears welled in my eyes. 'Scarlett's done something to you, Aric. She's twisted your mind—'

'My mind is clearer than it's ever been, and this conversation is over.' Aric raised his sword and approached the three surviving members of my party, his expression suddenly businesslike. 'Release Scarlett, or I will start killing your companions.' He considered Jadis, Odessa and Cassius for a moment. Then he said, 'Starting with the prince.'

Aric never had believed me, I realised with sudden clarity. When I had told him there was nothing between me and Cassius.

And now Cassius was going to suffer for it. But—

'We're all going to die anyway,' I said, raising my chin. 'I might as well make my death count.'

Aric's hold tightened on his sword. But it was Scarlett who spoke, her voice lightly chiding.

'I didn't come here to kill you, Mira.' Scarlett shifted slightly and I tightened my hold in response, warning her not to move. She went still. 'Despite everything, you're still my cousin. I wanted you gone from Ravalia, but I never wanted you *dead*.'

Her words brought back memories of our interactions in the Ravalian Court, and even the brief moments of softness I'd seen from her. But that softness had been just another manipulation.

Why else would she have ridden to the docks ahead of a host of Ravalian Warriors, intent on capturing me for the murder of

Emperor Kalias? If I hadn't sailed off before they reached me, I doubted I would still be alive.

'That would be more convincing if your Warriors hadn't almost killed me,' I said, ignoring the increasing weakness of my muscles. Soon, I knew, her poisonous magic would reach my heart. 'I noticed you didn't leave any of the clansmen alive.'

'I didn't want any witnesses to the offer I'm about to make you.' How did she sound so calm, so *reasonable*? 'Besides, killing all of them means you can tell the clans whatever you like. Ideally that Roran murdered them in an unprovoked attack.'

I pulled back just enough to stare into Scarlett's face. I wondered why it had taken me so long to see it before. 'You're insane.'

'Just calculated.' Scarlett's glacial blue eyes met mine, then shifted to my neck – to the dark tendrils that must be visible there. I could feel them spreading through my blood: draining my energy and muddling my thoughts. There was something almost hungry about the way Scarlett looked at me then, but all she said was, 'We both want Roran dead. It makes more sense to pool our resources and work together to end him.'

Adjusting my hold on the dagger, I placed it flat against Scarlett's throat – in the perfect position to slice it ear to ear. And I looked straight into her eyes as I said, 'I trusted you once. I won't make that mistake again.'

'Not even if it's a choice between trusting me and dying here?' It was half taunt, half what sounded like genuine curiosity.

Scarlett leant in closer, heedless of the way my blade nicked her skin, sending a thin trickle of blood rolling downwards. She placed her hand against my heart. Weaker – it was already weaker than it should have been.

'If you're not willing to do it for yourself, then do it for Lillian.' A hint of satisfaction laced her voice as she told me, 'Roran has her. She's his leverage to assure my cooperation – and Aric's.'

My grip tightened on Scarlett's shoulder – no longer a threat, but now the only thing keeping me standing. I was tired. So achingly *tired*, and I knew this was the real reason Scarlett had spared Lillian. Not just to drive a wedge between me and Aric – but because she'd planned to use her against me. Saved her up like a pawn to put into play at the perfect moment.

'You can work with me to save her,' Scarlett said, pressing her advantage. 'And not just her. These red and gold Warriors,' a gesture at the men and women around us, 'accompanied me from Ravalia and are loyal to me. As you might already have noticed, they're also particularly strong – thanks to the magic my mother granted them. They can help you and the shifters destroy Roran's loyal force down below.' Scarlett tilted her head, considering the black veins webbing across my skin. 'Or you can all die here. The choice is yours.'

The cold sapped the energy from my muscles, the heat from my anger. I glanced past Scarlett – towards my surviving companions – then down at the forest floor, where the shifters were still battling for their lives. This was about more than me and Scarlett. It was about Kalure.

And Lillian.

'I accept your offer of a truce. I'll work with you to kill Roran.' *And then I'll find a way of dealing with you.*

'Smart choice.' Scarlett's smile was positively feline. 'Perhaps in time you will come to trust me again. Aric has.' With that last verbal slap, she stepped away from me. I let out a gasp as warmth – lifesaving, wonderful *warmth* – flooded back into my body, the black veins disappearing as if they had never even existed.

Aric immediately moved to Scarlett's side, watching me with open wariness. I felt Cassius come to stand next to me, Jadis and Odessa taking defensive positions at my back.

'What can you offer as part of this alliance?' I lowered my dagger, addressing Scarlett rather than Aric. Somehow, it was easier to look at her – to face the coolness in her expression, and even the faint glimmer of enjoyment in her eyes. Anything was easier than seeing the hatred and distrust in his.

'Quite a lot,' she replied. 'In addition to my contingent of loyal Warriors, I'm living in the Kalurian palace with Roran. I have inside access that you desperately need, considering my brother has an uncanny knack for finding and killing Temple spies.'

Cassius folded his arms, regarding Scarlett with thinly disguised loathing. But even he didn't contradict her.

'Assist the shifters,' Scarlett ordered her red and gold Warriors. 'Leave none of Roran's force alive. Not a single Warrior can report back to him – is that understood?'

Arms slapped against armoured chests in a Ravalian gesture of obedience. Scarlett and I looked on as her Warriors began climbing down the trees. Ten remained to guard their princess, waiting across the central sky bridge.

'Wait,' I called and Scarlett glanced over her shoulder at me. 'How will you explain this to Roran? If Lillian's life is on the line—'

'It shouldn't be difficult to convince my brother that your people fought us off and I escaped with a severely diminished force. Especially when none of his loyal Warriors remain to contradict me.' The sound of steel grating against steel drifted up from below, and Scarlett's lip curled in satisfaction. 'Cassius managed to wound a few of the Warriors accompanying me back to Taiga, which should make my case even more convincing,' Scarlett added, with a cold glance at her younger brother. She turned back to me. 'But you just focus on surviving – you can't kill Roran if you're dead.'

With a cool smile for Cassius, and a nod for me, she strode towards her remaining Warriors. Aric matched her steps with unsettling synchronicity, his hand resting on his sword.

I looked on from a distance, my emotions in turmoil. My heart squeezed as I noticed the way Aric helped Scarlett down the treetop steps. Apparently his warmth and softness hadn't disappeared altogether.

It was just no longer reserved for me.

Cassius drew closer to my side, keeping his voice low. 'You realise this truce will dissolve eventually.'

'I know,' I said grimly. 'I'll be ready when it does.'

Cassius studied my face for a moment. Then he glanced back at Scarlett and Aric's distant figures, tracking their every movement with narrowed eyes. 'Will you be ready to stand against both of them?'

'Aric will come to his senses,' I said, my heart tight as a vice. More quietly, I said, 'He has to.'

'And if he doesn't?'

The continuing sound of fighting provided a welcome distraction.

Relief filled me as my shifters and Scarlett's Warriors gradually over-came Roran's forces, the tide of the battle turning, just as Scarlett had promised it would.

But I had no answer for Cassius. Not yet.

CHAPTER TWENTY-NINE

Scarlett

'You let the Volaris bitch escape,' Roran said coldly from a few metres away. 'That was a poor choice to make.'

I raised my head to glare at my brother. 'It wasn't just Mira. She had the Council of Ancients on her side—'

'I gave you three hundred Warriors. *Three hundred magically enhanced, battle-hardened Warriors.*'

General Harte backhanded me across the face with his gloved fist, and I spat blood onto the tiles, bracing my bound hands against the stone floor. 'The shifters have magic too,' I forced out. 'In their beast form, they're so strong that they smashed right through our lines. Like battering rams.'

Roran levelled me with a dangerous stare. If he suspected that I had let Mira go, he would allow General Harte to kill me here and now. But my loyal Warriors had already backed up my explanation under torture: that we had been met with overwhelming resistance and had been forced to flee for our survival.

Still, it didn't matter if Roran believed me. He didn't accept failure well.

I watched his gaze shift to General Harte and I tensed, anticipating whatever punishment he might give.

'This is still a victory,' I quickly reminded Roran. 'The shifters have been decimated and their village destroyed. They will be even less inclined to accept Mira's leadership now.'

'For your sake, you had better hope so,' Roran said, his voice filled with cold threat. 'Because if Kasmira becomes clan leader, I will feed

Lillian to Titus. And once Aric watches his sister die – *permanently*, this time – I will do the same to him. It might be entertaining to watch you beg for his life.'

'It won't come to that,' I said with a confidence I didn't feel. 'Mira will fail, and when she returns to the Temple in disgrace, we can use the division amongst the clans to weaken her politically. Once she's isolated from her allies, we can turn our attention to ending her—'

Roran slammed the model of a ship down on the ornate table in his war room. Then he picked up a dagger and advanced on me. 'I spared your life so that *you* could kill Kasmira. If you can't do that, what use are you?'

'I can return to the Wilds—'

'You expect me to send you back there after you allowed her to destroy almost three hundred of my best fighters? To humiliate me?' Roran's fingers twitched in a way that made me suspect he was debating whether to wrap them around my throat.

At Roran's glance, General Harte twisted my wrist and—

This time, I couldn't stay on my knees. I fell forward, and for a few seconds I was blinded by the pain. But I didn't scream. Not even as a healer reset the bones in my wrist.

I felt the agony of each one shifting back into place. I clamped my mouth shut, refusing to release so much as a whimper.

When the healer helped me into my previous kneeling position, my expression was as cold as the stone beneath me. Roran followed the movement of the death magic I could feel swirling impotently in my veins.

'I can kill Kasmira,' I told my brother, ignoring his faint smile. 'And I will. I still have time.'

'You have three weeks.' Roran's voice was the bite of steel, but General Harte's fist didn't meet my face.

I took advantage of the brief respite to glance at the figurines on the table – miniature versions of real military resources. Unfortunately, my position on my knees meant that I couldn't make out the whole picture.

'Interested in my plans, are you?' Roran's focus returned to me – precisely what I had hoped to avoid.

'*Our* plans,' I corrected him. 'I signed your deal; our interests are now aligned.'

'I suppose they are.' Roran crouched in front of me. It was the closest he'd dared come since my arrival, and I doubted he would have done it if my hands were unbound. 'But you should remember that you're only alive as long as you're useful. If the Council of Ancients give Kasmira their blessing, your punishment will be to watch Aric and Lillian die. But if someone else succeeds in killing Mira before you do . . . well, then I'll have no more use for *you*.'

He motioned to General Harte, who hauled me roughly to my feet.

Roran stood as well. Though he was still taller than me, he no longer towered over me like he once had.

'I failed to kill you when you were younger, Scarlett,' he said in a low voice, 'but I wasn't really trying then; terrorising you was just enjoyable. But now . . .' He leant in, almost close enough for our skin to touch, but not quite. 'You've finally succeeded in capturing my full, *undivided* attention. And if you fail me again, next time I will make you wish for death.'

Perhaps I should have felt afraid. But Roran had made a mistake, keeping me alive. I might not be able to kill him personally, but I *would* find a way of destroying him – and when I did, he wouldn't die quickly.

'It looks worse than it is,' I told Lillian, whose fingers hovered inches from my bruised cheekbone.

'What did Roran want from you?' she asked as she applied cosmetics to my skin, taking over Aella's usual role. There was an edge to her voice that made me wonder what she had felt through our bond. Whatever it was, I doubted that she could suspect the truth.

'Roran has decided to keep me alive, so long as I prove useful to him. But I'm more concerned about you.'

'I'm fine,' Lillian said with a soft smile. 'No one even visited my chambers while you and Aric were gone.'

I wasn't convinced by her assurances. A few days ago, Lillian had witnessed General Harte maim her brother – and then she had been forced to stitch up the bloody mess he had made of Aric's face. I might not be able to sense her feelings, but she had been exposed to too much blood and violence for it not to take a toll.

Lillian dusted some powder lightly across my cheeks and then set down the brush. After casting a furtive glance at the door, she met my gaze. Her blue eyes were filled with surprising resolve.

'Earlier,' she whispered, 'Aric told me that you let Mira escape. How did she seem to you?'

'How did she *seem*?'

'I mean . . .' The brush stilled in Lillian's hand. 'Was she unharmed?'

That was clearly the least of what Lillian wanted to ask. Her concern and longing for her friend was obvious. Even after Mira's apparent betrayal, Lillian still loved her. Would she feel the same about me, if she knew the truth? Was such a thing even possible?

I angled my head away from her. None of this was Lillian's fault, but I was suddenly furious with her for making me feel this way – for making me *feel* at all. I couldn't afford to feel. Not when it gave Roran yet another weapon against me.

'She seemed healthy enough,' I replied, my voice carefully level. Not mentioning the death magic I had used on her – or the dagger she had held to my throat.

A glance in the mirror showed me that the thin red line still lingered. A reminder of just how eager she had been to end my life.

The hope in Lillian's voice was difficult to hear as she asked, 'Do you think you'll be able to beat him? Roran?'

'I'll find a way to make Roran pay,' I vowed.

Shadows entered Lillian's eyes, and I knew that she was envisioning the many ways she wanted to make Roran suffer.

Vengeance was an emotion I was intimately acquainted with. But seeing it in Lillian's face . . .

I touched the back of her hand with cautious fingers. 'Try not to think about Roran. He corrupts everything within his reach; don't let his darkness corrupt you, too.'

I watched her until she had left my chambers, drumming my finger-nails against the vanity table as I cast an eye over the grand chambers my brother had assigned me. The same ones I had stayed in during previous visits to Kalure.

Including the visit when Roran had tried to drown me.

My gaze drifted to the frost-covered windows, which overlooked a frozen lake. A chill darted down my spine at the sight of it. I could never forget that lake; it haunted my dreams, my memories. Every time I looked in the mirror, I saw that startling ice-blue water reflected in my eyes.

A knock sounded on the door. Not General Harte, then – he wouldn't have bothered.

I crossed the stone floor, barely sparing a glance for the austere furniture. When my father had ordered the Kalurian palace rebuilt, he hadn't bothered to imitate the original. Instead, he had stripped everything back, as though he was emulating one of his military campaigns. No wonder Roran seemed so comfortable here.

His generosity was a show, of course – assigning me my old chambers, instructing Lillian to disguise my bruises, inviting me to tonight's banquet . . . it was all a pretence of civility before the inevitable, bloody ending.

Aric opened the door. I started to hurry towards him, but he shook his head, indicating that he wasn't alone.

'Your Highness,' Aric said with uncharacteristic formality, offering me his arm. I took it with a curt nod.

Warriors were stationed in the grey corridor. They bowed their heads at my approach, and I took note of their locations and numbers, even as my sense of hopelessness increased.

The impossibility of escape became even more pronounced when I reached the great hall, which was just as imposing as I remembered. My eyes lingered on the stone thrones my father and stepmother had once occupied, then rose to take in the life-sized sculptures spanning the space – the ancient Northern kings that my father had admired. Each armed and poised to deliver a fatal blow to an invisible enemy.

Passing between them, I turned my attention to the main wooden table, filled with Roran's favoured Warriors and generals. There were even some Kalurians in attendance – the privileged few that Roran was prepared to indulge and reward, so long as they proved useful.

Roran himself sat at the centre of the table, his broad shoulders made even broader with furs, and his crimson tunic pinned with military medals. He looked up, pinning me with those hateful, jade-green eyes. A sudden sense of deja vu engulfed me – but I was no longer the girl Roran had terrorised, stepping into the great hall barefoot and freezing.

I was something else – something powerful. Like the ancient kings surrounding me.

I smiled at the thought. Ironically, it was thanks to Roran I had the ability to pose a threat to him. If it wasn't for his attempt on my life, I wouldn't have death magic churning in my veins.

Roran stood at my approach, and my gaze went to the empty seat at his right. But he motioned for Aric to join him, forcing me to claim the seat opposite. Still careful to keep his distance.

I watched my brother closely through all four courses. He spent most of the time speaking with his generals, but he invited Aella into conversation just as often, flaunting her presence at his left side. Dressed in a low-cut gown, with an ornate mask covering the upper half of her face, Aella couldn't have looked more different to the demure attendant I had grown used to. And it wasn't just her appearance – it was the cunning smile that upturned her red lips, and the purring laughter that made it difficult to tell whether she was amused or mocking.

'It isn't poisoned,' Roran said to me, taking note of my untouched plate.

I forced myself to take a bite of the succulent meat. Roran looked away, apparently satisfied. But I kept my attention on him, even as I smiled where I had to and engaged in conversation when required. At one point, I thought I saw a familiar figure slip out of the hall – but she was gone too quickly to be sure, leaving me with only a glimpse of white-blonde hair. Was it possible that Mira had sent Odessa to keep an eye on me?

Given her Mask training, she *was* a logical choice. But I would have expected Mira to baulk at the idea of sending anyone to the Kalurian palace – especially after Roran had slaughtered her spies in particularly messy ways.

When the banquet was finally over, Aric escorted me back to my chambers. Even though it was better not to confirm our romantic connection in front of Roran's guards, I allowed him to follow me inside.

Brutal and awful though the scar was, it did nothing to diminish Aric's attractiveness. If anything, my attraction towards him had increased. Along with my respect.

Not just for the way he had unflinchingly faced down Roran – but also for the way he had handled seeing Mira again. I hadn't even needed to consider using his blood ruby against him.

Part of that was due to his determination to protect Lillian, of course, but I liked to think he was genuinely devoted to me as his future empress. That he believed in what I could accomplish if I ever had the power to make my own choices.

It was just a pity that a river of blood needed to be spilled first.

'Do you regret it?' I asked him quietly, and I knew Aric understood that I wasn't referring to the clansmen. Killing the Kalurian warriors hadn't bothered me; I wouldn't have been able to get to Mira otherwise, and I couldn't have dispatched one of them without silencing them all.

But the men, women and children in the village below . . .

'There was nothing we could have done to save them.' Aric's voice was heavy but resigned. 'We couldn't have stood against Roran's Warriors. Not without Mira and the shifters behind us, and there was no way we could have made an alliance before the killing started.'

That was true enough. And Roran would have sent his Warriors after Mira regardless, even if Aric and I had refused. A refusal that would have cost us our lives.

'Once Roran is dead,' I ventured, watching Aric closely, 'Mira will become a threat to me. You saw how close she came to ending my life.'

He was silent for a long time. 'I know.'

Do *you?* I almost asked him. *Could you really stand by and watch Mira die? Could you stand by and watch* me *kill her?*

'I serve you now,' was all Aric said – not quite an answer, but close enough.

I traced his scar with my eyes as he undid the laces of my dress, careful to keep my death magic contained within me. Shielding Aric from the poison only I could survive.

He pulled me closer, his lips moulding perfectly with mine. But when he steered us towards the bed, I forced myself to think of all the secrets between us – and the cost of keeping them.

Tell him, I told myself. *Tell him* now.

But there was something so painfully tender about the way he looked at me. And then his eyes darkened, and I knew that the bruise on my cheek was visible.

'I'll kill him for you,' Aric promised, cupping my face in his hands. 'For you – and for Kain.'

He claimed my lips once more, and I kissed him back just as hungrily, pulling him down on top of me.

My nails raked possessively down his back, and my arms strained to hold him close even though I knew I would soon need to let him go. Perhaps he knew it too, because I tasted desperation in his kiss.

Though whether that desperation was for *me* . . .

My eyes narrowed as I noticed his were closed. Perhaps in the passion of the moment—

Or perhaps because he wasn't thinking about me at all.

The death in my veins surged – begging to be released. Eager to lash out, to—

A chill that had nothing to do with the magic darted down my spine. *No,* I told the power within me.

Hooking my leg under Aric's, I shifted our positions so that I was on top. His eyes reopened and I allowed myself a small smile of satisfaction as I kissed my way down the chiselled V of his abdomen and lower, kissing and licking and—

At the first stroke of my hands, Aric's head fell back against the pillows. His groan was low – guttural. It reverberated through me, all the way down to my throbbing core. And the death in my veins quietened.

There was something thrilling about watching Aric come undone. Maybe it was because of how strong and capable he was, but whatever the reason, I delighted in being the one to dismantle his composure.

Sex was just another form of warfare, after all. It was all about understanding your opponent.

And I understood Aric very well.

A shudder went through his body as my tongue—

'Gods, your mouth,' he rasped. 'Scarlett—'

I pulled back slightly, raising my gaze to his. 'Yes?' I asked innocently, delighting in the expression on his face. The knowledge that he was entirely focused on me. *As he should be.*

Without warning, Aric flipped me back onto the bed.

'My turn.' His voice was low with promise.

Another delightful advantage of having Aric for a lover: he preferred to be the one pleasuring me.

The material of my dress ghosted over my skin as Aric lifted my skirts, the press of his fingers against my thighs making me shiver.

He touched me lightly at first, teasing strokes that made me shift with impatience. And then—

Pleasure and heat sparked within me at the first teasing flick of his tongue. This time, I was the one threading my fingers through Aric's ebony hair, as much for his sake – there was nothing men liked better than to know their efforts were appreciated – and because I suddenly desperately needed something to hold onto. Gods, it was too much.

He was too much. Too wonderful, too consuming.

Rapture beckoned, but I kept my eyes open, watching Aric's face, committing everything to memory – the maddening pleasure of his mouth, the feeling of his strong hands parting my thighs, the fierceness in his dark eyes as he looked at me. It was all precious.

And it was infinitely sweeter knowing that every caress, every kiss, every brush of our bodies, could be our last.

CHAPTER THIRTY

Scarlett

Two days had passed since my meeting with Roran. *Which means I'm running out of time to kill Mira.*

The thought settled like a stone in my stomach. But I kept my gaze on the manor up ahead, my hood carefully lowered to shield my features from view. Beside me, Aric and Lillian did the same.

It was fortunate that Mira had sent Odessa here. It had taken both my illusions and her assistance to slip past the guards stationed throughout the Kalurian palace and the city beyond. More than that, it had allowed me to put Aella under watch – a stroke of genius on my part.

The first few times Odessa had tailed Aella, we hadn't understood why she would leave the Kalurian palace in favour of an aged estate in the countryside. But the moment Odessa had laid eyes on the red-haired boy, it had all clicked into place.

No wonder Roran favoured Aella. Why wouldn't he, if she had provided him with a son?

Illegitimate, to be sure – but our father had made me part of the line of succession. Once Roran was officially crowned, and he could be sure the boy was safe, I felt certain he intended to do the same for his son.

Still, something didn't ring true. I could accept that Roran had seen an opportunity to lure Aella away from Zandri by seducing her. I could even accept that Roran had found a way to take Aella's blood ruby and free her from my mother's control. But how could Zandri not have noticed if one of her Masks disappeared for nine months?

It was far-fetched enough to make me wonder if Odessa had set all this up, either acting on her own or under Mira's orders. She had never liked me, and I wouldn't put it past her to come up with a plot to destroy me.

But if Odessa *was* telling the truth . . . well, kidnapping Roran's son was an opportunity too tempting to resist.

And if she was lying, I would happily kill her. Perhaps I could even use her death to win some favour with my brother.

'I'll deal with the guards around the back,' Aric whispered to me, and then he was moving.

A few minutes later, distant shouts and the clang of metal against metal rang out. As if that was her signal, Odessa slipped inside the manor – leaving three dead Warriors at the entrance.

'Stay here,' I instructed Lillian, who was concealed amongst the trees. 'Don't come out until we return.'

She nodded, her face pale.

I approached the manor carefully, taking note of the dead Warriors. Roran was definitely hiding *something* here. Maybe this was just his way of keeping his lover safe – but it had to be more than that. I refused to even contemplate that we'd risked this much for nothing.

My curiosity and wariness increased as I entered the dark manor. There were two more bodies on the floor in front of me, and seeing them reminded me of Zandri's warnings not to underestimate Odessa.

A scuffle sounded above.

I took the stairs two at a time, no longer bothering with subterfuge. I reached the landing in time to see the Warrior fall, a kerosene lamp falling with him.

Odessa's eyes met mine over the body. 'Come on,' she said brusquely. 'The boy is upstairs.'

When we reached the top landing, I told her, 'Let me go first.'

Without waiting for Odessa's agreement, I visualised my surroundings and called up an illusion of invisibility. Two guards were stationed outside the door at the end of the hall, and though their weapons were drawn, they didn't see my approach. It was a simple matter of touching their faces to transfer the death within me.

A few heartbeats later, I stepped over their bodies and pushed open the door.

Aella was in the shadows, but the lamplight illuminated her eyes – large and brown, luminous even in the semi-darkness. There was something odd about the way Aella was standing – as if she was trying to block someone from view. I shifted to the right, and there he was: the red-haired child Odessa had described, sitting up in the bed behind her.

I took a step closer to Aella, but my eyes were on the blades in her hands. Did she really believe she could stand against me?

'Roran is *using* you, you fool.' My voice dripped with condescension. 'Do you think you're the first to fall in love with my brother? Plenty of women think he's charming enough, at least until they end up dead—'

'By Zandri's hand, or on her orders,' Aella retorted, inching further in front of the bed, and the boy who was watching us with wide eyes. 'I should know, since I killed one of his lovers for her. Aurelia.' Without shifting her gaze from us, she said, 'This is Aurelius. Her son.'

I frowned down at the boy. He had inherited Roran's green eyes and distinctive red hair, but he had softer features. For a child of four or five, he was strangely solemn as he met my gaze.

'None of this matters,' Odessa said impatiently from behind me. 'We're here for the boy; we don't have time for—'

'Aurelia begged me to keep her secret,' Aella continued, her eyes locked on mine. 'Zandri forced me to kill Aurelius's mother just because she was close to Roran. What do you think Zandri would have done if I had told her about the boy? Whatever Roran is, the child is innocent.'

I could almost see Aurelius as she did: sweet and untainted by the sins of his father. But any child of Roran's would always be a threat to me. A threat I couldn't allow to exist.

'I told Roran about the promise I made Aurelia,' Aella said, her words coming more urgently now, 'and I vowed to protect their son if he freed me from Zandri's control. But while I may be Roran's lover, my loyalty isn't to your brother – only to Aurelius.'

'Really?' I tilted my head as I considered her. 'You seemed enamoured with Roran at the banquet.'

Aella narrowed her eyes. 'How do you think I've survived this long?'

Odessa crossed over to my side. 'I don't intend Aurelius any harm. All I want is to take him back to the Temple—'

'As leverage,' Aella finished, her voice hard.

Odessa had the grace to look apologetic. 'This war isn't over. Even out here, Aurelius may not be safe. He'll be protected in the Wilds. Not just from future battles – but from his father, too.'

How *convincing* she sounded. I might have believed her if we weren't planning to use Aurelius's kidnapping as a way of forcing Roran to invade the Wilds, where Mira and the clans would have an advantage. Which meant war would find Aurelius soon enough.

But Aella's shoulders slumped. She suddenly looked far more like my attendant than the cruel Mask I had seen standing at Roran's side.

I inhaled, and as I did, the acrid taste of smoke filled my lungs. The kerosene lamp. The one that had fallen on the level below—

'We have to go,' I said urgently. 'This entire manor is about to burn to the ground.'

I expected Aella to reach for her weapons and attack. But she only murmured something to Aurelius, and kissed him on his forehead. Aurelius climbed down from the bed, but she held him to her chest.

'I want your promise,' Aella said, her eyes burning into mine.

'We won't hurt him,' Odessa said immediately. 'You have my—'

'It's not your word I care about. I want *hers.*'

Aella looked at me with eyes like mirrors. Reflecting my every doubt, my every dark thought.

'You have a choice, Scarlett,' she told me. 'You don't have to be your mother. You can choose trust over fear.'

I glanced down at Aurelius. Trusting him was a fool's decision. How could I know that he wouldn't rise up against me one day? That he wouldn't grow into a threat just as terrible as Roran?

Simple: I couldn't. And I didn't need to promise Aella anything. Her guards were dead, this house was about to become a death trap, and she was outnumbered two to one.

Odessa must have had the same thought. She lunged for Aurelius, but Aella held him fast. She didn't even blink as Odessa raised her sword. Just kept her eyes on me as she said, 'Trust, not fear. That's what Severin would have wanted.'

It was the wrong thing to say. I moved towards her, my hand on my sword. 'What do you know about Severin?'

'I know that he chose to throw himself off the battlements rather than let Zandri kill him herself. I know that he didn't try to run from death, but faced it head on, hoping it would finally turn you against your mother.'

If I had thought Aella was lying, I would have run her through right then and there. But the sincerity blazing on her face . . . the way her words made a terrible, sickening kind of sense . . .

I closed my eyes, thinking of everything my mother had said to me. All her lies and assurances. The way she had ripped my heart right out of my chest. *He chose to die rather than be with you.* Her words resurfaced, smooth and relentless. *They all turn against you in the end, don't they? But I never have. And I never will.*

'How?' I asked Aella sharply. 'How do you know this?'

'Zandri had me use magic on every Artisan in the palace, so that if you asked them what happened to Severin, they couldn't say anything that would implicate her. And then . . .' Aella hesitated. I thought I saw a trace of pity in her eyes.

'And *then?*'

'I heard her gloating about it. About how Severin had sacrificed himself for nothing.' Aella's gaze was steady on mine. 'Apparently he asked Zandri how she convinced you to betray Mira. Even at the end, he didn't believe that you could have done it yourself. That you would have been so cruel.' Softly, she said, 'Zandri found it amusing that Severin died for someone who doesn't even exist. But I think . . . I think he saw something in you that your mother ignores.'

'Because you know me so well.' Sarcasm was thick in my voice.

'You'd be surprised. I watched you for a long time, Scarlett. I've seen how you behave when you're alone and when you're with others – particularly your mother. And Severin.'

Severin, who had always brought out a gentler side in me. A version of me he had believed in enough to—

It was suddenly difficult to breathe, and I knew it wasn't the smoke that clogged my throat and made my eyes water.

There would never be enough atonement for this. *Never.*

'You have my word,' I told Aella. Before I could reconsider, I sliced my palm with my dagger. *Making* my word true, and ensuring I couldn't go back on this promise later, even if I wanted to. 'I'll do everything within my power to keep Aurelius safe.'

Aella released the boy, and Odessa quickly grabbed him. But despite the increasing smoke, and the distant line of fire torches I could see through the windows – no doubt belonging to Roran's reinforcements – I couldn't make myself move.

I glanced at my former attendant. 'You're not coming with us, are you?'

'No,' Aella said with a soft smile. 'I'm not.'

'You don't have to do this. I can find your blood ruby—'

Aella shook her head. 'I won't live my life under someone else's control. Not Zandri's, not Roran's – and not yours.'

Odessa tugged on my arm, and I allowed her to lead me out of the room and into the hallway, which had turned into a smoking furnace. The curtains lining the windows went up in a blaze of flame and the glass shattered.

If Aella didn't leave now, she never would.

I looked back at her one last time – sitting on the edge of Aurelius's bed. Tracing his name embroidered onto a pillow.

Her brown eyes locked with mine. And I knew the conviction in her eyes would haunt me forever.

The certainty that she would rather die than be controlled. That she would rather die free.

Like Severin.

For a day and a half, we travelled through lush countryside in a stolen horse and cart. Only my illusions had saved us as we escaped from the burning manor, a few minutes ahead of Roran's Warriors.

His fury would be volcanic. Not only had he lost me, Aric and Lillian – but he had lost his son.

And Aella.

I didn't know why her death bothered me so much. I hadn't known her – not really – and she had made her own choices. But what she had revealed about Severin had shaken me to my core.

Severin had believed that I would hate Zandri for what she had done to him, and he was right. But I hadn't turned against her. Whether out of love or dependence or fear . . . I had allowed Zandri to manipulate me. Had allowed her to *comfort* me—

A warm hand brushed mine, and I quickly clamped down on my death magic as I noticed Aurelius staring up at me. He was relatively calm now; there were no more heart-wrenching questions about where we were going or why we had left his mother behind.

When I opened my palm, I saw that Aurelius had placed two objects inside it. Toy soldiers. No – toy Warriors, I realised as I saw the black armour. Roran must have had them especially commissioned for his son.

A foreign emotion squeezed my chest. I looked pleadingly to Aric for assistance.

Aric took the toy soldiers and set them up on his knee, arranging them in battle formation. Then he matched his Warriors against Aurelius's, until the boy was completely absorbed in the game.

His childlike laughter was painful. There was nothing of Roran's cruelty in him, and it felt wrong to contemplate using Aurelius like this. What would Severin think of me now, kidnapping a child and making an alliance with Mira that I intended to break?

I wondered what he had Seen, to make him so surprised that I would betray her. In the days leading up to Cassius and Mira's wedding, I had been certain that it was a choice between her or me. That if I let her leave for Kalure, she would be in the perfect position to threaten my rule.

But was any of that really true – or was it a result of my own para-noia? The fear and distrust that had hung over me ever since I realised how precarious my life in the Ravalian Court really was?

'Careful,' Aric said, and I turned to see him unsheathing his sword. Apparently, Aurelius had grown bored with the figurines.

He wasn't bored now. His eyes lit up with interest as his fingers brushed the steel and enclosed around the hilt. Aric kept a firm grip on the sword, so Aurelius couldn't hurt himself.

'Father promised to give me a real sword one day,' Aurelius said, and though he was speaking to Aric, his eyes were on the blade. 'I don't see him much.' This held a hint of sadness.

Personally, I thought he was fortunate.

I gazed at Aurelius, but it was Aella I saw in that moment: her eyes burning with conviction as she prepared to die. A choice she had made to escape Zandri's control as much as Roran's.

But this wasn't the time to evaluate the morals of the Orders. Reformation could come later, if I survived to see it through. Right now, I needed to focus on escaping to the Wilds alive – which would be much easier if I hadn't already strained my illusion magic to its limit.

'I don't know if I can do this,' I warned as the cart slowed to a stop. We disembarked, Aric helping Aurelius down.

'If you can't,' Odessa responded tersely, 'then we're all dead.'

We were on the edge of the countryside now, far from Taiga. To the north-east, I could make out the smaller settlement of Frør – the last point of civilisation before the Frozen Wastes. If there had been a mountain pass in Frør, this would have been much easier. Then again, the Kalurians who lived there weren't exactly welcoming to outsiders. Even my father had given them a surprising amount of freedom.

I turned my attention to the palisade of tall, sharpened posts in front of me. There was an iron gate in the middle – the only way into the no-man's-land that separated Kalure from the Wilds, allowing passage between the Archasian mountains. The checkpoint was lit with fire torches, intensely bright in the darkness, and manned by black-garbed Warriors.

Aric left to scout up ahead, Lillian taking over his position at Aurelius's side. She had been quiet during the coach ride, shooting wary glances at Odessa and watching Aurelius with fierce protectiveness.

'I want to go with him,' Aurelius said, tugging on Lillian's arm. 'I want to meet the Warriors.'

I crouched at Lillian's side – so that I was level with Aurelius's pale green eyes. A similar shade to Roran's, but with none of his coldness.

'When Aric returns,' I told him, 'we're going to play a new game. It's Roran's idea; a test of your suitability to become a Warrior one day. All you need to do is keep your eyes straight ahead and cross through that checkpoint without making eye contact with anyone. No acknowledging the Warriors, no speaking to them – nothing. Can you do that for your father?'

Aurelius nodded seriously. 'I won't let the emperor down.'

'I know you won't.' My answering smile was genuine. If he could stay quiet, maybe we could actually survive this.

'They aren't letting civilians through,' Aric told us quietly when he returned. 'Only Ravalian Warriors are allowed to pass.'

His words confirmed what I had already suspected. I closed my eyes and concentrated, recalling the mental images I had spent the past two days perfecting. When I reopened my eyes, I was staring at three Ravalian Warriors – and I knew that I was cloaked in the same dark armour, a sword gleaming at my side. But—

'I've never tried to work an illusion on a child before,' I said, eyeing Aurelius. 'The slightest slip could give us all away.'

Aric met my gaze steadily. 'It's still our best chance. And you only have to hold the illusion until they let us through.'

'I'll make it happen,' I assured him.

Aric took point at the head of our small group, followed by Odessa who adopted a convincingly bored expression. Lillian would usually be our weakest link, but I had disguised her delicate features and increased her height. It was Aurelius I was most worried about.

Lillian murmured soft instructions to the boy, reminding him to be quiet and follow her.

'Like a mission?' he whispered back.

'*Exactly* like a mission.'

I couldn't hear what Aric said to the Warriors at the checkpoint, but they let him and Lillian through easily enough. I followed just behind Aurelius, focusing my illusions on keeping him invisible. Warriors pressed in against us on either side but I walked past them with my head held high, my gaze fixed ahead – on the desolate mountain plateau beyond the border. We were almost across the threshold when—

I was a second too late to shift my illusion as Aurelius tripped, and there was nothing I could do to conceal his faint cry of pain. Acting on impulse, I grabbed his arm and sprinted the remaining distance.

Behind me, the Warriors shouted. They had only seen Aurelius for an instant – but the whole of Kalure was on the lookout for a boy of his description.

Arrows whizzed past my head as we ran – aiming high, so as not to hit Aurelius. I picked up my pace, my legs straining at the effort.

I let my illusions scatter as we reached a narrow barrier of snow drifts, disappearing into a powdery haze. The alpine tree line was close now, and I knew we would be safe from the Warriors, who were reluctant to follow into the Wilds.

But as we ran, I noticed that Aric's face was curiously pale. His left hand pressed against his back, as if he was in pain.

'You're hurt,' I said, studying the wound with worried eyes. 'How bad is it?'

'It's nothing.' Aric's voice was sharp. 'One of the Warriors landed a lucky shot, that's all.'

An arrow wound – and he must have pulled it out to keep running. An icy tendril of fear darted down my spine.

I slowed to match Aric's pace, letting him lean on my shoulder. The fact that he accepted my help told me it was much worse than he had made it seem.

'There are healers at the Temple,' Odessa promised, but her expression was pinched.

Neither of us mentioned the distance we still had to cover – or the blood staining Aric's tunic.

Neither of us had to.

CHAPTER THIRTY-ONE

Mira

My heart ached as I bandaged wounds and applied natural poultices. Some of the wounded were beyond help, and all I could do was kneel on the grass beside them and offer prayers to the Sorceress. Entreating her to ease their pain and guide them into the afterlife.

It felt sorely inadequate, but the shifters seemed to appreciate my prayers all the same. The young woman I had been praying for grasped my hand with weak fingers.

'Thank you,' she said, nothing more than a wheeze of breath. 'Your Majesty.'

No shifter had said those words to me before, and they cracked something open deep in my chest. *You should blame me*, I wanted to say to her. *You should hate me for bringing death and destruction to your home.*

But all I could do was smile, offering the only reassurance I could. 'You will be with the Sorceress soon,' I murmured, hoping that my words weren't a lie. Hoping that she really would find peace.

I squeezed her hand until it went limp in mine. Then I rose and approached the next.

And the next.

It was only when the lamps were lit that I realised how late it was. But I couldn't rest. Not while my people were suffering. If they could endure such unimaginable pain, then I could endure too. I *would* endure.

Thankfully, the woman in front of me wasn't as badly hurt as the others. Reaching for the poultice contained on a large leaf, I dabbed the thick green substance on the wound gouged in her shoulder.

She didn't even flinch, but her other hand rose to touch my face, drawing my gaze down to hers.

'My daughter . . .' Her voice faltered. 'Her name was Inola. Will you pray for her?'

'Of course,' I vowed, and I hated Scarlett in that moment. Hated her and Roran, and all the atrocities they had committed in the name of power.

'I should have known.' I looked up to see Cassius standing over me, his midnight-blue eyes searing into mine. 'What do you think you're doing, Mira?'

I blinked blearily up at him. Tired – I was so tired.

'I'm helping,' I said. 'In the only way I can.'

'No.' Cassius's voice was dangerous. 'You're past the point of helping.' His gaze raked over me, then the groaning shifters nearby. 'You look like you're about to join them. I'm of half a mind to set up a pallet for you right here.'

'Don't be dramatic,' I said, rising to my feet. 'I'm perfectly—'

Cassius took hold of me a second before my legs crumpled.

He muttered some choice words under his breath and led me away from the wounded, ignoring my protests. Approaching Sionnach, who was issuing orders to a group of female shifters, Cassius said firmly, 'I'm taking Mira to get some rest. I trust you have no objections?'

Sionnach's honey-brown eyes narrowed as they fell on me. It was the same intent expression she had worn when assessing the severity of the wounded under her care, and it was disconcerting to have it levelled on me. *And embarrassing.*

'Really,' I said, 'I'm fine. I only need to sit down for a moment—'

'You've been here almost as long as I have, and you have none of my experience or training as a healer. You are most certainly not fine.' Sionnach turned to Cassius as if I wasn't even there. 'Feel free to stay in any of the intact dwellings. Take whatever sustenance you need.'

Cassius nodded, but I pulled free of his steadying grasp. 'What about the ritual?'

Sionnach considered me. 'It can wait until tomorrow. There is too much to do as it is, and you need to be well rested to have the best chance of survival. Meet me here at dawn and I will escort you to the temple.' With that, she returned her attention to the healers gathered around her.

The dismissal was clear. It also rankled, since I didn't appreciate being treated like a child who needed coddling.

But I didn't argue as Cassius steered me between splintered wooden huts and blazing pyres for the dead Ravalian Warriors. And graves. So many graves.

'It's not your fault,' Cassius said softly, and I knew the anguish was obvious on my face. 'This was Roran's doing. You don't have to punish yourself for it.'

'I was trying to help my people,' I said, whirling on him. 'To save as many as I could—'

'I understand that,' Cassius replied, his voice frustratingly calm. 'But I also think that you blame yourself for what happened, and there's a kind of masochistic relief in pushing yourself to your limits.'

'And what would *you* know about any of that?' I retorted, not caring that I was being cruel. Not as people grieved and died around me, driving the dagger of my guilt in deeper.

'You think I don't know what it feels like to lose friends in battle?' A hint of anger sparked in Cassius's face. 'You think my father didn't make sure I learnt that lesson early – that being a ruler means making decisions that will cost lives? He hammered that lesson in, Mira, until everyone I cared about was taken from me. He hammered it in until I had to become desensitised to death or let it break me.'

I backed away from him, as if I could back away from that terrible truth. As if I could separate myself from it.

'Being a ruler comes with many luxuries,' Cassius continued ruthlessly, 'but peace of mind is not one of them. You have to decide if you're strong enough to accept that. If you're willing to bear that burden for the sake of your people's survival. Because that is the true weight of wearing a crown.'

Cassius said nothing else as he added food to our saddlebags and took a waterskin from beside a nearby fire, approaching the steps carved into the trees. He gestured for me to lead the way, positioning himself reassuringly at my back.

I climbed slowly, relying heavily on the vines for support. Though lamps gleamed from the overhead branches, and most of the dwellings were still intact, the treetops felt desolate and empty. Tainted by the absence of everyone who had died.

My eyes lingered on the central platform where Thoren had fallen. Where *Aric* had—

I cut off the thought. I didn't want to think about Aric – couldn't bear it.

Cassius paused in front of a small tree house that appeared undisturbed. It was clearly a calculated choice; facing away from the decimated village and over the forest beyond, the lamps casting everything in a warm haze.

Taking a seat on the high wooden platform surrounding the dwelling, I drew my knees protectively to my chest. Cassius unpacked the food he had brought: an assortment of native fruits and some skewers of meat still hot from the coals. The boards creaked as he took a seat by my side, stretching his legs out in front of him.

'Eat something, Mira,' he instructed in that light drawl of his. 'You're making me nervous.'

Rolling a red fruit contemplatively in my hand, I asked, 'Do you think I made a mistake? Asking Odessa to leave for the Kalurian palace?'

'I think,' Cassius said after a pause, 'that Odessa's Mask training makes her an obvious choice for clandestine work. If anyone can infiltrate Roran's palace and keep an eye on Scarlett, it's her.'

I sucked in a breath of the crisp night air. 'I still should have sent Jadis with her.'

'Jadis needed to return to the Temple, so she can inform Velanthe of the deal you made with Scarlett. Besides, without Mask training, she would only have been a liability to Odessa.' Cassius's tone was indulgent; he knew I was already aware of this. Just as he knew I needed to hear it again anyway. To try and rid myself of the guilt that came from sending my friends into danger.

'Careful,' Cassius warned as I reached for a discarded wineskin. 'You'll want a clear mind tomorrow, if this ritual is as dangerous as Sionnach seems to believe.'

'Actually,' I said, lifting it to my lips, 'I think a clear mind is exactly what I *don't* want.' I closed my eyes, delighting in the burn of the alcohol and the pleasant way it muddled my thoughts.

'What do you mean?'

Angling my face away from Cassius's too intent gaze, I refocused on the food he had laid out like a picnic. I snacked on a meat skewer, wondering if I could change the subject. But I already knew it wouldn't be that simple.

'To commune with the Sorceress,' I admitted, 'I have to be in a state near death.' Cassius waited expectantly for me to continue, his face giving away nothing. 'Apparently there's a body of water near the shifter's temple, where they worship the Sorceress. That's where they take the prospective clan leaders. They're weighted down somehow and kept underwater until they either drown – or the Sorceress saves them, and they resurface as clan leader.'

Silence descended, broken only by the creak of the wooden boards as Cassius stood. I deliberately kept my gaze on the lush forest in front of me, extending all the way to the darkening horizon.

'There are other options,' Cassius said at last. 'Ones that don't require you to face almost certain death.'

'What would you suggest?' I had once told Cassius that he had the uncanny ability to make light of absolutely *everything*. But there was nothing light or irreverent about the way he was looking at me now.

'You could leave Kalure.' The glow of the lamps highlighted the angular features of his face, and the concern shadowing his eyes. 'We both could.'

'You don't mean that. For as long as I've known you, you've wanted power—'

'What if I told you,' Cassius interrupted in a low voice, 'that I want something else more?'

The intensity in his eyes made it clear that *something* was me. For a second, all I could do was blink at him.

Then I laughed. It sounded slightly hysterical.

'If you expect me to believe that, you're—'

Cassius let out a frustrated sigh. Then he whirled around and kissed me.

It seemed like all the emotions that had consumed me lately were poured into that kiss. My teeth bit against his lips, and when he shifted so that he was leaning over me, I felt a jolt of adrenaline-filled heat. My hands tangled in his hair as I tilted my head back to receive his kisses, but all too soon he was pulling away, smiling faintly at whatever expression was on my face.

He traced my swollen lips with his thumb. 'Leave Kalure,' he told me again. 'Let my brother and sister fight amongst themselves, and let yourself be free.'

'I can't,' I said, staring up into Cassius's piercing gaze. 'I can't just walk away.'

Cassius watched me for a long time. He was so close that I could see every speck of blue and silver in his eyes, and though I had been this close to him before, this felt different. *He* felt different.

'I know,' he said finally, his voice soft. 'I know you can't.'

I frowned at him. 'That's it? You're not going to try to change my mind?'

'What would be the point?' Cassius asked with a half-smile, pulling back from me and standing. 'You've already decided. Besides, you're not the kind of person to turn away from a challenge. It's my second favourite thing about you.'

I knew I shouldn't ask. Asking meant that he had drawn me in, but—

'What's the first?'

Cassius didn't answer immediately. 'I wanted my father's throne for all the wrong reasons.' He leant back against the wall of the tree house. 'I realised that when you made a deal with me for your country's independence. You're a true queen, Mira – the kind of ruler who actually puts her people first.' He paused, then said quietly, 'It's an admirable quality. I just hope it doesn't get you killed.'

'That makes two of us,' I muttered. We said nothing for a while, and I suspected we were both consumed with thoughts of what tomorrow would bring. But I didn't want to think about tomorrow.

Possessed by a boldness born from recklessness, I allowed myself to truly take in Cassius – the proud lines of his body, the honed muscles of his arms visible even through his red tunic, the chiselled perfection of his face. Right now, after a day filled with death and suffering . . . I needed to feel alive again.

Rising to my feet, I approached Cassius. He went very still, and I knew his gaze was focused on mine.

I lifted his palm to the light, my eyes on the dirt encrusted beneath his nails. I recalled seeing him digging graves alongside Conall for hours. Recalled the begrudging respect in the way the shifters had looked at him.

Something fundamental had shifted in that moment, but I was only realising it now.

Slowly and deliberately, I kissed each of his fingers.

'Mira.' Cassius's voice was cautioning.

I looked up at him with a teasing smile. 'Yes?'

'I know where this is heading.' His body was very still – carefully still, as if it was taking considerable willpower to resist the invitation in my face. 'But it isn't the right time. Not when you're so exhausted, and definitely not when you're conflicted over another man.'

'Sometimes I hate how perceptive you are.' I pressed my body against his, delighting in his soft, almost imperceptible groan. Brushing a strand of golden-blond hair from his too-perfect face, I whispered, 'But Aric isn't the one I'm thinking about right now.'

Then I reached up and brought his lips down to mine.

I kissed him like he had kissed me outside the banquet hall – all force and fire. He huffed out a soft laugh as my hands roamed across his back, needing him even closer. Needing to feel the hardness of his body against mine.

Cassius lifted my hips, allowing my thighs to wrap around his waist as he pushed open the door of the tree house. His lips were firm and yet soft as they danced with mine, and I yielded to them, our tongues moving in tentative tandem. But when I met his eyes again, the charged intensity behind his stare made it difficult to breathe. I felt as if I could lose myself in those eyes – as if I could lose myself in *him*.

This time, he kissed me slowly and thoroughly, stoking a slow-burning fire in my chest.

'I told you what I want from you, Mira,' Cassius murmured against my lips. His teeth grazed the sensitive skin of my neck, sending shockwaves through my body. 'I want all of you. And I won't settle for anything less.'

Before I fully understood what he was saying, strong arms lay me down on a soft pile of furs—

And released me.

My eyes flashed open, staring at Cassius in stunned disbelief. He didn't so much as glance my way, changing out of his dirt-encrusted tunic with easy nonchalance while I lay there, breathless and aching. From everything I had heard about his exploits in the Ravalian Court, I hadn't expected him to turn down physical intimacy. And yet here he was, stopping *me* from taking things too far.

'And what if I don't *want* to give you all of me?' I snapped back, folding my arms across my chest like a shield. 'What if all I want from you is a distraction?'

'Then this won't happen again,' Cassius said, pulling on his trousers. As he did, I couldn't help but admire the contours of his muscles, remembering the feeling of his body against mine.

'Fine,' I said coldly as he climbed underneath the pile of furs. His warm hands took hold of my waist, drawing me close so that I was settled comfortably between his legs, my head resting against his chest.

Amusement entered his voice. 'Are you mad?'

'Why would I be mad?'

Cassius just shook his head like he didn't believe me. He even had the nerve to smile as he brushed a chaste kiss against my forehead—

As if he had won a game I hadn't realised we were playing.

CHAPTER THIRTY-TWO

Mira

I woke in the early hours of the morning, Cassius's strong arms wrapped around me.

Careful not to disturb him, I slipped out of his embrace. The tree house was dark, but I didn't dare light any of the candles or lamps. Dressing in fresh clothes, I braided back my hair and cracked open the door.

Cassius's breathing remained steady and rhythmic. With any luck, he wouldn't realise I had left until the ritual was over. He'd seemed to make peace with my decision last night, but I knew how unpredictable Cassius could be. With so many lives hanging in the balance, I couldn't risk him trying to stop me.

All seven council members were gathered at the edge of the village when I descended from the treetops. They nodded in respect, their faces silhouetted by the soft glow of dawn. The men wore their usual bone armour, and the women matched them in white woven dresses. I suspected it was a ceremonial colour.

'Follow me,' Sionnach instructed, turning on her heel. Her nut-brown hair was unbound today, cascading down her back in soft curls.

As we walked through the ancient forest, the lush trees curved above us, forming a gentle archway. Despite the thickness of the canopy, enough sunlight filtered through to illuminate my surroundings, and everything around me felt alive in a way I hadn't experienced before.

All too soon, the forest opened out into a glade filled with golden flowers, and I found myself staring at the ruins of a temple. Seven elegantly carved pillars were still intact, ivy and greenery intertwining with the stone so completely that only the occasional glimpse of white was visible.

And beyond those pillars . . .

My legs turned leaden as I followed Sionnach to a cliff above a circular sinkhole. The water was such a dark blue that it reminded me of Cassius's eyes, and it was impossible to tell how deep it was. If I was here under different circumstances, I might have found it beautiful. Might have asked Sionnach if there was a story behind how it had been formed.

But speech suddenly seemed impossible. Foreign.

A dip of my head was all the acknowledgement I could muster for Conall as he approached. My heart lurched as I saw the rusted iron cage beside him. Ready to be pushed into the water far below.

My breathing was coming faster now. It was one thing knowing what I would have to do – and it was another facing the reality. How was I going to clear my mind when I already felt so close to panic?

The distant hum of voices and thudding footsteps made me turn. Despite their grief and anger, despite whatever blame they might harbour for my role in Roran's attack, it seemed as if the entire village had come to witness me commune with the Sorceress.

Or die trying.

When they tried to move past the temple, the remaining five council members formed a barrier in front of them.

'No further,' one of the male shifters warned.

But his words had no effect whatsoever on Cassius. He strode through the crowd as if it wasn't even there, his narrowed eyes focused on the councillors keeping the onlookers contained. As if daring them to try and contain *him*.

Then his searing gaze rose to lock with mine. Clearly, Cassius hadn't been pleased to wake up and discover I was gone.

'Let me through,' he said to the shifters blocking his way – an order, not a request. The glint of Ravalian steel in Cassius's hand made me very nervous.

It had to be a bluff. He couldn't possibly intend to *use* that dagger, not when he was outnumbered and knew that doing so would risk his life. One of Cassius's strongest instincts was self-preservation.

But as I took him in properly, I wasn't so sure. His golden hair was tousled, as though he had been running his fingers through it, and his tunic was rumpled. I knew that his dishevelled appearance was an outward reflection of his mental state. And if someone as calculated and conniving as *Cassius* was out of ideas—

'According to your traditions,' I said, turning to address Sionnach, 'I am allowed one companion to stand by my side. Let Cassius be that companion.'

Sionnach's proud face softened as she studied me. Turning back to the waiting shifters, she instructed, 'Kasmira's consort may join her.'

I didn't correct Sionnach's assumption. Not when it allowed Cassius to push past, joining me on the edge of the cliff. His face was like stone as he watched Sionnach unlock the rusted door of the cage.

Projecting her voice to the listening audience, Sionnach said, 'As you know, communing with the Sorceress requires entering a state near death. Please bow your heads in prayer for our queen, and entreat the Sorceress to spare Kasmira's life if she deems her worthy.'

A chill darted across my skin as the shifters fell to their knees. Only the Council of Ancients remained standing, but their gazes were cast down to the ground.

'Let me get this straight,' Cassius said, not bothering to lower his voice. 'You're going to trap Mira in that cage – and somehow you expect her to survive?'

'If Kasmira is meant to survive, the Sorceress will free her from the cage.' More gently, Sionnach said to me, 'And if she does, you will emerge from the water reborn. The undisputed leader of the clans.'

I stared down into the sinkhole that could easily become my grave. But the potential rewards . . .

I removed my boots and slipped out of my fur-lined jacket, until I was shivering in my blouse and fitted leather pants, the bars cold and hard against my bare feet. Stepping inside the cage made my chest constrict, the bars seeming to press in against me.

The thought of Vølund and other clansmen facing this ritual buoyed my flailing confidence, as did the knowledge that their larger builds would have required them to crouch. In comparison, I was fortunate; the bars were a few inches above my head. Giving me at least the illusion of more space.

'Sionnach.' My throat felt tight as I curled my hands around the bars in front of me. Fighting not to think of how heavy this cage was, and how easily it could become my tomb. 'Do you have any last words of advice?'

The faint breeze blew her unbound hair over one shoulder. 'Just remember to clear your mind. Your best chance of survival is to stay relaxed. Trust in the Sorceress, and don't panic.'

It would have been better if I hadn't asked. In the Ravalian Trials, I had faced my death head on, and my bravery had never deserted me. But the thought of being submerged in this sinkhole, trapped and entirely dependent on *faith* to save me—

Cassius's grip tightened on the dagger strapped to his side. I hoped he wasn't planning to do something foolish if I was underwater too long – like attempting to force the key from Sionnach and dive in after me.

'Don't try to interfere,' I told him. 'If you do, this will all have been for nothing.'

I didn't have the chance to take in Cassius's reaction. My stomach dropped as Conall transformed into the hulking beast that had first greeted me. With one swipe of his paw, he could push the cage right into the chasm.

And yet I couldn't seem to say the words. Couldn't give Conall the order he was waiting to hear.

'Don't look at him,' Cassius said softly, approaching the cage until he blocked out everything else. Reaching through the bars, he raised my chin so I was staring into his midnight-blue eyes. 'Just keep looking at me.'

I swallowed as the sound of heavy footfalls rang out on my left, disturbingly close. But I kept my eyes on Cassius's, and as he rested his forehead against the bars, I felt steadier. Afraid, but no longer close to panic.

A test of bravery, I told myself as I willed my fear down. *That's all this is.*

'Do it,' I ordered without looking away from Cassius. Sucking in a deep breath, I trapped as much oxygen inside my lungs as I could. Knowing even as I did that it wouldn't be enough.

It wouldn't be anywhere *near* enough.

Cassius glanced over his shoulder, and from his expression, I knew Conall was only heartbeats away. 'I wish we could have more time,' he whispered against my lips. 'I wish you could have learnt to trust me.'

I do trust you, I wanted to say, only I couldn't. Couldn't release any of that precious, life-saving air.

Perhaps Cassius saw that answer in my face, because he smiled. His smile was the last thing I saw as something heavy hit the cage—

And sent me toppling backwards as I hit the water.

The cold slammed into me like a blow, threatening to steal the air I had so carefully trapped. But I kept my mouth clamped shut, even as the weight of the cage dragged me under at such a rate that it felt as if I was still falling, sending my body tilting and my brain screaming with panic.

I ignored every single survival instinct as my ears popped and the distant light of the surface shrank, growing smaller and smaller until it was little more than a pinprick high above.

Impossibly out of reach.

The cage hit the bottom with a thud that shook my bones. The pressure was so great that moving was an effort, and I knew the smartest thing would be to lie back against the cage and surrender. To calm my mind, as Sionnach had instructed, and embrace the possibility of death.

I righted myself instead and wrapped my hands around the bars. Clinging to the illusion of control, even as I fought to separate myself from my thoughts and fears.

Relax. I had to relax.

But already, the urge to breathe was clawing at my chest. The water had initially been so cold that it burned, and there had been some comfort in that. Now the cold was relentless as it tunnelled into my bones, making me shake and shiver, and my limbs—

I couldn't feel them. Could barely even feel the sliminess of the rusted bars.

I pushed against the bars, testing their strength. All I had to do was make it to the surface and I would be clan leader. What did it matter if the Sorceress saved me or I saved myself?

A few bubbles left my mouth as I slammed my shoulder against the bars. Rusted meant weakened, but there was no give in them. I hurled my entire body this time, throwing every ounce of my remaining energy into breaking through.

I started convulsing. This time, I couldn't stop the air from leaving my lungs. Couldn't stop myself from inhaling—

Water flooded into my mouth and down my throat in a surging, relentless torrent. I was choking on it, gasping and clawing for breath that wouldn't come.

Drowning. I was drowning.

But I'm not ready to die—

I was further away from the bars now. Drifting in the faint current, my body weightless and curiously untethered. For a moment, I could see myself as if from the perspective of an outsider: my black hair floating behind me like a halo, my eyes open but unseeing, my lips blue and parted, letting more water in. But there was no pain. No fear.

And then I felt it.

That familiar, inexplicable *pull*.

The same pull that allowed me to shoot arrows with uncanny accuracy or pick the correct card out of dozens of identical options. Just as I had all those years ago at the circus.

As my vision blurred, a memory of the Sorceress's card formed before my eyes. The red and gold outline, the elegant lettering—

The way she had winked at me.

It was that version of the Sorceress I trusted. Not the cold and unfeeling statue in the Temple that had never answered my prayers, but the woman I had seen on that card, with her beguiling, impish smile—

The water warmed against my skin, glowing with an aquamarine light that enveloped me like an embrace.

Bright, so bright. *Blinding—*

And then it faded.

And I was staring up at the sun.

CHAPTER THIRTY-THREE

Mira

I turned my head, feeling the soft brush of flowers against my cheek. It was only as I looked to the side that I recognised where I was: in the golden meadow surrounding the shifters' temple.

Only this temple was no ruin.

I moved forward slowly, reluctant to disturb the serenity that clung to this place. The sun shone down overhead, and I glanced up to see that the circular roof was open to the elements.

All the pillars were intact and unblemished, painstakingly decorated with beautiful carvings. The marble floor was cool beneath my bare feet as I approached, taking in the designs: all different, and yet all related to nature. Carvings of vines were most prominent, running down the sides of all the pillars, but my eyes skimmed over images of clouds and forests, blazing fires and endless oceans.

When I reached the first pillar, I placed my hand against the ancient stone. Though it should have been impossible, I could have sworn I felt it shudder at my touch. As if in recognition.

Movement in my peripheral vision made me turn—

It was as though the Sorceress had stepped right out of my imagination and into being. Her hair and eyes were the ebony of a moonless night, and her olive skin glowed as if she had consumed the sun.

'I was hoping it would be you.' The hint of a smile upturned Selussa's ruby lips. 'It's a pleasure to meet you, Mira. I have been waiting a long time for this moment.'

'If that's true, why haven't you appeared to me before now?' *Was it because you found me unworthy?*

'No, Mira,' she said, and I flinched with the realisation that she could read my thoughts. 'I couldn't be prouder of you. You've endured so much, and still you continue to fight for Kalure.'

Her gaze was steady on mine, filled with an acceptance that lifted a weight from my chest. Tears welled in my eyes, but I held them back with an effort of will.

'But *you* haven't fought for Kalure.' Part of me couldn't believe the words that had left my mouth. My ancestor, a virtual goddess, was standing before me – and yet I couldn't seem to hold back my rising resentment.

The Sorceress didn't seem offended by my accusation. She didn't even seem surprised. 'Even immortals can be defeated,' she told me. 'My body was trapped and hidden by one of Fennec's worshippers. Without it, there is little my spirit can do but watch this country suffer.' A deep sadness emanated from her. 'You know the responsibility that comes with being queen. The weight of all the lives depending on you. Imagine what it is like to feel the weight of that responsibility for over a century, all the while being unable to protect your people.'

What she described . . . I couldn't fathom the depths of that feeling. That *torture*.

'Please forgive me.' I dropped to my knees in the centre of the Temple. 'I didn't mean—'

'You meant it.' Selussa tipped my chin gently upwards. 'But there is nothing to forgive. The question was a fair one. Besides, I already knew to expect boldness from you.'

I smiled at what was clearly a compliment. Selussa's pale blue dress rippled like water as she helped me stand, and I realised it was the same colour as the aquamarine light I had glimpsed earlier. The same aquamarine light that surrounded the temple like a haze, obscuring my view of whatever existed beyond it.

'We're not really here.' Selussa followed the direction of my gaze. When she looked at me, her expression was serious. 'And you cannot stay for long without your body failing. When you return, you will need to take this back with you.' She opened her palm to reveal my locket. It hummed with power.

I took it from her and slowly turned it over in my hands. 'What did you do to it?'

'I imbued it with some of my healing magic. In time, it will help overcome the damage that blood magic has done to you.'

'Damage?'

Selussa considered me. Despite her youthful appearance, I knew she was much older than she appeared, and much more cunning. 'You have the natural ability to sense and connect with the world around you,' she told me. 'It's a precious gift that could turn the entire tide of this war. If you can connect with the Wilds, you could harness the power of nature itself.'

The intuition I had felt. That sense of connection . . .

'But blood magic is a perversion of nature,' she continued. 'I was born with great magical power. My blood, however, was entirely ordinary until Fennec cursed me with eternal life. Once Fennec took away my mortality, my blood ran black with power – but it is a twisted power that comes with consequences. If anyone else consumes it, they are cursed as I am cursed.'

Eternal life. Eternal damnation.

I wondered whether she had ever offered anyone that choice. And whether anyone had accepted the price.

'Someone did,' Selussa murmured, and I realised she had read my thoughts again.

'Who?'

'Do you really need to ask, Mira?'

'No.' I shook my head, sending my hair fluttering around me. 'It's not possible.'

'Didn't you ever wonder how Velanthe knew so much about me? Why she appears so youthful?'

'You lived over a century ago—'

'And Velanthe ingested enough of my blood to become equally long-lived. She has been chasing the shadow of that power ever since, which is why she created the Temple – to instruct the descendants of the Sorceress on blood magic, in order to collect their blood and channel their power for her own ends.'

I didn't want to believe it. But then I thought of Velanthe's insistence on using blood magic, and the blood I had donated for various Temple services. Was it possible that she had been *using* it to—

Selussa cocked her head and closed her eyes, as if she was listening to something I couldn't hear. For a heartbeat, I fancied that I could hear a distant whisper on the breeze.

'We're running out of time,' she said, her musical voice grim. 'You have to return to your body now.'

'I need your blessing first,' I reminded her, careful to phrase my request as respectfully as possible. 'To become clan leader.'

'You have it,' Selussa said, fixing me with her dark eyes. 'But in return, I need your vow that you won't use blood magic again. No matter the provocation.'

I hesitated. 'I don't know if I can promise that. It might be the only way to win this war.'

'The way to win this war is by embracing your natural magic,' Selussa cautioned. 'Your heart and magic are still pure, but already your use of blood magic has taken you to the precipice. I can reverse some of the damage, but even one more use of blood magic could tip you over the edge.'

A shiver of foreboding darted down my spine. 'What would happen then?'

'Most likely,' Selussa said severely, 'you would lose control. If that happened, you could destroy everyone around you – and yourself. There's a reason your father and grandparents tried to ban blood magic, Mira. It's dangerous. You have no idea how dangerous.'

It was impossible to doubt her sincerity. It radiated from her – and anger stirred in me as I wondered why Velanthe hadn't warned me about the consequences.

'I promise,' I said to Selussa.

She considered me for a moment and then nodded her assent. 'Return to your body with my blessing and my love. But you must hurry back to the Temple, Mira, or you won't survive long enough to lead your army against Roran.'

Before I could ask what she meant, the Sorceress was gone – as was the meadow.

And its precious air.

*

I opened my eyes to darkness and steel bars.

The need for air still pressed urgently against my chest, but my mouth and lungs were no longer filled with water. A glance down at my locket showed it pulsing with that beautiful aquamarine light.

The Sorceress was still helping me – but for how long, I couldn't be sure.

I turned my attention to the bars. It would have been more helpful if the Sorceress had charmed my locket to help me break them down, but after hurling myself against them, it was clear she hadn't.

And the locket's light was already beginning to dull, my need for air growing increasingly insistent.

I cast my mind back over our conversation, recalling what the Sorceress had said about connecting with my natural magic.

I released my hold on the bars.

It went against every instinct I had to stop fighting and stand in the middle of the cage without doing anything at all.

But a strange certainty kept me in place. The same certainty that had served me well all my life.

Don't look with your eyes, I reminded myself.

I closed my eyes, embracing my surroundings completely. And as I did, my intuition seemed to expand, until I was one with the elements.

I was the fire blazing in the braziers set around a temple that pulsed with power. I was the clear azure sky and the faint breeze that ruffled the hair and clothes of the shifters on the cliff above. I was the ancient trees of the forest and the golden flowers beneath their feet.

And I was the water.

I was its coolness, its slight current, its peaceful expanse that sheltered schools of fish and a thousand other organisms. I felt its depth and its mass. And I felt its power.

It was that power I called to me to lift the cage. Slowly at first, so that the bars hovered a few inches above the sandy bottom of the sinkhole. Then higher and higher, until fish darted around me once more and the surface was visible.

Still the water answered my call, until I was buoyed up on its current. Light and weightless and—

Floating. That was what it felt like as the cage broke the surface and I inhaled beautiful, wonderful, life-saving *air*.

When I glanced down, I noticed dark blue tendrils extending from the lake. They reminded me of hands as they pushed the cage upwards, propelling it towards the cliff face and my watching audience.

The first thing I saw was Cassius's golden-blond hair. He was being restrained by two shifters with gold medallions around their necks, but they released him at the sight of me.

There was a thud as the cage hit the grassy ground, the wisps of water returning quickly and silently to the sinkhole where they belonged.

I slipped between the bars like a wraith. As insubstantial as water and air and fire.

The shifters fell to their knees before me, Conall and Sionnach amongst them. Even Cassius was staring at me with awe.

Elements cared nothing for worship, so neither did I. But when Cassius extended a hand, as if he might touch me—

'No,' I said sharply. 'Don't.'

He drew back slightly, and I saw myself reflected in his eyes – my skin a kaleidoscope of colour: blues, reds, greens. I ran a hand over my palm, where the scar from the priestess's ceremonial blade should have been. There was nothing but smooth skin.

Reborn. That was what Sionnach had promised, and that was how I felt. Physically – but also . . . there was a lightness to me now. An emotional weight that had been lifted from my heart.

No – not a weight. A darkness that I hadn't even known was there until it was gone.

My fingers curled around my locket, imbued with the Sorceress's healing powers. Gratitude rose within me – the gratitude I should have felt the moment I saw her, but that had been clouded by whatever darkness blood magic had brought out in me.

I walked between the shifters towards the temple. Understanding what I needed to do without fully understanding why.

I placed my hand against the first pillar, where the Sorceress had emerged. A deep shudder went through the earth, and suddenly the magic I had felt . . .

It coursed into and through me. Like a conduit.

I closed my eyes, visualising the temple as the Sorceress had shown it to me: complete and beautiful and untouched. I felt the transformation as it happened. Felt the pillars increasing in size, the earth shifting and hardening beneath my feet, the open circular roof forming overhead.

And as it transformed, I felt everything around me wake up. As if I hadn't just revived the temple—

But the entire Wilds.

CHAPTER THIRTY-FOUR

Scarlett

'Save him.'

The priestesses visibly bristled. My words hadn't been a request. They were an order.

But the high priestess didn't seem to mind. She studied Aric, who was laid out in front of the Sorceress's altar like an offering. He had worsened during our journey to the Wilds, and had lost consciousness when we arrived at the Temple.

'He shouldn't have pulled out the arrow,' the high priestess – Velanthe – said at last, standing.

'It's done now,' I retorted, 'so that no longer matters. What matters is saving his life. Can you do that, or has Odessa overstated the abilities of your healers?'

'There will be no healers involved,' Velanthe said, her dark eyes capturing mine. 'It will take my particular skills to save your friend. That is, unless you would like to resurrect him and bind him to you. He would be easier to control if you did.'

I blinked at her. 'Pardon?'

'The bond cuts both ways. If you decided to, you could use it to control his sister – even more fully than a blood ruby would allow you to. No doubt the brother would prove more useful.'

Velanthe sounded like she had seriously considered this. But though her voice was measured, I could sense the test in her words. She was trying to determine whether I was a threat to her queen.

I tried to conceal my unease. How could Velanthe know so much about my powers?

'I can't resurrect Aric without releasing Lillian from our bond,' I said tightly, when it became clear that Velanthe was waiting for a response. 'And I have no intention of letting her die. Aric would never forgive me if I did.'

'You could force him to forgive you,' Velanthe said, no inflection in her voice. She tilted her head as she studied me, her auburn hair gleaming darkly in the firelight. 'But I suppose that's beside the point. You've made your choice – now it's time for me to make *mine*.'

And there it was. The price that I had been expecting.

'What do you want?' I asked, mentally cursing Odessa. She had made it sound so simple – that Velanthe would help without giving a thought to her own agenda. But no one was that altruistic. Especially not a high priestess.

'I want to know what you promised Roran in exchange for your life.'

Decades of practice kept my face expressionless. 'I convinced Roran that I could be useful to him. Then I seized my chance and escaped.'

'That's not the full truth,' Velanthe said, watching me closely. Like Zandri, I had the sense that her black eyes saw more than I wanted them to. 'I won't accept anything less than the entire truth in exchange for Aric's life.'

'And you would trust me to give it to you?' I asked, though I already knew the answer. Only a fool would trust their enemy to be completely honest with them – and Velanthe didn't strike me as a fool.

Sure enough, Velanthe smiled. Her smile transformed her face – she had to be older than Zandri, since I knew she had once tutored my mother in blood magic, but somehow she looked years younger. Her skin was smooth and unblemished, and everything about her radiated health and vitality.

'I'm afraid not,' she said in response. 'But I have a way of ensuring your honesty – and mine.'

I glanced down at her extended arm. Perhaps Velanthe *was* a fool, after all – or perhaps she didn't realise that my death magic spread through touch. I was careful not to react as I grasped her arm with my hand.

But rather than death magic, something else surged between us – an unfamiliar, alien power.

Velanthe's power, I realised as red tendrils encircled our arms. The moment those tendrils touched my skin, they sank in enough to draw blood. Just as Zandri had done to Mira during the third Trial.

'Lying,' Velanthe warned, 'is now a death sentence. For either of us.'

'What happens if we do?' I asked, staring down at the dripping blood with morbid fascination.

'We would bleed out in seconds. And before you think of using your death magic,' Velanthe said, drawing my attention back to her face, 'let me warn you that I taught your mother everything she knows. I have enough power to suppress your magic, Scarlett, which means you would die before you could kill me.'

'That's not possible,' I said, ignoring the way the red tendrils tightened – as if in wordless threat. It was painful, but the high priestess didn't react, and neither did I. 'I'm a descendant of the Sorceress; that's where my power comes from. But you—'

'I am a student of the Sorceress,' Velanthe replied, her voice level. 'I have studied everything she has ever written. Even those texts I haven't shown Kasmira or my own priestesses. I might not have magic of my own, but I can channel it from other sources. And your blood has enough power to sustain this for days.'

I narrowed my eyes as I stared into Velanthe's dark ones. 'Ask your questions, then,' I said, raising my chin. 'But for every question you ask, I will ask one of my own.'

Velanthe inclined her head. 'That seems fair.' A smile twitched on her lips. 'Aside from blood magic, what other magic do you possess?'

'Illusion,' I said promptly.

The high priestess tilted her head. 'Interesting.'

'What's interesting about it?'

'Magic says a great deal about the wielder, and is often influenced by our formative years. Illusion suggests that you became adept at changing to fit your surroundings. I imagine it was difficult, growing up in the Ravalian Court.'

I didn't dignify that with a response. 'And what does your power say about *you*?'

'I don't have power of my own,' Velanthe reminded me. 'I can only channel – a gift from the god I serve.'

'God?' I asked warily. 'Don't you mean goddess?'

Velanthe smiled. 'I mean exactly what I said.' She paused. 'Do you love this boy?'

Did I love Aric? I certainly cared about him – more than I should. But—

'No.' I hesitated, considering my next question. I settled on, 'Tell me more about channelling – and the limits of it.'

Not strictly phrased as a question, but Velanthe answered anyway. 'Energy exists all around us. If I touched the trunk of a tree, I could channel that energy as I wished, but if I used it up then the tree would die. The same principle applies to humans. However, *some* humans, like descendants of the Sorceress, possess much greater power reserves. Even a small amount of your blood can be channelled to great effect.'

'And a *god* gave you this power? In exchange for what?'

'I believe it's my turn,' Velanthe said, fixing me with her black eyes – as black as my mother's. As black as mine, after I invited death magic into my body.

And a suspicion began to take root.

Velanthe's smile widened as she watched me riddle it out. 'What did you promise Roran in exchange for your life?'

This was the question that would determine my fate. Either my answer would result in Velanthe trying to kill me – or it would result in her saving Aric. Either way, it was a leap of faith.

Not that I had much of a choice. Even now, I felt the bonds of Velanthe's magic tightening, blood dripping down my wrists.

'My life – in exchange for Mira's.'

The silence between us held. I couldn't tell what Velanthe was thinking – her face was utterly expressionless. But she hadn't tried to end our connection and murder me, so I supposed that was a good sign.

She waited expectantly for me to ask my question. I sensed that it would be my last.

'Are you Zandri's Mask?'

The bindings tightened around Velanthe's wrists. She didn't so much as glance down at them as blood welled, vivid against her white skin.

'Yes,' she said, and severed the connection.

I stumbled back from her, rubbing my bloody arms. Already the cuts were beginning to heal – at a significantly faster rate than should be natural. I felt a wave of dizziness.

'You killed King Arioch,' I said, as Velanthe knelt at Aric's side.

'I did,' she agreed without looking at me. 'I would have done it even if Zandri hadn't ordered it. Arioch abhorred blood magic – and as you have probably guessed by now, blood magic is what I and my senior priestesses truly value. We have a symbiotic relationship with the descendants of the Sorceress – they believe they need us to learn their magic, and we need their blood in order to connect with our god. I discovered that by accident, when the Sorceress was still alive.'

'You knew the Sorceress?' It seemed ludicrous. The last reported sighting had been over a century ago; even my mother had spoken of the Sorceress more as a legend than a real person.

'I was her first acolyte.' Velanthe's eyes were distant, even as she rested a hand – red with my blood – on Aric's wound. My dizziness increased as his skin stitched itself back together, and I swayed on my feet. 'Her name was Selussa. I believed in her once, but that was before Fennec revealed himself to me, and I learnt of the way she had betrayed him.' Her eyes cut to mine. 'Did you know that Fennec was once the patron god of Kalure? That shifters were once worshipped throughout these lands as his divine children?'

'No,' I said stiffly. 'I didn't.'

Velanthe waved a dismissive hand. 'I suppose that's understand-able, since the temples to the old gods were torn down so long ago. Casualties of the Sorceress's vengeance.'

I had heard the Sorceress's story before, but never quite like this. Usually Fennec was the villain in that tale.

'I don't expect you to understand. No doubt your religious educa-tion was severely lacking, considering Emperor Kalias's determination to silence anyone who believed in a power greater than his own. But if you could have experienced what I have, if you could have felt Fennec's presence and bathed in the purity of his love . . .' She closed her eyes as if remembering. 'The first time I ingested Selussa's blood, I had access to the world of the divine for a month. I've never experi-enced such a potent connection before or since.'

I crossed my arms protectively across my chest, wishing that Zandri had warned me about the Temple. My eyes darted to the ceremonial dagger lying in front of the dais and back to Velanthe.

'What happened to her? The Sorceress?'

'What do you think?' Velanthe's smile was positively ghoulish as she finally looked at me. 'I killed her.'

I took a startled step back, wondering if Velanthe was imagining cutting me open even now. Imagining what powers and divine access my blood might grant her – however temporarily.

Velanthe laughed softly at my reaction. 'I quickly realised that killing Selussa was a mistake – though Fennec was certainly pleased. Besides, a being granted eternal existence cannot die completely. I dispensed with her body, but her spirit remains.'

I followed Velanthe's gaze to the life-sized statue. I wasn't sure which was harder to believe – that Velanthe was old enough to have known the Sorceress, or that the Sorceress's spirit somehow still existed. But even as I had the thought, I realised that I did believe it. I could *sense* it – could sense *her*. Selussa.

I stared into the cold, unfeeling features of the statue. It looked lifeless, but surely it was the source of the energy I felt. Where else would it be coming from?

I glanced sideways at Velanthe, wondering if she could feel it too. But I suspected my affinity with death gave me the ability to sense what even the high priestess couldn't.

'The blood only works when it's fresh, and it's best when it's willingly given,' Velanthe continued, as if all of this was perfectly reasonable. 'Your mother used to provide some after Temple services – just a thimbleful here and there to allow us to communicate with Fennec and channel the power within her blood. We're not monsters.'

I wasn't convinced, but I was careful not to react. 'And Mira? What are your plans for her?'

'Your mother didn't tell you?' The high priestess sighed. 'Of course she didn't. Kasmira was supposed to unite the clans and the Temple, helping us to finally dispense with Roran. After that . . .' Velanthe shrugged. 'Well, Zandri never had any intention of leaving her alive.'

I remembered Zandri telling me that she had a plan to deal with Mira – and the Temple. It seemed that Velanthe knew about the first part of that plan, but hopefully not about the second.

Otherwise this visit could take a very unpleasant turn.

'Obviously, your deal with Roran changes things,' Velanthe continued, those eerie dark eyes still fixed on my face. 'My understanding with your mother extends to you – so it's better that Kasmira is dealt with sooner rather than later.'

'We made an alliance—'

'Yes, Jadis told me about that. Unfortunately, it's likely that Mira now knows the truth about the Temple, which means I can't let her return alive.'

Despite myself, I felt a flicker of pity for Mira. She really was nothing to Velanthe – and I knew the sting of betrayal well.

'Do you have an approach in mind?' I asked, keeping my voice level. If Velanthe was anything like my mother, she would already have put a contingency plan in motion.

'Her blood allows her to influence others – a dangerous gift, but like your own, it comes with a considerable cost to the wielder. If Kasmira attempts to use blood magic on a group of people all at once – as I instructed her to do with the Council of Ancients – there's every likelihood that it will destroy her.'

A shiver darted down my spine. Not just at the implications for Mira – but at the implications for *me*.

'There's no need for you to worry,' Velanthe said, correctly guessing my thoughts. 'Training you is part of the deal I made with your mother; once this war is done, I will teach you how to use your abilities safely, in a way that maximises their potential.'

I thought of what Velanthe had done to Mira, and I felt sick at the thought – and the realisation that Zandri hadn't even bothered to mention this to me. Doubts crept in, dark and insidious. I wanted to believe that my mother had no intention of handing me over to Velanthe, but I knew how much she valued power. I could only imagine what I would become under their combined tutelage.

'He will wake up soon,' Velanthe said, her fingers lingering on

Aric's pulse. When she turned to face me, her hand was extended. 'Give me his blood ruby.'

'No.' My hand dropped protectively to the ruby in my pocket. 'It stays with me.'

I sensed the priestesses before I saw them. I tried to reach for my death magic, but all that rose up was a kind of icy dizziness.

'Don't be stubborn, Scarlett,' Velanthe said serenely as I struggled against the four priestesses. Fury burned inside me, but my limbs were slow and non-responsive, and I felt so faint that it was suddenly difficult to remain standing. 'We all want the same thing.'

A priestess handed the blood ruby to Velanthe, who took it, her dark eyes glittering.

'What are you doing to me?' I tried to raise my voice, but it came out as little more than a sigh.

'You will be perfectly fine,' Velanthe said, with a cursory glance. 'I'm simply slowing your blood to make you more docile. It won't cause you any permanent harm.'

Her matter-of-fact tone chilled me – as did the scope of her powers. But I was more concerned with Aric as he stood, his eyes wholly black – as black as the blood ruby pulsing in Velanthe's palm.

'Release him,' I ordered, wrenching my arms free of the priestesses' grip.

'I can't do that, Scarlett. There's a possibility Kasmira will survive the Council of Ancients, but I doubt she will survive against *him*.' Velanthe murmured something to Aric, too low for me to hear. 'It's practically poetic. What better way to kill Kasmira than by using the person she loves against her? He's the perfect tool to ensure her demise.' She smiled at him, almost affectionately.

I took a step towards Velanthe, summoning every shred of energy I had left. 'If you do this, I will destroy you—'

'No,' Velanthe said softly. 'You won't.'

And then I was falling. Velanthe caught me before I hit the stone floor, lowering me to the ground. I tried to pull away but I couldn't move. I had never felt so cold before – or so utterly powerless.

The high priestess cradled me like a child, but her eyes didn't remain on my face for long. They dropped to my arms – to the blood staining my white skin. The hunger in her eyes stole my breath.

'No,' I breathed, and I hated that I was *pleading* with her.

The other priestesses closed in with sly smiles. Their beautiful, youthful features melted away to reveal glowing yellow eyes and sharp, pointed teeth. Not human at all, but—

Shifters.

I jerked back from them, imagining their daggers carving into my body and their teeth biting into my flesh. Killing me outright was one thing. But *this* – this was a fate worse than death.

'Shh,' Velanthe crooned, and the moment she touched my skin, my muscles went limp and boneless.

'I thought—' It was a struggle to form words. Even to *think*. 'I thought you said the blood must be given willingly—'

'It's more powerful that way,' Velanthe murmured, stroking my hair with sharp fingernails – wickedly sharp, and curved. *Like talons.* 'But this isn't about your blood. We'll harvest what we can now, and when you're dead, I will use it to resurrect you – ensuring that you're bonded to me. Consider it my insurance against Zandri.'

Horror gripped my stuttering heart. If she did that, I would never be free. I would be tied to Velanthe until she died. And she would be able to control me utterly, shaping me in her image—

For the first time, I was jealous of Aella and Severin. Jealous of the freedom they had found in death.

Because there would be none for me. Blood and power and control. That was all there was and all there ever would be.

Except that hadn't been entirely true. I thought of the companionship I had found with Aric and Lillian. Then I thought of the symmetry I had once noticed between myself and Mira, when we had first met in the Ravalian Court. The way we had both clawed to shape our own destinies against all the odds.

What would have happened, I wondered, if I hadn't betrayed her? If I had chosen to trust her instead?

I felt a brief spasm of regret at the thought.

What sorry fools we are, I thought as I watched Aric leave, off to hunt down the woman he still loved. The cousin I had never really had the chance to know. *What sorry, sorry fools.*

My eyes fluttered shut as the first dagger bit into my skin, but instead of pain, I felt a tiny flicker of surprise.

I had never imagined that Mira would be my final thought.

CHAPTER THIRTY-FIVE

Mira

We rode all through the night.

Cassius didn't question my breakneck pace, though I knew he placed less weight on the Sorceress's warning.

Despite my tiredness, and my screaming muscles, I wasn't taking any chances. Selussa had said that my survival depended on reaching the Temple quickly – and now that I was officially clan leader, I refused to risk victory slipping out of my grasp. With the Council of Ancients also having pledged their support, and that of all the shifters who answered to them, we finally had a real shot at defeating Roran.

When dawn began to lighten the horizon, Cassius and I dismounted to set up a makeshift camp – little more than a brief rest stop before we continued, allowing us to make use of the dried meat and apples the shifters had included in our saddlebags.

We ate in companionable silence as the forest seemed to wake up around us, filling with the trilling sounds of distant birds. Once I finished, I picked up my sword and ran through a series of practice movements until my arms were as tired as my legs, conscious of Cassius's gaze on me the entire time.

Neither of us had spoken about the night before my ritual, or how far our intimacy had almost gone. It was easier that way. Easier to pretend it hadn't happened – even if I couldn't seem to stop thinking about it. About *him*.

'What made you want to become a Warrior?' A seemingly idle question, but I could hear the curiosity in his voice.

I stepped to the side and executed a particularly fluid strike before parrying, imagining that I was blocking an invisible sword. 'I liked the idea of dedicating my life to a worthy cause. When the Warriors visited Aldara, they seemed so strong and fierce – untouchable. And I believed in their supposed values of honour and integrity. I thought that if I joined them, I could protect the people who needed it.'

Dark blue eyes slid to mine. 'Like you and your mother.'

I nodded. Cassius already knew about my transient upbringing – had asked me about the places I had travelled to, the various roles I'd embodied. I had the sense that he was fascinated by how different my experiences were to his upbringing in the Ravalian Court.

'And now you're a ruler,' he said after a contemplative pause. 'It seems you got your wish after all.'

I hadn't thought about it like that, but he was right. As queen, I could make a real difference. What worthier cause was there than dedicating my life to a country? To serving and improving the lives of an entire population?

'You mentioned that you wanted your father's throne for the wrong reasons,' I ventured, setting down my sword. It was a dangerous topic, and I almost stopped right there. But I pressed on. 'Do you still want to rule the Ravalian Empire?'

Cassius looked as though he was seriously considering the question. 'I love my country,' he said at last. 'I think it could become spectacular, under the right leadership. Look at the theatres we have in the capital, the craftsmen and artists. If we were to stop focusing on conquering and expanding and instead turn our attention inwards, Ravalia could be a golden example of a properous and enlightened country.'

I blinked at him. It felt almost as if I was seeing Cassius for the first time, and I realised that I had been wrong. It wasn't a matter of which version of him was real – the nonchalant prince who delighted in luxurious parties and sensation, or the more serious strategist I had come to know over the past few weeks. They were both part of him – two halves of the whole.

The soft grass brushed my skin as I rejoined Cassius in the middle of the meadow. 'The parties you threw, the dancers and artists . . . I thought it was just for show. For indulgence.'

A faint smile. 'I told you, Mira: in the Ravalian Court, you can't reveal what you truly care about. Far better for my family to think of me as a spoilt prince, spending their coin for my own entertainment. Not that it was all an act, exactly. Being a second son comes with a certain amount of freedom; it seemed a shame not to take advantage.'

'Of course it did,' I said dryly.

Cassius took hold of my arms and drew me back against his chest, just like he had that night in the tree house. I stiffened; there was something far more intimate about him holding me like this in the daylight. I knew I should pull away, but—

'You know,' he murmured against my ear, 'the Ravalian Court isn't as terrible as you think it is. The courtiers are like sheep; they follow the lead of whoever sits on the throne. My father empowered the generals and focused his attention on conquest, so the court had a high tolerance for bloodshed. My mother, meanwhile, elevated her own position through entertaining her favourite ladies and unleashing her petty brand of vindictiveness on the others. Between my parents, the court was both cruel and self-indulgent.'

I considered that in silence. Wondering whether some of the courtiers had a greater depth and kindness to them that might emerge under the right leadership.

Then I realised what I was thinking. I turned to confront Cassius. 'I hope this isn't your way of trying to convince me to restore you to the Ravalian throne.'

He held up his hands in a gesture of innocence. 'I would never presume such a thing.'

I suspected he would presume a great deal, where power was concerned. Rising to my feet, I studied Cassius. He leant back on his forearms, stretching out in a languid pose that masked that dangerous, calculating mind of his. His face was the epitome of handsome carelessness.

My eyes narrowed. How *guilty* I had felt about sneaking out the morning of the ritual – but I had been right to do it, just as I was right not to take him at face value now. Despite his supposed acquiescence, he had still tried to dive in after me. He was quite capable of promising one thing and doing another.

Cassius was watching me closely. 'I've been trying to do things differently. To prove myself to *you*.'

'And yet,' I retorted, 'you went against my wishes during the ritual. I saw the way the shifters had you restrained.' A hint of incredulous anger entered my voice. 'What were you *thinking*? The shifters could have killed you for trying to interfere.'

'I was thinking that you were dying.' Cassius's gaze, usually unreadable, was filled with searing heat. He stood and closed the distance between us in three easy strides. 'I'm more selfish than you are, Mira,' he said ruthlessly, pinning me between his body and the tree at my back. 'I would rather watch the world burn than watch you sacrifice yourself to save it.'

For a moment, I could only stare at him. My breathing quickened, but it was no longer from anger.

Cassius's eyes dropped to my lips, and I was suddenly very conscious of how close we were. But he looked away from me with an exasperated exhale, raking a hand through his golden-blond hair.

'Sometimes, Mira,' he said, 'I don't think you value your own life. But *I* value it. And I won't apologise for putting you first.' Without another word, he stalked past me into the forest.

I sagged back against the tree. Was Cassius right? Was I still punishing myself for everything I had done back in the Ravalian Court, and devaluing my own life as a result?

After ten minutes passed and Cassius didn't return, I picked up a waterskin and retreated deeper into the forest.

It was quieter here, and the sighing of the wind in the trees was peaceful. Grounding. Perhaps practising my natural magic would calm my mind further. Perhaps then I would be able to set aside Cassius's accusations.

I sat cross-legged on the mossy ground and closed my eyes. Almost immediately, I felt more attuned to my surroundings. To my surprise, I could sense the life around me: the insects on the forest floor, the birds in the trees, even a few larger mammals that I had no name for.

Time became meaningless as my awareness widened, stretching outwards until I seemed to leave my body behind. I was so much a part of everything around me that I—

A faint splash jerked me out of my trancelike state. I sat up suddenly, my body humming with irritation.

I wandered towards the sound, parting the branches in front of me until I saw a lake glistening amongst the trees. In the faint early morning light it was particularly striking, a clear sky blue that reminded me of the Sorceress's magic.

I noticed Cassius about the same time he noticed me. His gaze locked with mine as he resurfaced, water dripping invitingly down his face and onto the chiselled planes of his bare chest.

'You're welcome to join me, Mira.'

It was an invitation I would be reckless to accept. But Cassius's smile was full of the same knowing amusement as the night of the coupling dance, and I realised that he didn't think I was going to do it.

That made the decision for me.

Taking satisfaction in the flicker of surprise that crossed his face, I discarded my weapons on the bank. Then I slowly stripped out of my clothes, never shifting my gaze from his.

Cassius's intent stare heated my blood. I felt intensely vulnerable as it raked over my naked skin.

Whatever he might have seen of my body previously, this was different. An intense, considered appraisal that made me feel as if he was exploring every inch of me with his eyes, mapping out exactly where he would like to touch me – what he would like to do to me. With a start, I realised that I was imagining it too: the places his lips and hands might linger, the sensations he would stir to life—

Deliberately looking away from him, I dropped my filthy clothing to the ground. It had been almost two days since I last had the opportunity to bathe, and the lake did look dangerously inviting.

Especially with Cassius in it.

He continued watching me as I slipped into the cool water. I wasn't as tall as Cassius; the water came up to my collarbone, but at least I could rest my feet against the sandy bottom.

I swam a few lengths of the lake, trying to warm up and delighting in the feeling of gliding through the fresh water. On my next lap, I almost collided with Cassius, who had apparently grown bored of watching me swim. I narrowed my eyes as I stared up at him, but whatever irritation I'd felt earlier was gone, eclipsed by the knowledge of how close his body was to mine.

Cassius's eyes glittered down at me. 'I'm surprised you haven't developed an aversion to water.'

'Only to sinkholes.'

His laughter was unexpected and surprisingly genuine. And the appreciative way he looked at me . . . It made my chest constrict. My breath hitched as Cassius moved even closer, until there was only a few inches between our bodies. His fingers grazed my cheek as he smoothed my hair back from my face.

I fought back a shiver at even that simple touch.

'What do you want from me, Mira?' he asked softly.

This was my chance to hesitate; to walk away before I did something I couldn't come back from. Getting close to Cassius felt too much like tempting fate – like being drawn to a flame and expecting not to be burned.

But I was tired of playing it safe. Tired of fighting the attraction between us, even if it was ill-advised.

Even if it threatened to consume me whole.

'You know what I want,' I told him, and claimed his mouth. Hungry, demanding, devouring – my kiss was all of those things, and Cassius matched them tenfold. His hands tangled in my damp hair, wrapping it around his fist. Drawing my face up to his.

'Have you thought about my terms?'

My pulse picked up speed – perhaps from the way he was looking at me or the way he held me immobile in his grip. I had never thought that something so possessive could be so arousing.

But my voice hardened as I said, 'Your ultimatum, you mean.'

'"Ultimatum" is such a strong word. I like to think of it as an offer.' Before I could respond, Cassius lifted me smoothly out of the water and set me back on the bank, so that I was half reclining.

For an instant, I thought he was going to leave me there, furious and dripping, much like he had the other night. But the seductive promise in his smile said otherwise.

'So many options,' he said, those calculating blue eyes roaming over my exposed body. I'd thought I felt vulnerable before, but it was nothing compared to how I felt now. I moved to change my position, but Cassius stopped me. 'No, no,' he said, brushing his thumb over my lips. 'I want to see you. To admire you. You are . . .' A trace of hunger darkened his expression.

Yet his touch was surprisingly gentle as his hands traced the path his eyes had travelled a few moments before. I swallowed in anticipation as fingers ghosted over my breasts and then downwards, his touch so light that a high, needy sound left my mouth. I didn't have it in me to be embarrassed. Not as his mouth replaced his hands, fire licking at my skin just like he licked—

'Oh, Gods,' I breathed as his tongue flicked over my peaked nipple, sending a rush of heat straight to my core.

And his hand—

I flinched as it grazed the centre of me, tensing at the knowledge of how wet I was. Cassius made an approving sound low in his throat, his mouth still occupied worshipping my breasts.

His hand continued touching me, pleasuring me, but never quite—

I shifted, desperate to get the friction I craved. The gleam in Cassius's eyes was positively sinful.

'Don't hold back,' he told me – an order. 'I want to hear you.'

'I—' Whatever I was going to say was forgotten as he slid a finger inside me.

Cassius rewarded my moan by adding another finger, curling it in a way that robbed me of coherent thought. I pressed against him, instinct making my hips rock as he drew his fingers in and out of me, making the pleasure build until it was utterly *torturous*.

He was so good at this, knowing exactly where to touch me to drive me insane. Varying the pressure so that I was never entirely sure what to expect, never quite getting enough—

And then he stopped.

A sound close to a snarl left my mouth until I felt the hardness of him against me. I jerked my eyes up to meet his, and the intensity of his expression made me shiver – in anticipation or nerves, I didn't know. Probably both.

'Tell me you're mine, Mira,' he said, his lips brushing my ear. 'Because I'm yours. In all ways.'

Commit myself to him. That was what he was really asking – and beneath the sensual promise of his words, I knew there was a lethal edge I couldn't see yet. A blade waiting to be drawn.

I didn't care. His kiss was claiming, consuming, and I was beyond caring about the consequences – about whatever insidious agenda he might have. Let him demand a place at my side. Let him believe he could win power through me.

Let him believe anything if it meant he wouldn't stop kissing me, touching me, pressing his body against mine—

Light flared, and I glanced down to see strange elemental currents flowing through my body – just as they had after my ritual.

'Cassius,' I warned, but he was already reaching for me. Tracing those currents gently with his hands, studying them with eyes filled with reverence.

Beautiful. I could have sworn I saw the thought in his face. His face, which was completely absent of fear, even as the kaleidoscope of light flared beneath his fingers. Coming alive at his touch.

His lips curved, revelling in the way my body and magic responded to him. But when he looked at me, there was a challenge in his gaze. 'What now, Mira?'

Aching pleasure swept through me as he shifted his hips, making his point clear. *How far do you want to take this?*

Beyond the question, there was an intensity that was almost frightening. An unspoken promise that there would be no going back after this.

I placed my palm against the hard muscles of his chest. Something flared in his eyes – and I realised that he thought I was about to push him away. For a moment, I thought so too.

Then my hands were pressing against his back. Drawing him even closer, so that his face was poised over mine, and the lower half of his body—

I swallowed as I took in the large length of him, sudden apprehension battling with the heady pulse of my desire.

'Don't worry,' Cassius said, his dark eyes intent on mine. 'I'll be gentle. *This* time.'

He slid into me slowly, watching every bob of my throat, every flutter of my eyelids. A gasp left my lips at the sensation, but it wasn't a sound of pain. I was so ready for him, needing his fullness, needing the feeling of him moving in and out of me.

My nails raked down his back, making my demand clear. Cassius laughed, not concerned in the least about the blood trickling from the cuts. My gasp turned into a moan as he withdrew, then kissed my neck and filled me in a single thrust that had stars exploding before my eyes.

'Tell me,' Cassius said as he thrust into me again, each stroke slow and controlled until the pleasure was almost unbearable. Until I was desperate for him to move faster, harder, to stop being gentle and *ravish* me. 'Tell me what I want to hear, Mira. Tell me that you're mine, and I'll give you what you crave so badly.'

Even though he felt so good, even though my body was arching into his like a moth to a flame, I hesitated. 'I can't—'

'You can.' He punctured each thrust with his lips. Claiming my mouth, my jaw, my neck.

I could barely think – could barely remember the history between us. Brutal schemes and bad blood wrapped up in an attraction so intense that it was all tangled together. Impossible to unravel.

Instead, I thought of other things. The way he had dug graves alongside my people, how he had counselled me through ruling, the image of him fighting to reach me on that cliff face—

The sincerity in his words as he told me had been trying to do things differently. To prove himself to me.

'Yes,' I said, and my stomach lurched just as it had in that cage, when I had toppled into the water below. Looking into Cassius's dark blue eyes, I felt like I was falling all over again. 'Yes, I'm . . .'

A smile curved his lips as he stilled inside me. 'You're *what*, Mira?' he asked, stroking a strand of damp hair back from my face.

'I'm yours.' This time, my voice was steady. Filled with startling resolve.

Triumph lit his eyes. Without releasing my gaze, he ran his hand teasingly down my thighs – and then lifted them, so my legs were almost level with his shoulders.

And this time, he wasn't gentle.

My head fell back and my moans rent the air as he buried himself in me, hitting a place so deep that it threatened to fracture my already tenuous control. Again and again, until I was delirious with the relentless pleasure, until I was shaking with it, until my thoughts and worries were torn away in a tidal wave of bliss—

Until I knew nothing but him.

CHAPTER THIRTY-SIX

Mira

The days passed in a pleasant blur, filled with travel and conversation. And the nights . . .

My face heated at the thought of how he took me in the darkness, sometimes gentle and slow, other times faster and rougher, but always stoking my passion to new heights. It was a little embarrassing how much I desired him. How much I *craved* him.

I'd hoped that it would be the opposite – that after our coupling he would have lost whatever hold he had over me. Instead, I couldn't seem to get enough. Was that normal?

I glanced across the clearing, where Cassius was preparing a rabbit he had snared, heedless of the mess staining his fingers. Even *that* was attractive to me. Without Warriors to delegate to, it was clear just how capable he really was.

Striding deeper into the forest, I tried to focus on collecting fire-wood. But my attention soon began to drift back to Cassius.

The emotional distance I'd been waiting for . . . it hadn't come. And now I was growing used to sharing a bedroll with him, trusting him enough to drift off to sleep in his strong arms. It might even be my favourite part of our newfound closeness – and that was downright terrifying.

Because physical intimacy was one thing. But growing attached to his presence, needing him close in other ways . . . That meant I was starting to care. Starting to truly mean the words I had said to him in that lake.

I'm yours.

Easy to say in the moment, but I hadn't expected it to feel like this. Hadn't expected the softer, more attentive side to Cassius – the way he seemed willing to open up to me, sharing not just his body, but also precious insights about his past. Insights that made me feel as though he really could lay a claim to me.

When I returned from collecting firewood, I found Cassius throwing knives at a tree across the clearing – a skill that Jadis had taught him when we'd first travelled into the Wilds. Jadis's throws had been perfect, hitting the trunk dead centre. Cassius's were far less precise, but there was a faint smile on his face all the same.

I started to smile too, until I heard the thunderous sound of hoofbeats. I barely had the chance to turn before a hulking black stallion burst through the trees, its rider's sword flashing down towards me.

Dropping the bundle of firewood, I rolled, only just avoiding the sword and the horse's trampling hooves. Cassius sprinted across the clearing, his sword drawn, but he was too far away to help me.

The stallion turned and charged.

I ran for my life, cursing my decision to discard my sword by the fire. I could hear Cassius shouting, but I blocked him out, focusing on the stallion galloping after me. Its grunting breaths told me that it was gaining, but I didn't dare look over my shoulder – and I didn't try to run to Cassius, knowing that I would never make it in time. My best chance of survival was to get out of the open.

I fought to calm my mind. To expand my awareness, until I was one with the forest around me.

The tree line was close – *torturously* close – when the stallion caught up to me. The rider's sword arced through the air, but just as he was about to strike, vines wrapped around the horse's hindquarters.

Horse and rider fell heavily to the ground with a thud that shook the nearby branches.

The swordsman rose to his feet almost immediately, picking up his discarded sword as he advanced on me with murder in his face. As he stepped out of the shadows, recognition speared through me, followed closely by horror.

No, no—

My hold over the vines shattered. I stared into his face, drinking it in like someone dying of thirst. His features were the same: his golden-brown skin, the determined slant of his mouth, the dark brows and hair. But his eyes . . .

There was something wrong with his eyes. They had never been this dark, and certainly never this furious, filled with rage and bloodlust—

'What is this, Aric?' I demanded, but he didn't answer. Merely lunged at me with his sword, and while the motion was beautiful and familiar in its elegance, *this* was something the Aric I'd known never would have done. Raising a sword against an unarmed opponent went against everything he believed in. Everything he had ever taught me.

I dodged as best I could, reminded of the times we had sparred together in Aldara. He had taught me to dodge then too – taught me much like this, by swinging at me. But that had been a lesson.

This wasn't.

Without a weapon, without the focus needed to summon my natural magic, I was no match for him. All I could do was keep backing away, hoping that my speed and reflexes might keep me alive for a few more moments.

'Don't you want to discard your blade?' I shouted at him as I stumbled backwards. 'Make this a fair fight?'

Aric didn't answer, his sword swinging towards me with a speed and force that I wouldn't be able to evade. I wanted to close my eyes, desperate to block out the sight of the hatred twisting his face. But I couldn't look away from him as I waited for the blow to—

A bloody gash erupted as a silver knife sliced into his unprotected face. Aric whirled to face Cassius, who stood calmly with his sword drawn, his stance filled with challenge.

Despite Cassius's height and steeliness, Aric's burlier build gave him a clear advantage. Yet as I looked between them, I was reminded of a Kalurian axe against a Ravalian dagger. Both deadly in their own ways.

And if they fought each other . . . only one would be left alive.

I closed my eyes, but this time I wasn't focusing on the forest. I was focusing on the gentle breeze swirling around me, willing it to strengthen until it was no longer a breeze but more of a gale, whipping my hair into a frenzy as I stood in the centre of its vortex.

Aric was running towards Cassius now, charging with his sword extended—

I raised my hands and redirected the gale. Unleashing the full force of it on Aric's distant form—

Sending him careening into a nearby tree with a sickening thud. The magic slipped out of my grip.

'*Aric!*'

I ran to his side, panic pounding at my skull. His skin was pale as his chest rose and fell—

Then stopped altogether. Along with his laboured breathing.

I took hold of his shoulders and shook him. He didn't move.

'Gods no . . .' Tears dripped down my face and onto his. I was furious with him – for abandoning me, for blaming me, for whatever *this* was – but I didn't want him to die. The thought of him dying was more than I could handle. 'Wake up, Aric! You have to wake up!' I pounded on his chest, but nothing happened.

Then I remembered what Sionnach had done when a wounded shifter had stopped breathing.

Pinching Aric's nose, I tilted his head back and pressed my lips against his, blowing air into his mouth.

Not enough. It's not enough on its own—

I pounded on his chest, but this time it was a rhythmic motion, pumping his heart with the heels of my hand.

He sucked in a gasping, heaving breath—

I held him close as he leant on his side and coughed. When he looked up at me, his words were almost unintelligible. 'Kill me, Mira,' he rasped. 'You have to kill me.'

I stumbled back, but he was already rising to his feet, blocking my defensive movement towards his sword. The fury in his eyes was almost as terrifying as the realisation that they were entirely black.

I knew I was right then. Knew that this wasn't him.

Relief and terror surged within me, because if he didn't really want to hurt me . . .

'You have to fight this,' I begged him. 'You're being controlled—'

Aric's only response was to reach for my throat. A whimper escaped my lips as his hand wrapped around my windpipe and squeezed.

I clawed at his hand, my teeth gritted with the effort of holding him off. My eyes darted past Aric – to the figure coming up behind him.

Aric didn't notice. He was so full of rage that his entire attention was on me, with no hope of defending himself against Cassius's blade.

My eyes locked with Cassius's midnight-blue ones. I couldn't talk, couldn't say a word, but I begged him just the same.

Don't kill him.

Please.

Cassius's jaw clenched as he raised his sword, and I braced myself for it to slice through Aric's neck.

At the last moment, Cassius shifted his grip on the sword – and hit Aric over the head with the diamond-studded pommel.

Aric collapsed face-first into the dirt.

I sucked in one painful breath. Then another. My knees buckled, and I would have joined Aric in the dirt if Cassius hadn't taken hold of my shoulders. His eyes were murderous as they lingered on the bruises ringing my throat.

'He was going to kill me,' I whispered, staring down at the unconscious body of the young man who had been my best friend and my first love. 'He was really going to kill me.'

Cassius could have driven the point home, but he didn't. He merely held me close and let me break.

CHAPTER THIRTY-SEVEN

Scarlett

I dreamt of ice.

At first, all I could see was white. Then, as the snow seemed to clear, I saw someone else.

The young woman was dressed in cream-coloured furs, so light that she almost blended into the scene around her. But her dark hair was vivid against all the white, cascading down her back. And there was something oddly familiar about the way she knelt in the middle of a frozen lake, staring down into the eerie blue ice.

An overwhelming curiosity drew me closer, but something held me back. Something a whole lot like fear.

And yet, if this was *my* dream, what was there to fear?

Slowly, the woman began to turn—

Black eyes met mine. They bored into my face with surprising intensity.

I tried to back away, unnerved for a reason I couldn't put into words, but my legs were heavy and leaden.

The young woman stood and walked towards me calmly, her bare feet making no sound against the ice. When she was close enough to touch, her image seemed to waver, until I was staring at myself. The version of myself that I had seen when I drowned in Kalure.

Another blink, and the dark-haired woman was back – her olive skin bearing a striking resemblance to Mira and Zandri.

'I thought it was about time we met properly,' she murmured, and understanding speared through me.

'You saved me. When I fell beneath that ice.' And I had been so convinced that I had survived on my own merits.

'Not quite.' The woman tilted her head almost playfully. 'It was my power that saved you then, not me personally. But this time . . . *this* time, it will be me.'

And before I could move, before I could scream, the ice collapsed beneath my feet.

At the very last moment, the Sorceress grasped my hand. Her grip was unnaturally strong; up close, her eyes weren't black at all, but a very dark brown.

'You said you would help me,' I said desperately, staring up at her.

'And I will.' Selussa's expression softened, until her features were achingly sad. 'I can't save you from Velanthe, but I'll keep you alive for as long as I can.'

Strong hands pulled me to safety, until I lay panting on the ice. I twisted to look at the Sorceress. I had so many questions – so many things that I wanted to know. But as my memories came flooding back, so did fear.

'If I fall . . . Velanthe will resurrect me, won't she?'

Selussa nodded. 'I'm afraid so.'

A fate worse than death. That was what waited for me – a control so absolute that everything I was would cease to matter. Velanthe would use me to kill whoever she wanted, to gain any scrap of power, and eventually my mother would have to decide if bowing to the high priestess's demands was worth my life.

I rested my head back against the ice. The cold seeped into my skin, but I knew it wasn't real. It was a mental manifestation of my body, which had probably been drained of most of its blood by now.

'How did Velanthe defeat you? You're supposed to be immortal.'

'She disposed of my body, not realising that I had the power of astral travel. It's the only reason my spirit isn't trapped as well.'

'But if—'

'Shifters aren't the only species that worship Fennec. My body is far from here, guarded by beings considerably more dangerous than Velanthe and her priestesses.' Selussa's voice was tight. 'It's beyond even my reach.'

We said nothing for a while. Even my teeth were chattering now. How much longer did my body have?

I gripped Severin's teardrop necklace with chilled, aching fingers. It was curiously warm beneath my touch, the glacial blue glowing as if lit from within – as if it was trying to comfort me.

As if a sliver of him was here with me even now.

Glancing sideways at the Sorceress, I studied her carefully. If the legends were true – and I was beginning to suspect they were – the woman in front of me had destroyed a god, brick by brick, prayer by prayer. She had been the embodiment of revenge.

And yet she had also been capable of great kindness. Why else had she remained in Kalure after falling in love with a human man? Why else had she safeguarded her descendants and shared her secrets with the Temple?

I knew what it was like to live apart from others, yet still crave connection. And I knew what it felt like to have your kindness rewarded with betrayal.

It occurred to me that Selussa and I had a great deal in common. Maybe that didn't make us friends, exactly, but alliances had been built on far less. And with the Sorceress on my side . . .

I could obliterate my enemies. I could make the entire world *tremble*.

'Perhaps . . .' I hesitated, unsure what my offer could cost me, but equally sure that I was running out of time. Given a choice between certain death and a shot at survival, I knew which option I preferred. 'Perhaps we can help each other.'

Selussa had turned away, dangling her legs in the icy water. But now she twisted to look at me – and the full force of her appearance hit me like the very first time. Sharp angles, graceful limbs, and the kind of face I could believe a god would create another immortal for: blood-red lips, elegant high cheekbones, and a shock of long black hair, so dark it was almost blue.

'Perhaps we can,' the Sorceress said—

And smiled.

CHAPTER THIRTY-EIGHT

Mira

'He's regaining consciousness,' Cassius warned, checking the bindings that secured Aric to the base of a particularly thick tree.

I crouched down so that I was at Aric's eye level – though I was careful to remain just out of his reach. Cassius strode to my side and drew his sword, the silver gleaming threateningly in the midday sun.

'Put that away,' I said sharply, my chest constricting at the sight.

'You should let me end him,' Cassius said, his hard gaze trained on Aric. 'He's a danger to you – as long as he's being controlled, he won't stop until you're dead. He isn't the person you once knew, Mira. Not anymore.'

But when Aric looked up, it was the young man I remembered staring back at me – not the black-eyed monstrosity he had become.

'Mira,' Aric murmured, and he said my name the way he used to. When we had meant everything to each other.

'Your eyes . . .' I studied the familiar, warm brown, and tears slid down my face. Not just because of how close Aric had come to dying, but because it felt as if I was seeing him for the first time in months. 'They're back to normal.'

Aric gave me a wary frown. 'What happened? The last thing I remember, I was in the Temple with Scarlett after kidnapping Roran's son—'

Cassius's significant glance confirmed my suspicions.

'It's Scarlett,' I said grimly. 'It has to be. I knew she was twisting your mind somehow, but it seems she's moved beyond that now. She's actively controlling you – forcing you to hunt me like an animal.'

'I don't—'

'You don't remember riding here and attacking me? If Cassius hadn't knocked you out, you would have killed me.' I tilted so that he could see the bruises mottling my skin. Bruises in the shape of fingerprints.

I watched Aric swallow. Watched doubt enter his eyes, followed by recognition – and something darker. For the first time, it occurred to me that perhaps it wasn't a good idea to force him to remember.

Aric shook his head firmly. 'Scarlett couldn't have done this. She wouldn't.'

'How can you *know* that?' I hissed, standing until I was looming over him. 'She's Zandri's daughter – she could have all sorts of abilities you know nothing about. And she's already betrayed me once.'

The words came flooding out – everything that had really happened the night I had escaped Ravalia. I held nothing back. I recounted my every thought and emotion from the moment I had bought that blade from Madam Mandrakes to the moment Aric had confronted me at the docks.

A few times it seemed as though Aric might interrupt me, but he didn't. And with every confession, every recollection, his face began to darken. Not magically – there was no trace of the eerie blackness that had shadowed his eyes earlier – but with slow-dawning realisation.

'You really didn't—' He stopped, unable to finish the sentence.

'I told you.' There was a bite to my voice. 'I gave up my revenge. For *you*.'

Aric said nothing, just watched me carefully. Gods, if he *still* couldn't see the truth—

'Whatever you think of me,' I pleaded, 'whatever cause I've given you to doubt me – I've always been honest with you. And I'm being honest with you now.' I didn't know how else to convince him. What else to say to make this right.

My heart squeezed as Aric looked away – as if he couldn't bear to look at me. But when he spoke, it wasn't to protest. 'I wondered, when I found out she had the power of illusion, but . . .'

'But you didn't want to believe it,' I said, my voice cool. Whatever relief I'd felt at the knowledge he believed me was gone. 'Far better to believe *I* had betrayed you than your precious Scarlett.'

Aric's eyes met mine, and the pain in them dissolved some of my anger. 'Far better to believe you had betrayed me,' he said at last, 'than to accept I had thrown away everything we had based on a *lie*.'

'Mira,' Cassius cautioned, but I wasn't listening. My focus was entirely on Aric – on my best friend and my first love.

I'd never told him that, had I? Never said those three precious words. I'd meant to at the Ravalian docks, but I'd never had the chance. And now . . . How *did* I feel about him now? After everything he had put me through, after everything I had shared with Cassius and everything *he* had shared with—

'That's why she did this,' I told Aric, raising a hand to his scarred cheek. Just the sight of it filled me with an unexpected tenderness – and sadness, too. 'Scarlett *knew* that I still cared about you. And that you still cared about me.'

That last part was more of a question than a certainty, but the moment Aric's fingers intertwined with mine, I knew it was true.

I had no intention of kissing him before I did it. It just happened, surprisingly natural, surprisingly sweet. As though I was trying to reassure him.

As though I still loved him.

And I did, I realised. I had never really stopped.

And neither had he.

The kiss only lasted for a handful of seconds, but it felt electric all the same. I stepped back, blinking at him as he studied me in silence. His warm, tentative smile felt like coming home.

'You can fight this,' I told him, low and fierce. 'Whatever hold she has on you – you're stronger than it is. You're stronger than *she* is.'

'I'm not sure that I am.' His words were nothing more than a whisper. 'I'm starting to remember. Bits and pieces – flashes. When I was trying to kill you, it was like a haze came over me. Nothing felt real except the compulsion to . . .' Aric closed his eyes, as if he was in pain. When he reopened them, they were still brown, but they were no longer warm. 'Even now, I can feel my clarity slipping.'

'And that's your cue to leave,' Cassius said pointedly, pulling me to my feet. 'Go – while he still has control over himself.'

Guilt surfaced as I met Cassius's eyes. I had forgotten about him entirely – hadn't even given a thought to his feelings when I kissed Aric, and yet he was still here. He hadn't left me alone and defenceless.

'I can handle this,' Cassius said again, his hand wrapping firmly around my arm in a way that made his intentions perfectly clear.

Whatever guilt I felt dissolved, replaced by anger. 'I already *told* you – I won't let you hurt him.'

Cassius's expression shuttered so completely that for a moment, I could almost imagine *he* was the one under Scarlett's influence. I tensed, preparing to step in front of Aric and shield him with my own body.

'You would choose him, then?' There was no inflection in Cassius's voice. No hint that what we had shared had meant anything to him.

But I knew him well enough now to find the evidence of his true feelings. My eyes lingered on the hard set of his mouth as I said, 'This isn't about *choosing* anyone. It's not as simple as that.'

'Isn't it?' Cassius's words were cutting. 'You gave yourself to me. You drew a clear line between your past and future. Let me dispense with that past once and for all. Nothing good can come of letting him live.'

I glanced past Cassius to where Aric was watching me. The comprehension on his face, the hurt and understanding . . .

'You didn't.' His jaw clenched, so hard it looked like it might break. 'Not with – not with *him*.'

Cassius's hold tightened on my arm. His eyes were glacial as he turned to Aric. 'Given your romantic entanglements with my sister, and the fact that you just tried to kill Mira, you no longer have the right to an opinion. You forfeited that right when you threatened her back in Ravalia.'

Aric's expression was anguished, but he didn't try to argue.

'No matter what you feel for him, Mira,' Cassius continued, tipping my chin so that I was staring up into his face, 'he's a liability. If he cared about you at all, he would beg me to end him.'

I refused to even entertain the idea. 'I'll find another way.'

'Maybe . . .' Aric's voice was soft, but my attention instantly returned to him. His eyes were on Cassius's hand, still wrapped around my arm. I shifted out of his grip, but it was too late. Something sad and indefinable shadowed Aric's gaze. 'Maybe you should let him finish this.'

My voice was low and imploring. 'You don't mean that.'

'Even if you're right, and Scarlett *is* behind this, you can't kill her. Lillian's life is tied to hers.'

'It doesn't matter,' I said firmly. 'There are other things I can do to her. I don't care what it takes, I *will* find a way of convincing Scarlett to release you. But until then, you need to keep fighting. Promise me.'

Aric nodded once. But then his eyes went past me – to Cassius. As his eyes darkened to black, he gritted out, 'Do it.'

Before I could intervene, the pommel of Cassius's sword came flashing down. Aric went motionless once more.

We reached the Temple just as night descended, and I had the sense we were all relieved to dismount.

Cassius had led Aric's horse the entire way, with Aric bound to the saddle. He had dozed most of the trip – which was probably for the best, though I had continued shooting him concerned glances throughout the journey. Glances that had further contributed to Cassius's foul mood.

This was far from the triumphant return I had imagined. Even the Temple itself was eerily silent.

None of the refugees emerged from their makeshift dwellings, and the Kalurian warriors gathered in front of the sandstone steps were curiously still.

'Just when I thought this place couldn't get any creepier,' Cassius muttered.

I frowned. I had never found the Temple unnerving before, but I was unnerved now – and it didn't help that Aric lay unmoving on the horse tethered behind us. When I moved to let him down, Cassius placed his hand over the restraints. Stopping me.

'Aric is Scarlett's most effective tool to kill you,' he reminded me. 'It's safer to leave him here.'

I reluctantly conceded the point. Together, we climbed the sandstone steps to the Temple complex. The clansmen showed no reaction to our presence. They were as still and silent as statues.

'Mira.' Cassius's hand grazed mine, and I went still. 'They're enchanted.'

A shiver went down my spine. Their eyes weren't black like Aric's, but they were eerily empty, unblinkingly reflecting the firelight.

'Could Scarlett have done this?' I whispered to him, not taking my eyes off the warriors.

'I don't know.' Cassius hesitated, and in that hesitation, I saw the worry he was trying not to express.

I didn't ask Cassius where he thought his sister would be. If I was Scarlett, I would have claimed the most powerful place within the Temple – and the most fortified. The Inner Sanctum.

Darkness greeted us as we entered the courtyard. A shiver crawled down my spine as our footsteps echoed, unsettlingly loud in the absolute silence. All the fire braziers were out, and a few had been toppled over.

A flicker of movement made me turn towards the looming pillars of the colonnade. For an instant, I could have sworn I saw a pair of golden eyes watching me. Eyes that weren't quite—

My foot connected with something soft. I looked down, choked back a scream, and stumbled backwards.

I had stepped on a *person*.

No – not just any person. Nausea consumed me as I crouched down at Elian's side. *Please be alive. Please, please—*

I turned him over, and my stomach sank. Even in the semi-darkness, I could see the blood coating his neck. Had someone slit his throat on Scarlett's orders? Because she knew that Elian and Jadis were loyal to me?

Jadis. My blood ran cold. Darius's death had been bad enough, but to lose her *brother*, her *twin*—

'Come on, Mira.' Cassius gave Elian's body a cursory glance before raking his gaze over the bloodstained courtyard. 'We can't stay here.'

'But Elian—'

'Elian is dead.' A cold statement of fact. 'If we survive, you can see that he receives a proper burial. Until then, I would rather focus on not joining him.'

He strode ahead, weaving his way between the bodies. All of their

throats were slit, and when I leant in to examine one of them . . .
I jerked back in shock.

'What is it?' Cassius asked sharply.

'Their throats – they've been *torn* out. As if by teeth or claws.'
I turned in a slow, wary circle, trying to keep the colonnade in my
sights. Searching for those golden eyes.

All that greeted me was darkness, but my skin prickled – as if
something was still watching us. Watching *me*.

Cassius followed the direction of my stare. I wasn't sure if he had
seen those golden eyes too, but his voice was resolute as he said, 'We
should retreat. You can send a message to the shifters, and—'

'By then, it will be too late.' I pushed through the heavy bronze
doors. 'I have to help my people. There must be survivors.'

Cassius cursed but followed me up the curving staircase, his presence steadying at my back.

The route to the Inner Sanctum was filled with more blank-faced
clansmen and priestesses. We gave them a wide berth, and they
didn't try to stop us as we passed, though I could have sworn their
eyes followed me. Was Scarlett watching us even now? Following our
progress through the eyes of her living puppets?

Cassius heaved open the heavy doors leading to the heart of the
Temple, and my grip tightened on my sword, expecting an attack.
But the Inner Sanctum was as still as the rest of the Temple. Only
two figures were visible, their bodies lying in front of the Sorceress's
dais—

'*Lillian!*'

I sprinted the rest of the distance, heedless of possible threats.
Falling to my knees beside my friend, I searched for a pulse. It thumped
faintly beneath my fingers, in time with her shallow breathing.

'What happened to you?' My eyes canvassed her pale form.
There was no sign of a wound; no obvious explanation for her
weakened state—

Until I noticed the young woman lying next to her.

Scarlett's body was riddled with scars, as though a person – or
multiple people – had cut her open and left her to bleed out. Her
unnaturally pale skin was chalk-white, the skin beneath her eyes deathly

purple. Only her red hair possessed any sort of vibrancy, and even that was darker than usual, silhouetting her body like a shroud.

Cassius crouched next to his sister, reaching for her wrist. An indefinable expression crossed his face.

'She's dying,' I whispered. His sharp nod confirmed it.

Lillian's hand brushed mine. I glanced down to see her eyes flutter open, the clear, uncomplicated blue that I remembered. 'I don't have long,' she breathed. 'Neither of us do.'

'Don't try to talk,' I said, clutching her hand to my heart. Tears welled in my eyes but I held them back.

'She's fighting it.' Lillian's voice was little more than a rasp. 'The Sorceress is helping her.'

'The—?'

The doors swung open and Velanthe marched in, a blank-faced Odessa at her side. In front of her was a little boy, and one glance at his red hair told me this was the child Aric had mentioned kidnapping – Roran's son. Velanthe kept a possessive hand on his shoulder, though he seemed to be enchanted in the same way as the others.

'*You*,' I hissed, drawing my sword.

'Me,' Velanthe agreed, and when she smiled, I saw that her teeth were stained red with Scarlett's blood.

CHAPTER THIRTY-NINE

Mira

'I'm glad you made it back to me, Ḳasmira,' Velanthe said conversationally. 'You have so much raw power – it would have been a shame for it to go to waste.'

I glanced over at Scarlett, at the red lines criss-crossing her skin, and I felt sick to my stomach.

Selussa had warned me about the priestesses' interest in blood magic, but I had never imagined *this*.

'I trusted you,' I snarled, advancing on Velanthe.

'Of course you did.' She looked faintly bored – as if she had stopped thinking of me as a real person the moment she sent Aric to hunt me down. Or perhaps she had never thought of me as a real person at all. Just a tool – to be used and then discarded. 'You had lost everything when you came to me. You were desperate for guidance – and that was what I offered you.'

I raised my sword and pointed it at Velanthe. The only thing stopping me was the child in front of her.

'Instruct the boy to move.'

'You can't kill me with *that*.' Velanthe eyed the sword with distaste, as if non-magical weapons were beneath her. 'But if you want a fight, I can easily give you one. I have your army of clansmen under my influence – with a single thought, I can summon them to my side. You're their leader now, aren't you?' Her lip curled. 'I wonder – will you be ruthless enough to cut your way through hundreds of your own people?'

We both knew I wasn't. But—

'Try it,' I challenged, 'and find out.'

Before she could respond, I lunged forward—

And ran her through.

Velanthe didn't try to avoid the fatal strike. She merely pulled me close, until her lips were at my ear. 'Is that the best you can do?'

With a smooth motion, she pulled out the sword, hilt-first. The moment it left her body, her skin stitched itself back together. Velanthe met my shocked stare with a serene smile.

Then pain erupted in my neck.

I didn't realise what had happened at first. Not until I brought my hand up to the ceremonial dagger embedded in my skin.

I stumbled back from Velanthe in horror.

'I'm disappointed in you, Kasmira.' This time, the high priestess was the one who advanced on me, forcing me to concede step after step. 'I taught you better than this.'

My nerves sang with pain as I took hold of the dagger. But I paused, terrified that it might be all that was keeping me from bleeding out.

'Let me,' Velanthe said, and in a lightning-fast movement, she tore the dagger from my neck.

Blood sprayed, splattering the high priestess's face. Light-headedness told me that I was moments from losing consciousness.

But then Velanthe's hand was on my wound, her black eyes inches from mine as my wound stitched together just as hers had.

'How?' I breathed, watching in disgusted disbelief as she brought some of my blood to her lips. Licking it off her fingers – only . . . I stared at the black, curved talons that extended from her hands. Exactly like a bird of prey.

'I told you.' Velanthe's eyes glittered, terrifying in their utter delight. 'Never underestimate the power of blood magic.'

Cassius lunged at the high priestess, his sword aimed high – as though he intended to sever her head from her shoulders. Seconds before he could make contact, Odessa slammed into him from the side – her face blank and soulless.

'Don't kill her!' I shouted to Cassius as Velanthe hurled my sword across the room. It clattered to the floor far from my reach.

'*She's* trying to kill *me*,' Cassius snapped back, avoiding a particularly nasty strike to his stomach. Odessa responded with a slashing motion that threatened to slice him in two—

'It's a shame you don't have the stomach for magic, Kasmira,' Velanthe said. 'You could have been magnificent.'

The door opened and more blank-faced priestesses poured in, ceremonial daggers clutched in their hands. I started as I realised Jadis was amongst them. Covered in blood and wearing a glazed expression – but alive. For now.

'Are you controlling all of them?' I asked, looking back at Velanthe. 'The Sorceress seemed to believe some of your priestesses knew the truth.'

'My senior priestesses do,' Velanthe replied. 'But I ordered them out of the Inner Sanctum when I knew you were coming – let them tide themselves over by making a few sacrifices of their own. I didn't want to risk them killing you too soon. Now that you're here, I want your blood to *last*.'

Pragmatic, if terrifying. And it told me what I wanted to know: once they were released from Velanthe's control, these priestesses would no longer pose a threat. But—

Sacrifices. I understood then – exactly what she was. What all the senior priestesses must have been, if those golden eyes were any indication. Shifters – but the less benign kind.

'Not even your god can save you from me,' I warned. Velanthe's answering smile was laced with vicious amusement. 'Release the magic,' I told her, my one attempt at resolving this peacefully. 'Free these people from your control, and I will spare your life and the lives of your senior priestesses.'

Velanthe barked out a harsh laugh that was unlike anything I'd heard from her before. 'What a terrible queen you are. So weak that you don't even have the stomach for vengeance.'

'I prefer justice these days,' I replied calmly. 'And I didn't say that you would go free. The Council of Ancients will determine your punishment.'

'As delightful as it is to see you finally coming into your confidence, Kasmira,' Velanthe remarked, 'you can't kill me. I'm every bit as immortal as the Sorceress. *You*, on the other hand . . .'

I backed away, summoning my natural magic. Holding it tight as she prowled towards me – a predator relishing the chase.

When Velanthe was in the right position, my eyes darted behind her – to the Sorceress's statue. She turned just as the cracks began to appear, spiderwebbing through the ancient, life-sized statue. And not even Velanthe was fast enough to hurl herself out of its path as it toppled, burying her in a cloud of dust and rubble. Beneath tonnes of ancient stone.

I coughed and rubbed the grit from my eyes as I took in the damage. It had been a gamble, but Scarlett and Lillian were untouched – and mercifully, so were the pillars holding up the ceiling. I whipped my head around, hoping it might have bought us even a few minutes—

'Not bad,' Cassius shouted, and I saw he was still battling Odessa, 'but not quite enough to stop her influence. I don't suppose you have something else in mind?'

I was spared from answering as Jadis and a handful of acolytes strode towards me, their blades glinting. I wasn't too concerned about the priestesses, but Jadis was another matter – and without my sword . . .

The groaning of rock made me risk a glance over my shoulder. My heart sank as a section of the statue rose—

And splintered apart, sending chunks of stone raining over my head. I threw my hands up instinctively, protecting myself from the worst of the onslaught.

I rose to see a wolf crouched in the middle of the ruins, its reddish-brown fur coated with grey remnants of stone. Its hackles rose as it fixed me with eyes black as tar.

My fingers twitched towards the dagger at my side. But Velanthe had made it very clear that I couldn't win against her with conventional means.

The high priestess's steps shook the ground as she moved, and – was it possible that she was even bigger than before?

Swallowing down apprehension, I held my ground – refusing to give her the satisfaction of watching me run. Even in her wolf form, I could have sworn Velanthe was smiling. Her claws left gouges on the smooth obsidian floor as she approached, scraping against it with a sound that jangled my already shredded nerves. Showing me exactly how easily she could tear open my flesh.

Could I use my natural magic to create some sort of cage? No – Velanthe's shapeshifting ability made her impossible to contain, and her immortality made her impossible to kill. My only chance was to access her mind.

And the only way I could access her mind . . .

I glanced across the hall. Cassius was no longer just holding off Odessa but also the other priestesses, whose numbers would soon overwhelm him. Lillian and Scarlett were moments away from death, and even if Velanthe didn't intend to kill me now, she would eventually – along with Jadis and anyone else who was loyal to me.

Unless I destroyed her first.

For a heartbeat, I thought of the Sorceress's warning. She had been very specific: don't use blood magic again, no matter the provocation. But whatever the consequences were, at least I would be alive to face them. And so would the people I loved.

My decision made, I suddenly felt very calm. It was surprisingly easy to connect with the blood pulsing beneath Velanthe's skin – as if the magic was eager to take hold of me again. To have another taste of my heart and soul.

And a part of *me* was eager too – eager to embrace that darkly seductive power and everything it offered.

I dived headfirst into sensation.

As I had hoped, there was so much of my blood inside Velanthe that accessing her mind was as simple as opening a door. In front of me, the wolf's black eyes widened – understanding what I intended and trying to fight me. But her blood magic was channelled from *my* power, and it was my will that mattered. Not hers.

A hall of memories appeared in front of me. It was like being in an art gallery, except the paintings were memories. I paused in front of a few of the more recent ones, observing Velanthe's last interaction with Scarlett. Despite everything, the fear and dawning horror on Scarlett's face made something tighten in my chest. No one deserved an end like hers.

The hall seemed to stretch on forever, and as I took in the furthest memories, I caught glimpses of Velanthe as a child.

But I wasn't concerned with understanding Velanthe. Only destroying her.

The moment I had the thought, the hall began to crumble around me, the memory paintings smashing, one after another after another.

As the painting in front of me toppled, I caught a glimpse of the memory contained inside: a vision of a stunning man with long, russet hair and cruelly perfect golden eyes. He was sitting atop a heavy throne in a dark cavern, surrounded by beautiful, cavorting subjects who I might have mistaken for human if it wasn't for their animalistic features. Fennec seemed to look right at me, his mouth opening in a snarl that displayed razor-sharp teeth.

And maybe I was every bit as self-destructive as Cassius believed I was, because I picked up that painting and hurled it against the crumbling wall. Shattering the memory of Fennec into a thousand jagged shards.

Somewhere far away, I heard Velanthe screaming. But I didn't stop. Not until I had torn her entire mind apart – as completely as she had intended to destroy me and my friends.

I opened my eyes to an empty shell. No longer a wolf but a husk of a woman – as beautiful and eternal as ever, but mindless.

And as I looked past Velanthe, my magic seemed to expand, until I was no longer just connected to the people in front of me but to everyone inside the Temple. Hundreds of minds and hearts that were now mine.

Mine to influence or break or shape as I desired.

All mine.

Though Scarlett hadn't woken, colour entered her cheeks the moment Velanthe's hold over her snapped.

Lillian, however, quickly returned to normal. Soon she was sitting, and then she was standing and hugging her brother, whose eyes had returned to their usual brown. But despite my happiness to see my friend returned to her usual healthy self, and my relief to know that Aric would no longer be hunting me, Scarlett's comatose state left me with a strange dilemma.

Thanks to my experience with Velanthe, I knew that I could enter

Scarlett's mind – and I suspected I could use such a connection to guide her back from the brink of death.

I just wasn't sure whether I *should*.

If I left Scarlett like this, both Aric and Lillian would be free. And I would have no competition for the Ravalian throne. A throne that I would have to claim, just as I had promised Vølund, if only to stop future bloodshed. The only way for Kalure to be truly free was if both countries were united under my rule.

Cassius could prove problematic to that plan – but I trusted him a hell of a lot more than I trusted his sister. If his devotion to me was genuine, then perhaps we could come up with a deal that suited us both. If not . . . well, I would face that when it became necessary.

Scarlett, however . . .

Across the room, my new high priestess was watching me knowingly – but if Odessa had an opinion, she kept it to herself. Concern shadowed her gaze as she returned her attention to Jadis, who was kneeling over Elian's body. I had ordered him brought to the Inner Sanctum, where he could be prepared for burial.

Jadis looked up at me, her jaw clenched with emotion. I felt for her – she had lost a father figure in Darius and now her brother was gone too. Accompanying me to Kalure had cost her everything.

Well – maybe not *everything*.

Odessa put a reassuring hand on Jadis's arm as she stood. 'I want Elian to be laid to rest beside Darius,' Jadis said to me. 'And I don't want the priestesses anywhere near him. No one touches my brother except me.'

I nodded, choosing not to mention that the remaining priestesses were innocent. Grief wasn't always rational. 'I'll see to it personally.'

Jadis's brown eyes swam with tears that she didn't allow to fall. 'Thank you.'

This time, when she returned her attention to Odessa, there was no trace of the grieving sister – only the capable young woman I had tasked with coordinating security of the Temple. It was a decision I'd made to keep her mind off Elian, and because I needed someone I trusted to keep an eye on Nari and the clans.

Jadis had worked efficiently, imprisoning the mindless Velanthe and sending a raven to Conall and Sionnach – warning them about the senior priestesses, who had fled before I could deal with them. With any luck, the Council of Ancients would capture the priestesses and punish them according to shifter laws.

But with the Temple out of immediate peril, and the clans willing to obey my commands, I could no longer put off this reunion. My gaze shifted to Aric and Lillian, who was murmuring something to the boy – Aurelius. He shouldn't really be here, considering the dust and debris, not to mention Elian's body, but he had refused to leave Aric. Aurelius stayed so close to him he was like Aric's miniature, red-haired shadow.

My body tensed as I walked over to them. There was so much that needed to be said – that needed to be explained – and I felt suddenly uncertain.

That uncertainty slipped away as Lillian looked up at me and smiled, the love between us making conversation unnecessary. I threw myself into her arms, and after a slight pause, Aric embraced us both.

I closed my eyes as I hugged my two best friends tight, feeling at peace in a way I hadn't in a very long time.

Eventually Aric pulled back from Lillian, but he let our closeness linger. He hesitated, as if assessing my response, and then threaded his fingers through mine. Like an unspoken question.

I answered it with a reassuring squeeze.

Aurelius tugged on my leg, drawing my gaze down to his oddly solemn one.

'This is Mira, remember?' Lillian said. 'She's a queen. She rules this place.'

He immediately cast his eyes to the ground and bowed, like a proper courtier. 'Your Majesty.'

His age made the display a little unsettling – but no doubt he had started etiquette lessons young.

I crouched down so that I was at his level. 'It's nice to meet you properly, Aurelius,' I said gently. Odessa had given me a brief overview of his kidnapping, and my heart went out to him. 'There's no need for formalities with me. I'd like you to think of me as a friend. Like Aric and Lillian.'

Aurelius's smile was timid. He considered me for a moment, then reached up – daringly touching my forehead. Tracing the crown Velanthe had inked across my brow. 'I've never seen a crown like this before.'

'No,' I agreed. 'It's a Kalurian custom.'

'Father says Kalurians don't have rulers.' He glanced around the Inner Sanctum, and I could almost see it like he did: as something huge and alien. 'He says . . .' Aurelius hesitated. 'He says they're barbarians who rebelled against the empire, and now it's his role to bring them back into line. To save them from themselves.'

My smile tightened. 'I'm sure he does. But politics are more complicated than that. Not everything is solved by conquest.'

Aric took hold of my arm, drawing me back to my feet. 'Can you do something for me, Aurelius?'

The boy's nod was eager.

'Wait with Odessa for a while. Lillian and I need to discuss something with Mira.'

I watched Aurelius until he was out of earshot. But as I turned back to my friends, my gaze fell on Scarlett – and Cassius, kneeling at her side.

Lillian watched me steadily, and I knew this was what she and Aric had wanted to discuss. 'Scarlett has been like this for days,' she said. 'Velanthe cut her up with the intention of resurrecting her, but she just remains in this comatose state. I think it might be some kind of defence – only she doesn't realise Velanthe is no longer a threat.'

I stared down at Scarlett. Like this, she looked younger and oddly vulnerable – and I now knew that she hadn't been responsible for Aric trying to kill me. But that didn't make her trustworthy.

'If I leave her like this . . . you could be free.' I took no pleasure in the words, but they needed to be said. 'She's not technically dead, so you won't die, but she also can't pose a threat to you. Or to any of us.'

'Yes,' Lillian said softly. 'But that's not you, Mira. You're better than that.'

'*She* isn't,' I said, glowering at Scarlett. 'You don't know what she's done—'

'I do, actually. I started to put it together when we were in the Western Lands.'

Aric glanced at his sister in shock. 'And you didn't think to tell me?'

'I hoped Scarlett would. She felt so much guilt about her deception, and she did give me a second chance at life.' Lillian tilted her head as she considered Scarlett, and I had the sense that she wanted to be by her side, even now. 'Scarlett regretted what she did to you, Mira – and I know she regretted lying to us. She never felt like she truly deserved my friendship – or Aric's.'

I dropped Aric's hand as though it had burned me. 'It was a bit more than *friendship*, though, wasn't it?'

'Scarlett and I . . .' Aric hesitated, his expression conflicted. He settled on, 'It never would have happened. Not if I hadn't believed—'

'If you hadn't believed her lies,' I said tartly. I shifted my assessing stare to Lillian. 'And now you want me to wake her up? To bring her back into our lives?'

'I never said she was perfect. But neither is he,' Lillian said, with a nod at Cassius. 'You've given him a second chance.'

'After locking him in the dungeons for two months,' I said heatedly, though I kept my voice low, so Cassius wouldn't hear me. 'Since then, he has worked tirelessly to prove himself to me—'

I stopped talking at the look on Aric's face. It was a look that I recognised instantly, because the same darkness had reared up inside me when Lillian had spoken about Aric's *friendship* with Scarlett.

'Perhaps Scarlett will prove herself just as her brother did,' Lillian said mildly, though I knew she had noticed the sudden awkwardness between me and Aric. 'There were times when she wanted to tell me the truth – and you, Aric. But she could never quite bring herself to trust us.'

I couldn't believe what I was hearing. I had known that Lillian was soft-hearted, but—

'Scarlett is a gifted manipulator. How can you be sure anything she felt was actually genuine?'

'Because the bond doesn't lie.' A hint of steel entered Lillian's voice. 'Her guilt was real. And so was my friendship.'

I stared at her in disbelief. Then I shifted my pleading expression to Aric, who rubbed his temples.

'Lil—'

'No,' she interrupted coolly. 'You can be angry with Scarlett all you want, but I'm entitled to my own feelings.'

'So you think her guilt excuses everything? You died because of her! Mira and I haven't spoken in months—'

'That says more about you than Scarlett.' Lillian's eyes bored into Aric's, and they were no longer soft. 'You were so quick to believe that Mira had betrayed us. Granted, I was as well, but . . . I still would have heard her out.'

'I was out of my mind with grief,' Aric said, more to me than to Lillian. 'That night, at the docks, I had just watched my sister die in front of my eyes. I had *seen* you – or someone who looked *exactly* like you – cut down the emperor. And you had made so many decisions that I . . .'

He trailed off, but I knew what he would have said. I couldn't even blame him for it. Still—

'If you're able to excuse your actions by saying you were out of your mind with grief, then I should be able to say the same thing. I crossed lines in the Ravalian Court, but in the end, I made the decision to turn away from revenge. I *chose* you – you and Lillian.'

'I know,' Aric said softly, keeping his gaze level with mine. 'And I am so sorry I believed the worst of you.'

I nodded but said nothing more. I would need time – time to let his apology sink in, time to unravel my very complicated feelings. But hearing that from him . . . it gave me hope.

And that was enough. For now.

'What do you think?' I asked Aric, motioning towards Scarlett. 'Do you think she deserves a second chance?'

'I think . . .' He paused, weighing his next words. 'I think she gave my sister one.'

Which was a yes. I turned to Lillian.

'We need her,' Lillian said firmly. '*You* need her.'

I wasn't convinced of that. If our roles were reversed, and Scarlett had the shifters and clans on her side, not to mention Roran's son as leverage . . . I highly doubted she would raise a finger to help a potential rival. But I wasn't Scarlett. And a part of me felt relieved at being talked out of making a monstrous choice.

But it wasn't just Aric's and Lillian's opinions I had to take into account.

Though Cassius wasn't touching Scarlett, his gaze was focused on his sister's face. No longer did he look like the cool, unruffled prince I had first met, so effortlessly in control of the world around him. There was a realness to him now – a depth of emotion that stirred something deep within me.

We looked out for each other. Cassius's soft words from the dungeons resurfaced. *When I was young, I relied on her more than I* . . . In my mind, I saw Cassius's face harden. *It doesn't matter. She proved I was right not to trust her in the end.*

It seemed Scarlett was talented at behaving in a manner that destroyed her relationships – whether she intended to or not. But I knew it wasn't always easy to stop caring about someone. Even when they hurt you.

Without looking at me, Cassius said, 'I thought it would be a relief to see her like this. No doubt she would have been a problem, but . . .' He smiled – a humourless twist of his lips. 'It seems I've forgotten my own advice. When she was considering killing her fiancé, I warned her that she needed distance to succeed. It's harder to kill someone if you're looking into their eyes.'

I crouched next to him, touching his hand briefly with mine. 'I'll do whatever you want me to.'

To my surprise, Cassius shook his head. 'The decision should be yours. It will mean more that way.'

'I'm not sure—'

'I tried to kill Scarlett once. If she believes you did this for me, she'll be suspicious of my motives, and that suspicion will transfer to you. But *you* . . .' Cassius paused. 'I saw the way she looked at you in the Ravalian Court. The admiration and curiosity. She needs to know that you saved her – not because you were told to or because you had an agenda, but because it was the right thing to do.'

I frowned at him. 'I think you're overestimating my value to her. And I'm not sure my motives will make a difference.'

'They will.' Cassius's midnight-blue eyes met mine, filled with unexpected certainty. 'I know they will, because they made a difference to me.'

CHAPTER FORTY

Scarlett

I sensed my cousin before I saw her.

It was different to the awareness I had when Lillian was close – more like a tether. The same tether that had drawn me out of the icy void Velanthe had condemned me to.

For two days, I had been conscious but unable to move, anchored to life only by that tether.

By *her*.

My cousin, my rival, my . . . *saviour*. How strange it was to think of Mira that way.

I could hear her now, speaking with the guards stationed outside my chambers. It occurred to me that Mira could have summoned me to her. A barbed reminder that she was the ruler here and I was nothing.

It was what *I* would have done. Instead, she had come to me.

Not alone – no, that would have been too much to hope for. Cassius and Lillian flanked their precious queen as she stepped inside, and I suspected Mira had doubled the warriors outside the door. Something indefinable shadowed Cassius's gaze as he took me in, his eyes lingering on the scars marring my arms. Fully visible thanks to the dress I wore.

The smile I gave him was barbed. Doubtless he believed I had gotten exactly what I deserved.

I looked past Cassius and Lillian, but there was no sign of Aric. He knew everything now – and his absence felt pointed. Anger and hurt, demands for the truth – those responses meant that he still cared.

That I had been more than a consolation prize to him, a way of forgetting Mira. Outright dismissal, however . . .

'Forgive me if I don't get too close,' Mira said, leaning against the window and folding her arms as she regarded me.

I crossed the receiving room in a few easy strides, ignoring the way Cassius tensed protectively at my approach. No doubt Aric and Lillian had shared all my secrets – including what they knew about my death magic. But I had no intention of harming Mira. At least not right now.

'Apparently I have you to thank for saving my life,' I replied. 'Killing you would be a poor way of expressing my gratitude.'

Mira didn't seem convinced. Fair enough; trust didn't come easily to me, either. 'And what of your deal with Roran? Your life – in exchange for mine?'

I blinked. 'How did you—'

'I saw some of your memories when I brought you back.' Mira's tone was carefully unreadable.

'Which ones?' It was difficult not to feel violated. How could she have intruded so deeply into my mind without me sensing it?

'I didn't see very much. Given your in-between state, your mind was disorganised – the memories were more like flashes. But I did relive your last interaction with Velanthe.'

I went still. If she had relived that, then she would have experienced my fear. My vulnerability. Worse – she would have heard my last thoughts about *her*. The regret I had felt over my betrayal.

But perhaps that would engender some much-needed trust. Mira hadn't locked me up, after all. Instead, she had come to my chambers in person – a decision my brother clearly didn't agree with, given the open suspicion in his expression.

'I had the opportunity to kill Mira at that treetop village,' I reminded Cassius. 'I chose to offer her a truce instead. A truce that I haven't broken.'

'*Yet*,' Mira said, sharp and clipped.

'Yet,' I agreed, suppressing the urge to smile. My gaze went past her – to the beautiful, cloudless day beyond the windows. 'How about we take a walk? I'm interested to explore the Temple. I might have been here for over a week, but I've spent most of that time unconscious.'

Mira frowned at me. I could tell that she disbelieved my flippancy, and she was right to. But I didn't want to think about how hopeless I had felt when Velanthe and her priestesses had cut into me, and I didn't want to think about the emotions Mira's presence had stirred to life.

I just wanted to *walk*. To burn off the reckless energy coursing through my veins.

When I looked up, I saw that Mira's eyes were on my forearm – where my fingers were tracing the raised scars. It was an unconscious gesture, and I was surprised Mira had noticed it.

Irritated with myself, I let my hand fall.

Mira's voice was oddly hesitant. 'What Velanthe did to you . . . no one deserves that. *No one.*'

Not even you. That was what she really meant, wasn't it?

'It doesn't matter,' I said tightly. 'My mother always told me it's better to be feared than to be loved. I suppose I can finally test that theory.'

'You're still beautiful—'

'Don't lie to me. And don't you dare pity me.' My voice was filled with enough warning that everyone in the room tensed. I barked out a soft laugh. 'Now, how about that walk?'

Mira glanced at Lillian – who nodded, apparently satisfied that I had no immediate plans to murder her best friend.

Cassius moved to follow as we left my chambers, but Mira shook her head. 'I'll be fine,' she told him with unexpected softness.

There was nothing soft about the stare he levelled on me. A warning – and a threat.

I brushed past him without a glance. It hardly seemed necessary for him to be so concerned for Mira's safety; fighting leathers covered every inch of her skin, leaving only her face exposed. I doubted I would be able to touch her before the clansmen cut me down.

Four of them fell into step behind us as we walked, and I resisted the urge to make a quip about how much security she seemed to need. It was flattering, really, that she considered me so dangerous.

'I meant what I said the last time we met,' I said conversationally. 'I want to work with you to kill Roran. He forced me to make that deal – if I hadn't signed it, he would have killed me along with Aric and Lillian. As it was, he still let General Harte brutalise Aric's face.'

Mira's gaze hardened as it met mine. 'Is General Harte still alive?' At my nod, she smiled. 'Good.'

I knew she was already planning what she wanted to do to him. All the ways she wanted to make him suffer.

She would have to get in line.

But all I said was, 'I can't kill Roran myself, but you can. Once he's dead, I won't have to uphold my end of the bargain. You and I can—'

'Go our separate ways?' Mira asked, with a faint, sceptical smile.

'I suppose that depends.'

'On . . .?'

'On whether you have designs on the Ravalian throne.'

Silence descended, broken only by the distant hum of conversation drifting from the main courtyard. Mira's silence told me everything I needed to know. A pit grew in my stomach.

What I had told her was true – I didn't want her dead. I never had, and now that she had saved my life, I was even less eager to think of her as an enemy. There was so much that we could achieve together.

But the Ravalian throne was *mine*.

'I am willing to sign a treaty that gives you absolute control over Kalure,' I said. 'I have no interest in fighting you for this country. My only interest is Ravalia. My birthright.'

'And Cassius's.' Mira's voice was mild, but her words were not.

I stopped in my tracks, forcing Mira to turn and look at me. 'I don't want to be your enemy. I don't even want to be Cassius's enemy. But you have to understand – I've bled and sacrificed and killed for this. I've also proved myself to my people. I won a victory in the Western Lands, and my mother has the court onside. If Cassius returns to Ravalia with the intention of usurping the throne, he *will* die.'

Mira's mouth twisted – in something close to disgust. 'And to think,' she said, her voice cutting, 'that *Cassius* chose to give you a second chance at life. The very brother you're talking about killing.'

Irritation warred with surprise. I hadn't expected Cassius to advocate on my behalf, and it unsettled me. Clearly, he had made that decision before he knew of the deal I had made with Roran – but I wondered why he would make such a decision at all. Surely he knew he would never claim the throne with me alive.

I shook off the inconvenient thoughts. I had loved Cassius once. I had loved him and fought for him and protected him, and he had thrown that love back in my face. His motivations were no longer my concern.

'Let's focus on the present, not the future,' I said to Mira after a pause. 'At least for now, we all want the same thing.'

'Roran's death,' Mira murmured. I followed her over to the walls of the Temple and braced my arms against the sandstone as I peered over.

An army was out there: thousands of clan warriors and hundreds of shifters, all readying themselves for battle. I glanced sideways at Mira, who smiled faintly at the look on my face.

'If Roran wants a war,' she said, her voice fierce, 'then I intend to give him one.'

Mira didn't bother assigning guards to watch me.

Maybe she realised how pointless it was to try and contain me – or maybe she was trying to establish some goodwill between us. If it was the latter, she should have invited me to join her strategy meetings. What use was an asset if you refused to use it?

Still, I knew that Mira's people were reporting my movements to her spymaster – and I knew Cassius wouldn't hesitate to act if he believed I was a threat. But I felt certain my brother had more pressing matters on his mind.

My lips curved. How it must *irk* him to have Aric back in the picture, and to be unable to dispense with his rival without losing Mira completely. It was almost worth relinquishing Aric to see Cassius in such an irritating predicament. By the time I turned my attention to taking the Ravalian throne, at least I wouldn't be facing off against Mira and Cassius together.

What a challenge *that* would have been.

I walked idly through the Temple, curious about Mira's life here. But the opulent surroundings held no answers. There was nothing of my cousin in the elaborate tapestries and stone carvings of the Sorceress.

Nothing of my cousin – but plenty of Selussa.

Despite the unpleasant memories associated with the Inner

Sanctum, I found myself drawn to it. Seeking the peace I had felt in Selussa's presence.

Today, I deliberately timed my visit to coincide with Odessa's. It was strange to realise that she truly worshipped the Sorceress: she was every bit as devout as the priestesses who hadn't known the truth about Velanthe. I supposed there was a comfort in feeling part of something greater than yourself. A comfort that she would have needed, after watching her parents executed.

Odessa was kneeling before the Sorceress's altar, near where the massive statue still lay in pieces. I watched her for a moment, wondering what she prayed for.

'You know that Mira needs to reach out to Roran,' I said, shattering the silence. 'To use his son to convince him to come to the Wilds, where we will have the advantage.'

Odessa glanced up at the sound of my voice, instantly wary. I took her silence as an invitation to continue.

'The message should come from me. Roran will be more likely to believe Aurelius's life is in danger that way. He won't expect the same level of ruthlessness from Mira – or from Cassius, considering how closely their fates are intertwined. Cassius's future power is dependent on ingratiating himself with her.'

'I know,' Odessa said tightly.

'Then perhaps you can tell your queen to hurry things up. If she's concerned about what I might say, she can watch me write the message herself.' I smiled at Odessa, ignoring the suspicion in her face.

'You came all this way to tell me that?'

'Would you believe me if I told you I came for absolution?' At Odessa's faint snort, my smile widened. 'As it happens, I did have an alternative agenda.' I handed over a piece of parchment.

Odessa took it with hard eyes. 'Where did you get this? And why are you giving it to me?'

'Read it.'

I waited expectantly for Odessa to recognise the Sorceress's handwriting. To understand the significance of what she was holding.

'But this is . . .' She trailed off, and I took some satisfaction in watching her struggle for words.

'It's one of the missing excerpts from the Sorceress's grimoire,' I finished. 'Information Velanthe deliberately removed.'

'I've searched the Temple top to bottom since becoming the high priestess, and I never came across anything like this. How did you find it?'

'I didn't find it. I *wrote* it.'

Odessa stared at me as though she had never seen me before. 'But this handwriting – it's the Sorceress's. And the Sorceress has been gone for years.'

'Powerful beings have a way of returning.'

'Returning?' Odessa's fingers tightened around the parchment.

'Well,' I said, smiling, 'she couldn't stay gone forever.'

I left Odessa standing there, staring down at words that shouldn't exist. As far as demonstrations went, it was a slightly theatrical one.

But it was only right that the Temple should know of Selussa's existence. In time, and in a way that suited my purposes.

I made my way to the dungeons next, making full use of my illusions. The guard in front of Velanthe's cell barely even flinched when I brushed a finger along his cheek, and when he collapsed, I borrowed the key from his belt. I hadn't used enough power to kill him, which meant that I needed to act quickly.

I slipped inside Velanthe's cell.

The ex-high priestess was sitting in the far corner, her knees drawn up to her chest, her face blank and her eyes unblinking. A platter of food lay untouched in front of her.

Given the way Velanthe had influenced the other priestesses, Mira hadn't questioned her control over Aric. And though Velanthe had been stripped of her weapons, I was pleased to discover that my suspicions had been right – Aric's blood ruby was still there, concealed in a hidden part of her robes.

I rolled it in the palm of my hand. With Aric's blood ruby in my possession, I could make him love me like he loved Mira. Or I could make him seduce and kill her – perhaps during her sleep, when she was unsuspecting and defenceless. Not even Cassius could protect her if she chose to let Aric into her chambers.

But Mira *had* saved my life. Repaying that kindness with murder seemed like something my mother would do.

And I was trying to be different to Zandri. Different to Velanthe and Roran and my father.

When I returned to my chambers, I held the blood ruby out over the balcony. If I dropped it, no one would be able to control Aric again. Not even me.

It was a risk. I hadn't seen Aric, not once, since regaining consciousness. Lillian had assured me that he would come around, but Lillian was optimistic to the point of foolishness. It was far more likely that he wanted me dead.

But Severin and Aella had chosen to die rather than be controlled. Thanks to Velanthe, I now knew what it felt like to have my autonomy ripped away from me – to realise that my life was no longer truly my own.

Trust over fear, I told myself—

And let the blood ruby fall.

CHAPTER FORTY-ONE

Mira

'You can't avoid her forever,' Lillian told me as we walked amongst the clan warriors and shifters outside the Temple.

'Not forever,' I replied, stopping to observe the clansmen shooting at their targets. 'Just until the battle. I trust Scarlett to use her death magic against Roran and his Warriors, but I don't think it's wise to be alone with her.'

Bows pulled taut as the archers took aim, the next batch of arrows whistling through the air. They embedded in the circular straw targets with a resounding thud.

Across the field, I saw Nari and Aric sparring, surrounded by a ring of onlookers. From Aric's hand motions, I knew he was explaining where best to strike Ravalian armour. He had been an invaluable teacher these past few days, sharing inside knowledge of Roran's battle techniques and how to counter them. Roran still had numbers on his side – but I hoped the Wilds would afford us an advantage.

The thickness of the forest meant that the bulk of Roran's forces would have to take the main path to the Temple – where they would be headed off by our calvary and the shifters in animal form. The clans had already constructed traps and obstacles along the way, including sharpened pikes creating a bottleneck for our archers to pick off Roran's men.

I felt cautiously optimistic about our chances. Now that the shifters had joined with the clans, Roran and his magically enhanced Warriors would have a true war on their hands.

But I frowned as I caught a glimpse of Aurelius's distinctive red hair.

He was watching Aric spar with obvious fascination, kept under close observation by Jadis.

Lillian was watching Aurelius too. 'Should he be out here? Surely this isn't the best place for a child.'

'The sooner he gets used to being around the clansmen and shifters, the better. I'll keep him at the back of the army, but he will see battle soon. I need him as calm as possible when that happens.'

Lillian shot me a reproachful glance. She had protested against using Aurelius as a bargaining chip, and I knew she was still appalled by the letter Scarlett had sent to her brother.

Its harsh wording had been enough to make even *me* believe Aurelius was in real danger. Hopefully it would make Roran believe the same.

Yet as I had assured Lillian multiple times, Aurelius was safe and under my protection. I would never harm a child. I hadn't even contemplated locking him away, despite Cassius's attempts to convince me otherwise.

As if the thought had conjured him into being, my attention shifted to a shirtless warrior twirling his sword through the air. The crowd parted, and I saw that Cassius was surrounded by a group of female spectators, though he wasn't instructing them.

At least not yet, I thought, my mind conjuring unwelcome images of exactly what kind of instruction he could offer them.

I wondered why he hadn't tried to hold me to the promises I had made him, or attempted to warm my bed these past few nights. Perhaps I should have been relieved, but I found his distance unnerving. I might have thought he was plotting something, if I hadn't already warned him not to act against Aric.

'Come on, Mira,' Lillian said, her grip tightening on my arm. 'Let's watch Aric and Nari.'

I pulled my eyes away from Cassius, but he was already striding over, an irritatingly smug smile on his handsome face.

'You're welcome to join me, Mira,' he said, and I knew he had chosen those words to remind me of our time in the forest lake.

Heat flooded my cheeks, but his presumption amused me. I had faced warrior after warrior on this sparring field, and aside from Aric, none had bested me. I doubted Cassius would be the exception.

'By all means,' I replied, unsheathing my sword. It would do Cassius good to learn some humility.

And it would do *me* good to vent some of my frustration.

The onlookers moved back to give us space, and I noticed Conall amongst them. He was the only member of the Council of Ancients who had joined us, Sionnach and the others remaining behind to hunt down the senior priestesses and protect those who couldn't fight. Lillian moved to stand at Conall's side, though I could feel her disapproving stare on me.

Cassius shifted smoothly into a fighting stance. Perhaps that should have been my first clue – but I had never considered Cassius a warrior on par with Aric or Roran.

I was forced to reconsider that assumption as our swords met. Cassius disengaged with a flourish, effortlessly sidestepping my follow-up blow. His fighting style was an outward reflection of his mind: every move calculated but possessing a ruthless edge. I appreciated his skill even as it frustrated me.

Cassius's midnight-blue eyes raked over my body, anticipating my every move. I unleashed a barrage of vicious attacks, but he blocked me each time, countering my advance with unsettling ease.

Our audience swelled as we battled back and forth. I was dimly aware of settling into a rhythm; a familiar push and pull that reminded me of our interactions off the battlefield. I had once thought of fighting as a dance – and Cassius was a talented dancer, the two of us so evenly matched that one of us triumphing over the other seemed impossible. Even our breathing was synchronised as we exchanged blows, our bodies moving in exhilarating tandem.

Cassius whirled to the side and struck, fast as a viper. I countered with my sword until we were locked together, our faces inches apart. When I met his eyes, I saw that they were filled with fierce appreciation.

I slowly stepped away, my breathing uneven. Cassius and I studied each other as we lowered our swords.

'Impressive,' Nari said from behind me, and I whirled on my heel, feeling guilty for a reason I couldn't fathom. 'It's rare to see warriors so evenly matched.'

Aric stood stiffly at Nari's side, his face unreadable as he and Cassius locked eyes. The tension between the two men was so thick that I half expected one of them to challenge the other to a duel. But Cassius strode off through the training field without a word.

I stared after him, unexpectedly conflicted. It felt as if our sparring match had cracked me wide open – as if Cassius and I had shared something far more meaningful than practising our fighting skills. I had known he was capable – physically as well as mentally. But the realisation that he could match me with a blade, that he was my equal in that arena—

I noticed Aric watching me, a question in his gaze. I forced myself to focus on him instead.

'If you want someone to practise with,' he said with forced lightness, 'I'm happy to oblige.'

Before I could tell him that I was done for the day, Nari cut in, 'Actually, I would like to see that. I missed your last two sparring matches.'

A much bigger crowd formed to watch Aric and I cross blades. The old ease returned as we exchanged blow after blow, a sense of rightness and familiarity blooming between us. But no matter how hard I tried, I couldn't beat Aric, and I hated knowing that he had to hold back in order to keep the match going. He never used to hold back with me.

Still, even after my eventual defeat, we were both smiling. Reminded of the moments we had shared on Aldara.

'I missed this,' Aric said as we returned to the Temple. 'I missed *you*.'

I smiled back at him. 'I missed you too.'

If the history between me and Cassius was bathed in blood, then the history between me and Aric was like that mountain meadow back in Aldara – filled with shared confidences, laughter and plans for the future. *That* was how I would always think of Aric – as the boy who first gave me a sense of purpose. And hope. Hope for a better future – with him.

I took in his broad shoulders and the determined lines of his face. As always, the scar on his cheek hit me like a blow – not because it detracted from his attractiveness, but because I hadn't been able to protect him from it.

That was what he had always been to me, after all – my protector. The one person I had trusted without question.

'You're staring.' The hint of a smile pulled at Aric's lips.

'I'm thinking about old times.' A trace of sadness entered my voice as I gazed up at him. Servants had lit the fire torches in preparation for nightfall, but in the dusk light, every inch of Aric's appearance stood out in sharp relief – including the Warrior black he wore. 'All I wanted back then was for you to *see* me. To realise how perfect we could be together.'

'We still can be.' He leant in, until his lips were inches from mine. Warm and familiar and beckoning.

But though I craved Aric's touch . . . My eyes darted to the chambers next to mine. *Cassius's* chambers.

'I was such a fool,' Aric said, his fingers brushing my cheek and drawing my gaze back to his. 'Gods, Mira, I feel like I've been slowly dying for months, and I'm only just realising it now.'

'I know,' I breathed back. 'It's the reason I decided to run away with you. Back in the Ravalian Court, when I tried to stay away from you . . . I felt like half a person.'

'And when we were together?' Aric stroked my hair back from my face, his golden-brown eyes intent on mine. Searching.

To my surprise, I saw that there was vulnerability within them. Hadn't he *known* how incredible that night was? How special?

'It felt like the beginning of something. Something wonderful.'

Aric's smile was the slightly crooked one that always melted my heart. The one that reminded me he had once been like the air I breathed. That I had needed him like I had needed water and sunlight – in a way that was vital to my survival.

I didn't know if he kissed me or I kissed him, but suddenly his hands were in my hair and my lips were on his, and our bodies were fusing together with the same desperation that I had felt back in the Ravalian arena, when he had been the only thing holding me together.

Aric kissed me like he wanted my lips to be the last thing he tasted, like he wanted to brand himself into my soul. My head fell back against the sandstone wall, and suddenly it was only Aric's strong arms that were keeping me upright, our bodies pressed so close together that it was difficult to believe we had spent months apart.

And I knew that if I let him, he would make love to me like I was something precious and delicate he couldn't bear to see shatter. He would whisper endearments and promises of eternity in my ear, and everything that had happened would be forgotten. I would be home again.

A ship returned to its safe harbour.

'We belong together,' Aric murmured against my lips, his arms holding me close. 'Let me show you how it could be.' His voice turned rough as he kissed my neck. 'How it always should have been.'

As good as he felt, as tempted as I was to say yes, the knowledge of what he was really asking gave me pause.

Tell me you're mine, Mira. Cassius's voice resurfaced in my mind, smooth and dark and accompanied by the sensation of his lips brushing my ear. *Because I'm yours. In all ways.*

This time, Aric noticed my glance in the direction of Cassius's chambers. He stepped away from me so abruptly that the absence of his touch was like a physical ache. 'I see,' he said, and his voice was stiff. 'You'd prefer to be with *him*, then? Is that what this is really about?'

'It's not that simple,' I said quickly, filled with sudden fear. I didn't want to lose Aric again. Not when we had just come back to each other. 'I just need time – to sort out my feelings.'

'*Feelings?*' Aric's expression was incredulous. 'I knew you had a – a *dalliance*, but you can't be foolish enough to believe he's really interested in you. He's a monster. A manipulator.'

'He was there for me after I came to Kalure,' I shot back. 'After *you* abandoned me.'

'And I'm sure he didn't expect anything in return.' Aric's smile was twisted. 'Can't you see that this is exactly what he wants? Anything you believed was real was a *lie*, Mira – carefully crafted to lure you in. To show just enough vulnerability to make you let down your guard.'

I folded my arms, as if I could shield myself from his words. 'Are you talking about Cassius or Scarlett?'

'Does it matter?' Aric retorted. 'They're both liars.'

For a moment, we only stared at each other, our breathing heavy and slightly uneven.

A distant part of me acknowledged that we weren't being exactly *quiet,* and we were standing dangerously close to the guards stationed outside my chambers – and Cassius's. The thought of him listening to this and smiling, the possibility that Aric was right, and I had fallen for yet another one of his manipulations . . .

Maybe Aric saw the anguish on my face, because his turned to stone. 'Do you love him?'

Was he seriously asking me that? Now, after I had just said I needed time to figure out my feelings?

'I should have put it together earlier.' Aric ran a hand through his hair. 'When I saw the way you looked at him.'

'I didn't say that I *loved* him!'

'You didn't deny it, either. What about me, Mira?' His voice was carefully measured. 'Do you love me?'

'That's not fair. Not after everything that's happened. Not when you've only just come back into my life—'

'Answer the question, Mira.'

I took a deep breath. 'I don't know. I *did* love you – I was going to tell you so, that day at the docks.'

Aric's eyes closed, and I saw how deeply that knowledge cut him. I watched him take it in, like a wounded man being dealt yet another blow.

I reached for him instinctively, taking his face in my hands. 'I care about you. I . . . I *want* you.'

A mocking smile twisted Aric's lips as he opened his eyes. He fixed me with a searching stare. 'Do you even know *what* you want, Mira?'

He didn't wait for an answer.

I stared after him as he walked away, wondering how everything had gone so wrong in a matter of minutes.

'Your Majesty.' The warrior outside my chambers bowed deeply and opened the door for me. If he had overheard my argument with Aric, his expressionless face gave no sign of it. 'The food you requested has been brought up from the kitchens. It should still be hot.'

'But I didn't order any . . .' My voice trailed off as I had my first glimpse of my transformed chambers—

And the young woman sitting at the head of my dining table.

Exactly what I need right now, I thought bitterly. *To spend time with the person responsible for all of this.*

I had a handful of seconds to decide on my next move – to allow this farce to continue, or to inform the warrior of her presence and have her forcibly removed.

Scarlett cocked her head as she watched me, apparently curious as to what I would decide.

I closed the door behind me and crossed through my suite. Candles burned along the mahogany table, which was filled with silver platters and crystal decanters of wine. Scarlett had even dressed for dinner, in an elegant silver gown that had most likely been provided by the priestesses. I took a seat at the other end of the table, far from Scarlett and her poisonous touch.

'I'm not really in the mood for whatever *this* is.'

'I know. You weren't exactly subtle – I heard every heated word you and Aric exchanged. I'm sure my brother did too.'

My eyes darted to the far wall of my chambers and then away. Since Scarlett clearly wasn't leaving – not unless I threw her out – I decided to hear what she had to say. Maybe it would distract me from the mess I'd made of my relationships.

'You didn't have to go to so much trouble,' I said warily, unsure how to react to the ostentatious display in front of me. I supposed it had been naive of me to expect someone as powerful as Scarlett to respect my boundaries. Or to tolerate being ignored.

Scarlett merely smiled. 'Consider it a token of my gratitude.' She plucked the lid from a silver tray, the mouth-watering smell of cooked meat wafting across the table.

I made no move to do the same.

'Nothing is poisoned, I assure you.' Scarlett tipped some wine from its decanter, a dark red that reminded me of blood.

'I know about your powers,' I said after a pause, 'but I'm not sure that you know about mine – or the full extent of them. For instance, right now I'm attuned to the beat of your heart. It would be a simple matter to slow it – or stop it entirely.'

Scarlett didn't so much as blink. 'We could make such trouble for each other, you and I,' she said with an amused curl of her lips. 'But as we've already established, I don't want you dead. So long as you feel the same, there's no point bothering with threats. I'd rather talk about your plan to defeat Roran.'

'I've seen you watching the warriors from the battlements. Surely you've already deduced most of it.'

'Do you know what Roran's biggest advantage is?' she asked idly, setting down her fork.

'His overwhelming numbers?' I said, my voice dry. 'His magically enhanced Warriors and his fleet of ships?'

'Not quite.' Scarlett leant back in her chair, utterly at ease. 'His *Artisans*. They give him the ability to know exactly what we're planning – and how best to circumvent those plans.'

My heart sank at the reminder. I had done my best not to think of the Artisans – mostly because there was no way of dealing with them.

'I'm assuming that you brought this up for a reason?'

Scarlett pushed a note halfway across the table. In the firelight, the scars criss-crossing her arms were particularly horrifying. Some of my anger dissipated at the sight, though I was careful to keep any trace of pity off my face, knowing she wouldn't appreciate it.

I reached for the note. My throat tightened as I recognised the heavy, blocky script.

'Roran replied to my letter,' Scarlett drawled. 'With his usual sweet charm.'

Aurelius is a bastard child like you, and just as expendable. Tell Mira that if she wants Kalure, she will have to come to Taiga and match her army against mine. I did promise her a spectacular homecoming.

'What does he mean, a "spectacular homecoming"?' Scarlett asked.

My voice was tight. 'He promised to mount my head on a spike. To display it on the gates of the Kalurian palace.'

'Ah.' To my surprise, a tinge of amusement coloured the word. 'Well, this is good news in one respect.'

'How is any of this *good* news?'

'His Artisans must have warned him that meeting us in the Wilds was a bad idea. Which meant your forces stood a chance of winning.'

'But not in Taiga, it seems.' I threw the note to the side of the table.

Scarlett hummed in thought. 'Artisans can't See futures until decisions have been made. I could have warned you it was useless to set up all those traps in the Wilds. Roran would have expected them all.'

I slumped back in my chair. 'I suppose he knows I have no intention of killing Aurelius, too.'

A shrug. 'It was worth a try. I was hopeful that Roran wouldn't be willing to gamble with his son's life. Seeing the future isn't an exact science – especially when there are so many people and eventualities to consider. There's a reason Roran relied so heavily on Severin for information. He was . . .'

I stared at the narrow column of Scarlett's throat, watching her swallow past something that looked dangerously like genuine emotion.

'He was in a different league to the rest of them,' she settled on. 'Without him, even with so many Artisans at his disposal, Roran won't be able to account for every eventuality – and thankfully, we haven't planned for a battle in Taiga. If we don't make too many specific plans, the Artisans won't be able to warn Roran to expect them. The battle will play out on more equal footing.'

'That's your suggestion?' I asked, extremely underwhelmed. 'To march to Taiga without a plan and hope for the best?'

'You've prepared the shifters and clan warriors as best you can. Perhaps it's time to trust in their abilities. And your own.'

'My magic, you mean,' I said without inflection.

The awareness that had grown after killing Velanthe hadn't stopped. Even now, I could sense the heartbeats of not just Scarlett and my guards, but the priestesses in the Temple and even the warriors in the open field beyond. There was something so tempting about that power, but the consequences of using it terrified me.

Scarlett was watching me knowingly. 'I don't mean blood magic. I mean your natural magic – like my illusions or my mother's ability to control. I think I can help you master it.'

'What makes you say that?'

'Velanthe never wanted you to embrace your full potential, and she didn't want anyone else to discover the Sorceress's knowledge, so she hid her original grimoires. But not well enough.'

A headache throbbed at my temple. 'I don't have time to comb through stacks of books—'

'You don't have to. I already know the most important parts. For instance, did you know that the Sorceress could connect with other people's minds?' She leant in, bracing her forearms against the table. 'That means it was one of her *natural* abilities – not one that comes from blood magic. If it's safe for you to use, then it could make a big difference to the war. Imagine if you could get close enough to influence Roran. You could force him to surrender, and save thousands of lives in the process.'

Accidentally, my mind brushed Scarlett's. Excitement and hope rose up, along with a touch of longing.

There was nothing to suggest her offer was less than genuine.

'If we use Aurelius,' she continued, 'we can draw Roran out. He might claim not to care, but bastard or not, Aurelius is still his son – his only son. That means something to him, or he wouldn't have gone to the effort of keeping him close and hidden. And I have another surprise in store for my brother – one that I will tell you about when it's too late for him to change his strategy.' Scarlett's smile widened, revelling in the knowledge that *I* now needed *her*.

'Even you can't turn the tide of an entire battle.'

'No, but I can certainly help.' Her smile turned impish – reminding me of how she used to smile at me, when she had magically disguised herself as Sabine. 'Just imagine what we can achieve together.'

I frowned at Scarlett. Lillian believed I had avoided her out of fear, but that was only partly true. There was humanity within Scarlett, even if she didn't care to admit it – and that humanity bothered me more than her death magic ever could.

'You're afraid of me.' Scarlett sounded disappointed by this realisation.

'You unnerve me,' I corrected. 'I don't know how to react to you. After you betrayed me, it was easy to think of you as my enemy. But *this*—' I waved a hand at the books and food spread out in front of me— 'this attempt at civility is far more unsettling. Because I don't know when it will end.'

Our eyes locked, and a strange affinity passed between us.

'Has it ever occurred to you that I felt the same?'

'I'm sorry?'

'When we met in the Ravalian Court,' Scarlett clarified, drumming her steel-tipped nails against the table. 'I wanted to believe that we could be allies, if not friends. But you have to understand . . . I don't have the best track record with family. In the end, I couldn't trust you not to turn against me.'

'I wasn't your enemy until you made me one.'

'I know,' Scarlett said softly. The candlelight glinted in her cold eyes, adding a deceptive warmth to them. 'But once you made an alliance with my brother, you became a threat. And when your engagement was announced . . .' She sighed. 'I couldn't allow you to marry my brother.'

'So everything you said, your offers of working together—'

'They were genuine. At first.' A rueful smile. 'But when you finally decided to trust me, it wasn't to work together as I had intended. It was because you wanted my help to escape to Ravalia, where you would have become a rival queen, in the perfect position to attack my country.'

'I wouldn't have—'

'No?' Scarlett tilted her head. 'You made no secret of your hatred for the Ravalian Court. Even now, your sights are set on Ravalia as much as Kalure. You don't trust me any more than I trust you.'

'Can you blame me? You framed me for Emperor Kalias's murder.'

'I made a choice out of fear. And once I did . . . I didn't believe there was any going back. For either of us.'

There was something strange and searching about the way she looked at me. My power brushed against her mind, and memories surfaced in a flash of colour. The ballroom from the first Trial. Sabine's smile as I descended the steps with Cassius's crown on my head. The two of us running from the party, arm in arm, filled with adrenaline and excitement—

'You liked me once,' Scarlett murmured. 'When I was Sabine.'

She was right – I had liked Sabine. Had considered her a friend, at least until Scarlett had revealed it was all a lie. Except that wasn't what she had told me. She'd told me it was real to her as well. That she cared about me, not just as her friend, but as her *cousin.*

And I had believed her. Had *wanted* to believe her – to believe that I could have a family again.

'What happened to the real Sabine?' It had never occurred to me before, but Scarlett couldn't have been impersonating her from the very beginning. I had seen Sabine during the Choosing Ceremony – talking to a group of Artisan candidates. And Scarlett had been there too, looking on from her throne along with the other royal patrons.

'I never wanted to hurt her,' Scarlett said, watching me closely. 'I kidnapped her before the first Trial, but when I returned, I found her dead. She'd accidentally sliced her wrists when she tried to undo the ropes. My mother . . .' Her throat bobbed as she swallowed. 'My mother threw her off the balcony afterwards. She told me to leave her there after casting an illusion over her body, but I couldn't. I stayed by her side for hours.'

Was she really trying to stir my sympathy by making me believe that Sabine's death had hurt her? A death she was at least partially responsible for?

I almost left. But when I had brought Scarlett back, I had seen some of her memories. I didn't remember everything, but I remembered enough: Zandri's cold presence overshadowing her childhood, the love and responsibility she still felt for Cassius, despite her pretence not to feel anything at all. I even knew that she had come to care for Aric and Lillian. Perhaps not in the same pure, uncomplicated way that I did, but the emotions were still there. Still genuine.

It had been difficult to hate her after discovering that. But it was equally difficult to forgive her.

Scarlett stood. She walked towards me slowly, cautiously, as if she was giving me the chance to back away.

She wants me to trust her, I realised. That was what this whole display was about: not an attempt at control, but an attempt at a reconciliation.

Scarlett paused less than a metre away. 'I don't want to be like Zandri, and I know you don't want to be like Velanthe.' She raised her chin defiantly. 'So let's choose to do things differently. Their way doesn't have to be ours.' And she extended her hand, palm up, like an offering.

I stared at her in shock. Scarlett knew I was aware of her death magic. She couldn't expect me to—

But clearly, she did. Her eyes glittered down at me, filled with unexpected sincerity. 'Choose trust, Mira. Not fear.'

I wanted to. And perhaps the first step to defeating Roran was trusting Scarlett. Banishing the animosity between us.

But if I was wrong . . .

I stood and faced her, my heart beating a thunderous rhythm against my ribcage.

And I took hold of her outstretched hand.

CHAPTER FORTY-TWO

Mira

Conall barrelled through the forest like a battering ram. Even with a week of practice, and a woven saddle on top of his bone-plated armour, it took all my concentration to stay on his back.

Scarlett didn't have any such issues. She sat, straight-backed and proud, on a slightly smaller shifter, an exhilarated smile curving her lips. Her red hair streamed out behind her like a bloody banner as she urged him forward, still driven by the desire to compete with me.

A week ago, the shifters' warmth towards Scarlett would have bothered me. But Scarlett and I had spent nearly every hour of the past seven days together. The mornings had been reserved for practising magic in a secluded glade near the Temple, where Scarlett took point, guiding me with information she had apparently learnt from the Sorceress's grimoires. The afternoons were my domain, spent discussing battle strategy with Aric, Cassius and the shifters and clansmen, while Scarlett looked on from a slight distance, content to listen and observe. And since I had been avoiding Aric and Cassius during the evenings, those had become a time for Scarlett, Lillian and I to share, trading conversation while we ate dinner together in my chambers – often joined by Aurelius, who was becoming increasingly talkative and comfortable in our presence.

But even seven days of this hadn't entirely dismissed my wariness where Scarlett was concerned.

Cassius had been clear: take advantage of Scarlett's knowledge and abilities, but don't allow her to outshine me in front of the Kalurian people. I could only imagine what he would say if he saw Scarlett riding beside me.

The shifters were proud creatures, and until today, only Nari and I had been invited to ride them in animal form. I had no idea why *this* shifter had made such an offer to Scarlett. Maybe it was her Kalurian blood, or maybe it was more than that. Despite the distance that Aric and Cassius had advised I keep from Scarlett, it was impossible not to get drawn in. Not to notice all the traits that I suspected the shifters had – her single-minded focus, her confidence, her fierceness.

They were all traits that she had used against me, and could use against me in the future. But right now, as partners, they were traits I had come to appreciate. Or perhaps I had simply come to appreciate *her*.

By the time I dismounted, my legs were trembling and my hair was a mess of leaves and twigs.

'How is it you look so composed?' I asked Scarlett, who jumped down from the saddle and murmured something to the shifter in a soft voice. Even in animal form, she treated him as if he was still human. And arguably with more respect than she treated most humans.

I had never met anyone so full of contradictions. Though Cassius came close.

Scarlett shrugged. 'I suppose I avoided most of the trees, since Ferox is lower to the ground than Conall.'

'Ferox?'

'That's his name.' Scarlett smiled fondly at the four-legged beast and then strode over to me. 'At least I'm pretty sure that's what he said. He sort of growled it at me.'

I raised an amused eyebrow but said nothing else as we left the shifters to privately change back into human form – something that Conall had told me was sacred, and usually kept between them. It made me feel privileged to have witnessed him change in their village.

The trees parted to reveal a long line of Kalurian clansmen and shifter warriors. We had left the Temple this morning and began our march to Taiga; already we were on the very edge of the Wilds, and tomorrow we would travel through the Archasian mountains to meet whatever was waiting for us in the capital. No doubt Roran knew we were coming, and would be prepared with an overwhelming show of force.

Priestesses and warriors turned as Scarlett and I passed, the novelty of seeing us together still not having diminished. Cassius's warning rang in my ears, but I ignored it.

'Are you nervous?' I asked.

'No.' Scarlett smiled faintly at my sceptical expression. 'You forget – I spent months in the Western Lands, where skirmishes erupted almost every day. Battles are like anything else. Once you've experienced enough of them, they lose their power. And I'm eager to fight against Roran.'

That made two of us. I just wished I could be so certain of a positive outcome.

'But if *you're* nervous,' Scarlett said, 'that's nothing to be ashamed about. A lot is riding on tomorrow.'

Like my life, and the lives of my friends. Not to mention the freedom of an entire country and the fate of my crown.

Scarlett paused outside her tent. It was at a slight distance from the warriors and main campfires, but I caught her yearning glance at Aric, Lillian and Odessa, who were eating with a group of clansmen. Taking Lillian with us hadn't been my first choice, but the bond between Scarlett and Aric's sister made separating them impractical. So instead, I had done my best to ensure she would be well protected – and the warriors assigned for Lillian's protection had sworn to defend her with their lives.

'Do you want to know how I'm really so calm?' Scarlett asked, turning back to me. 'It isn't because I'm used to war, or because I'm eager to end Roran. It's because I'm confident that we can.'

Even in the darkness, her icy eyes were fierce. Despite my fears, I felt some of her conviction seep into me. 'How can you be so sure?'

Scarlett smiled, as though she had been waiting for me to ask. 'Think about it: the most powerful people in the empire have tried to control us. Zandri was so threatened by you that she intended to use you to kill my father and then kill you afterwards. Velanthe was so threatened by me that she tried to resurrect me and bend my will to hers. And Roran . . . Roran tried to use me to end you, because he believed that only someone as magically powerful as me could kill someone as magically powerful as *you*. Individually, we're a danger to all of them. But together? We're a force to be reckoned with.' She let that sink in for a moment and then she said, 'I'm not afraid of this battle, Mira. And you shouldn't be, either.'

'I'm not.' I was startled to realise that it was true. 'Not with you by my side.'

Scarlett blinked at me with surprise. A hint of a flush coloured her cheeks at the compliment.

'Goodnight, Scarlett,' I said, and I was still smiling as I turned away.

Yes, it was definitely too late for distance. Because something unexpected had happened over this past week.

I had started to *like* her.

I spent the night walking amongst my army, stopping to chat by campfires, smiling at the warriors and shifters I passed.

Aric remained close at my side, even though I suspected he would have rather been with Lillian. But Lillian was safe with Odessa and had seemed perfectly happy conversing with the priestesses.

And as the night wore on, Aric seemed to relax. Somehow I did too, though every minute that passed brought war closer.

But I stiffened when Ulrik, the imposing, bearded leader of clan Skjöldr, stood from a nearby fire and approached me. None of the clansmen had blamed me for Thoren's death – not after I had told them Roran was responsible, as Scarlett had recommended. Even Gunnar, who had replaced Thoren as head of clan Asbjørn, treated me with the respect I was owed as leader of all the clans.

Yet Ulrik had always seemed rather cool towards me. I suspected he felt that I was a poor substitute for Vølund – and that he still harboured some animosity towards my Ravalian companions.

I exchanged a glance with Aric, whose expression was inscrutable. But I felt his tension all the same.

Ulrik wasn't as tall as some of the clan warriors, but his bulk more than made up for it. I raised my chin as he considered me, conscious of the battle axe he wore and the clan leaders watching from the fire.

My heart sank as the public setting suddenly made sense.

Duels weren't uncommon amongst the clans, but to challenge me now, to force me to fight him to hold my position as clan leader the night before a war that could determine Kalure's fate—

He sank to one knee before me.

I blinked down at him in shock. Without releasing my gaze, Ulrik said in a great, booming voice, 'It will be an honour to follow you into battle. Should even one warrior of clan Skjöldr survive, he or she will ensure that your victories are etched into the sword you bear.'

I glanced at the sword strapped to my hip. *Vølund's* sword, marked with runes that depicted the battles he had fought and won.

They are your victories now, he had told me when he gifted me this sword. *As your victories will in turn be mine.*

'Thank you,' I said to Ulrik, my voice slightly choked. 'I hope to do Vølund proud, and to honour his legacy.'

Ulrik nodded and stood, but I was no longer looking at him. I was looking across the fire – at Nari. Her kohl-lined eyes were intent on mine, but there was no trace of hostility within them. No indication that my magical influence had faded.

She inclined her head to me. 'My brother would have been proud.'

I forced a smile that felt false. Did she really mean that? Had my blood magic tampered with her mind *that* much?

Since leaving now would offend Ulrik and the clan leaders, I took a seat between Nari and Gunnar. Aric accepted a flask of alcohol from one of the clansmen, drinking it down in a stoic way that resulted in laughter and approval. I took a generous sip, fighting not to splutter at the resulting burn.

It was pleasant to listen to tales of previous battles, and as the flask and wineskins were passed around, the atmosphere become increasingly welcoming. I looked on with interest as various competitions sprang up amongst the gathered clansmen – knife throwing, drinking contests and even marksmanship.

'Shall we give it a try?' Aric murmured to me, aware that we both excelled when it came to hitting marks.

I smiled and reached for my bow. The conversation around the fire faded, and I knew I had everyone's attention now. Not that I needed to prove myself – I had already done that when I had returned with the

Council of Ancients' approval and the shifters, not to mention all the sparring matches I had won – but it seemed like a harmless way of joining in the fun.

'There,' I said, pointing at a tree trunk in the distance and taking aim. I thought I had accounted for the breeze, but my arrow hit the mark slightly off-centre.

Aric's hit dead centre.

'Show-off,' I said with a smile that he returned.

Nari clapped Aric warmly on the back and passed him the wineskin, which he took a quick swig from.

'My turn to choose the target,' he said, pointing at a particularly difficult one – a thin branch at an odd angle.

I watched Aric take aim, the firelight illuminating the concentration on his face. When he released the bow in a smooth, seamless motion, his arrow struck the branch – but glanced off and toppled out of sight.

'You can't win them all,' I said as I lined up my shot. My arrow thudded into the branch—

And stayed there.

It was my turn to be clapped on the back. My turn to take a victorious swig from the wineskin.

But when Nari invited us to go another round, I shook my head. 'I'd rather keep it as a draw.'

Together, Aric and I strode back through the encampment. It had been a few days since we'd been alone like this, but tonight it felt easy, and I wondered if Aric had found a way to set his jealousy over Cassius aside. In the lead-up to the battle, I had the sense the two of them had come to something of an understanding. At least, I had caught snatches of civil conversation between them.

Perhaps war had a way of putting everything into perspective. It had certainly helped Scarlett and I set our differences aside.

'Will you wait here for me?' I asked Aric when we reached my tent. 'There's something I have to do.'

Maybe Aric knew what I had in mind, because he nodded and said nothing.

It wasn't difficult to locate Cassius. He was leaning against a tree, his arms folded as he watched the revelry. I knew he would have been welcome around any of those fires; his strategic mind and public demonstrations of physical skill had won him the respect of the Kalurians, and his charm had done the rest. But tonight, he seemed content to observe from a distance.

He didn't turn as I approached, though he must have heard me coming. Even cloaked in shadow, he was strikingly handsome. I took a breath, steeling myself against the weakness I had for him. The weakness that had made me delay this conversation for so long.

'You don't have to say it,' Cassius remarked, and finally he looked at me. 'I know you've made your choice.'

'There was never a choice to make. You have to understand – I never really stopped loving Aric.'

'Of course you didn't,' Cassius said. 'Aric is your first love and your best friend. He's comfortable. It makes sense that you would go back to that.'

'You think I want Aric because he's the safe choice? Because he's *comfortable?*'

'Don't you?'

'No!' I took a step closer to Cassius, infuriated by his mild expression. By the knowing glint in his dark blue eyes. 'Aric is attractive, intelligent, kind-hearted, passionate—'

'He sounds thrilling,' Cassius said dryly. 'Yet here you are, talking to me.'

'Not for long,' I said, turning on my heel. Then I paused and glanced back at him. 'You must know that we never had a chance. What did you think was going to happen when this war was over? That we were going to rule Ravalia together? How would that even have *worked?*'

'Are you asking me, Mira?' A light, taunting question. 'I thought you'd already made your choice.'

'I have,' I shot back, more sharply than I'd intended.

Cassius's half-smile was difficult to read. 'Since you asked . . . I had something special in mind. An offer I don't think you would have refused.'

The evaluating way he looked at me then, the certainty in his eyes . . . It reminded me of Aric's warnings. His suspicions regarding Cassius's motives.

It was better not to know. Whatever offer he would have made, it was clearly intended to draw me in. To ensnare me.

'What offer?'

'In the Kalurian tradition,' Cassius said, watching me closely, 'women are the monarchs. I was considering renouncing my own claim to the Ravalian throne in favour of becoming your consort and father to our eventual heirs.'

My face heated at the mention of *heirs*. At the knowledge of exactly what he was proposing.

'With me by your side,' he continued, heedless of my reaction, 'you would have a legitimate claim to the crown. A great deal of bloodshed and civil unrest would be avoided, and both our peoples would be safe.'

How *clever* it was. He knew I would baulk at marriage after our last proposal, so instead he had come up with something new. A way of proving himself to me.

Except what was he really giving up? As advantageous as this could be for Kalure and Ravalia, for *all* the people in the empire, once Cassius and I were bound together . . . he could easily turn against me. He could undermine my rule in so many ways, many of which I was sure hadn't even occurred to me.

But one certainly had.

'If we had an heir,' I said at last, 'you could kill me and rule as regent until they came of age.'

Something close to hurt flickered across his face. 'Do you think me that much of a monster?'

No. No, I don't. The answer was on the tip of my tongue, but I held it back. Because how could I trust my own feelings, my own perceptions, where Cassius was concerned?

'Everything you've just said . . .' I inhaled a sharp breath. 'It depends on trust.' *And I'd be a fool to trust you blindly.*

'You trust me. You're just terrified to admit it.' Cassius tilted his head, his blond hair gleaming in the firelight. 'Aric betrayed your trust too,' he reminded me, his words smooth and remorseless and brutally true. 'Even if he hadn't left you, I saw you together in the Ravalian Court – he was always doubting your decisions, blaming you for everything that you did to survive. If you want to rule, Mira, you need to be with someone who understands that ruling comes with tough decisions. Someone who respects you enough to respect your choices – and not blame you for them.'

'Someone like *you*. That's what you really mean.'

'Maybe I do.' Cassius's voice was measured, but I knew the anger was still there. 'Who better to understand the pressures of ruling than me? We're the same, you and I. But Aric – he's a warrior, through and through, without the stomach for court politics. He might have suited the girl you once were, but he won't be enough for the queen you've become. He never will be, and yet you persist with this charade. Why? Because you don't want to trust me? Because you don't want to admit what's right in front of you?'

'None of that matters,' I replied, gently and yet cruelly. 'I love Aric.'

'You love me, too.' Cassius's voice was whisper soft.

'No,' I said firmly. 'I don't.'

Cassius considered me for a moment. 'You've never been a good liar.' His eyes hardened. 'Which of us do you love more, Mira? Or do you not even know yourself?' He strode off into the darkness, leaving me staring after him.

CHAPTER FORTY-THREE

Scarlett

Whatever animosity I had harboured towards Mira had faded over the past week – a whisper rather than a roar. And I could ignore a whisper.

Most of the time.

When the third group of warriors went silent at my approach, I gave up entirely on being social. They would have welcomed me if Mira had been by my side, but without her . . . well, I was still a Ravalian princess. Still Zandri's daughter.

I started to turn away when Odessa's voice called me back. 'Join us,' she invited, motioning towards Jadis, Lillian and a handful of priestesses.

'Not right now,' I said, my gaze darting to Mira's tent – and the young man waiting outside.

I could feel Aric's heavy stare on me. He hadn't been pleased about my new understanding with Mira – or her agreement to practise magic with me. But we could both die tomorrow, and I didn't want to leave anything unsaid.

'Wait,' I said before he could disappear again. 'I have something I need to say. It won't take long.'

Aric waited expectantly. He was as attractive as ever, and under different circumstances, I would have spent tonight with him – passing the remaining hours until dawn in his arms. Perhaps that was why the loss of him felt particularly fresh. No doubt I could find a replacement if I craved that particular kind of distraction, but somehow, I still found myself missing *him*.

'I understand if you despise me for what I did,' I began haltingly. I wasn't used to apologising, and I hadn't felt a desire to apologise to anyone since Severin. 'I shouldn't have impersonated Mira, and I shouldn't have used the situation to drive a wedge between you both.' Aric still appeared unmoved, so I added, 'And I shouldn't have lied to you about it.'

It occurred to me that I was still omitting a few things; the way I had manipulated him in the Ravalian Court, how I had bribed the stableboy to orchestrate the fall that had nearly killed him. I wondered if Lillian suspected my role in his accident – but surely she wouldn't have kept my secrets if she'd known *everything* I had done.

Aric shook his head, his expression unreadable as he glanced away from me. 'I should have left,' he said finally, more to himself than me. 'The moment I survived the Trials.'

'Emperor Kalias would have sent Warriors after you. Masks, too. You wouldn't have made it very far.'

'Maybe not,' he said quietly. 'But at least Lillian wouldn't have come to Ravalia. She wouldn't have—' He stopped, but I knew what he was going to say.

At least she wouldn't have died.

At least she wouldn't have become tied to you.

'And what about Kain?' I asked, frustrated with Aric's attitude. 'Or have you forgotten about him?'

That woke him up. Aric whirled to face me, his eyes inches from mine, his breathing uneven.

'Everything I've done,' he said tightly, 'has been with Kain in mind. *Everything.*'

'*Then prove it,*' I snapped. 'You know exactly who is responsible for his death, and you have the perfect opportunity to make Roran pay. So blame me if you need to, but don't regret the decisions that brought you here. Focus on avenging your brother, so you and Lillian can finally be free.'

Aric barked out a harsh laugh. 'Except we'll never be free, will we? Even after this battle is done, Lillian will always be bound to *you*. She will have to follow wherever you go, and if I want to ensure my sister is safe, I will have to do the same. Regardless of my own desires.' He glanced across the encampment – to where I glimpsed Mira talking with Cassius.

That glance said enough of Aric's desires. Mira was still in his heart, and she always would be.

It didn't hurt as much as I had expected. I had always known that Aric wasn't truly mine, but I had never wanted to destroy his happiness. To turn myself into a villain in his eyes.

'I'm sorry,' I said, looking him straight in the eyes. Trying to show him just how much I meant it.

A bone-deep sadness entered Aric's expression. For a heartbeat, he looked at me how he used to, when I had still been precious and untarnished in his eyes. When he had been my protector and I had been his lover.

Then the heartbeat passed.

Though he hadn't stepped away, it felt as though a yawning chasm had opened between us. 'I'll do my best to keep you alive – for Lillian's sake. But that's all I can promise.'

His words were as hard as his face. Whatever softness he felt towards me was gone – banished by sheer force of will. And I somehow knew that I would never see it again.

'There's one last thing.' Aric moved towards me, almost close enough to touch, but his cold voice was a mockery of his closeness. 'If you betray Mira or try to harm her, you will have me to deal with. And I will dedicate my life to ensuring that you regret it.'

His skin beckoned, temptingly close. A single touch, and I could send him to his knees. It wouldn't kill him, but it would certainly prove a point. But I resisted the urge. Instead, I nodded back at him – sharp and perfunctory.

'Goodbye, Aric,' I said, turning decisively on my heel. 'I hope you and Mira are very happy together.'

I made a beeline for the trees. Once I was out of sight, I broke into a run – not bothering to swat the branches out of my way. Blood dripped down my face. Blood – in the place of tears.

I had never wanted or intended to care so much. I had learnt to harden my heart, to see others as disposable. That was the lesson of the Ravalian Court: power was all that mattered, and emotion was weakness. Emotion was death.

But I had forgotten that lesson with Aric and Lillian. And I had learnt it too well with Severin. Severin, who I had lied to and used again and again. Severin, who had died not knowing that I loved him.

The forest opened up into a clearing – deserted except for a shadowy figure leaning against one of the trees.

'What are *you* doing here?'

'Trying to find some solitude,' Cassius drawled. 'An attempt that seems doomed to failure.'

I glared at him. 'Shouldn't you be with Mira?'

'And why would I be with Mira?'

Of course he had to answer my question with another question. It was like he was *born* to antagonise me. 'I saw you talking to her earlier. And she hardly goes anywhere without either you or Aric watching her back.'

'Mira has made it clear that Aric will be taking over that duty from now on. So I suppose I will have to find other ways to occupy my time.' As I came closer, Cassius studied me – taking in my dishevelled appearance and the scratches marring my face. But he said nothing, and I realised that he had probably seen me speaking with Aric and deduced the rest. The realisation was not a comfortable one.

'He's a good match for her,' I said, unable to resist needling him. 'Aside from the obvious – like looks and fighting prowess – he's also reliable and *stable*.'

'You're implying that I'm not?' Far from sounding irritated, he sounded faintly amused.

'A murderous prince who still has designs on his sister's throne? I think Mira can do better.'

Cassius said nothing for a moment. 'I told Mira I was willing to give up my claim for her. To become her consort while she ruled as empress.'

I frowned at my brother, expecting to see a mocking smile curving his lips. But there was none.

'How noble of you,' I said tightly. 'And how ultimately pointless. Neither of you will get close to the Ravalian throne. You know that I will never stop fighting for my birthright.'

'I know.' Cassius's voice was soft.

'Do you still mean to challenge me for the crown?'

We surveyed each other for a long moment. It was impossible to tell what was going on behind that calculating dark blue stare, but I wondered if Cassius – like me – was wondering what it would be like to turn our blades against each other. Wondering who would be left standing in the end.

'I could be convinced to stand down, if you were to grant me a position at court – one with lots of influence and very few irksome responsibilities. One that keeps me far away from Mira and Aric.'

'You know that Zandri would never allow you to return to the Ravalian Court.'

'I thought I was negotiating with you,' he said mildly. 'Not your mother.'

'And what about your precious Mira? If you relinquish your claim to the Ravalian throne and put your support behind me, she won't have the legitimacy she needs to rule in my place – not without a horrifying amount of bloodshed and upheaval. Knowing her, she will consider that cost too high. She will be forced to remain in Kalure. Is that really what you want?'

'I want Mira far away from Ravalia. Far away from *you*.' The sincerity blazing in Cassius's face almost convinced me, but this could all be a ploy – a scheme he and Mira had hatched together.

Except where would Aric fit into such a scheme? The moment Mira had chosen Aric over Cassius, she had turned her back on Cassius's offer. We both knew she wasn't cold enough to force Aric to become her lover, while Cassius sat publicly at her side as her king consort.

'You really expect me to believe you've decided to give up years of in-fighting and scheming? Just like that?' My eyes narrowed. 'You tried to *kill me*, Cassius. Whatever you said to Mira to convince her to save my life doesn't change that. It was clearly nothing more than a temporary lapse in judgement.'

Cassius shrugged. 'Believe what you want. My ambitions no longer include killing my way to power.'

I wanted to believe him, but Cassius hadn't said that he *didn't* want the crown. Just that he preferred not to murder me over it. I had thought Cassius above killing me once – and I had nearly died for that mistake.

'Tell me something,' I said after a pause. 'How can you forgive Mira for locking you up for months, when you could never seem to forgive me for – what did you call it? Stealing our father's love?'

'That really hurt you, didn't it?' Cassius peered at me through the darkness, his expression irritatingly superior. 'I didn't realise you were so eager to stay in my good graces.'

I strode right up to him, and even in the shadows, I could see the way his eyes narrowed at my closeness. As if expecting me to lash out.

The anger I felt drained away, replaced by a painful ache that I hadn't felt in years.

'I would have done anything for you, Cassius,' I said, my voice cracking. '*Anything*. Do you even know how many times I put your survival ahead of my own? I promised to protect you, and every day I fought to keep that promise. I eased your fears, shielded you from Roran, and placed you above my own ambitions. I made myself even more of a target for *you*, because you were the only true family I had. And how did you repay me? By betraying me. By scheming against me and threatening my life.'

'I did what I had to,' Cassius hissed back, though he made no move to push past me. 'For every one of your petulant, rebellious acts, Father punished me in your place. Roran was the heir, and you were his precious and only daughter, but me? I was nothing to him. You didn't protect me, Scarlett. I was a fool for believing that you could. And you were a fool for making a promise you couldn't keep.'

'I didn't know.' I stepped back from him, more shaken than if he'd hit me. 'Why didn't you say anything?'

'Because I didn't want your pity. And because there was nothing you could have done.'

Silence descended between us. I inhaled the crisp night air, trying to banish the emotions Cassius's words had stirred in me.

'He did it deliberately, you know,' I said at last. 'Because he knew that I loved you. Do you know what Father said, when you first turned against me? He said, "That's what you get for trusting family".'

My unstable emotions called to the death magic inside my body. It surged through me like an icy wave.

Cassius watched me, silent and unblinking. If he was thinking that

I looked like a monster, with black veins winding up and down my arms, I couldn't see any disgust on his face.

'Perhaps,' he murmured, 'it's time for us to call a truce of our own.'

'Shall we shake on it?' I asked, allowing the black veins to swirl prominently against my skin.

To my surprise, Cassius laughed. But all he said was, 'Not today, Scarlett.'

He turned to leave. I watched him stride through the trees, and then I called, 'Try not to die tomorrow.'

I heard Cassius's booted footsteps pause, then resume. The briefest crack in his armour.

'You too,' I thought I heard him whisper, and then he was gone.

CHAPTER FORTY-FOUR

Mira

The moon was large and full overhead, casting our surroundings in a silvery haze. It reminded me of the nights we had spent in our mountain meadow on Aldara, staring up at the stars.

Do you see him? Aric had asked me once, pointing up at a constellation that resembled a lone figure. *That's the Traveller. Wherever you are, Mira, however far you go, he will always guide you home. He will always guide you back to me.*

Yet neither of us had expected I would travel this far.

I leant further back against Aric's chest, gazing up at the night sky – visible through a circular gap in the canopy. But while the stars were beautiful, they were also entirely unfamiliar. *Alien.* Even as the ruler of Kalure, this country was still a mystery to me.

That thought felt like a betrayal of my parents. A betrayal of everything they had fought and died for.

'What are you thinking about?' Aric's voice was soft, but his arms were warm and firm around me. Secure in a way that felt comforting – like anything could come for me and I would be safe, because I had him.

It had been a long time since I had felt that security. I hadn't realised how much I had missed it until now.

'I'm searching for the Traveller,' I said, and I wondered if Aric could hear the sadness and longing in my words. 'I can't see it from here. Do you think we will ever find our way back again?'

'I think if we want it enough, we can.'

I knew we were no longer talking about constellations. No longer talking about Aldara, even.

Aric tugged me even closer, and I buried my face in his neck. 'I love you, Mira,' he murmured against my skin. He had said those words to me before, but it was no less special hearing him say them again. 'I don't expect you to say it back after everything I've put you through, but I need you to know that my feelings for you haven't changed. I've loved you since the first day I saw you on Aldara.'

'Since I kicked Nikolas Atwood in the groin, you mean?' I said, with no small amount of amusement.

He smiled. 'Since the moment you looked up and I saw your face. I had never seen anyone so fierce – so vibrant. So alive. And then I asked if you needed any help, and you told me that you had it handled.'

'I'm failing to see the romance in that.'

'The point is, you were completely different to any girl I had ever met. That was why I offered to train you. Because I knew you had a warrior's heart, even then.'

Heat flooded my body. Heat – and tenderness.

'I love you too,' I whispered, looking up into his warm brown gaze. The brown of freshly tilled soil. 'Even when I was with Cassius, even when I hated you for breaking my heart . . . I never stopped loving you. I don't think it's possible for me not to love you.' *You're so much a part of me.*

But even as I had the thought, another memory surfaced. One of midnight-blue eyes and a cool, knowing voice that had burrowed deep into my soul. *Which of us do you love more, Mira? Or do you not even know yourself?*

The hope on Aric's face brought me back to reality. It didn't matter if Cassius was right and I loved them both. What I had said to Aric was true – I had never stopped loving him.

And I never would.

He was so close that I could hear his breathing. So close that I could smell the leather and woody scent of him. He smelt like home.

Aric kissed me like he had kissed me back at the Temple – as though I was the only thing keeping him alive. I moved so that I was straddling him, his back against the trunk of a tree – but he shifted our positions almost immediately, laying me gently against the forest floor.

Damp leaves and grass brushed against my bare skin as he removed the furs from my shoulders and unzipped my fighting leathers, but the cold could no longer touch me. Not as his hands glided down my body, warming me in a way that made it impossible to think about anything else.

His face was a picture of love and determination and passion as he settled over me, and for a moment we only stared at each other. I couldn't see the stars; could only glimpse the moon shining down on his dark hair. But that didn't matter. He was the only constellation I needed.

I helped him tug off his tunic and then he brought his lips crashing down on mine. No longer tentative or unsure – not like that very first time, and I knew we both felt the difference.

We were equals in this, and I loved everything I learnt about Aric as I rediscovered how and where to touch him – just as his hands and mouth explored my body, tender and reverent and filled with wicked delight. Every single touch a revelation – a second chance I had never thought we would receive.

My breathing quickened as he shifted once more, the heat of his body now against my back, his arms wrapped around me in a way that made it feel as though he was embracing me even as I felt him move *inside* me—

My head fell back against his neck, my eyes fluttering closed as he lavished my neck with kisses that sent fire shooting through my veins. It was sweet and wonderful and Gods, how could I have expected it would be anything else?

'We're meant to be together,' Aric murmured as the pressure and heat built between us, as my chest tightened until I could barely breathe. 'I – Gods, Mira, I love you. *I love you so much.*'

I couldn't speak – not as he picked up his pace, our bodies moving together in an urgent, thought-obliterating rhythm. But as he continued moving, harder and faster, driving into me with the force I craved—

'Aric, I can't hold back much longer—'

'Don't hold back,' he breathed against my ear. 'Not with me. *Never* with me.' The raspy edge to his voice told me he was seconds away from succumbing as well.

That realisation was all it took. A blinding wave of pleasure swept through me, made all the sweeter as I clung to Aric, my friend and first love. My forever love.

And as we tumbled over the edge, all I could think was that we had found a way to forgive each other. That we might actually have a chance to find our way back to the people we used to be.

Dawn arrived too soon.

I nestled closer to Aric, watching the first hint of daylight brighten the canvas walls of my tent. I could hear the sounds of my army preparing to march through the Archasian mountains: the low hum of voices, the thud of booted footsteps, weapons and armour being prepared. Their war preparations drowned out the sighing of the wind in the trees, the distant growls of forest cats and the chirping of birds.

Aric's arms tightened around me, anchoring me in the present moment. If there was fear, it couldn't reach me. Not with him here.

I tilted my head, tasting his lips. They were soft against mine, and laced with the tartness of the wine we had shared.

I could taste them forever.

But while I wasn't afraid of the coming battle, or the possibility of my own death . . . I was afraid for him. For *us*.

'Promise me,' I said with a sudden urgency. 'Promise me that this wasn't the last time. I just got you back. I can't lose you again.'

'You won't,' Aric murmured, even though we both knew it wasn't a promise he could make.

Perhaps that was the reason I said what I did. The knowledge that all we might have was this moment, and I couldn't bear to waste it.

'Rule Kalure with me.'

Aric went still.

'It's incredibly selfish of me, I know,' I said quickly, even as a part of me deflated at his hesitation. 'You're fierce and independent, and you shouldn't be tied to overseeing a country and all the tedious politics that go with it—'

'I would do anything for you, Mira.' He shifted so that he was looking straight at me, his expression so earnest that it was impossible to doubt his devotion. His willingness to sacrifice his own hopes and dreams for mine. 'You know that.'

I *did* know that – of course I did. Yet for some reason, I found myself thinking of Cassius's warning. *Aric – he's a warrior, through and through, without the stomach for court politics. He might have suited the girl you once were, but he won't be enough for the queen you've become.*

'You shouldn't have to change your life just for me.' It was difficult to say – because if he didn't accept this offer, what would our future look like? Would we even *have* one? 'This is a decision you need to make for yourself. I don't want you to hate me years down the track. I don't want to . . . I don't want to turn you into someone you're not.'

Aric considered me seriously. 'Even when I tried my hardest, I could never hate you. I don't think there's anything you could do to make me hate you. As for ruling – how could I turn down an opportunity to be by your side?' But he pulled back from me. 'Still, you're right – it is something I need to consider seriously. And I'm not sure this is the right time.'

'Then when is?'

'Not before a battle,' he replied. 'Once it's over. Once you're not so afraid of losing me. I don't want us to commit to a future out of fear, Mira. And not when you've just told Cassius goodbye hours earlier.'

I felt my face flush, though I couldn't argue with his reasons. 'You're annoyingly honourable sometimes. You know that, don't you?'

Aric smiled against my lips. In the distance, a horn blared – the signal that we were preparing to move out.

We reluctantly climbed out from underneath the furs and splashed water on our faces from the washing bowls. Once we were dressed, Aric stepped briefly outside, returning with a group of aides who rushed in with food and water. Even as we hurriedly ate, we stayed close to each other, some part of us always touching.

I had never thought that putting on battle armour would be sensual. But with Aric helping me, *sensual* was exactly the right word. His hands ghosted over my body, tightening straps and slipping weapons into their sheaths.

I withdrew my dagger, eyeing my hair consideringly. I had kept it long because it looked more regal, but long hair was only a hindrance in battle. I lined up a section with my blade—

And sliced it off.

'Nice,' Aric said, eyeing my now shoulder-length hair.

'It was time for a fresh start,' I said, and I meant it in more ways than one.

I admired Aric as we left the tent, his silver armour bright even in the faint rays of dawn. I was dressed similarly; I hadn't bothered with a crown or any other reminders of my station as queen. Today, I was one with my army.

Conall was already waiting, transformed into his animal form. Scarlett was beside him on Ferox, her hair braided into a crown on top of her head. I smiled faintly at the sight.

My smile quickly died as I searched for Lillian, only to remember that she was at the back of the army along with Odessa and the priestesses. And Aurelius, who was here as leverage.

Leverage I would be a fool not to use, though the thought of threatening a child still bothered me.

'Lil will be fine,' Aric whispered, and I nodded back at him, grateful that he understood me so well.

Then he turned in the direction of his saddled stallion, which was waiting obediently next to Cassius and Jadis's mounts.

My heart lurched. 'Stay close,' I told Aric as I climbed onto Conall's back.

'Always,' he promised.

CHAPTER FORTY-FIVE

Mira

A marching army was not quiet.

It was the sound of thousands of heavy footsteps. The thud of enormous war horses and beasts.

I was immensely grateful to be riding Conall, who traversed the steep mountain pass with no discernible effort. Beneath my gloves, my hands were numb and chilled, and I was starting to lose feeling in my legs. Beside me, the icy wind had all but undone Scarlett's braid, whipping her hair into a tangled mess of red.

I had the sense we were all relieved when Taiga came into view, though that relief was short-lived.

It was one thing to imagine or plan for a battle. It was another to see thousands of Ravalian Warriors and soldiers spread out in front of me in uniform, precise killing lines. Their ranks inhabited the entirety of the rocky plain, extending all the way to the grey fortress of the Kalurian palace.

And beyond them . . .

'Whose ships are those?' Cassius said sharply, his eyes fixed on the distant harbour.

I shielded my face against the sun, which had peeked out from between the grey clouds. Even squinting down over the bowl-shaped valley, I could barely make out the smaller naval force approaching the harbour – but the colours . . . I blinked as the red and gold sails caught the light.

Ravalian ships. Either reinforcements for Roran's already impressive fleet, or—

'Did Zandri mention sending a force?' I asked, twisting to glance at Scarlett, who looked as shocked as I felt.

'No,' she said after a pause. 'But it's possible. Zandri has ways of controlling Order members – maybe she sent loyal Warriors to stand against Roran. Pitting the Ravalian fleet against itself sounds like a strategy she would employ.'

Either way, we couldn't wait to see what reception those ships received. We marched on until we reached the foothills leading down from the mountain pass, where we had decided to make our stand.

'We have the high ground,' Aric reassured me.

I nodded, not trusting myself to speak. Not as I took in Roran's black-garbed Warriors and the thousands of red and gold soldiers in the front. Looming over them on a raised platform was their ruler, armoured ostentatiously in gold imperial armour, his distinctive red hair blowing faintly in the wind. He hadn't bothered with a helmet – a deliberate choice. His way of daring me to face him.

'His arrogance is astounding.' Scarlett sounded disgusted. 'Doesn't he even care that he's made himself a target?'

'He doesn't think we can kill him.' Which was deeply concerning. If his Artisans had *Seen* us lose . . .

I frowned as I noticed something else. A ripple of silver surrounding Roran – people wearing silver armour, perhaps? It made me uneasy in a way I couldn't put my finger on.

Irritated with myself, I returned my focus to Roran's army. I could barely see the cavalry sitting astride hulking Zigilian stallions, but I knew they would be there. Roran's frontlines were already in formation: a closed wall of armed men crouching behind their shields.

Aric had warned me of their effectiveness. Many armies had been broken apart by formations like this one. *But not mine.*

Determined brown eyes fixed on me – waiting for my signal.

'Do it,' I told Aric, and he rode forward to two shifters at the very front. Janwar and Ursa.

My whole body tensed. Even though this was necessary, it felt wrong to send them to almost certain death.

'They volunteered,' Cassius said in a low voice. 'They know what they're risking, and in beast form – it's possible they will survive.'

He glanced at me, his midnight-blue eyes communicating his thoughts perfectly. *This is one of those difficult decisions we discussed. The kind of hard choices that rulers have to make.*

I nodded. We had already covered this – and I had agreed with Cassius's reasoning. Far better to risk two lives than thousands. Even though the rocky plain *looked* safe, there could be any number of concealed traps.

The shifters charged across the battlefield, moving with impressive speed. I watched with bated breath as they drew enemy fire, the arrows bouncing off their armour just as we'd hoped – but all it would take was one arrow slicing through their unprotected throats or into their golden eyes to kill them.

'Very good,' Aric said with a grim smile as he rejoined me. 'Roran has just exposed the position of his archers.'

I allowed myself a small smile too, following the torrent of arrows to the thick forest bordering the steep sides of the valley. Once the archers had thinned our ranks, the frontlines would open to let Roran's deadly calvary through – and then close once more, sealing his army from our reach.

Except his archers didn't have long to live.

I closed my eyes, allowing my awareness to drift around me. I couldn't see the archers, but I *felt* them, just like I felt the animals in the forest and the trees and plants around them.

My attention focused on the vines and creepers twining around the distant trees. At my command, they began to unwind and snake across the ground. I gritted my teeth and willed the vines to snake upwards, winding around the archers until they encircled their throats.

And then I instructed them to squeeze.

It felt like a cowardly way of killing, but each of these men had the potential to kill scores of my own. They had to be eliminated.

An agonised roar snapped my concentration before I could take them all out. Horror flooded through me even before I opened my eyes to see the larger shifter – Janwar – topple. One look at the arrow embedded in his pupil told me he had died instantly – and that the roar had come from Ursa, who had paused beside his body. A faint whistle announced the next wave of arrows from the ramparts of the Kalurian palace.

With another agonised roar, Ursa whirled around and galloped towards us, outracing the death flying towards her. When she reached our army, she transformed into human form and raced towards me. Her hazel eyes were clouded with tears but her voice was steady as she reported, 'No traps – camouflaged or otherwise. It's safe for us to advance.'

'Thank you,' I told her. 'Janwar's sacrifice will be remembered.'

Ursa bowed her head and retreated back to the frontlines. How many more would we lose before this war was through?

'I don't like this,' Cassius said, peering at the rocky plain. 'Roran should have set up *some* traps. If he hasn't, it means he doesn't feel the need to. Which means—'

'He has something else planned.'

'Exactly.' Cassius glanced back at me, and the serious expression on his face chilled my blood. 'You can't cross this terrain, Mira. It's exactly what he wants you to do.'

I glanced towards the raised platform Roran had erected. This time, the silver ring around him became clearer.

Priestesses. *Velanthe's* senior priestesses.

Their silver gowns billowed in the wind, creating the illusion of movement. And their placement around Roran made their intentions perfectly clear.

'*That's* his plan,' I said at last. 'He thinks he doesn't need traps – because he has them.'

'A group of shifter priestesses? Roran's lost his mind if he thinks they'll do anything against us. We have an entire *army* of shifters.' Scarlett impatiently tossed her red hair over her shoulder. 'Give the order, Mira. Let's get this over with.'

I tightened my grip on Conall and glanced sideways at Aric. He nodded in assent. 'We're as prepared as we can be.'

My gaze lingered on Aric's resolute one before shifting to Cassius. There was a hint of emotion in his dark blue eyes – emotion that he would never have allowed me to see before this. Not jealousy or disappointment, but something deeper that reminded me of how afraid I had been that I might lose Aric again.

I swallowed down unwise words. This wasn't the time for sentimentality.

It also wasn't the time for drawn-out speeches. That wasn't the way of the shifters – and it certainly wasn't the way of the clans.

So instead, I looked over the army around me – the male shifters in beast form, ready to charge through Roran's lines; the females preparing to transform into birds of prey and attack from the air; the clan warriors ready with swords and axes, most sitting astride hardy war horses.

'You all know what Roran has cost us,' I shouted. 'Now, we have the chance to avenge our fallen and to punish him for his brutality and arrogance. Together, we are a force to be reckoned with! Together, we can make him rue the day he ever set foot in Kalure!'

Shouts and roars erupted around me. And then the shifters were moving.

The force of their strides shook the ground as they raced down the foothills towards the no-man's-land between our armies. Conall loped after them at a slight distance, Scarlett and Ferox staying close to my side – along with Aric and Cassius on their galloping stallions.

It was Cassius who saw it first. 'Look at the priestesses!'

My heart sank as I followed his gaze to the distant platform, where the priestesses had joined hands. Flickers of strange russet light crackled around them, and as the sky darkened, a sense of wrongness swept over me.

'You have to give the order to retreat.' Scarlett said, twisting to look at me. 'You have to give it *now*.'

Except it was already too late. I looked on with bated breath as the shifters hurtled across no man's land – an impressive show of force. But seeing them all in one place, with Roran's forces making no attempt to advance—

A deep rumbling sounded in front of us.

'What was—'

'GET BACK!' Scarlett shouted, trying to turn Ferox as the earth split open with a deafening crack and the screams of falling shifters. Cracks spiderwebbed towards us even as we fought to put distance between us and the fissure in the earth—

And the flames that erupted from it in a wall of searing heat.

The shifters closest were immediately incinerated, but the rest were packed together so tightly that soon most were ablaze, agonised howls and keening wails rending the air – along with the smell of burning flesh. Through the strange russet flames, I saw Roran's forces advancing. Trapping the shifters between them and the pulsing wall of fire at their backs.

I didn't need to look at Aric to know this was a disastrous situation. The shifters were supposed to break through Roran's lines – but burning and weakened, Roran's soldiers were butchering them, cutting them down without honour and dignity. Tears welled in my eyes as winged shifters spiralled down on burning wings. The ones that weren't burning were being shot out of the sky by Roran's archers.

I reached for my locket – then dropped my hand, remembering that it was now little more than a pretty ornament.

Summoning my natural magic, I tried to connect with the wall of fire – to diminish it somehow. But as soon as my mind connected with it, a wave of dizziness and lethargy overcame me.

Draining me. It was *draining* me somehow, sapping my strength and my magic.

Panic clawed at my chest. *I can't* release *it—*

Hands came down on my armoured shoulders, shaking me. I opened my eyes to see Scarlett's glacial blue ones. 'Don't try that again,' she warned. 'Whatever that fire is – it isn't natural.'

As I stared at it, the fire seemed to waver – until I saw a fox in the flames, watching me with eerie golden eyes. *Familiar* golden eyes.

The fox disappeared as a group of burning shifters lurched through the flames, bellowing and howling in agony. Screams sounded as some of the shifters attempted to turn back into human form, the fire devouring their skin just as easily as it devoured their hide.

Despite Scarlett's warning, I tried to connect with the fire again – to bend it to my will.

Nothing happened.

I reached out towards the harbour next, but the water was too far away to summon, and when I tried to reach for air—

The flames only increased, licking at the shifters' blistered and blackened skin. No screams now – only moans of pain. I crouched at their side, wanting to ease their suffering but not knowing how.

'Mira, the shifters are already doomed.' Scarlett's voice was choked. 'We have to get out of here.'

'Scarlett is right,' Cassius said, his horse veering in front of me. He swung down from the saddle, forcing me to look up at him – and not at the burning shifters. 'This is the trap we were expecting, and if we don't get clear of it soon, we won't survive the fallout.'

A faint whistle warned me as the next hailstorm of arrows hit. *Fire* arrows.

They streamed down like a deadly rain. Cassius's shield arched overhead as he crouched at my side, protecting me from being sliced to ribbons. Others weren't so fortunate.

My stomach constricted as I listened to the pained groans around me. How many more had been lost?

Pushing Cassius off me, I angled my shield over my head and rose to my feet – searching for Aric and Scarlett. My heart sank as I saw that Ferox had taken an arrow to his throat and was lying in a crumpled heap in front of Conall, who was mercifully unharmed – though I could sense his anguish from here. Aric had managed to reach Scarlett in time, and had shielded her like Cassius had shielded me. But we couldn't stay here much longer.

Sending my awareness out in front of me, I shifted my focus to the earth beneath my feet. To my relief, I could feel it – could sense it just like any other natural element. I gritted my teeth in concentration as I instructed the earth to stitch itself back together – forming a walkable path through the fire.

Scarlett's expression was difficult to read. Not concern exactly – but something close. 'You really should retreat.'

'I'm not retreating. None of us are.' I raised my chin, turning my stare on the others. 'Roran believes that our army is stuck – but there's a chance he doesn't know I killed his archers in the forest. Scarlett and Cassius, take a force through the forest and encircle Roran from behind. Aric, take the bulk of our army to higher ground, and be ready to mount an attack on my signal.'

'It's a sound plan,' Aric said, 'but if we can't get through the fire—'

'Let me take care of the fire.' My voice was steel. No hint of the uncertainty I felt – or the knowledge of who those golden eyes belonged to. 'You have your orders. I need to trust you to follow them. And you need to trust me to see my part through.'

The next stream of arrows forced me to duck under my shield. My arm buckled under the onslaught but held.

Smoke clogged my lungs as I sucked in a desperate breath and surveyed the damage. Most of my army had taken cover in time – but not all. I couldn't afford to wait another moment.

'Mira!' Cassius grabbed for me a second too late. And there was fear – real, undiluted fear in his eyes as I approached the wall of flame.

'Go,' I shouted back without turning my head. 'That's an order!'

I didn't hesitate to see what they decided. I strode forward – into the fire and its searing heat.

Where I knew Fennec would be waiting.

CHAPTER FORTY-SIX

Scarlett

Leaves crunched beneath hooves as we guided our horses between the snow-dusted pines.

My fingers tightened uneasily around the reins as I scanned my surroundings for threats. So far, we had encountered no resistance. No sign of anyone living.

Just bodies.

The metallic taste of death flooded my mouth as we passed the archers Mira had killed. Some were slumped on the ground and others were strung up from the trees, dangling overhead like grotesque marionettes. But all of them had vines curled around their necks, their chests, their vital organs.

It was those vines that had killed them – squeezing the life from their bodies. The pressure had been such that some of their eyes had popped from their sockets.

'What are the chances Roran's Artisans missed this?' I asked Cassius, just to dispel the eerie silence clinging to this place.

'Highly unlikely,' he replied. A sentiment that would have been useful for him to share with Mira earlier, but I doubted it would have made any difference. We all knew this was a gamble – but it was the only chance we had left, after Roran's fiery display.

Which was how I knew Roran's Artisans would have Seen this. Roran had planned everything out – every last detail. He would know every decision we made, unless those decisions surprised even us.

'Stop,' I ordered as the trees opened out into a clearing filled with dead archers.

Behind me, I heard Ulrik shout something to the clansmen under his command. The sound of hoofbeats immediately paused.

'What is it?' Cassius asked impatiently, reining in at my side.

'Priestesses.' I pointed towards the edge of the trees, where glimpses of rippling silver were visible. It was almost a relief to see them – to finally face the danger I had known was coming.

The six priestesses moved forward slowly, their timing too perfect to be anything but planned. As they entered the clearing, they joined hands – and I saw that their fingernails were long and black, hooked like talons. The hairs on the back of my neck rose as they began chanting in a language I didn't recognise.

Darkness exploded out from the priestesses without warning. Everything dulled. Sound became strange – echoey and distant. My body felt slow and lethargic, and it took an incredible amount of effort to reach for Cassius. I threaded my fingers through his as we dismounted.

'We need to regroup.' Cassius's voice sounded like it was under-water. 'Ulrik was right behind us.'

Without a better plan, I allowed Cassius to lead us forward. The darkness wasn't so complete now; my surroundings were beginning to come into focus. I almost wished they hadn't.

Something had killed the horses. No – not killed them. Horror filled me as I realised they had been ripped apart, their internal organs spilling out onto the blood-soaked ground.

'What could have done this?' I breathed.

Cassius's expression was grim, and he was dragging me forward now. Moving with an urgency that told me he was truly unnerved.

A high-pitched scream rang out from somewhere to my left, but when I turned, it suddenly seemed to come from my right. Then from in front of us – and then from behind. And all around me . . . bodies. Clansmen that had been torn open just like the horses, their chain mail ripped off and their skin marred with deep slashes that leaked red-black blood.

Death was everywhere. So strong now that I could feel my own magic surging to meet it, those icy black veins frantically spiderwebbing across my skin. Cassius cast me a glance and I knew he was seeing them too.

'Can't you do something?' he said tightly. 'Dissipate the darkness somehow, or punch through it? There has to be a way to fight the priestesses' power. Ideally before we face whatever did *that*.'

He motioned towards the pile of bodies on either side of us. Flanking our path like a morbid honour guard. As if whatever had done this was delighting in showing us what they were capable of.

A roar cut through the unnatural stillness. A roar that sounded like—

Before I could think better of it, I was moving towards it. I reached Ulrik just in time to see him fighting against darkness made form. At first, I thought I was staring at a phantom human soldier – but when it turned, I saw that it had the head of a jaguar and hands that were definitely claws.

Ulrik charged with his axe, but the weapon went right through the jaguar-headed man as if he was as insubstantial as smoke. Yet he seemed perfectly capable of slicing into flesh.

Blood spurted and Ulrik's scream split the air as the creature tore off his arm. Ulrik collapsed to his knees.

I could have sworn the jaguar man smiled at me before he wrenched Ulrik's head from his neck.

Cassius's breathing was coming as fast as mine. We didn't release our hold on each other as Ulrik's murderer approached, his bare feet making no sound against the blood-stained ground.

'How touching.' The words echoed strangely around me, as though they were coming – not from underwater, but from inside a large cavern. Was that where he had been, before the priestesses' darkness descended?

Acting on impulse, I released Cassius's hand and knelt in front of a dead clansmen with a ripped-out throat. Drawing death into me, I embraced the cold power it offered. When I was done, I no longer felt afraid of the monster standing over me. I felt sated, whole, utterly invincible.

I looked up, expecting to see a pair of ancient golden eyes staring back at me. Instead—

'Beautiful,' Severin said, a smile curving his inked lips. They glittered faintly with the gold paint he had always favoured. And his eyes – those striking, mismatched eyes . . . they were exactly as I remembered them. *He* was exactly as I remembered him.

I took a step closer, inexorably drawn to him. Severin's smile widened until it flashed teeth.

'Scarlett.' Cassius's voice was sharp. So was his grip as his fingers enclosed around my arm. 'That isn't him. It isn't Severin.'

I paused. He was right – of course he was. *My* Severin had never smiled at me like that – with such mockery and arrogance. And his voice . . . it had never sounded this smooth and inhumanly cold, like an unsheathed blade.

'*Stop wearing his face.*'

'Suit yourself.' Severin's form wavered – until I had a glimpse of long russet hair and unnatural golden eyes. Skin so pale it was almost a match for mine, emanating a faint silvery light.

A single thought brought my death magic swirling to the surface. I felt those inky veins darkening my skin, and I knew he saw them too. Knew he understood how eager I was to use that power against him.

Yet there was no flicker of wariness. Nothing except predatory amusement as he said, 'Your show of force would be more impressive if I could die.'

I swallowed, unnerved by his words – and their implications.

He strode towards me and Cassius. We stayed very still, holding our ground even as Cassius's fingers clenched around my arm and my legs tensed to run. It was better not to move. Even with the jaguar features gone – for now – there was something animal-like about the god, something predatory.

And predators relish the chase.

'Would you like to see your beloved again?' Fennec asked as he stalked towards me, still smiling, daring me to try to run. 'I could bring him back for you.'

I didn't need to see Cassius's warning shake of the head to know it was a lie. Fennec was a trickster god, after all.

'That's impossible,' I said, holding that ancient gaze. 'Not even the Sorceress could bring someone back after they were dead too long—'

'I granted the Sorceress her powers. Do you think anything is impossible for me?' At my hesitation, Fennec smiled widely – a red slash that reminded me of the clansmen whose throats he had slit. 'All you have to do is join my priestesses and unleash your death magic against your brother and cousin. Is that really such a high price to pay? You know you will have to kill them both after this battle is done.'

The hitch in Cassius's breathing was a like a heart murmur. Sharp and sudden and telling.

Fennec watched me knowingly. 'Already he doubts you. And I know you doubt him, despite your pitiful thoughts of promises and family loyalty. What hope is there for peace between you? Peace is a fairy tale. A dream.'

An image of Severin formed at Fennec's side. I quickly looked away, refusing to let the god use my feelings to manipulate me.

Gentle fingers tilted my chin upwards. No longer insubstantial, but warm. Real.

As real as the compassion and sadness on Severin's face. So genuine that I knew those emotions couldn't possibly belong to Fennec. Knew that whatever magic had formed this in-between place . . . it had somehow allowed Severin's spirit to reach me. To share a few precious heartbeats together.

'This isn't a hallucination, is it?' I asked, my voice whisper soft. Cassius and Fennec glanced around, clearly wondering who I was speaking to. But the fact they couldn't see him didn't deter me.

'No, Scarlett.' Soft and melodious. 'This is real. *I'm* real.'

Severin leant in and stroked a strand of hair back from my face. He was all I could see. Fennec and Cassius faded, along with the darkness and the bodies.

But Fennec's offer remained, tempting and terrible. What he was asking me to do was monstrous – but what wouldn't I do for Severin? If this was what it took to save him – wasn't it worth the lives it would cost?

'Is he telling the truth? Can I bring you back?'

Severin shook his head, and something in my chest tightened – and loosened, all at once. 'There's a reason the Sorceress couldn't bring someone back after they had been dead too long. By that point, they would be a shell of what they once were – a reanimated corpse, nothing more. What Fennec is offering isn't a gift. It's a curse.'

He cupped my face in his hands and brushed his lips against mine. The ghost of a kiss.

'Don't go,' I begged, reaching for him even as he stepped back. 'Please. I can't lose you again. I *need* you.'

A hint of a smile. It held a slightly wry edge. 'You've never needed anyone.'

'That's not true,' I said immediately. 'I need you. I . . . I *love* you.'

Answering emotion sparked in his face, in those piercing, mismatched eyes that seemed to stare right into my soul. And as I looked into those eyes, into the light and wonder and compassion within them, I knew he saw a soul worth loving.

'As I love you,' Severin said, resting his forehead against mine. A tear dripped down my cheek. He wiped it tenderly away. 'For eternity, Scarlett. I will love you for eternity. *And you will never be alone.*'

I opened my eyes to darkness. To Cassius and Fennec staring at me as though I had lost my mind.

'Have you made your decision?' Fennec asked, a hint of impatience hardening his voice.

'I have.' I stared him down. 'Some fates,' I said, echoing the words Severin had once said to me, 'should not be changed.'

Darkness whipped out from Fennec with impossible speed, spearing towards me like a javelin. I shoved Cassius to the side and faced it, knowing that this wasn't something I could avoid. If it killed me, so be it. At least I would be with Severin. At least I would have died fighting for something that mattered.

Aquamarine light exploded from the necklace Severin had given me, brighter even than Fennec's darkness. It shattered through the priestesses' power and even the image of Fennec himself, wiping away the darkness in a single brilliant flare. When I dared move my hands from my eyes, it was to see a grey sky above me, the sun peeking out from one of the clouds.

Behind us, our army of clansmen was decimated. A thousand lives callously and brutally taken.

But the priestesses . . . I stared down at their motionless forms. It seemed ludicrous that six people could have been responsible for this level of destruction. And yet, those six priestesses had almost destroyed any chance we had at winning this war.

Perhaps a thousand lives was worth the cost of taking them down.

At least now we had a fair chance.

'Do you think Roran's Artisans would have Seen this?' I asked, helping Cassius to his feet.

A year ago, Cassius would have pushed me away – would have spurned any assistance I offered. Today, he gave me a nod of thanks before turning in a slow circle, taking in the destruction.

'I don't think so,' he said at last. 'Roran wouldn't have sent the priestesses if he knew they would be killed. I don't think even Artisans could See past whatever *that* was.'

'I think it was a place.' I thought of what Velanthe had told me, about how blood sacrifices had brought her closer to the divine world. 'A kind of in-between, where the priestesses could commune with Fennec. Somewhere the mortal and divine realms come close to touching.'

'Disconcerting,' Cassius remarked, 'but as good an explanation as any.' He cast me a curious, assessing glance.

'What's that for?' I asked as we made our way through the morbid pile of bodies – searching for survivors. A horse would be useful, but I wasn't holding out much hope. Fennec seemed to have torn through them first.

'You could have dived out of the way and left me to bear the brunt of Fennec's burst of power.' His tone was carefully unreadable. 'Instead, you held your position and used precious seconds to push me out of its path. You saved my life.'

'You saved mine,' I reminded him, thinking of the way the priest-esses had carved into me.

Cassius's lips curved. 'Let's call it even, then, shall we?'

I smiled back with genuine warmth. I had missed this – working with Cassius rather than against him.

But his expression turned serious as his attention returned to the bodies. 'Mira will be expecting our army to outflank Roran's forces. This defeat could cost us the war.'

'Maybe not.' I knelt beside one of the dead horses. If everything Velanthe had told me was true, blood magic was destructive – corrosive. She had thought it would destroy Mira if she used too much, and there was no reason to believe it wouldn't do the same to me.

But my mother had used blood magic a great deal, and she was still in seemingly perfect health. I doubted she would have been so determined for me to embrace magic that would only kill me.

The horse answered my call almost immediately. It stirred and clambered to its feet, its eyes wholly black – as black as the blood that dripped from my palm. It tossed its dark mane and lowered itself onto the ground, allowing me to climb on.

'Take my hand,' I said to Cassius and hoisted him up.

His warmth settled behind me, but I could hear the dryness in his voice. '*That's* your plan – to charge Roran's army with one horse? As much as I admire your boldness, Scarlett, I was hoping for something slightly less suicidal.'

I didn't answer, too busy taking in the dead. Thousands of bodies that could turn the tide of this battle.

Mira's blood magic hadn't been limited to touch. Perhaps neither was mine – not if I embraced it completely.

As if the horse was an extension of my mind, it trotted slowly between the piles of bodies. I sliced my palm with my dagger and let my blood drip steadily down onto the ground.

And then I waited.

Cassius shifted impatiently behind me. But he must not have seen what I had – the black blood thickening and beginning to move, snaking across the ground towards the bodies. When I saw the inky veins spiderwebbing across my arms and hands . . . My smile felt like Fennec's. Powerful and calculated and more than a little hungry.

Cassius jerked as the pile of bodies shifted. With a groan, the dead clansmen began to rise. One after another they broke out of those piles and straightened, snapping to attention as they looked at me. Their eyes were so dark that they burned.

There was wrath in those eyes. Wrath that needed to be directed.

Their heads swivelled to fix on Ulrik, as if recognising his authority. Then their focus returned to me.

Kill them. It was nothing more than a thought, but I felt it echo around me, deafening in its power. *Kill Roran and everyone loyal to him. Make him pay for what his priestesses did to you.*

Their bodies lurched as they moved into formation, flanking me and

Cassius, whose grip tightened almost painfully around my waist. And as we reached the edge of the forest, Roran's immense army coming into view, I no longer felt even the slightest flicker of fear.

What was there left to fear? I was the master of death, and death was what I planned to offer my enemies.

'Let's go kill our brother,' I said to Cassius and my army of the dead. And then we were moving.

It seemed only fitting that my rule as empress should be built on Roran's bones.

CHAPTER FORTY-SEVEN

Mira

Pain.

Blistering, terrible pain that made it impossible to think. Impossible to do anything except scream.

I pushed against the barrier of fire with everything I had. Desperate to make it to the other side—

'Don't bother. It won't let you through.' The flames in front of me reformed into a man with hair the colour of fox fur and arresting golden eyes. There was no mercy in those eyes as they studied me. Nothing but darkness and ancient cruelty. 'Did you think you had seen the last of me, Kasmira? That I would allow you to smash my servant's mind without consequences?'

'I didn't give any thought to you at all,' I gritted out, even as my vision began to blur and I struggled to remain standing.

Fennec's teeth flashed in a feral grin. 'A fatal error.'

I couldn't bite back my agonised cry. The fire was inside my mind, my heart, my veins. The sound of my flesh sizzling hissed in my ears, and I knew I was dying. Failing, even as I fought with every ounce of my remaining strength to succeed, to help my people—

I took a step forward. Then another.

Fennec's raspy laugh echoed around me, amused and terrible. That laugh told me that I had seconds left to live.

But a strange instinct kept me moving towards him. The same uncanny certainty I had felt when I had communed with the Sorceress and connected with the elements.

I closed my eyes, blocking out the emotions that would kill me

· 362 ·

that much sooner. As my intuition expanded, I could sense Fennec's toxic presence in front of me. I could feel the fire licking at my skin, threatening to devour me.

The fire felt like destruction. Fennec felt like fury.

My eyes snapped open. And I felt it again. The *pull*.

I reached for Fennec's arm, heedless of the fact I was about to touch pure fire. Pure *power*.

Fennec's smile said that touching him would burn me up that much faster. But—

It was just like at the circus, when I had used my mother's locket. The flames engulfed me, hungrily licking at my clothes, my skin, my hair, but though I felt their heat, Fennec's power no longer hurt me. How could it?

I *was* Fennec.

I was his hunger. His fury. I felt his urge to consume, to devour, to *destroy*, but I could temper that urge.

So I did.

I drew that urge into me, containing it within my body. And as I did, the image of Fennec exploded in a shower of sparks.

The remaining fire flooded into me or died completely. As the flames disappeared, I became aware of the extent of the destruction. So many dead. Butchered – because of Roran.

My gaze lifted to the raised platform, where he was smiling down at me. My mother's murderer, confident in the knowledge that he was out of reach. So certain of his victory and my defeat.

'Kill her,' his booming voice rang out – and then I heard nothing except the thudding of thousands of boots as Roran's frontlines advanced in perfect, murderous formation.

A formation that would cut right through me. *If* I let it.

I shot Roran a smile that was little more than a baring of teeth. The sound of hoofbeats told me that Aric was charging towards me with the rest of the forces he had taken to higher ground.

They would reach me soon – but not soon enough to protect me from those swords and spears. I had no delusions about what I was facing: we had known it would take all our shifters to break through Roran's perfect killing formations. But I didn't need to break through his lines.

Already, that sense of connection, of *oneness*, was fading. It was taking more and more effort to hold onto Fennec's power, to keep it contained inside me.

Just a few more moments, I told myself as the Warriors advanced, their spiked black armour absorbing the sunlight. *Just a little longer—*

Arrows rained down as the archers in Roran's main force began their onslaught. Somewhere behind me, I could hear Aric screaming my name. I probably looked insane, standing in their path without raising my shield.

But I could *sense* the arrows in a way I hadn't been able to before.

With everything I had, I pushed back on the arrows, forcing them off course until they were threatening Roran's forces instead. Forcing the frontlines to stop their advance and raise their shields.

My army was nearly at my side, but I continued walking forward. A few of Roran's soldiers had gone down – but already they were regrouping, their formations as strong as ever.

Let's see how strong they are after this, I thought and released Fennec's power.

It detonated out of me in a searing tidal wave that instantly vaporised Roran's frontlines, cooking them alive in their amour. Chaos descended, breaking those disciplined lines as soldiers and Warriors fled, trying uselessly to outrun the death at their backs.

Their inhuman screams reminded me of the agonised sounds my shifters had made as they burned alive. Bile clogged my throat at the realisation I had unleashed something equally horrific.

But every time one of the Ravalian soldiers died, it meant that one of mine might live.

My eyes locked with Roran's furious ones. He unsheathed his sword and whirled on a man standing next to him on the platform. I flinched as the man was cut down without mercy, not understanding until I saw something fall from Roran's hand. A red jewel. *A blood ruby.*

I stared at the Artisan's body in horror. Had Roran really expected him to See outcomes that were influenced by the decisions of a god? A being that didn't even exist on the mortal plane?

'Hail Queen Mira! Hail the Sorceress!' The shouts of the clansmen were almost as loud as their galloping mounts. I turned to see Nari and Gunnar leading their remaining forces, a few paces behind Aric and Conall.

'Get on!' Aric shouted, leaning across his stallion and pulling me onto Conall's armoured back – just in time.

My stomach sank as the fire began to disperse. Barely even singeing the first lines of Roran's calvary, which parted to let through—

'Hounds.' Aric's voice was like a death knell. 'Charge!' he ordered the others. 'CHARGE NOW!'

Conall barrelled forward, leading the way as he broke through the remaining lines of foot soldiers, with Aric close behind. But then Roran's calvary was there, colliding with our forces in an explosion of toppling bodies and spurting blood. I clung to Conall with everything I had as the world descended into a nightmare.

The screams of fallen warriors and dying horses rent the air – theirs, ours, I couldn't tell. It was deafening. Disorientating. A mess of blood and death and howling hounds that made horses rear up and toss their riders – allowing Roran's army to ride through and slaughter the unseated clansmen.

'WATCH OUT!' I shouted to Jadis – too late.

A hound leapt up and tore out the throat of her horse, hurling Jadis to the ground, where I immediately lost sight of her. All around me, horses and clansmen went down in a tumble of blades and hooves.

I swung my sword viciously as one of Roran's Warriors aimed for Aric, separating the Warrior's head from his body. Aric gasped out something that I took as thanks before engaging his next opponent.

Time blurred as the fighting wore on. So did faces.

I forgot them as soon as I killed them, turning my attention to the next – and the next. Butchering myself a path through Roran's army as I set my sights on the raised platform where Roran would be waiting.

The sooner Aric or I killed him, the sooner the fighting would stop. I knew we both felt the weight of that responsibility.

Shocked yells erupted from across the plain, and I squinted to see—

'They did it,' I shouted to Aric, relief flooding me at the sight of the thousand clansmen descending on Roran's ranks from behind. Taking them by complete surprise.

Roran's soldiers scattered, fleeing as Scarlett and Cassius led the charge on a horse that looked half dead. No – there was no *half* about it. The horse was riddled with gaping wounds, its eyes either wholly black or torn out of their sockets.

Ducking under the next sword that came at me, I dispatched the rider and risked another glance at the clansmen under Scarlett's command. Now that they were closer, I could see the same evidence of fatal wounds as the horse. One of them had a gaping hole in his chest where his heart should have been. Another was missing an arm. And Ulrik . . . Ulrik was missing his *head*.

'Undead!' A cry rang out from Roran's side of the army. 'She's created an army of the undead!'

More voices rang out, echoing similar cries of horror and dismay as Scarlett's forces circled around and began killing their way towards the platform. Leaving nothing but corpses in their wake.

'*Hold your formation!*' Roran bellowed.

His order might have worked – if not for me. When I was connected to my surroundings, I willed the ground to burst open. Sending Warriors tumbling down the yawning chasm in a roar of falling rock and screeching horses.

The remaining Ravalians shifted into practised formations.

I exchanged a glance with Aric, wanting to help Scarlett but not wanting to leave him.

'Go!' Aric ordered me. 'Use Conall to break down their lines!'

Conall didn't just break down their lines – he shattered them apart, tossing horses and Warriors aside like rag dolls. My sword cleaved through the air as I helped him, blood spraying in a vicious arc. It splattered across my face like warpaint.

Even Roran's seasoned Warriors backed away at my approach. Some turned and broke ranks entirely.

A war horse barrelled towards me from an angle. I turned slightly too late, but before the Warrior could skewer me, Scarlett was there. She smoothly lopped off his head and jumped off her horse, leaving Cassius to ride on ahead. I dismounted too, and Conall roared as he raced past Cassius, clearing him a route to Roran.

Scarlett and I fought back-to-back, and what Scarlett lacked in swordsmanship, she made up for in cunning and magical prowess.

Warriors fell to her illusions and her death magic, until I could see Cassius once more. Scarlett paused, reaching down to touch one of the Warriors she'd killed. Topping up her magic, I realised, when I noticed the black veins darkening her skin. A perfect match to the dark veins spiderwebbing across the skin of the undead clansmen.

A heartbeat later, we resumed cutting our way through Roran's personal guard and onto the platform. We were so close that I could see the perspiration beading on General Hare's forehead as he battled Cassius back, and the promise of murder in Roran's eyes as he advanced on his younger brother.

And then it happened.

I watched Roran's sword sing out – and connect with Cassius's armour, the impact hurling him to the ground.

'*Cassius!*'

I was too far away to help him. Too far to stop General Harte as he raised his lance and brought it thudding down, right through Cassius's weakened armour.

He crumpled to the ground, only to be dragged to his feet by Roran, who tore aside the broken armour and placed his dagger directly over Cassius's heart.

'I'll make this simple for you,' Roran said, his hateful green eyes searing into mine. 'Surrender, or I will kill Cassius. And believe me, it will not be easy to watch. I know exactly where to strike to draw out his suffering for as long as possible.'

'Do that,' I said coldly, crossing the platform, 'and I will make sure Aurelius suffers as well. You will never see your child again. You won't even have the chance to bury him.'

Roran only laughed. 'Don't bother with threats you can't enforce. I know you won't kill an innocent.'

'What about me?' Scarlett moved to stand at my side, her red hair billowing in the wind.

Brother and sister considered each other for a moment. The tension between them was so thick I could feel it crackle around me.

'You,' Roran said at last, 'I can believe. But having an heir only matters if I live through this battle – and if I do, I can always sire another son. Kill Aurelius if you wish. Either way, I have no qualms about ending our brother.' His jade eyes glittered in dark satisfaction as they shifted to me. 'I think I would rather enjoy it, actually. Carving Cassius up slowly and watching you try to be strong for him. I'll tell you a secret, Kasmira: loved ones always break in the end. They can't stand to watch someone they care about in pain.'

'You underestimate my importance to her,' Cassius said tightly. 'I've never been her first choice.'

Something in my chest cracked open at his words – at the rawness of them. Months earlier, he never would have allowed any trace of vulnerability to show.

Roran looked truly amused. 'Oh, I think Kasmira cares more than she lets on.' He sliced his dagger slowly down Cassius's chest. A groan left his lips as blood bubbled from the wound, but I almost didn't hear it, my scream was so loud.

Aric grabbed me from behind, stopping me before I could run to Cassius. 'Don't,' he murmured in my ear. 'It's what he wants.'

Roran looked at me with open satisfaction. And Cassius . . . I thought he saw how much I cared about him then. That he realised I would hand Aurelius over if it gave him even the slimmest chance of survival.

'You're a monster,' I told Roran.

Roran clucked his tongue. 'How unoriginal.'

He slammed his elbow into Cassius's face. This time it wasn't just blood that spurted from his nose and dripped from his mouth. He spat a tooth onto the platform.

'Is that all you've got?' The Cassius that looked up at Roran was the prince from the Ravalian Court. The one who had worn nonchalance like a mask and wielded disdain like a shield. 'Our father hit me harder than that.'

'A glutton for punishment, aren't you?' Roran's dagger bit into Cassius's side. *No, no, no.*

Blood everywhere. So. Much. Blood.

My eyes found Cassius's. *What are you doing? Why are you* baiting *him?*

'I love you, Mira,' Cassius said, his eyes steady on mine.

I realised what he was about to do a second before he did it.

'No!' I shouted. '*Don't!*'

But not even Roran was fast enough to stop Cassius as he grabbed the dagger and sank it deep into his stomach. Sacrificing himself so that I could act against Roran—

Yet even as I knew that . . . all I could see was Cassius's head thudding back against the ground as he went still. Utterly still.

I was so attuned to his heartbeat that I felt it weaken. Slower . . . *slower* . . .

The crevasses around us widened, the ground shaking with the force of my anger. Cracks spiderwebbed towards the platform.

Towards *Roran*.

'Stop it, Mira!' Scarlett hissed, taking hold of my shoulders. 'If those crevasses get much wider, you'll kill us all. You need to—'

I didn't listen to whatever she was going to say. 'Stay with Cassius. Do what you can for him.'

And then I was moving – sprinting after Aric, who was already spearing towards Roran.

But I couldn't let Aric get to him first.

Roran was *mine*.

CHAPTER FORTY-EIGHT

Mira

I pushed Aric out of the way and swung violently at Roran with my dagger. '*You don't get to win.*'

'First your mother,' Roran taunted, dodging my desperate slashes, 'then Darius, and now Cassius. Who should be next, do you think? Aric – or Lillian, perhaps?'

'You'll be dead before you touch them,' I growled, vaguely conscious of Aric crossing swords with General Harte nearby. But I couldn't look at him. Couldn't risk shifting my focus for even a sec—

Roran thrust my blade away from him, slamming his other fist into my face.

My head snapped back, my mouth filling with the metallic taste of blood, but I attacked him like an animal, kicking and punching and dodging. My next kick connected, and I delighted in Roran's grunt of pain.

We traded savage blows until both of us were bleeding and breathing heavily. A roar of frustration left my lips as he dodged my next strike and slammed into me, so hard that I felt a rib crack at the impact.

I clawed at every part of him I could reach. I was so much stronger and more experienced than I had been when I'd faced Roran the last time, but it still wasn't *enough*—

'That's right,' Roran gloated. 'You can't beat me, Kasmira. And when you die, Cassius's sacrifice will be meaningless. I will mount all your heads on the Kalurian gates, and those members of your army that do survive will spend their—'

The platform lurched to the side, sending Roran tumbling amongst the bodies of his personal guard. I lunged after him, landing on his chest and squeezing my hands around his throat. I wanted him *dead*. I wanted him motionless and bleeding and broken—

But he was already rallying – using his magical Warrior strength to prise open my fingers and reverse our positions. Roran lifted me like a rag doll and then smashed me back down once, twice, three times. I couldn't breathe. Couldn't see, couldn't think. When I tried to cough, only blood bubbled out. I spat it in his face.

He was smiling as he wiped it away. As he reached for the very blade that had dealt my mother a fatal blow.

And then Aric was there.

I sucked in a painful, heaving breath, unable to look away as the two best swordsmen I knew went head-to-head, moving so fluidly I could barely see their blades.

Watching Aric fight was like watching Kain reborn. His muscles rippled as he forced back blows that would have shattered any other opponent. He never stopped moving, pushing back and deflecting in a way that allowed him to remain out of Roran's reach.

They threw everything at each other, holding nothing back. It was brutal and terrible and seamlessly natural. A dance, like all the best fights were. Only Aric was the one leading, driving Roran towards the inevitable conclusion.

Frustration made Roran sloppy – relying on brute force where he should have known better, being baited into taking openings that were really traps. I had the sense that Aric was playing now, his blade darting out and opening wounds like I had once done with Nikolas Atwood – small cuts here and there, just to enjoy the look on Roran's face, the rage.

I watched Roran's threats crash over Aric like a wave. He didn't even flinch as Roran mentioned Kain, and Lillian, and everyone Aric loved, because all Roran was doing was reaffirming Aric's decision to end him. There was nothing Roran could do or say to rattle him now.

He was beyond Roran, and I realised that I was watching a master in action. A swordsman beyond equal.

Aric disarmed Roran with ease. Even Scarlett was looking at Aric as though she had never seen him before, and I saw a glimmer of awe on her face. Roran watched him with hatred and confusion. He didn't understand how Aric could possibly have bested him.

Pride rushed through me as Aric advanced on Roran with his sword raised, forcing him closer to the end of the platform. Beyond it, I saw that the battle was won: my forces had triumphed, and Roran's had fallen. I relished the dawning realisation that crossed his face as he surveyed the carnage.

'I told you,' I said, walking over to join Aric. 'You don't get to win. Not this time. Not against all of us.'

Roran's hateful eyes darted past me – to where I could feel Scarlett at my back. And Cassius, lying wounded beyond her.

Scarlett, Aric and I moved closer, forming a barrier that Roran couldn't hope to break through. He stared at us and then glanced over the edge, where my clansmen and remaining shifters waited. Scarlett's undead warriors were closest to the platform, their eyes empty husks, their skin streaked with black veins. An army of unfeeling faces and dead, blackened skin. Hideous. Terrifying.

Wonderful.

'I promised them revenge against you,' Scarlett said to Roran. 'For what the priestesses did to them. It won't be pretty.'

Roran looked at his sister, searching for softness he wouldn't find. Then he looked back at the mob – and finally at me. 'Not like this.'

It sounded almost – *almost* – like a plea. But there was no mercy left in me.

I glanced at Aric. 'Would you like to do the honours?'

Aric stepped forward, until Roran teetered on the very edge of the platform. Just below, hundreds of sharp hands waited to drag him down into their midst.

'I'm sorry for what I did to your brother,' Roran said desperately to Aric. 'But he wouldn't have resorted to this. He was a rebel – a reformer. He would have wanted a trial or even an execution—'

'You have no idea what he would have wanted,' Aric said, and pushed Roran off the platform.

Before he even finished falling, I saw the clansmen and shifters converging. Roran's screams rang out as they descended on him—

Trapping him beneath a mass of vengeful bodies.

Reducing him to bits of blood and bone.

CHAPTER FORTY-NINE

Mira

The instant Roran fell, General Harte mounted a horse and galloped away. Fleeing with the remaining Ravalian forces.

I hesitated, torn between chasing them down and helping Cassius. My legs chose for me.

I ran to Cassius's side, Scarlett and Aric hurrying after me. Even for a Ravalian, he was pale – unnaturally pale.

And his pulse . . . it was so slow. Faint and fading, but still there. Barely.

Thump . . . thump.

Thump.

'Hold on,' I whispered to him. 'You can survive this. You *have* to survive this.'

Aric was watching me, but in that moment I didn't care. All I could think about was the vulnerability in Cassius's voice when he had said, 'You love me too.'

And my answer: 'No. I don't.'

My last words to him had been a lie.

'If he . . .' I could barely say it. Barely even *think* it. 'If he dies, you have to bring him back.' It was an order, not a request. 'The same way you resurrected Lillian.'

'It doesn't work that way. I would have to . . .' Scarlett's wary glance at Aric said enough.

She would have to sever her bond with Lillian. The bond keeping my best friend alive.

I gathered Cassius's unresponsive form in my arms, frantically searching for a sign of life. A sign that I could still reach him, still *save* him—

I found it. A hint of warmth – not in his expression or his cold body, but in his veins.

'You promised the Sorceress.' Scarlett's voice was soft, little more than an exhale of breath. 'No blood magic.'

'I don't care.' Promises and consequences meant nothing to me if I could save Cassius.

And despite Scarlett's warning, I knew she felt the same. She said nothing else as I closed my eyes, focusing on Cassius's heartbeat. On the blood pumping weakly through his veins.

Dimly, I was aware of Aric moving to meet what was left of Roran's personal guard as they reached the platform – buying me as much time as he could.

Scarlett caught my left wrist, understanding what I was about to do. 'Don't—'

I pulled out the dagger.

Blood bubbled out, red and thick and terrible. If I was wrong, then I had just killed Cassius with my own hands.

'Don't die,' I begged him, pressing my hands over the wound. 'Please.'

Thick, reddish warmth stained my hands and skin. But the blood wasn't mine. It didn't belong to me.

Return to him, I willed it with everything I had. *Save him.*

My mind felt as though it was fraying at the edges, but I held onto the magic, refusing to let go.

I didn't notice the change at first. Not until the bleeding began to slow, and then stop entirely. The wound was still open, but it began to close in tiny increments. Like Velanthe had once done to me.

Scarlett watched with wide eyes as Cassius's wound healed. But as colour and warmth returned to his skin, I felt colder and harder. Brittle. As if the magic had cost me something crucial this time.

My apprehension faded as Cassius opened his eyes, midnight-blue and every bit as piercing and alive as I remembered.

We looked at each other for a long moment. Scarlett murmured something as she helped him stand, and Cassius's mouth opened, forming words. Words I didn't have the chance to hear.

A Warrior broke through Aric's defences, his spear raised. I cut him down without pause, and as his blood sprayed, my senses seemed to sharpen. It was like what had happened with Velanthe in the Temple. I was connected to everyone around me, to their blood and their minds and their beating hearts—

Including Roran's fleeing forces.

And General Harte.

My power hardened into ice at the thought of his name. And my focus narrowed to vengeance.

I raced down the steps of the platform and ran towards Conall, heedless of the distant shouts of my name. I would be damned if I let General Harte make it to the harbour with Roran's remaining soldiers. If they escaped on those ships—

I refused to finish the thought. They wouldn't escape. *I won't let them.*

My magic erupted from me as I rode towards the harbour, connecting me to Roran's remaining force. Blood rushed through my ears until it was all I could hear. All I could feel.

Power thrummed through my veins, warm and electrifying and addictive.

Puppets. They were all puppets, and I had hold of their strings.

With a single thought, I severed those strings.

Dozens of bodies collapsed ahead of me, spreading out through Roran's fleeing army like a contagion.

And as Roran's forces fell, the clansmen joined my pursuit. Their heartbeats reverberated through my ears, loud and tempting and distracting. I resisted the urge to stop them. They were *my* warriors. Mine to protect.

It occurred to me that I shouldn't have had to remind myself of that fact. That perhaps using so much blood magic had skewed my perceptions.

But my entire being rebelled at the thought of releasing the magic. Roran might be dead, and his army destroyed, but this war was far from over. General Harte needed to pay for what he had done.

Then I would stop. But only then. When I knew he couldn't hurt me – or anyone I cared about. When I knew Kalure was truly safe.

I descended on the harbour ahead of my warriors, though I could sense Scarlett gaining on me, Cassius and Aric close behind. What I had seen before at the clifftop was correct: Ravalian ships had been set against Roran's armada. Despite their superior numbers, somehow it was Roran's fleet that was decimated, the proud ships leaning on their sides and taking on water, some blown apart entirely, with only floating debris left behind.

It was a power I had seen once before – on Aldara. When Zandri had blasted apart the tents in the circus.

Conall stilled as General Harte and six of his officers shuffled into view – wounded and with none of the confidence I had observed earlier. Zandri rode behind them, Emperor Kalias's bone crown glinting ominously on her head. Its golden tips jutted cruelly upwards, like death dipped in gold.

A cool smile greeted me as Zandri swung down from the saddle. She hadn't bothered with armour, instead donning her usual black fighting leathers. Warriors, Masks, Artisans – they all flanked her, giving me pause.

'Congratulations on a decisive victory, Kasmira,' she said in her razor-sharp voice. 'It seems any further assistance is unnecessary. At least I was able to apprehend these cowards for you.' A nod at General Harte and his senior Warriors.

I eyed the crown she wore as I asked pointedly, 'Did you come here to help, or to challenge me for the Kalurian throne?'

'I assure you,' Zandri said smoothly, 'there's no cause for concern. Ruling Ravalia is more than enough for me.'

'I thought that was Scarlett's intention.'

Zandri merely smiled. 'Does it matter? Do you care what happens in Ravalia, so long as your country remains free?'

I trust Scarlett a great deal more than I trust you, I thought. Out loud, I said, 'I suppose not.'

Let Zandri think that I believed her assurances. At least I had the larger fighting force.

I returned my attention to General Harte, who had the audacity to collapse to his knees, his head bowed in surrender. The rest of his men followed suit, discarding their weapons.

I laughed. A harsh, callous sound. 'What would you have done if *I* had surrendered?' I asked, stalking closer. 'Would you have let me live?'

General Harte said nothing. I saw the truth reflected in his eyes as he met my gaze, and that truth was all it took for my blood magic to rise up.

Blood rose with it. Pouring from General Harte's eyes as he writhed on the ground, his fingernails clawing at the dirt.

'Enough,' Aric said from behind me. 'That's *enough*, Mira.'

'Are you seriously trying to stop me?' I asked, twisting to look at him. 'Don't you remember what General Harte did to you?'

'I remember,' Aric said in a low, measured voice. 'But you're not yourself right now. Scarlett told me about the blood magic; I think you've used too much. It's affecting you more than you realise.'

I shifted my gaze to Scarlett. Despite Aric's words, she was watching General Harte with an impassive expression and didn't seem too bothered by my actions. Cassius stood at her side, silent and still, but his gaze was intent as he studied me, filled with unexpected gravity.

'I know what kind of queen you want to be,' Aric said again, 'and this isn't it.'

'You're wrong,' I said defiantly, willing the blood to flow more readily. Willing General Harte to experience the same pain he had inflicted on Aric and Cassius.

The General crawled to me, his hands outstretched as if he might beg for mercy. But when he opened his mouth, only blood came dribbling out. It poured from his ears and eyes and even his nose. Choking him.

Killing him.

I felt nothing but satisfaction as his heart finally stopped. Out of the corner of my eye, I saw one of his companions dash for the forest. The remaining five exchanged a panicked glance and bolted after him.

Nari's warriors didn't try to stop them.

My teeth ground together, but I didn't turn my ire on Nari or her people. I merely watched General Harte's Warriors run.

The sight reminded me of Darius – of how Roran had given him a glimmer of hope, only to wrench it away at the last moment. I let

General Harte's Warriors flee until I felt that same hope emanating from them. Then I stopped their hearts one by one, laughing as I wrenched that hope away. Laughing as they fell, only a short distance from the tree line. From escape.

'Bring me Roran's son,' I ordered Odessa. The priestess tensed at my words and glanced at Scarlett.

Scarlett frowned, the first glimmer of emotion she'd shown so far. 'Aurelius is resting. I don't think he—'

'I don't care what you think. I gave my high priestess an order, and I expect it to be followed.'

'What are you going to do with him?' Scarlett asked, utterly unfazed by my anger.

'I'm going to execute him.'

Scarlett stared at me. She was looking at me like *everyone* was looking at me – as if I had lost my mind.

'Mira—'

'He's Roran's *son*,' I reminded her, irritated that I had to spell it out. 'Kalure won't be safe until he's dead. And neither will you, not if you intend to claim the Ravalian throne. You should be thanking me. I'm finally making the hard choices – isn't that what you and Cassius told me I needed to do?'

'Aurelius is a child.' Scarlett took a deep breath, and I had the sense it cost her something to say, 'No matter who his father was, he deserves our protection. He's an innocent.'

'There's no such thing.'

Odessa returned with Aurelius – and Lillian, her arms draped protectively over his shoulders.

'Bring him over here,' I said, unsheathing my sword. 'I'll make it quick. He won't feel a thing.'

Aric stepped in front of Lillian and Aurelius, protecting them with his own body. I turned towards him, and another unstable laugh bubbled from my lips. 'Are you really going to fight me? To commit treason against your queen?'

'Do you see a sword drawn?' Aric asked steadily. 'I won't fight you, Mira. But if you want to harm this boy, you're going have to kill me.'

My body shook with a mixture of rage and hysterical amusement.

'He's not a boy! Can't you see that? He's a threat that has to be put down—'

'Release the magic, Mira,' Cassius interrupted, his voice low and imploring.

I lifted my gaze to him – and I laughed again, only this time, it sounded choked. 'Since when are *you* the voice of reason?'

'Since right now,' Cassius said, taking a step closer. 'Aric is right; this isn't you.'

Things must have been bad, if Cassius was agreeing with Aric. But just because they agreed didn't mean I had to *listen* to them—

Movement made me turn.

Conall and the remaining shifters were leaving. Betrayal speared through me – quickly followed by rage as I noticed the clansmen disappearing into the trees. Nari led them, stiff-backed and purposeful. She didn't even spare a glance for me, her queen.

Her dismissal stung. It was happening all over again; the same outcome, the same betrayal, only I had done everything right this time! I had reversed all my mistakes, and yet somehow my warriors were still leaving. The shifters had already disappeared, and the priestesses and Ravalian Warriors were watching me like – like—

'You broke your vow,' Odessa said, moving out of Aric's shadow. Behind her, a dozen priestesses looked warily between her and me. 'You promised you wouldn't use blood magic again.'

'I did it to save *his* life,' I said, pointing angrily at Cassius.

'And I'm very grateful,' Cassius replied, his tone light – though his eyes were filled with calculation. His hand rested on the hilt of his sword, ready to draw it. 'So don't make me fight you.'

'*Fight* me?' I stared at him incredulously. Had everyone lost their minds? 'You can't fight me. My magic is—'

His sword sliced towards me, and I hissed in irritation as I was forced to used blood magic to slow his heartbeat. Cassius's attack paused, but I could still feel him testing the limits of my concentration. Stopping me from turning my attention to Aurelius.

'Could it be the magic? Or . . .' Aric trailed off, his attention shifting to Scarlett, who was watching Zandri with an odd expression. 'It's your mother, isn't it?' Aric said, stepping away from Odessa and Aurelius.

Leaving the boy exposed. 'She's controlling Mira somehow. Like Velanthe did to me.'

I didn't listen to Scarlett's response. I wasn't being controlled, but if they were distracted by the possibility, perhaps I could finally deal with Aurelius. I raised my sword and stepped towards the boy—

Cassius smoothly moved in front of me, blocking my path. 'You need to work on your concentration, Mira.'

I glared at him. Before he could attack again, I slowed his heartbeat, sending him toppling to his knees.

But his gaze darted past me, towards—

I dodged as Scarlett lunged for me, avoiding her poisonous touch by a matter of centimetres.

Her eyes were fixed on mine, and her lips were moving. *Stop this. Or I'll stop you.*

I laughed a little at the arrogance of her words, before realising that I couldn't actually hear them.

I couldn't hear anything—

Panic threatened to overwhelm me, but I fought it back. What did it matter if I couldn't hear what Scarlett and Cassius were saying? Listening to them would only distract me from my true purpose. Aurelius.

Scarlett circled me, waiting for an opening to strike. Was *this* what Scarlett had intended all along – to weaken me so that her mother could swoop in and take over? Was this yet another betrayal?

'Stop this, Mira.' Scarlett's voice was cautious. 'You won't get to Aurelius. I won't let you.'

But I didn't need to get any closer than I was. I didn't even need a sword to deal with Aurelius. I only needed my magic.

My senses extended, until I was attuned to his heartbeat as well as Cassius's.

A single thought was all it would take.

Yet I hesitated. The connection between the boy in front of me and the hatred I felt didn't quite match. Everything had seemed so clear a second ago, but now—

A force swept across the field, blasting me backwards and whipping my hair across my face.

When I looked up, I was shocked to see Aric lying on the ground a few metres from Zandri, his armour dented and abrasions covering every inch of his exposed skin.

Horror speared through me. How hadn't I noticed that Aric was fighting *Zandri*? How hadn't I noticed the danger he was in?

But I knew the answer. It was pulsing brightly in Zandri's hand. Red and mesmerising and terrible.

'Aric!' I shouted, sprinting towards him. 'Get away from her! *Run!*'

Aric's eyes met mine briefly, and the relief in them – the *love* – stole my breath. But he didn't run. His gaze returned to the blood ruby in Zandri's grip, his face filled with single-minded focus.

Zandri said something too low for me to hear, but I knew it was a warning. And I knew she wouldn't give it twice.

I ran even harder, but my body was sluggish and unresponsive. I felt like I was caught up in the middle of a nightmare – too far to do anything but watch as Aric advanced on Zandri, his sword raised.

As if a *sword* would do anything against Zandri. As if he stood a chance.

'RUN!' I screamed again, with everything I had left in me. So loudly I felt my throat tear. 'YOU HAVE TO RUN!'

I reached desperately for my blood magic, but either I was burned out or Zandri was blocking me somehow, because nothing happened. She didn't even look at me as she waved her hand in an almost nonchalant gesture.

For an instant, I thought nothing had happened. Then Aric turned to face me, and I saw the thin crimson line ringing his throat.

No. I wasn't sure if I gasped it or screamed it, but it ripped apart my soul. My entire being.

Aric stumbled towards me, just like Darius had done. One step. Then another.

I already knew he wouldn't make it. Blood seeped from the grisly wound around his neck.

A gaping, reddish smile.

CHAPTER FIFTY

Mira

I reached Aric as he fell, my hands slippery with his blood. So much blood, and I couldn't seem to stop it.

Zandri must have used her own abilities to amplify my blood magic. Now, without her control through the blood ruby, I was drained. Spent. *Useless.*

I was *useless* to him.

'Help him,' I begged Zandri. 'I don't care what it costs. I'll do anything. *Just help him!*'

Zandri looked on in silence. An unmoving, unfeeling pillar of shadow. And I knew then – there was nothing I could offer her. Nothing she wanted, except my death. And Aric's.

'AURELIUS!' Lillian's scream made me turn in time to see the little boy streak towards Aric.

Aric, who he had liked and admired. Aric, who had played with him and held him and told him stories by the campfire—

Zandri's dark eyes sharpened, and I saw the same hunger that I had felt earlier – the fierce need to end a potential threat. But that hunger had never been mine.

It had been *hers*.

Scarlett stepped forward, as if she might try to stop her mother—

Zandri moved too quickly to be natural. In an instant, her hands were on Aurelius's shoulders – a mockery of Lillian's gentle affection. Lillian's pleas were heart-wrenching.

'Don't do it,' Scarlett said, her face ashen. 'Aric was bad enough, but a child . . .'

'A child grows into a man.' Zandri's voice was as cool as her expression. Aurelius was trembling beneath her tight hold, his eyes wide with terror. 'What good is your victory against Roran if it's incomplete?'

In a quick, efficient motion, she lashed out with her dagger. Aurelius's small form slumped in the grass, the toy soldiers he had liked to play with spilling out of his pockets. Lying overturned in a pool of red.

My tears dripped down onto Aric's upturned face. He tried to speak – maybe to say Aurelius's name – but all that came out of his mouth was more blood.

I felt the moment it happened. Aric's chest went cold and still beneath my touch, and when I pressed my ear over his heart, I heard nothing but silence.

An agonised sound tore from my lips.

Hands took hold of me; warm and steadying and familiar. Dimly, I realised that Cassius had used Zandri's focus on Aurelius to reach my side.

'Mira,' he said, his voice low and urgent, 'we have to get out of here now. Without your Warriors, we're outnumbered by Zandri's forces. And the priestesses . . . Zandri is speaking with Odessa right now. I think she might be about to—'

'I don't care,' I said, not looking away from Aric's pale face. 'There must be something I can do—'

'There isn't,' Cassius said ruthlessly.

'If I saved you, maybe I can save him—'

'He's *dead*, Mira!'

I flinched away from Cassius, unwilling to believe it. There had to be a way. There always was.

Even as I had the thought, I sensed something. A lingering presence. *He's still in there. Or part of him is.*

I acted without thinking, guided by the instinct that had allowed me to connect with Scarlett and Velanthe – following that shred of presence to its source. Allowing it to act as a bridge between our minds.

Darkness enveloped me. There was no gallery of memories this time – everything was chaotic, and I found myself drifting in a violent sea of untethered thoughts and feelings. But there were flashes of clarity: a glimpse of Zandri's cold stare. A stab of fear.

The memory of Lillian's face. Then mine.

An intense feeling of regret crashed over me like a wave. *Aric's* regret, that he wouldn't see either of us again. That he wouldn't have the chance to build a life with me.

His last thought had been of me.

Something changed with that realisation. The violent sea calmed, and an awareness entered his mind. An awareness that he was no longer alone.

Mira?

Yes. If I could have cried, I would have. *I'm here. I need you to come back with me. We don't have much time.*

I don't think I can. My thoughts are . . . fading. My mind is . . . A pause, then, *I'm dying, aren't I?*

No, I thought back fiercely. *No, I won't let that happen.*

'Mira, you have to come back!' Cassius's voice was followed by the distant sensation of hands pressing against my chest. Had my heart stopped? If it had, shouldn't I have felt it?

You have to go. Aric's thoughts were filled with resolve – and the tang of sadness. *Return to Lillian and Scarlett and Cassius. They need you. Your people need you.*

Before I could protest, the darkness around us lightened. I stared in awe, recognising the mountain meadow on Aldara, where we had practised sparring together. Where we had dreamt of becoming Warriors.

Where I had first begun to fall in love with him.

But I knew what Aric was doing. He had always tried to protect me – and not even death could rob him of that instinct.

I can't do this alone, I thought to him, my heart aching. *Don't make me do this alone.*

Aric looked at me, his brown eyes sparkling, his skin sun-kissed and vibrant and *alive.*

You're not alone, Mira, he replied, his thoughts gently brushing mine. *And you never will be.*

'Gods, Mira, come back!' This time it was Lillian's voice that reached me, high and sweet and terrified. 'We're losing you, do you hear me? We're *losing you,* Mira!'

Aric smiled at me, wreathed in golden light and heartbreakingly beautiful. *Go, Mira,* he told me. *Live. Make my death mean something.*

Aric—

He shoved me out of his mind and back into my own.

My eyes opened to chaos.

Cassius was frantically pounding my chest, ignoring the Ravalian Warriors closing in behind him. Over his shoulder, I saw Lillian – restrained by Odessa and her priestesses. Her face was streaked by tears, but she fought against them with everything she had, cursing at Scarlett, who stood at Zandri's side, her expression inscrutable.

So Scarlett had made her choice, then. But I was too exhausted for rage. Too exhausted to feel anything.

I turned onto my side and gasped, air flooding my lungs. Aurelius's lifeless face was next to mine and the sight of his small body hurt. As did the knowledge that Aric had lived just long enough to see Zandri kill him.

When I was able to breathe again, I looked up – into a pair of dark blue eyes. The shock and relief in them told me how close I had come to dying.

'Deal with Kasmira, would you?' Zandri said callously to Scarlett, and I felt Cassius tense.

He climbed to his feet, preparing to fight. I stood too, but only to reach for his sword and lower it.

'Don't,' I told Cassius, my eyes sweeping over the Ravalian Warriors under Zandri's command, the priestesses who were obeying her orders over mine. 'There's been enough death today.'

Icy fingers enclosed around my shoulder. Fear raced through me as black veins wound up my arms, and as I stared up into Scarlett's glacial eyes, I wondered how I had ever doubted she would kill me.

'You must be pleased,' I whispered, as I felt her death magic enter my bloodstream. 'Now the throne is yours. You've got everything you wanted.'

Scarlett shook her head. The pity in her face hurt more than her betrayal ever could.

Her death magic threatened to pull me under. I fought against that pull, trying to summon the energy to meet Lillian's gaze one last time – to tell her that I had done my best to save Aric and to beg her to forgive me.

But I couldn't manage a single word. I could barely keep my eyes open.

The world tilted on its side, until all I could see was the grass against my cheek. I raised my head—

Aric's eyes stared back at me. Glassy and beautiful and somehow peaceful in death. I hoped I would see him again soon.

Then all I saw was blackness.

And I was grateful for it.

CHAPTER FIFTY-ONE

Scarlett

Most people, when faced with the ultimate betrayal by their mother, would be furious.

When I thought about it, all it really seemed was inevitable.

I stood in the throne room of the Kalurian palace, staring out over the crowd of priestesses bowing before the throne – but I wasn't the one sitting on that throne. I wasn't the recipient of those bows and lowered eyes.

Instead, I was standing beside my mother. Cast off to one side, just like always.

Zandri dismissed the priestesses until we were alone in the echoing hall – alone except for Odessa. My mother smiled at her, a fond smile, and murmured in her ear. Odessa nodded and glided from the hall without sparing a glance for me. I wasn't privy to the deal they had made – whether because my mother had decided against trusting me or simply because she was too used to keeping secrets – but I knew that Zandri had put this into motion a long time ago.

I followed in Zandri's wake as she strode through the stone fortress and down the stairwell leading to the dungeons.

'What happens now?' I asked, my chest tightening with every step. Was she taking me to the cells? To where Mira and Cassius and Lillian would be waiting?

'Kasmira and your brother will be executed at dawn.' Zandri's voice was calm, the words matter-of-fact. 'Odessa would like the honour of drawing first blood, as payment for Kasmira's involvement in the deaths of her parents. I promised her that months ago, when I visited her in the Ravalian dungeons. But the final strike will be yours.'

'Mine?'

Zandri glanced at me. She was still dressed in blood-stained fighting leathers, but my eyes went to the crown on her head. Just the sight of it felt like a knife twisting in my heart.

It hurt almost as much as the realisation that Zandri had killed Aric. That she was now responsible for murdering two of my lovers.

And that I had been unable to save either of them.

But I didn't let Zandri see the devastation on my face. Better that she thought I had swallowed her lies, that I still believed Severin had chosen to end his life without any assistance from her.

'Yes. Yours.' Cool fingers took hold of my face, until Zandri's eyes were inches from mine. Dark and unreadable and as black as Velanthe's. 'If you want Kalure, you must be the one to execute Kasmira. To show your people that you are a ruler to be feared.'

To show *her*.

That was what she really meant. I knew it, because Zandri had once tried to force me to make a similar choice. Had thrown me in the dungeons with a rebel and a dagger.

'*All you need to do is take one life. One life, Scarlett, and you will have access to your blood magic. You will be* magnificent.'

Except I hadn't been able to do it. Not when I stared into the woman's face, lined with sadness and compassion. 'What did you do to end up here with me?' she had asked. 'Why is the head of the Order of Masks punishing a child?'

I hadn't tried to explain that in Zandri's mind, this wasn't a punishment. It was the ultimate act of love, from a mother determined to make her daughter invincible.

Zandri had left me in there for two days until she finally relented. And then she had killed the rebel anyway. Just to prove how useless my attempt at mercy really was.

But she had never forgotten my reluctance. Her displeasure had hung over me ever since.

'I never intended to rule Kalure,' I reminded Zandri. 'I intended to rule the Ravalian Empire.'

'And you will,' Zandri said, her tone placating. 'Once you prove yourself by executing Kasmira, I will make you my heir. You *will* rule the Ravalian Empire, Scarlett – just not as soon as you hoped for. But Kalure is still a prize. And it will be all yours. Yours to shape as you wish.'

Severin had warned me. He had told me that Zandri would always be the puppet master. And now here she was, pulling my strings. *Dance, puppet, dance.*

But what was she actually offering me? I would rule Kalure in her name, and supposedly I would inherit the Ravalian Empire one day, *if* she ever decided to give it up. If she didn't find a way to cling to eternal youth like Velanthe had. I wouldn't put such a thing past her.

In the meantime, I would have to wait. Be patient. Trust in her promises.

Trust wasn't something that came naturally to me.

'I didn't expect such hesitation,' Zandri said, her eyes intent on mine. 'It's a generous offer.'

'But not what you promised.'

Zandri smiled – a flash of white teeth. A hint of a threat. 'I promised that you would be empress one day. That promise still stands.'

An empress of ashes. That was what I would be – because that was all that would be left to rule over.

I tensed as we reached the level where the cells waited. But Zandri continued deeper into the bowels of the earth, the darkness broken by the magical flame blazing in her palm.

'This is the only part of the original palace that still exists.' A trace of pride entered her voice as she slowed to a stop.

I knew immediately who this workroom belonged to.

Like my mother's austere tower in Ravalia, the benches were cluttered with jars and vials – ingredients for her magical experiments. As I walked amongst them, I noticed other things: remnants of Zandri's past. There were very few; letters discarded in a pile, a woven tapestry depicting her hunting prowess. But it was the portrait on the wall that captured my attention.

It was clearly meant to be a family portrait, probably commissioned by the king and queen of Kalure at the time, who stood proudly behind their two children. Yet their faces were burned and charred beyond recognition.

Only the daughter's face was visible, her dark eyes glittering coldly down at me. And I knew that the painting of Zandri's family was nothing more than a reminder of her failings – and her strength in cutting them down.

'Why did you bring me here?' I asked, turning to look at the adult version of my mother.

'Despite my best efforts,' she said, 'there is a weakness in you. A humanity. I wanted you to see that I was the same once. I had a family I cared about, who ultimately betrayed me – all because I hesitated to do what needed to be done. If I had killed my brother when I had the chance, I would have ruled Kalure, and a great deal of bloodshed could have been avoided. I'm giving you the chance to learn from my mistakes.'

'No,' I said, my voice hard. 'You're testing me.'

Zandri raised her chin. 'I'm making you strong. As I always have.'

I had noticed the wrongness of Zandri's eyes before, hadn't I? But I had never known the true implications of what that colour meant. Not until I met Velanthe.

I thought of Velanthe now, of the hunger in her black eyes as she had prepared to cut me open. Like Velanthe, Zandri was willing to do whatever it took to succeed. Even betray her own daughter.

And still a treacherous part of me yearned for her approval. Clinging to the belief that we were a team. That she loved me.

'What happens if I don't execute Mira and Cassius?'

Zandri laughed, as if I was being ridiculous. 'Why wouldn't you? All your life, you've been surrounded by obstacles. I'm simply giving you a chance to cut them down – like you've always wanted.'

Except Cassius and I had come to an understanding. Except Mira and I had started to form a friendship. Except—

Cool fingers took hold of my hands, turning them over. I stared uncomprehendingly at the black veins darkening my palms, remembering how I had used up all the death magic I had invited into me.

'That's not possible,' I breathed, even as Zandri's skin darkened, my deadly power flooding into her without my consent—

I immediately snatched my hands out of her grasp. A few seconds later, the veins faded – but my horror didn't.

You become as poisonous as the death you wield. The seer's warning was deafening in my mind.

I felt sick as I watched the black veins webbing across my skin. I had thought I could control this power – could keep my death magic contained within me. But if I couldn't . . . I would kill anyone who touched me.

And I would be alone. Completely and utterly alone.

'Look at how powerful you are,' Zandri crooned, also watching those black veins – but with satisfaction rather than wariness. 'No one other than me could hope to stand against you now. Certainly not Kasmira or your half-brother.'

'And if I fail?' I had asked her this question once before – before I assassinated my father. In her silence, I had heard the answer: there was no room for failure. Failure meant death.

That time, the threat of death had come from Emperor Kalias and his Warriors. This time, the threat came from her.

'If you fail, you would have proven yourself unworthy. And I will choose someone else to rule Kalure in my place.'

'And what happens to me then?'

Zandri shrugged, but her eyes remained cool and assessing. 'I suppose that would no longer be my concern.'

I couldn't quite believe her. I wanted to, but the painting above me was a grotesque reminder of how Zandri dealt with threats – she killed them.

'But none of this matters, because you won't fail.' Zandri's gaze softened, and the strength of her belief surprised me. It reminded me of the way she had looked at me before I left Ravalia. Her certainty that I would succeed.

'How can you know that?'

'Because you remind me of myself. Of who I used to be.' Zandri ran a finger along a jar with a human heart trapped inside. 'I told you that I was unsure, once. But I chose power over love. Magic over mercy. And I know you will do the same. I know you will, because I've watched you make similar choices for years.'

The truth of her words hit home. I had chosen power over Severin. I had chosen magic over countless lives.

All I had to do was make the same choice once more, and I could have Kalure. And if my mother didn't give me the Ravalian Empire . . . then in time, I could *take* it. Perhaps that was what she intended all along.

A final demonstration of my ruthlessness. A final test.

Or perhaps, if that day ever came, she would kill me. After all, she was the one who had always advised me to choose power over love. And she had already let me die once.

'Compassion is weakness,' Zandri reminded me, turning away from the doomed family that looked down at us from above. 'Rulers need to be able to do what is necessary, even if that means sacrificing others. If the roles were reversed, Kasmira and your brother would have to make the same decision.'

That much was true. But they wouldn't choose this – an execution and a coronation in one.

I thought of Cassius telling me he didn't want to kill his way to power. I thought of how Mira had saved me when she could have left me in a comatose state.

They weren't as ruthless as Zandri. I knew that now.

And no longer did I feel the same need to arm myself against them. To commit monstrous acts in the name of my own protection.

'What if . . .' I glanced up into my mother's coldly perfect face. 'What if I don't want to be like you?'

'Then you've already lost.'

I didn't follow Zandri back to the main palace. Instead, I found myself walking through the dungeons.

It was difficult to read Cassius's expression as I paused outside his cell, but there was no trace of the warmth we'd shared during our battle with Roran.

'Can you save her?'

I saw how much those words cost him. Cassius had always hated asking me for anything, and he would hate it even more now that he was at my mercy. But still he asked – not for himself, but for the woman he loved.

'Why would I?' I said at last, keeping my voice cool. Conscious of the guards listening to every word.

'Because Mira saved your life, and you owe her.'

'Not a good enough reason.'

'She's also your cousin. Your family.'

'What makes you think I care about that?'

Cassius tilted his head. 'I think we both know you do. Just like we both know you weren't working with Zandri. Mira might believe you betrayed us again, but I saw your shock. You weren't expecting her arrival any more than we were. And I doubt you were expecting to see her wearing our father's crown.'

I didn't reply, but my lips curved into a tiny, bitter smile that I knew Cassius would take as confirmation.

'When will it happen?' he asked, approaching the bars. 'The execution?'

'Tomorrow morning,' I replied without inflection. 'I'm to be your executioner.'

'You can tell Zandri no,' Cassius said with unexpected softness. As though he somehow felt sorry for *me*.

It was too much. I almost turned away from him, but instead I pressed closer to the bars.

'No one tells Zandri "no",' I said, projecting my voice for the guard's benefit. 'Not without consequences.'

Intrigue sparked in Cassius's dark blue gaze as my fingers brushed his – too quickly for my death magic to harm him. A seemingly innocent gesture from a sister who was saying goodbye.

I didn't look back as I swept out of the dungeons. But I knew that when it was safe, Cassius would unfold the note I had written him.

Six short, hastily scrawled words that would change everything.

I have a plan.

Trust me.

CHAPTER FIFTY-TWO

Scarlett

Hours.

I had hours left until dawn. Until I would be forced to execute Mira and Cassius – or face the consequences of failing my mother.

Fear tugged at me as I slipped inside my mother's workroom and locked the door behind me. A weak, selfish part of me begged me to reconsider, to go back on my promise to Cassius and follow my mother's orders. If I did, I would be protected from everyone and everything – except her.

What I was contemplating . . . I wasn't sure that I could do it. I wasn't selfless like Mira, or noble like Severin—

Severin. The thought of him gave me strength. I envisioned his face: his beautiful tattooed skin, those mismatched eyes that had stared right through me and into the person I was at my core.

For some reason, he had loved that person. Had seen something in me worth loving.

And he had died for Zandri's ambition.

It would be far too easy to let affection and dependence stay my hand. But Severin deserved justice. He deserved *vengeance*.

And he deserved to have died for something. A cause – much more powerful and enduring than a single person ever could be.

But with Zandri in control, nothing would change. She would continue Emperor Kalias's legacy of conquering new nations, and she would rely on ever harsher policies to subjugate the countries under her rule. Severin's dream of a better world would die with him.

Unless I stopped Zandri and took her place.

My fingers tightened around Severin's necklace, and something powerful and slumbering stirred at my touch. Ever since that aquamarine light had exploded from the locket Severin had given me, I had known the truth. Known how precious his gift really was.

I felt Selussa's warmth and encouragement. She was eager for me to do this – eager for me to honour the vow I had made when she had kept me from Velanthe's reach.

A vow that I had intended to honour decades from now. When I had lived my own life fully and completely. When I was finally ready to trade my individual freedom for the eternal existence she offered.

I wasn't ready for that now. Not even close.

But my death magic wouldn't be enough on its own. If I tried to face my mother as I was, she would kill me and proceed with Mira and Cassius's executions. There would be no one left to oppose her.

I looked up into Zandri's punishing gaze – unsettling and yet somehow fitting, even for a girl of twelve or thirteen. My eyes went to Queen Leanna, affectionately touching her daughter's shoulders. Then I noticed Zandri's hands – intertwined with her brother's. Mira's father, King Arioch.

Zandri was responsible for the deaths of everyone in this portrait, and she had made the decision to kill them when she had burned their faces to ash. There was so much anger and hatred here. The room seethed with it.

This was who Zandri thought I was at my core. The kind of person who resented her own powerlessness so deeply that she was willing to murder her own family. The kind of person who was every bit as dark and twisted as she was.

I had proven her correct when I had killed my father. But I had been desperate then; I hadn't seen another way out, and if I was being honest, I still didn't. Emperor Kalias's death had been necessary.

But I refused to condemn Cassius and Mira to similar fates. Executing them would be the actions of a coward and a monster. And I wasn't a coward.

As for being a monster . . .

I saw so much of myself here, in my mother's past. But that didn't mean her past had to be my future.

I turned decisively away from the portrait. From the hatred and darkness I could feel polluting the air around me.

I had made a promise to work with Mira – to choose trust over fear. I intended to keep that promise.

I'm ready, I thought and released Severin's necklace. Letting it fall against my skin in a blaze of aquamarine light.

As that light flooded into my body, filling me with warmth, I tipped my head back and embraced the Sorceress. Embraced everything she was and everything she offered.

In that moment, I was no longer afraid. Whatever doubts I had harboured were gone, replaced by certainty.

Together, Selussa and I could do more than tear down an empire. We could *build* one.

I felt like I was floating as I moved through the Kalurian palace. It was Selussa who directed me through the halls, urging my exhausted limbs forward even as tiredness threatened to overwhelm me.

I slipped silently into Odessa's chambers – and nearly walked into Odessa herself.

For a moment we merely stared at each other.

'If I call for the guards,' Odessa said, her voice unreadable, 'they might throw you into the dungeons along with Mira.'

'I'm merely visiting an old friend,' I replied with a saccharine smile. A smile that didn't quite fit this new version of me. 'What's wrong with that?'

Odessa didn't play along. Dressed in black, like the Mask I remembered, she looked fierce and strong – but her skin was paler than usual, almost unhealthy looking. 'We're not friends. We never were.'

'Fine. We're not friends.' My tone was light, conversational. 'But I am the daughter of your new empress, so why don't you indulge me for a moment?' When Odessa said nothing, I continued, 'You asked me something once. If there was anyone I loved – anyone I would be willing to sacrifice everything for.'

'And we established there wasn't.'

I thought fleetingly of Severin. Of how different things could have been if I had embraced my love for him earlier. But no one could change the past. Not even the Sorceress.

Though apparently she had a sense for the future. Which was why I was here – trying to save Odessa's life, when Zandri could visit my chambers at any moment and find me missing.

I must have lost my mind.

But all I said was, 'I'm not the one who needs to answer that question. *You* are.'

Odessa's expression shuttered. 'If you're talking about Jadis—'

'She won't forgive you if you allow Mira to be executed.'

'She won't forgive me anyway.' For the first time, a hint of regret entered her voice.

'Mira has forgiven me for worse. I think Jadis will do the same.'

'You can't know that.'

'You're right. I can't. But I do know that you need to choose between love and revenge. And if you won't make that choice for Jadis, then make it for the Sorceress. Because I know your dedication to her is real. I can *feel* it.'

I let Selussa rise up inside me, allowing Odessa to glimpse the Sorceress for a handful of seconds – her dark eyes and hair briefly overshadowing my own.

'That's not possible,' Odessa said through bloodless lips. 'You can't be—'

She took a step back from me, but beneath her shock was a yearning so deep that it was almost painful. And I felt an answering affection stir in Selussa. As if she really had heard Odessa's prayers, and more than anything, she wanted to grant them. To give her some measure of peace.

'I'm not asking you to stand against Zandri,' I told Odessa gently. 'I'm only asking you not to stand against me.'

'Why?' Odessa whispered. Her voice was faint – but her eyes were intent on mine, desperate to know the answer.

'Because,' I said, surprised by the conviction in my words, 'the Sorceress believes you're worth saving. And so do I.'

CHAPTER FIFTY-THREE

Mira

My fist slammed into the wall.

Again.

And again.

'Stop it,' Lillian said severely from the cell next to mine. 'None of this is your fault.'

I didn't believe that, and I wasn't convinced she did either. Zandri might have killed Aric, but he had died because of me. Because I had lost control.

'You should eat something,' Lillian murmured. 'You need your strength for . . . for what comes next.'

I didn't need strength to face my death. Death was easy – an escape from all my mistakes.

But I couldn't tell Lillian that. I hadn't been able to meet her eyes, not once, since I had regained consciousness in this cell, the memories of Aric's final moments replaying in my mind. An endless, torturous loop.

At least Lillian was safe. Zandri wouldn't kill *her* – not as long as she was bonded to Scarlett.

'Kalure still needs you,' Lillian tried. '*I* need you. If an opportunity presents itself . . .'

'Zandri will have planned this out to the last detail. She won't give me the opportunity to escape.'

'Scarlett might—'

'Scarlett can't do anything.' My voice was flat. 'Even if she wanted to help, which I doubt, she recognises a losing battle when she sees one.'

'That's not true,' Lillian shot back. 'I can feel her through the bond. She has a plan.'

'A plan to save me? Or a plan to save herself and take the throne?'

Lillian's silence said enough. She didn't know. But still she pressed on. 'I've seen the way Cassius looks at you. It's possible that he—'

'Cassius hasn't returned from wherever the guards took him,' I said harshly. 'He's probably already dead.'

I sensed Lillian's disapproval, but I had no energy for hope or scheming or anything else. My guilt over Aric's death made me sick. It still didn't feel real – but I had seen it happen. I had watched the life drain from his eyes, and since Lillian was alive, I knew that Scarlett hadn't resurrected Aric. Which meant he was far beyond my reach.

'We should have had more time,' I murmured, more to myself than Lillian.

'Life is short,' Lillian said ruthlessly. 'Particularly in times of war. Aric knew that. He could have died at any point during the battle – but he lived long enough to avenge Kain and to die for you. He would expect you to keep on fighting, Mira. To honour his sacrifice by reclaiming your country and destroying Zandri.'

I let her words settle over me. There was truth to them, but—

'Aric isn't the only person I failed,' I whispered. 'I failed the clansmen and the shifters. Even the priestesses turned against me.'

'They turned against you because of *Odessa*,' Lillian said sharply.

'Partly,' I agreed. 'But they might not have if I hadn't used blood magic. And I used it even before Zandri started controlling me.'

'You can't know that.'

I thought of my panic when Cassius had fallen. My determination to save him – no matter the cost.

'I do know that,' I said. 'It was my decision. And it was a selfish one. It cost me the loyalty and respect of my people.'

'The real question,' a familiar voice drawled, 'is whether you would take it back. Especially considering your feelings for my ex-fiancé.'

I turned to see Odessa studying me from the other side of the bars. Somehow I hadn't heard her approach, and judging by the surprised look on Lillian's face, she hadn't either.

'Quite the role reversal, isn't it?' Odessa continued, her eyes hard.

'I've thought about that moment many times, Mira. The kindness I thought you showed in stopping outside my cell in the Ravalian Court. The way I *thanked* you.' The bitterness in her voice made my heart ache.

'I never wanted your parents to die,' I said, approaching the bars. 'You must know that.'

'Do I?' Odessa tilted her head, and I noticed that her pale hair was unbraided like it had been back in Ravalia. Though she was still dressed in the robes of a priestess, any softness and warmth had disappeared – discarded like a useless mask. 'You might be naive, Mira, but even you had to realise what would happen once you framed my father as a traitor.'

I forced myself to meet her gaze. It was easier than looking at Lillian – easier to see loathing staring back at me rather than sadness or forgiveness. Odessa's eyes were a mirror to all the dark emotions constricting my chest.

'Cassius told me he would advocate on your behalf. That you and your family would be banished.'

Odessa's eyes flashed but she said nothing. Just stared at me with all the contempt she could muster. All the contempt I deserved.

'How long have you known?' I asked, hoping that perhaps some of her friendship had been real.

That hope was dashed as Odessa said, 'Before you rescued me from the Ravalian dungeons.'

All this *time* . . .

'Don't look at me like that.' Her voice was cutting. 'You weren't my friend any more than I was yours. You only pretended to care about me to absolve your guilt.'

'That's not true,' I said immediately. 'I did care about you. I—'

'Save your breath,' Odessa interrupted. The anger on her face faded all too quickly, replaced by something tired and resigned. 'It doesn't matter now. You'll pay for your crimes soon enough.'

Before I could say anything else, she motioned two guards forward. They unlocked my cell and tightened manacles around my wrists.

I glanced over at Lillian. 'Is she coming too?'

'No,' Odessa said, with a thin smile at my obvious panic. 'She stays. Scarlett doesn't want her to witness this.'

Which meant no chance to say goodbye. To hug her tight.

Tears welled as I met Lillian's gaze. My pulse thudded in my ears but I forced my voice into steadiness as I said, 'I'm sorry that it came to this. More sorry than you can ever know.'

Lillian extended her hands through the bars. I grasped onto them like a lifeline.

'No matter what,' she murmured, repeating her long-ago words, 'you'll always be my sister.'

The guards wrenched me away, but I was grateful for the chance to hide my face. To hide my grief.

'Hate me all you like,' I said to Odessa as we walked, 'but make sure Lillian is looked after.'

'You have some nerve,' she muttered, 'asking *me* for a favour. I don't even like Lillian.'

The coolness of her voice might have convinced someone else, but it didn't convince me. '*Everyone* likes Lillian.'

Odessa said nothing, which I took as reluctant agreement.

'Who will do it?' I asked at last, wincing as we stepped out of the stairwell into the blinding Kalurian afternoon. 'Zandri?'

'Scarlett.'

I blinked. Trying to imagine what it would be like to see Scarlett standing over me, a sword slashing down – or perhaps it would only take one touch. One touch to poison me with the death in her veins.

'But I claimed the right to first blood,' Odessa continued, her gaze dark. 'So you'll be facing me first.'

I wanted to rage at her, but instead I said softly, 'Jadis will never forgive you for this.'

'Don't mention Jadis.'

'Why? Because you're afraid it might weaken your resolve?'

Odessa stopped and the guards did too, pulling painfully on my manacles. This close, Odessa's face was highlighted in icy, unforgiving detail. 'You still haven't put it together, have you? Every smile, every laugh, every shared confidence – *it was all a lie*, Mira. I never stopped being a Mask. I imagined killing you a thousand times over.'

'You had plenty of opportunities. You could have buried a blade in my back so many times—'

'Zandri offered me a far more satisfying end, in exchange for my assistance.' Odessa smiled at me. A pretty smile that concealed the darkness lurking beneath. 'It's so much better like this – to watch you die at a public execution, just like your mother. Just like *mine*. Practically poetic, wouldn't you agree?'

She resumed walking, pulling me along by the chains, until the central Kalurian courtyard came into view, a crowd already in attendance. My people, waiting to watch their queen lose her head.

And at the front, smiling pleasantly at me—

My cousin and executioner. Scarlett.

My gaze went past her – to Zandri. The woman who had murdered Aric and who had ordered the death of my father.

I desperately tried to summon the anger and vengeance that had kept me alive in the Ravalian Court, allowing me to survive against impossible odds.

Nothing came. My fire had finally burned out.

And that was how I knew—

This was the end.

The knowledge didn't frighten me. If I had to die for my mistakes, then so be it.

But I refused to die chained and on my knees. No matter how defeated I felt, I would die fighting.

Like the warrior queen I had become.

CHAPTER FIFTY-FOUR

Scarlett

'You made the right choice,' Zandri said as we swept into the austere courtyard, in perfect tandem with the first rays of dawn.

I wondered if she had chosen dawn for the symbolism. It seemed like the sort of thing she would do – an auspicious way of heralding in a new reign. Though this particular reign would begin on the heels of an execution.

'I know I did,' I replied, and it was true. I felt at peace with myself and my decisions in a way I hadn't for years. Perhaps ever.

I twirled a strand of hair curiously around my finger. It was a darker red than it had been a day ago; a subtle difference to anyone else but a significant one to me. Whenever I passed mirrored surfaces, I was surprised that I didn't look more different.

But some differences weren't meant to be seen. Only felt.

'I'm proud of you, Scarlett.' Zandri touched my armoured shoulder, and I reluctantly turned to look at her. 'I know this won't be easy. But it must be done. And once it is, you will finally be free.'

The certainty in her voice was convincing – but then, it always was. How many times had she said something similar to me? Strengthened my flagging conviction with her own?

I stared into my mother's black eyes, searching for some warmth in them. Some undertones of dark brown, or a hint of colour that could only be seen in the natural light. There was none.

'Why are you looking at me like that?' A flicker of suspicion crossed Zandri's sharp face.

My fingers traced the scars marring my arms. Fading, thanks to

Selussa's influence – but still there. And I knew a part of me would always feel them, even if they disappeared entirely. 'Did you agree to hand me over to Velanthe for magical tutelage?'

Zandri seemed as surprised by my question as I was. I hadn't intended to ask – had believed I'd made my peace with my mother's propensity for deception.

'I did,' Zandri said cautiously, 'but it was a promise I never intended to keep. I always intended for Velanthe to die.'

I considered that in silence for a moment. 'I suppose Odessa told you what Velanthe tried to do.'

'Yes.'

'So you know that she attempted to kill me? To resurrect me and bind me to her?'

A nod. 'I'm relieved it didn't come to that.'

But what if it had? I wanted to ask her. *What if Velanthe had succeeded – what would you have done* then?

'All the secrets I've kept . . .' Zandri hesitated, and despite everything, that hesitation – that hint of vulnerability – drew me back in. 'They've come at a cost. I see that now. I'll do better, Scarlett. I promise.'

'I want you to treat me like your daughter,' I muttered. 'Not a weapon.'

'How about a queen?' Her hand rose to adjust the crown on my head – the very one she had instructed her attendants to provide, when they had dressed me this morning. A smaller, daintier version of the crown she wore. 'You were always meant for great things, Scarlett. It pleases me to finally be able to give them to you. To see you elevated to the station you deserve.'

My heart ached. It was easier to think of Zandri as cold and unfeeling – but with me, she was more than that. And I didn't want to hurt her. I couldn't begin to put into words how much I didn't want to hurt her.

'The coronation will happen immediately after the executions,' Zandri continued, her hand falling away, and her softness with it. 'Once I'm crowned, I will announce your new position as heir to the Ravalian Empire, and queen of Kalure. I doubt anyone will protest – not with Kasmira dead. But if they do, they can be dealt with easily enough.'

She took her position of honour on the dais above the sandstone steps. A throne had been brought in – a heavy stone throne that reminded me of the one in the Ravalian throne room. Sitting on it, Zandri looked regal and untouchable. *Invincible.*

I stood at her side as the courtyard slowly filled. The Kalurian people didn't seem any more eager to attend today's gathering than they had under Roran's rule, when they had lined the path from the docks to the palace. Even those of noble blood and wealthy means, resplendent in their fine gowns and tunics, were stiff with resentment as they bowed before the dais.

And yet Zandri smiled contentedly next to me, a self-satisfied expression that said she couldn't care less.

That she believed she'd won.

When the priestesses were assembled – save Odessa, who was bringing Mira from the dungeons – Zandri stood. Everyone went still.

My mother was a skilled orator, even if most of her speech was made up of lies – or what she would deem twists of the truth. No matter their feelings, the Kalurians listened in rapt silence, as if they were only now remembering that she was King Arioch's sister, born and raised amongst them.

Zandri spoke of the perils of blood magic and the importance of peace between Kalure and the Ravalian Empire. She turned her banishment into a grievous injustice, and made Mira seem like an extension of a conniving and power-hungry father – an unstable young woman who had been twisted by tainted magic. Dozens of priestesses looked on serenely from the audience, their occasional nods lending credibility to her words.

And then Cassius was brought out. His guards hadn't bothered with chains, allowing him to walk freely between them. Zandri's attendants had dressed him in courtly Ravalian clothes, and Cassius's determination to face his death with poise lent him an aura of arrogance.

The crowd hissed as he passed, shouting for his head. There was enough vitriol that I wondered if some of them had mistaken Cassius for Roran.

His gaze met mine as he was forced to his knees in front of the dais.

I didn't look away – but I didn't soften my stare. The time for reassurances and niceties had passed.

But I tensed when Odessa pushed Mira into view. She *was* chained – on Zandri's orders, most likely to make this even more of a spectacle.

I descended the steps, a gloating smile on my lips. Playing the role my mother expected.

Mira glared up at me from her position next to Cassius. Behind her, Odessa tore open the back of Mira's tunic and unsheathed her dagger.

'For my parents,' Odessa declared, and sliced the blade down Mira's back in a bloody, jagged trail.

Mira didn't so much as flinch. Not even when Odessa circled in front of her and slid her sword free.

I moved to intervene. Despite my conversation with Odessa this morning, part of me was afraid that she was about to kill Mira.

Instead, she sliced through Mira's chains.

An act of mercy. From one warrior to another.

Odessa glanced across the courtyard at Jadis, who was being restrained by two armed warriors. Then she met my eyes briefly, her expression conflicted. She hadn't done this for me – she had done it for Jadis and the Sorceress. But she had made her choice, which was all that mattered.

Mira stood, and suddenly we were both facing each other. There was resolve in her gaze – a resolve that told me she intended to fight for her life.

This time, my smile was genuine. I had been worried that Aric's death might have broken her.

'Are you going to run?' I taunted for the benefit of our audience. 'Are you that afraid of me?'

Mira squared her shoulders and stood tall. 'I'm not afraid of you.'

I waited for something to happen – for her to summon her natural magic and split the stones beneath my feet, or use blood magic to slow my heart. Then I remembered that Zandri still had her blood ruby.

I forced a laugh, and walked past Mira – to my brother. 'I wonder if you'll be so brave when I kill him in front of you.'

Cassius didn't react to my words, or to my presence. He kept his gaze straight ahead, and I wondered if it was because part of him doubted me, even now. The thought frustrated me, even though I knew he was probably trying to sell the ruse. Whatever the reason, it was difficult to keep my sword steady as I placed it against the back of his neck.

He shuddered as the metal touched his skin. Mira hurled a slew of curses at me, but I could hear the fear in her voice. And I knew that if I did this, she really would break.

I wondered if Cassius knew that too. His gaze shifted – to Mira's. And the softness in his eyes was all for her.

I raised my sword—

And twisted to cut down the nearest Warrior in a spray of blood. The second drew his sword, but Cassius was already there, taking hold of the weapon and running the other man through.

The gathering erupted into chaos. Warriors converged on us, but before I could even think about dealing with them, Mira was moving in front of me. Blocking my route to the dais.

To my mother.

Zandri surveyed me from her throne, her expression remote. She rolled Mira's blood ruby between her fingers as she said, 'You betrayed me.'

'You made it an easy choice.'

The moment Zandri stood, the crowd and the Warriors went still. I thought they were reacting out of fear, until I realised their bodies were frozen in place.

But their eyes—

'They can see and hear what is happening,' Zandri remarked as she descended the dais steps, ignoring the hundreds of eyes that followed her. 'They just can't intervene – at least until I will them to.' She paused beside Cassius's frozen figure, wrenching the blood-stained sword from him. 'Let's try this again, shall we?' she asked, handing the sword to me.

My fingers curved instinctively around the hilt, but I wasn't looking at the sword or my brother. I was looking at the ruby in my mother's hand.

There was something compelling about it. Something . . . familiar.

I realised then.

I *understood*.

'You never trusted me at all, did you?'

Zandri smiled thinly. 'Trust is overrated. I hoped it wouldn't come to this, but . . .' She shrugged. 'Perhaps this is for the best. Now you don't have to feel guilty about killing them. You can simply blame me.'

'If you do this,' I said, fighting back rising panic, 'I will never forgive you. You'll have to kill me.'

Zandri watched me for a moment – and then she laughed. 'I can *make* you forgive me. In fact, I can make you forget that this ever happened. I've done it once before.'

I went very still, understanding what she meant even before she continued, her voice lethally soft.

'I told you that I had a plan to use Mira against your father, didn't I? I even told you it had something to do with your power of illusion.' Zandri's amusement cut into me like a blade. 'Didn't you ever wonder what that plan was? Didn't you ever think to *ask* me?'

'No,' I said in a choked voice. 'It was my idea to frame Mira—'

'It was *mine*.' Zandri's smile was twisted. 'I always knew you would be too weak to do it yourself. How any daughter of mine could be so soft-hearted, I will never understand. Fortunately, you have me to help you make the tough decisions.'

Her grip tightened on the blood ruby, and as it pulsed with light, my reality shifted—

My conviction along with it.

CHAPTER FIFTY-FIVE

Scarlett

My right arm ached, and blood dripped from the sword in my hand.

Had I fought against someone? I must have, but then, why couldn't I remember?

A young man stared up at me from his knees, his courtly clothes covered in blood. Even though I didn't know who he was, part of me recognised that he meant something to me. And so did the young woman kneeling at his side, her face contorted with impotent despair.

Why were they looking at me like that? With a mixture of resignation and . . . *pity*? They pitied me, yet I was the one holding the sword. None of this made any sense.

Except the black-garbed woman watching from the dais. She made sense. Zandri. My mother, my empress, whose orders I obeyed without hesitation or question—

Except I was hesitating.

I was hesitating, because the young man was talking – describing moments from our shared childhood, moments that left fleeting images in my mind. I didn't remember the girl he spoke about, but the truth of his words reached me all the same. The sincerity of them.

I don't want to kill him.

That realisation sank into me, and I tried to lower my sword. My hands didn't move an inch.

Wrong. This was all *wrong*—

'Kill him.' Zandri's voice echoed through the courtyard, cool and controlled. 'Do it now.'

It was an order. I knew that because my body moved without my consent, my arms tensing to swing—

Midnight-blue eyes met mine, bright with emotion. With understanding. 'It's alright, Scarlett,' Cassius murmured. 'I love you. I forgive you.'

I saw a glimpse then – a glimpse of the boy he had been. The boy I had sworn to always protect.

'Cassius.' Memories unfolded like flashes; spots of colour and happiness in an otherwise dark childhood. Tears dripped down my face as I remembered. 'Cassius, I don't want to do this . . .'

'Then don't.' Calm and resolute, as though it was that simple. 'You have the strongest will of anyone I know. If anyone can stand against Zandri, you can.'

My arms trembled with the effort of holding the sword in mid-air. I had my orders, and those orders said to let the sword cut through his neck, but—

Since when did *I* take orders?

My scream of pain and fury reverberated through the courtyard. With all my strength, I hurled the sword aside.

And then I turned to face my mother.

Zandri held up the blood ruby so that it gleamed in the morning light. Brilliant and bloody and familiar.

Mine.

But I was no longer the sum of that blood ruby. I was no longer the person I had been, and that blood ruby only had power over me if I let it.

The compulsion to strike down Cassius and Mira returned – along with the temptation to give in, to surrender to the oblivion Zandri offered. But what she offered wasn't real.

It was an illusion – a trap. And I refused to be controlled or manipulated. *Never again.*

As I advanced on Zandri, I saw something like shock enter her eyes. Shock – and a trace of apprehension.

But she strode to meet me, until she was almost close enough to touch. Almost, but not quite.

I held out my hand, my palm outstretched. 'That belongs to me.'

It was impossible to tell what Zandri was thinking. Her eyes were dark and unfathomable, any trace of emotion wiped from her expression. But I knew my mother, and I knew what she respected most was strength. By resisting the effects of the blood ruby, I had proven myself worthy of claiming it as my own.

She dropped it into my palm, careful not to let our skin brush.

I stared down at the blood ruby in my hand, and as I did, I felt the Sorceress surface inside me, lending me her strength and power.

I crushed the blood ruby to dust.

The wind picked up around me, and some of the red dust went with it, whirling through the air. Zandri watched intently, and when she looked at me, the hunger in her gaze was finally laid bare.

'I underestimated you,' Zandri murmured. Despite the softness of her voice, I wasn't fooled. This was the calm before the storm. I knew it – and so did our silent, unmoving audience.

'Yes,' I said, because I couldn't afford for her to know about Selussa. 'You underestimated me – and I've proven that you can no longer control me. So what happens now?'

'You already know the answer.'

My heart cracked at her words, but I nodded. I had always known that my mother's love for me was conditional. Now I knew the limit of that love.

I didn't rage at Zandri, didn't scream, didn't try to run. It was always going to come to this.

My skin prickled, sensing her mounting power. But I raised my chin and said, 'I have one condition.'

'And what might that be?'

'We settle this between us. No outside involvement – not Cassius or Mira or the Kalurian warriors.'

'I suppose that's acceptable,' Zandri replied, too readily and too conciliatory.

I should have known then. But nothing could have prepared me for the force that detonated out from her, blasting me across the courtyard and hurling me into the far wall.

Pain erupted in my back and shoulders. Then I fell forward, slamming brutally into the ground. I was certain I would have broken something if it wasn't for Selussa and her regenerative powers.

Embrace me fully, her voice whispered. *Let me help you.*

But I resisted. It was one thing, sharing my body with the Sorceress. It was another giving over control.

Right now, she was little more than an inconvenient passenger. For her to become an active participant, I had to willingly surrender to her – and the thought of doing that terrified me.

Yet if I didn't—

I dodged the next blast of power, aware that my mother was merely unleashing her anger on me. When she decided to strike in a more targeted way, that was when I would really be in trouble. Even I didn't know the full extent of her abilities, and if *Velanthe* had been terrifying . . .

Focus on what you can control, I reminded myself. *Not what you can't.*

Darkness pooled in my hands, my death magic desperate to reach Zandri. But she wouldn't allow me to get close. Was there a way to use my magic without touch? Like I had with the clansmen I had brought back to life?

'You might be powerful, Scarlett, but you're no match for me. Do yourself a favour – surrender before I lose what's left of my patience.' Zandri's dark eyes raked over me, lingering on the crown I still wore. 'I'll forgive you for challenging me. I'll even allow you to live.'

'You won't,' I said, in a voice that sounded dead even to me. If I lost, I could be sure of one thing: she would kill me. My own mother would kill me. 'You have no use for a daughter you can't control.'

Zandri's silent agreement broke what was left of my heart.

Whatever part of me that is still capable of love will always love you.

The treasured memory of those words rang in my mind. I still believed that she had meant them – but this wasn't love. Severin had shown me what love really was, and it wasn't about power and control. It was about caring more about someone else than you cared about yourself.

I wasn't sure that Zandri had ever known what love was.

It was almost instinctual, the letting go. Like releasing a pent-up breath, or a weight I had been carrying so long I had almost forgotten it was there.

'*Selussa*,' I breathed—

In welcome.

And in surrender.

It happened in the space of a blink, but when my eyes reopened, the world around me was brighter, sharper. Changed.

And so was I.

My fingers rose to explore my face. The shape felt the same, but my skin was no longer cool to the touch, and I had the unsettling sensation of being somewhere in between myself and Selussa, no longer entirely one or the other.

'How?' Zandri asked as I shattered her control over the onlookers.

Cassius and Mira moved to stand at my side, but no one else did more than straighten or shift their feet. The crowd was no longer under Zandri's influence, but fear still held them immobile.

'We had an agreement,' Zandri said when I didn't answer her question. Her black eyes flicked warily between me and Mira. 'No outside interference.'

'Our agreement still stands.' I took a step towards my mother, shaking my head when Mira started to follow.

'Zandri's too powerful,' she protested. 'You shouldn't have to face her alone.'

'I'm not alone,' I replied, smiling faintly at the look of confusion on Mira's face and the concern on Cassius's. They clearly thought I was making a mistake, but they stayed back, respecting my decision.

I walked slowly towards my mother, waiting for her to make the next move. To determine the method of battle.

I was unsurprised when she reached for her daggers.

Mira would have been suited to this method of attack, but Zandri had always bested me when we had trained together, her enhanced strength and reflexes outmatching mine.

She whirled on me, her daggers slicing through the air, but Selussa seemed to slow time itself, until Zandri was moving at a sluggish pace. It was easy – effortless – to sidestep her first throw. The second I didn't even bother to avoid. The dagger had barely left her hand before I snatched it from the air and walked past her.

When time resumed once more, I was standing behind my mother with the dagger pressed to her throat.

'It seems fitting to do it this way,' I said, and somehow my voice was steady. 'For Aric.'

'I killed Aric with magic,' Zandri bit out, 'not a mundane weapon. If you're going to end me, Scarlett, at least have the decency to use your death magic.'

It was so like my mother to criticise me in her last moments that I almost laughed. 'Fine,' I said, resting my finger on her pulse.

The moment I released the dagger, pain sliced across my neck in a burning line.

Mira shouted my name, and I knew what she was seeing: the same magical wound that had cost Aric his life.

Zandri's timing was perfect, ensuring that her murderer would die along with her.

But now that I was one with the Sorceress, I was as endless and eternal as Selussa herself.

I felt the pain disappear, and I knew that the wound had disappeared along with it.

Zandri's lips parted in wordless shock. No, not shock – awe. And something else. Something like envy.

'The Sorceress,' she breathed, reaching up to touch my unblemished neck. 'You invited her spirit into your body . . .'

'I did it to stop you.'

I held Zandri close as her body weakened, refusing to let her fall. I lowered her to the ground and cradled her in my arms, feeling her skin cool beneath my touch as the death magic took over.

It wouldn't be long now.

My awareness of Selussa receded, and I knew she was giving me this moment with my mother. Mira and Cassius were staying back too, the tenuous calm over the courtyard holding. It felt like Zandri and I were in a protective cocoon of our own, where no one and nothing else mattered.

'How does it feel?' I whispered, shifting so that I could look into her face. 'Is it painful?'

A note of anxiety entered my voice. It seemed strange that I should care so much, since I was her killer.

But I did care. And it no longer seemed like a weakness.

'I stopped feeling pain long ago,' Zandri said, her eyes fluttering open. 'Velanthe taught me how to strip away human frailties like pain and sickness. Since then, I haven't felt much of anything.'

Sadness gripped me. She had discarded so much in the pursuit of power – never giving any thought to the cost.

'Was it worth it?' I had asked Zandri this once before, and I could still remember the way she had looked at me – as though I was a fool for even asking the question. But I wondered if her answer might have changed now. At the end.

'I have to believe it was,' Zandri said, her voice even fainter than it was before.

My throat tightened as I felt my death magic reach her heart. When her eyes reopened, some of that cloying blackness had faded away. In its place, there was a glimpse – just a glimpse – of the woman she could have been. The mother who could have loved me like a daughter deserved to be loved.

With her whole heart.

Zandri's hand tightened around mine. 'Forgive me, Scarlett,' she rasped. 'Please.'

I thought of everything she had done – to me, to Severin, to Aric. She had caused so much pain, but in that moment, I felt some of my splintered heart begin to heal. Just the fact that she was able to ask for my forgiveness – that she cared what I thought about her – made all the difference in the world.

'There's nothing to forgive,' I whispered. 'You're my mother, and I love you.'

Zandri's hand went cold and limp in mine. I held onto it tightly, unwilling to let go.

I couldn't remember the last time I had truly cried. Even when I had wanted to, the tears hadn't come. But they came now. Relentless and painful and somehow cleansing.

As I cried over my mother's body, I wished that she hadn't had to die. But I also knew that she couldn't have lived.

I had needed to kill my past in order to embrace my future.

And now . . .

Now I was finally free.

CHAPTER FIFTY-SIX

Mira

One week later

It was surreal being back on Aldara. Even more surreal carrying Aric with me – his ashes contained in an urn that hadn't left my possession.

I could see islanders lining the cliffs: fishermen and nobles alike. Somewhere amongst them, Governor Atwood and his son would be watching. I intended to deal with them personally.

'You look particularly regal today,' I said with a sideways glance at Scarlett. She was resplendent in a gown of red and gold, Emperor Kalias's bone crown glinting on top of her coiled hair. An empress in the making.

'I thought it best. If I'm going to start issuing orders, I might as well look the part.'

'Thank you for this,' I murmured. 'It means a lot to me, and I know it would have meant the world to him.'

I couldn't bring myself to say Aric's name, but Scarlett nodded. She glanced at the urn in my arms, and I realised I was hugging it protectively to my chest.

'It's a new concept for me, allowing a country – or an island – to have more control,' she said with an ironic quirk of her lips. 'I have no doubt my father would have disapproved. But that's the point, I suppose – doing things differently. Trying to be better than my parents.'

'You shouldn't have to try too hard,' Cassius drawled from behind me. 'They set the bar extremely low.'

I narrowed my eyes at Cassius's less than tactful comment. He gazed innocently back at me, but his eyes flicked cautiously to Scarlett – who laughed. A soft, genuine laugh that surprised us both.

'Yes,' she said. 'They certainly did.'

We stood shoulder to shoulder as the boat approached the harbour – Scarlett on my right and Cassius on my left. In my wildest imaginings, I had never dreamt that I would return with two members of the Ravalian family by my side.

Lillian's footfalls rang out as she emerged from the cabin. Scarlett shifted slightly, allowing Lillian to join me as the boat docked, our hands intertwining. Ravalian Warriors leapt off to tighten the ropes tethering us in place, and all too soon we were disembarking.

A glimpse of white drew my gaze to the cliffs, where Lillian's mother was hurtling down the path to the docks. Eliana opened her arms wide and Lillian flew into them, tears streaming down her face.

My heart clenched at the sight and I tightened my grip on the gold urn.

'Let's give them a moment,' I said, my gaze shifting towards two unwelcome figures.

Nikolas Atwood relied heavily on a cane as he approached, his face filled with loathing as he watched me. He was exactly as I remembered him – his clothing immaculate, his ash-blond hair and grey eyes striking.

At his side was Stacia, a pretty noblewoman who had always fawned over Nikolas. A large diamond ring glittered on her dainty finger, but there was nothing dainty about the scowl twisting her face.

'Your Majesty,' Nikolas said, inclining his head to Scarlett, who didn't react in the slightest.

Cassius moved to stand next to me, watching Nikolas with a thin smile. Nikolas's gaze narrowed at the sight of him, no doubt recalling how Cassius had taken my side over his in the Ravalian Court.

'Nikolas,' Cassius said pleasantly, when no one else seemed inclined to speak. 'I was expecting your father.'

'He's dead,' Nikolas said shortly. 'I'm Lord Atwood now.'

'Ah,' Cassius said, his tone utterly uncaring. 'My deepest condolences – or congratulations, depending on how you want to look at it.'

I resisted the urge to elbow Cassius in the stomach. He was having a little too much fun needling Nikolas, and despite the fact that Nikolas had once tried to kill me, I no longer harboured animosity towards him. Perhaps I really had changed from the person I used to be. Or perhaps Nikolas seemed tame in comparison to Roran.

'I'm afraid I have some bad news,' I continued. 'You can keep your title, but as for being the Aldarian Governor—'

'You can't replace me,' Nikolas interrupted coldly. 'You don't have the power to make those decisions.'

'No,' Scarlett said, her voice smooth, 'but I do. And I've decided to abolish the Provincial Governors.'

Nikolas blinked at Scarlett. I wondered if she had rendered him speechless.

'That means there will be no Governor of Aldara, at least not until the Aldarians decide to appoint one themselves. You can put yourself forward for the position, of course, but . . .' She trailed off, her silence pointed. We all knew that Nikolas wouldn't be a popular choice.

His cheeks reddened with rage. 'And my assets? My father's manor house? What will happen to those?'

'I have no intention of stripping you of your inheritance. Everything that belonged to your father will remain yours – except the manor house. That belongs to the Governor of Aldara, or whoever ends up being in charge. It was never intended to be passed down through families.'

'Emperor Kalias promised—'

'Emperor Kalias is dead.' Scarlett took a step towards Nikolas. She was a few centimetres shorter than he was, but somehow still towered over him. 'I am in charge now, and those are my terms. My Warriors will help you remove your things from the manor and relocate elsewhere.'

Nikolas's eyes darted past Scarlett – to the black-garbed Warriors backing up her order. He stiffly nodded.

Though Scarlett's expression didn't change, I had the sense that she was enjoying herself.

She brushed past Nikolas and followed the winding path towards the cliffs, Cassius and I at her side. I heard Lillian murmuring softly to Eliana as they followed, and I knew she was gently breaking the news of Aric's death.

As we walked through the streets, we were greeted by curious and awed stares. When the islanders saw that Lillian and Eliana were with us, the mood lightened into something less formal. People came up to welcome us, and I was surprised to realise they were as eager to speak to me as they were to Scarlett. It was strange being the centre of attention when I had once felt so inconsequential here. So certain that my life would never amount to anything unless I did something drastic to change it.

'Smile, Mira,' Cassius instructed from beside me. 'Relax your shoulders. You want to look like you're amongst friends.'

'It's just . . . hard, being back here,' I whispered. 'Without him.'

Was it my imagination, or were people staring at the urn in my hands? Did they understand what it was – what it *meant*?

'No one blames you for Aric's death,' Cassius said, equally quietly – though he kept a smile on his lips for our audience. He was good at this – a natural, his warmth impressively genuine and not overdone.

Maybe he was right – maybe the islanders didn't blame me for Aric's death. But maybe they should.

Lord Atwood's manor looked the same as I remembered, a realisation that only increased the ache in my chest. I remembered dancing in these grounds with Aric, lights twinkling around us as we celebrated the eve of the Choosing Ceremony. It felt like another lifetime.

'Come on, Mira,' Lillian said, gently taking hold of my arm.

The white-washed buildings faded from view as I followed Lillian and Eliana past the manor house, leaving Scarlett and Cassius to deal with Nikolas Atwood. We reached the open field where the circus had pitched its tents, and I was saddened – but not surprised – to find the field empty. It made sense they would have moved on after all the destruction Zandri had caused.

But I felt closer to my mother here. There was more of her on Aldara than there ever had been in Ravalia or Kalure. I could almost hear her sweet laugh on the breeze, and smell the scent of her perfume: sweet and mysterious but with an edge. When I reopened my eyes, my surroundings were blurry with tears.

And then we reached the meadow where Aric and I used to spar.

'Are you sure it's alright to scatter his ashes here?' I asked. 'If you have a special place—'

'Here is perfect,' Eliana said, her voice thick with emotion. Her hair – the same light shade as Lillian's – was shot through with grey, and only now, in the midst of her grief, did I realise how much she had aged since I last saw her. 'Aric used to look forward to those moments of escape with you. Sometimes I think this meadow is the only place where he felt truly at peace.'

I might have thought Eliana was saying that to be kind, but I believed it too. There had been something so open and unguarded about Aric here, and he hadn't been that way in the presence of the townspeople.

Handing the urn to Lillian, I crossed the meadow, giving Lillian and her mother the chance to share private remembrances. Tears dripped down my face as I paused on the bank of the mountain stream where Aric had tossed me in.

All around me were memories.

There – there was where he had helped me to my feet, and I had looked up into his eyes, hoping he was about to kiss me. That patch of grass was where we had lain down together, staring up at the sky, talking about our plans to compete in the Trials and become Warriors. To protect those who needed it and make a real difference.

We had done that. We had become everything we had wanted to be – and more. So much more.

The ashes scattered on the wind. Lillian and Eliana left the last of them for me, withdrawing with a soft smile from Lillian and a kiss on the cheek from Eliana. Small signs of affection that meant the world to me, because they showed that Lillian and Eliana still thought of me as family.

I knelt in that meadow until the sky darkened, gripping onto the urn for dear life.

I knew that I needed to release my hold on it – to release my hold on *him*. But I couldn't.

Hours passed. The meadow grew even darker, illuminated only by the faint moonlight overhead – and the distant glow of candles in the windows of houses. And then I heard it. The sound of booted footsteps.

Cassius's arm brushed mine as he knelt at my side. Letting me know that he was there if I needed him.

'I can't do it,' I whispered, my voice too loud in the silence. 'I *can't*, Cassius.'

Cassius didn't press me. He just waited, knowing that I needed to continue.

'He shouldn't have died like that.' The words came out as a sob. 'He was a warrior – a better warrior than any of us. It isn't fair that he was the one to die. It isn't *right*.'

And then—

'It should have been me.'

There it was. The guilt and self-loathing that I had been carrying ever since I had watched Aric bleed out in front of me. It was a relief to finally give voice to it.

Cassius didn't say anything immediately. When he did, it wasn't what I expected. 'I'm sure Aric felt the same about his brother. And I'm sure you would have tried to convince him that there was nothing he could have done.'

I looked up at Cassius. 'Did you ever meet Kain?'

'No,' Cassius said softly. 'I wasn't involved in that particular campaign. My father knew better than to station me under Roran's command; he liked the idea of having a spare heir too much to send me to be murdered. But I witnessed my fair share of bloodshed, and I can tell you that the best death a Warrior can hope for is to die in the place of someone they love. To know – in their final moments – that they have given their life so that person can live.'

Silence descended between us. My hands were ice-cold wrapped around the urn, but I didn't move or speak.

'You gave Aric that, Mira.' Cassius paused, letting his words sink in. 'You gave him the end he deserved. The end he would have wanted.'

Tears were flowing down my cheeks now, but I didn't swipe them away. Cassius helped me to my feet, his arms warm and steadying as they enclosed around me.

'Don't diminish Aric's sacrifice,' he murmured in my ear. 'Honour it – honour *him* – by living.'

My hands tightened around the urn one last time – and then I released the contents onto the breeze.

I felt lighter when it was done.

Lighter in the knowledge that Aric had died as he had lived – as a true warrior. In every sense of the word.

And that he had been laid to rest here, on the island he loved. His island home.

CHAPTER FIFTY-SEVEN

Mira

I spent the night at Aric's house with Eliana and Lillian. Cassius had walked me to the door and left without a word, respecting my need for space.

But something had woken me in the early hours of the morning. A suspicion that had me hurriedly throwing on clothes and lacing my boots. A suspicion that was proven correct when I discovered that Cassius and Scarlett were no longer at Lord Atwood's manor house – and neither were their belongings.

I caught up with Cassius just as he reached the docks, his blond hair a beacon of light in the darkness.

'You're leaving without saying goodbye?'

I watched his black-garbed shoulders stiffen. 'I thought it would be easier that way.'

'Easier for who?' I challenged. 'For me – or for *you*?'

'I never pretended to be above self-interest,' Cassius retorted. 'I'm not *him*.'

And there it was. The real reason Cassius couldn't stand to look at me. The real reason he was leaving.

The words left my lips before I considered the sense of them. 'You could stay.'

'And do what, exactly? Spend my life as your spymaster?'

'Not my spymaster.' I shook my head, my dark hair rippling in the breeze. 'My lover.'

Cassius turned to face me. 'Is that really what you want, Mira? Or is that your grief talking?'

I said nothing. I honestly didn't know.

He smiled mirthlessly and shook his head. 'You chose him in the end.' The pain in his voice said more than words ever could. 'I respected your choice. I still do. If it was a matter of giving you time, of letting you heal from your loss . . . I could do that. But it isn't just Aric holding you back.' His midnight-blue eyes bored into mine. 'Can you truly forgive me for the past? For all the mistakes I made back in the Ravalian Court?'

Truthfully, I had forgiven Cassius a long time ago – and that realisation had terrified me.

He had terrified me.

Perhaps Cassius saw a glimmer of that fear in my face, because his softened. He ran a finger across my cheek. 'If you tell me there's a chance for us, I will spend the rest of my life earning back your trust. But I want all of you – your whole heart.' He paused, and I had the sense he was steeling himself as he asked, 'Can you give me that, Mira? Will you at least *try*?'

Staring up into his eyes, I wished I could say the words. I wasn't afraid of my feelings for him anymore, and I wanted to give this – to give *us* – a chance. But with Aric gone, it felt like a betrayal to commit to Cassius. Aric deserved more than that – and Cassius deserved someone who would put him first.

In the silence we both heard it. My answer.

Cassius kissed my forehead – nothing more than a brush of his lips. 'Goodbye, Mira,' he said, turning resolutely away from me. I watched him board the waiting Ravalian vessel with a heavy heart.

And so did Scarlett. When she glanced back at me, there was a trace of recrimination on her face.

'My invitation to Cassius was just as much for you,' I said, walking over to her. 'You don't have to leave.'

'I've stayed too long as it is, Mira. I have to return to Ravalia, but you're always welcome to visit. And so is . . .' In her hesitation I heard Lillian's name.

'She'll miss you,' I said, and I knew it was true. 'Don't you want to say something to her?'

'What is there to say?' Scarlett's voice was carefully even. 'Now that Selussa has dissolved the bond between us, Lillian's life is no longer tied to mine. Given the choice between accompanying me to Ravalia and returning to Kalure with you . . . I know which option she'd prefer.'

I felt for Scarlett. Beneath her confident facade, there was something so alone about her – and I worried that her sense of isolation would only grow when she returned to the Ravalian Court, surrounded by subjects who obeyed her commands but didn't truly care about her. Not like Lillian cared about her.

Not like *I* cared about her.

'I should go,' Scarlett said, and I could sense her withdrawing even now, trying to distance herself from her emotions.

But she didn't move. And neither did I.

We stood in silence for a long time, staring out over the natural harbour. The water was beautiful and clear, lapping against the wooden dock, which occasionally shifted position beneath my feet.

It was peaceful. Not even the fishermen were up yet, though they would be soon, casting their woven nets.

'Will you be happy, do you think?' Scarlett asked softly. 'Ruling Kalure?'

I considered the question. And I knew she saw the painful, disloyal truth reflected on my face.

It was ironic; I had fought so hard to reclaim my throne, to follow in my father's footsteps, but I would always be an outsider in Kalure. It had never felt like my home – not in the same way as Ravalia.

'I don't think I'm meant to rule Kalure,' I said at last. It had been a difficult decision to come to, but I knew it was the right one. 'The Kalurians have always wanted independence from the Ravalian Empire, and they will always associate me with Ravalia. Now that Roran is no longer a threat, I'm thinking of letting them choose their next ruler, if they decide they want one at all. They may prefer some kind of elected council – one that represents the whole of Kalure, including the Wilds. I'll go back to oversee the transition, and I'll need to make amends with the clans and the shifters, but after that . . .'

Scarlett raised an eyebrow. 'I hope you don't expect me to follow your example in Ravalia.'

'Of course not,' I said, smiling. 'I know you'll make a wonderful empress, and an empress needs an empire. But you're the one who gave me the idea. When you relinquished control of the Western Lands.'

'I suppose I did, didn't I?' Scarlett smiled dryly. 'Some rulers we are, releasing countries left and right.' Then the smile slid from her face. 'What will you do? When the Kalurians have a new leader or council, and you're no longer needed?'

'I thought about becoming an emissary – negotiating alliances with other countries on Kalure's behalf.'

'Like the position I offered Cassius in Ravalia.'

'Exactly,' I replied. 'I never thought I would like politics, but it's grown on me. And I like the idea of visiting other countries.'

'It also gives you an excuse to visit Ravalia more often,' Scarlett with a knowing smirk. 'And my brother.'

'This has nothing to do with Cassius. It's over between us.'

'Is it?' Scarlett studied me for a while. 'You should give him a chance,' she said gently. 'Cassius isn't the same person you first met in Ravalia. And . . .' She hesitated. 'I hope you know that I'm not the same person I was, either.'

It was the closest she had ever come to an apology, but the time for apologies and recriminations was over. Scarlett had more than proven herself to me.

'None of us are the same people we were. You showed that when you stood against your mother – and when you convinced me to allow Odessa to remain part of the Temple.'

'Under Jadis's supervision,' Scarlett reminded me.

I nodded, thinking back to my last interaction with Odessa. I hadn't told anyone how I had offered her my knife, giving her the opportunity to avenge her parents. For a moment, I had thought that she was going to kill me – and I had been prepared to let her, if that was what it took to atone for my mistakes. But she had let the knife fall and walked past me without a backward glance. Her decision gave me hope that perhaps we could all move on from our bloody pasts.

'For what it's worth,' I said to Scarlett, 'I've made plenty of decisions that I regret. But you're right; we can't blame ourselves. We have to look forward – to focus on who we want to become.'

Scarlett smiled faintly, and I wondered if she thought me naive. But she said, 'I like the thought.'

She turned towards her waiting ship – but then she changed her mind and embraced me instead. I didn't flinch away from her touch, and I knew she noticed the difference. That she felt the same thing I did in how close we held each other: the trust and friendship we had established.

'Thank you,' Scarlett said when she pulled back from me. Her eyes weren't as cold as they had once been – still glacially beautiful, but the emotion within warmed them and set them sparkling. '. . . Cousin.'

It was the first time she had addressed me that way. The first time she had acknowledged me as her family, and it meant more to me than I could express.

A Ravalian Warrior extended his arm to help Scarlett onto the ship. She ignored him and brushed past without assistance, the crew bowing deeply at the sight of their future empress.

The sails were already unfurled, and in a matter of moments the ship was drifting away from the docks. I looked on as it sailed out of the harbour, but I wasn't looking at the ship or its crew.

I was looking at them.

For the first time, they seemed like true siblings. Cassius cut a striking figure in courtly clothes of black and red, and Scarlett's gold dress billowed in the breeze, her hair blazing out behind her like a crimson banner.

She looked every inch the Ravalian royal. And so did he.

I didn't expect them to look back, and they didn't. That wasn't who they were.

But I no longer felt the same urgency to keep them with me. It didn't matter that a sea separated us: family was family, and they were never really gone. I might have lost my parents, but I had gained a family of my own with Scarlett and Lillian and even Cassius. A family I had chosen – and who had chosen me in return.

And as dawn brightened the horizon, I knew it was heralding in a better world.

CHAPTER FIFTY-EIGHT

Scarlett

I had won.

That was the thought going through my mind as I climbed the steps of my mother's austere tower, the raven I had once resurrected circling high overhead.

I had achieved everything Zandri had convinced me I should want: the Ravalian Empire was mine, and my coronation was to take place in less than a week. The nobles who had once sneered and dismissed me now bowed before me, and it wasn't only respect or deference that made them bow. It was fear.

Selussa's presence had wiped away the taint of blood magic within me, but even without my death magic as a barrier, none of my subjects ventured too close.

My mother would call me a fool for wanting their love. *Love is fickle*, she would say. *Far better to be feared.*

I walked past the benches in her workroom, still cluttered with jars and vials. I had left everything exactly as it was, and part of me expected Zandri to sweep inside, ready to lecture me about neglecting my lessons or all the ways I needed to consolidate my rule.

I missed her more than I thought I would.

The servants couldn't understand why I spent so much time in my mother's tower. I had already destroyed her store of blood rubies in the cavern, freeing the members of the Orders from magical control and allowing them to choose to serve me. There was no reason to come here except to torture myself.

But ruling was emptier than I expected.

It didn't matter that I held weekly petitions to address the concerns of my subjects, or that I regularly visited the Lower Districts, supervising construction to raise living standards. It didn't matter that my nobles were desperate to impress me with lavish gifts, or that I had hundreds of suitors vying for my attention, throwing feasts and dances and fighting matches in my honour.

There was something missing. Something crucial.

My whole life had been about conflict. Someone or something had always stood in the way of my goals. Without an enemy to fight, a threat to be dealt with – perhaps I didn't know *how* to be happy.

The only times I had felt content were the moments I had spent with Severin. Moments when I hadn't been thinking about plots or countries or crowns. Moments when I had simply *existed*.

But I tried not to think about Severin. I avoided the battlements where he had died, and of all the Orders, the hardest to deal with were the Artisans. Only Selussa's soothing presence kept the memories of him at bay. The sadness.

You're wallowing, Selussa said softly. *This is your victory. Savour it.*

I took her advice. I let my ladies in waiting bathe and dress me, and I tried to relish the sensation of silk against my skin, to delight in the fact that I no longer had to concern myself with poison or attempts to kill me. I was protected now. Safe.

Just like I had always wanted. Except I now knew that what I had realised in Damar was true.

I had wanted all the wrong things.

I sat on Emperor Kalias's throne that evening, the sharp steel talons on my fingers tapping against the armrest. The satisfaction of claiming my father's place had faded. Even staring out over the crowd of nobles no longer excited me. They belonged to me now – this entire empire belonged to me – but that was precisely the problem. There was no challenge.

I supposed I could visit my brother at Caleah Fortress. He hosted nightly parties for nobles and visiting diplomats, and by all accounts, they were quite entertaining. But though I had made Cassius my heir and Crown Prince, I didn't want to intrude on his domain – and I knew he used those parties to gather useful information. People would be less likely to talk if their empress was in attendance.

So I remained where I was, my focus drifting around the hall until it settled on Lady Verne. She was speaking with a dark-haired woman – Lucia. She had been the newest addition to Empress Ivalene's ladies, and the most outspoken when I had banished them to the desert along with their mistress.

It was Lucia, I suspected, who had finally killed Ivalene. Though I was sure Lady Verne had been the mastermind.

'More suitors are arriving tomorrow,' Lady Verne told me when she reached the dais. She didn't curtsy – she knew I found such displays irritating – but she did incline her head in respect. 'I do hope you will entertain a few of them this time. The nobles are already whispering about how quick you were to dismiss—'

'Let them whisper,' I cut in. 'The nobles only have power because *I* decide to give it to them.'

Lady Verne raised an eyebrow. 'May I be frank, Your Majesty?'

'I've never known you not to be,' I said dryly. Lady Verne had never pretended to like me, but she did take her position as adviser seriously, and I had come to appreciate her candour.

'Certain traditions come with ruling. Marriage is one of those traditions.'

'I defeated Roran and Zandri without a husband at my side. Perhaps you can remind the nobles of that.'

'The nobles already know how powerful you are,' Lady Verne replied. 'They don't need to be reminded of your military victories. They need an assurance that you will provide them with an heir.'

I smiled at Lady Verne, and though I hadn't done it to scare her, I delighted in her unease all the same.

'I already have a successor,' I reminded her. 'There will be no children, and no heir. Cassius is the only person I am willing to entrust the empire to.'

Not that I had any need for a successor. The Ravalian throne was mine – and it would be for centuries, now that the blood of the Sorceress ran through my veins. *Immortal* blood.

Lady Verne nodded and backed away, but my satisfaction at her deference quickly faded.

Centuries. I had *centuries* ahead of me – and I was already sick of ruling.

It hadn't even been a month.

I should have remained in the Ravalian Court, ruling my kingdom by overseeing hundreds of tedious decisions. Instead, I sailed around the continent and rode towards the Western Lands.

Selussa didn't try to convince me to return. A sense of relief radiated from her – and something else.

Anticipation.

I remembered that Zigilia had dedicated entire temples and monuments to the Sorceress. No doubt Selussa had a particular fondness for the Western Lands, and I wondered if she missed exploring the world. If the restless itch beneath my skin was coming from her or from me.

Perhaps it was coming from us both.

Selussa wasn't the only one who had been trapped. I had been trapped and controlled for so long that I didn't even know what freedom – *true* freedom – felt like. But this came close: the sensation of the wind whipping through my hair as I galloped across the desert dunes.

The city of Damar was ordered and calm. Riding through the dusty streets, I noticed signs of stability: the people were quicker to smile, flowers bloomed in the terracotta pots crowning the flat mud-brick roofs, and I heard the distant laughter and shrieks of children at play.

When I reached the palace, I expected the guards to stop me. They merely bowed and opened the ornate double doors.

Their lack of surprise was disconcerting. I hadn't sent word of my arrival – but I supposed Malek had told them to expect me. The benefits of visiting a king who was also a seer.

Cool air greeted me as I was brought inside the main hall, but Malek was nowhere to be seen.

'Your Majesty,' Avril said with a deep bow and a rare smile. 'I've been looking forward to your arrival.'

My gaze swept over her, noting how *well* she looked. Her dark skin glowed with health and vitality, and her white linen dress suited her much better than the black combat clothes she had worn as a Mask.

'I was going to ask how you're enjoying being back in Zigilia,' I said wryly, 'but I don't think I need to. Still—'

'You want to know if I will return to Ravalia with you. If I will become the head of the Order of Masks.'

'Did Malek tell you that?' I asked with a hint of exasperation.

Amusement warmed her eyes to a golden brown – almost the exact shade that Aric's had been. I felt a slight pang at the reminder, but it was no longer painful. For the most part, I had made my peace with those I had lost.

'I'm sure you've heard by now that I destroyed the blood rubies,' I continued, 'but there will always be a need for the Orders. You have a keen mind for politics; it seems a waste for you to serve here when you could be a leader back home.'

'This is my home,' Avril replied, softly but firmly. 'And my abilities aren't wasted here. Already, Malek and I have done a great deal to improve relations between Ravalia and the Western Lands. I intend to ensure there is a lasting peace between our countries.'

'You? Not Malek?'

Avril's smile widened, but all she said was, 'You can ask him yourself if you like. He's expecting you.'

She escorted me through the palace and into the lush central courtyard. Somewhere amongst the foliage, I heard the gentle bubbling of a water feature.

Malek inclined his head at my approach but didn't bow. He was dressed in the Western fashion Severin had always preferred – a crimson vest trimmed with gold and loose linen pants – and the sight made something in my chest ache. His hazel eyes raked over me as if he was taking me in just as intently. No doubt he had heard a great deal about my exploits. And Seen even more.

'Scarlett,' he said with startling informality. 'Come with me. I have something to show you.'

A pebbled path wound through the courtyard. I followed a few steps behind Malek, conscious of Avril's receding footsteps.

'You brought me here to admire the gardens?' I asked, bemused.

Malek simply continued on, an expectant smile upturning his lips. 'What do you think?'

I frowned at his enthusiasm, not understanding the reason for it. And then I took in my surroundings properly.

I walked past Malek, momentarily speechless. A selection of Ravalian plants and flowers enveloped me: all colourful, deadly and familiar. Some of my favourites from the greenhouse in Ravalia. The greenhouse I had destroyed, except – here it was. Brought back to life.

'Severin would have loved this,' I breathed, thinking of the precious moments we had shared together. How he had loved exploring it with me and telling me the names of the flowers. 'Was that why you did it?' I asked Malek, unable to tear my gaze away from the plants. 'To honour him?'

'I did it to honour you,' a deep, melodious voice said.

Every inch of my body went still. Taut and tense as a wire.

I turned slowly, tentatively, not daring to believe it. But there he was, standing amongst the greenery, dressed in the same clothes Malek had been wearing a few seconds earlier. He looked as devastatingly beautiful as I remembered, but his expression was infinitely softer as he regarded me, his mismatched eyes intent on mine.

'Hello, Scar,' he murmured.

I didn't move. I hardly even breathed as my eyes swept over him: the tattoos creeping across his dark skin, the kohl darkening his eyes, the gold dust glittering invitingly on his full lips.

'You're dead.' It was all I could think to say. 'Zandri killed you.'

'Do I feel dead to you?' Severin asked, bringing my hand up to his chest. The warmth of his skin met mine, and so did the rhythmic thump of his heartbeat.

I tried to respond – to ask the obvious question – but the words wouldn't come. I just kept staring at his chest, watching the way it rose and fell beneath my hand. Had he – had he been masquerading as Malek this *entire time*?

Severin took hold of my shoulders and gently eased me down, until we were sitting side by side on the edge of a cascading fountain.

'Everything I told you about my past was true,' he said softly, his eyes never leaving mine. 'I grew up in the Western Lands – and I was the only survivor of a massacre that claimed the lives of my family and my village.

But on that day, I fought my way to our temple and begged the Sorceress to save my family. As I lay dying from my wounds, her voice answered me – impossibly clear. She told me that it was too late for them, but that it wasn't too late for me. If I was willing to accept the price.'

I felt Selussa listening, and I knew that every word was the truth. Somehow, she had saved Severin's life.

'She led me to a vial of her blood. There was only enough for me, but I hoped – somehow, I still hoped that I could find a way of saving my family as well. When I returned, my parents and sister were dead, and my village had been razed to the ground.' Severin paused, but he didn't look away from me. Allowing me to glimpse the true depth of the pain – and guilt – he carried. 'I removed the blade from my mother's body, intending to use it to join her. But my wound healed. *Every* wound eventually healed.'

'So,' I said through numb lips, 'when you fell from the battlements . . .'

'The fall wasn't fatal – though I made sure Zandri believed it was. I even took a corpse from the infirmary for her to burn. One that resembled me enough to ensure she was satisfied.'

'Because you thought she would try again.' It was the only explanation that made sense. He started to say something but I spoke before he could, my voice rising. 'Why didn't you come to me? I would have helped you. I would have protected you from my mother.'

'You would have tried. But what would Zandri have done,' Severin asked gently, 'if she discovered you were working against her? Or if she discovered the full extent of my regenerative abilities?'

I shook my head, unwilling to concede the point. 'If you had come to me, if you had trusted me with your secrets—'

'I wanted to,' Severin interrupted, his voice soft, 'but I couldn't. I—'

'You didn't trust me.'

'It was more complicated than that. I knew you would have to make a choice – a choice that had the power to destroy or save nations.' Severin's eyes were filled with unexpected gravity as he studied me. 'There were many visions of the future, Scarlett, but only one in which Kalure didn't fall. Where you and Kasmira weren't at odds – but working together to reshape your worlds. That vision only came to pass if you understood who Zandri really was.'

'You *wanted* me to believe you were dead,' I said, my voice trembling as the full ramifications of his words sank in.

'Would you have turned against Zandri otherwise?'

I stood and took a step back from him. I didn't care what he thought I might or might not have done – he had never given me the chance to find out.

'I am sorry for the pain I caused you,' Severin said, standing as well. It was impossible to doubt the sincerity radiating from him. 'There were many times when I wanted to reveal myself, to help guide your path forward. But you had to make your own choices. I couldn't make them for you.'

'It seems you tried,' I said coolly. 'Why else would you have shown me the vision of your death?'

Severin didn't deny it. He took a step towards me—

I shoved him. Hard.

He stumbled back, and the lack of surprise on his face was infuriating. He had probably Seen that, too – which meant that he was *choosing* to let my anger play out.

Gods, why had I fallen in love with an *Artisan*?

Severin moved closer, undeterred by the glare I levelled on him. My traitorous heart lurched at his proximity.

'I hate you,' I told him, but there was no heat in the words.

'No,' Severin whispered against my lips. 'You love me.'

'Sometimes it feels like the same thing.'

He chuckled. 'I know.'

I might have kissed him, or he might have kissed me, but suddenly our lips were intertwined and we were falling to the ground, our bodies tangling together. My hands threaded through his soft, ebony hair, and he tore away the layers of clothing separating us, until all I could feel was his bare skin against mine. Until I couldn't tell where his body ended and mine began.

All I knew was that he was somehow here with me. Real, tangible, *alive*. A miracle, except I had never believed in miracles until now.

Until *him*.

He kissed away the tears streaking my cheeks with heart-wrenching tenderness. But I wasn't in the mood for slow, languorous kisses and sensuous lovemaking. I needed him like I needed air, and I knew he needed me in exactly the same way.

There had never been anyone else for either of us. I had always known that, but now . . . now I felt the truth of it in my entire being. The others had only touched my body.

Severin touched my *soul*.

Our eyes never shifted from each other's, every kiss and caress and exquisite spark of pleasure a choice. A promise.

There would be no going back after this.

You're mine, I thought to Severin. *And I'm* yours.

Always. His voice was warm and familiar and somehow inside my mind. *Always, Scarlett*.

A joining – that was what this was. Powerful and sensual and deliberate, and as I felt Selussa stir within me, the necklace I wore beginning to glow, I knew that Severin could feel her too. Knew that when he looked into my eyes, he was also looking into hers.

And she was looking into his.

The three of us connected by a shared history – or perhaps something far greater. Fate.

Passion crackled between us like lightning, and as Severin moved inside me—

I knew I was home.

Afterwards, we lay sprawled out amongst the greenery, listening to the songbirds and the soft trickle of water.

It was all achingly familiar, and with him here, it felt like something out of a dream. One I never wanted to wake up from.

'You . . .' I paused as something occurred to me. 'You tricked me into making you a *king*.'

'A Provincial Governor,' he corrected.

'Oh no,' I said, twisting to look at him. 'You knew I would give Zigilia its independence. You made yourself a *king*. Benevolent King Severin of the Western Lands.' I should have been furious, but somehow, I was smiling.

Amusement deepened Severin's voice. 'I thought you would appreciate the cleverness of it.'

I leant back against his chest. 'Is this what you always wanted? To rule Zigilia?'

'No,' Severin said evenly. 'All I wanted was to set Zigilia back on a more traditional path, restoring the rule of the seers. I hid some of them from Zandri when I was sent to hunt them down. Now that the Western Lands are more stable, and Ravalia is no longer a threat, it's my intention to install one of them in my place.'

'Do you have someone in mind?'

I felt Severin's lips curve against my neck. 'Avril.'

'Avril?' That made no sense. 'She's a *Mask*, not a seer—'

'Can't she be both?'

Now that he'd said it, I remembered that Avril was Zigilian. But—

'Will the people accept her?'

'They will.' No hesitation in his voice. 'I've Seen it. Avril and I have already put the necessary steps in place.'

It smarted, somehow. Yet another plan that he had set into motion, this time with someone I had trusted. A Mask who had been concealing her true intentions from me for *months*—

Severin's slight smile told me that he knew exactly what I was thinking. He shifted so that his back was to the trickling fountain behind us. 'Avril didn't know any more than you at first. As you're aware, Artisans – or seers – can't See the future of others like them. But after I took over Zigilia and began working with her, I told her everything.'

I shivered as his fingers brushed my skin. An almost absent-minded gesture, except—

'And this?' I asked as Severin lifted the aquamarine necklace I wore. It wasn't lost on me that it was the same shade of blue as my eyes. As the Sorceress's power. 'You didn't buy it at a stall, did you?'

'No.' A reverent note entered his voice as he said, 'This revealed itself to me in Kalure as pure light and energy. It materialised over an icy lake – directly above the young woman drowning beneath.'

I went very still.

'Before then, I didn't like you very much.' Severin's mouth curved. 'I didn't see your struggles – only your privilege. But when I felt the Sorceress's spirit, and when her spirit became this necklace . . . I knew she was giving me a message – that I had to help you. And when I started to look out for you, to help you understand your magic and keep you safe from your mother and brothers . . . I started to see who you truly were. Who you had the potential to become.' He shifted so that we were looking at each other. 'It was impossible not to love you then.'

It's not a ring, Severin had told me when he had given me this necklace. *But perhaps you can think of it as a promise. Because I want to be with you, Scar. There's nothing I want more.*

'When you gave this to me . . .'

'I gave you my trust,' Severin finished with aching gentleness. 'I gave you the power to destroy the world – or to save it. And . . . I gave us a way to remain connected. Even when I couldn't physically be with you, I knew I could use this necklace as a tether. To appear to you if you ever truly needed me.'

Like he had during the battle with Roran. When I had contemplated taking Fennec's deal and Severin had appeared to warn me.

I closed my eyes, revelling in the warmth emanating from Severin and Selussa, banishing any trace of death magic and cold from my veins. And as I leant back against Severin's chest, there was something so special about this moment that I wondered if it had always been meant to be.

If the three of us were always meant to find each other.

'I suppose you already know what's going to happen next?' I asked, peering up at Severin.

'You still have choices to make,' he said, his fingers stroking my hair. 'I can tell you what those choices are – but I think you already know.'

'We could return to Ravalia and rule together.'

Severin nodded, his expression inscrutable. 'We could.'

The thought seemed far more enticing with him by my side, but I still hesitated, unsure if that was what either of us truly wanted. The moment Zandri had died, my thirst for power had died with her. No longer did I feel the same desperate need to prove myself to my family or my subjects. Nor did I need a crown in order to feel protected.

Between Severin and Selussa, I had everything I would ever need. Everything – and more.

Perhaps it was time to discover exactly who I was outside of my mother's reach and that of the Court. To truly become my own person.

'You once told me,' I said softly, 'that there's a whole world beyond the Ravalian Empire. Civilisations and religions and magic just waiting to be discovered.'

I had the sense that Severin was holding his breath. 'What are you saying?'

'We're finally free,' I said, my hand tightening around his. 'So let's embrace that freedom. Together.'

'I love you,' Severin murmured to me, and for the first time, hearing those words filled me with happiness rather than fear.

'I love you too,' I replied, and I meant it completely. Wholeheartedly. Which was how I knew I was making the right choice. 'I think the Ravalian Empire will thrive under Cassius's guidance, at least for the next few decades. And we'll have plenty of time to rule if we want to.'

I felt Severin smile against my ear. 'We have eternity.'

That thought had terrified me once. It didn't terrify me now.

'Eternity,' I whispered as I claimed Severin's lips once more. 'I like the sound of that.'

CHAPTER FIFTY-NINE

Mira

'Are you sure about this?' Lillian asked as we joined the line of richly dressed nobles.

'Yes,' I said, with more certainty than I felt. 'I couldn't miss Cassius's coronation.'

'I'm not talking about the coronation tomorrow.' Lillian tilted her head at me, her silver hair pieces glittering in the torchlight. 'Appearing unannounced at a public coronation is one thing, but this is Cassius's *private* party,' she reminded me, as if I could have forgotten. 'We shouldn't be here. And Caleah Fortress is . . .'

I followed her gaze to the forbidding structure of alabaster stone, looming on the hill like a pale spectre.

'It's nicer inside,' I told her. 'You'll see.'

Lillian frowned at the reckless smile on my face – and then at my clothing. She had created this outfit at my request: a crimson dancer's outfit with a beaded top cut above my navel and a slitted skirt. It was very similar to the one I had worn during the first Trial, though I hadn't explained that part to Lillian.

Unlike me, she was dressed to blend in with the nobles, wearing a stunning blue gown that matched her eyes. It was a mixture of the fitted Ravalian style and the looser, wrapped silk that Aldarians preferred. Judging by the admiring, covetous gazes the other ladies shot her way, they were already wondering who her dressmaker was.

'You should take some time to mingle,' I murmured. 'All these women are potential customers.'

'I thought the plan was only to stay in Ravalia for a few days,' Lillian shot back. 'Or is there something you're not telling me?'

I was saved from answering as the line moved again, making private conversation impossible.

Two Warriors guarded the entrance to the grounds. As I watched them check their lists, I was reminded of the first Trial, when Aric and I had waited in a line just like this one. I smiled slightly as I thought of Scarlett – who had been disguised as Sabine – and how she had used her wit to get us past the Warriors. I didn't have her help this time, but I didn't need it.

'Names,' the male Warrior said in a bored voice, his brown eyes canvassing my face and then Lillian's.

'I'm Thalia – one of the dancers,' I said, remembering the name Scarlett had once used. 'And this is Lady Verne.'

'I happen to be familiar with Lady Verne,' the Warrior said, his gaze narrowing on Lillian. His eyes returned to me. 'Do you want to try that again, or shall I escort you off the premises?'

My mental suggestion was subtle. So subtle it barely felt like magic at all – but the effect certainly was.

The Warrior waved us through without a second glance.

'Did you just—?' Lillian's expression was horrified.

'Relax,' I told her. 'I used my natural magic. I've learnt my lesson – I won't ever use blood magic again.'

Lillian looked slightly appeased. I linked my arm casually through hers, following the glittering crowd into the manicured gardens. A few musicians played outside, and I saw servants milling about with trays of spiced wine and finger food. Plenty of the guests seemed content to linger outside in the balmy, firelit evening.

I wasn't one of them. Caleah Fortress might look uninviting, but I was eager to get inside – to where the true party would be in full swing.

I virtually dragged Lillian along, and as soon as the ballroom came into view, I saw him.

Cassius was sitting on his throne, holding court over a group of fawning nobles. Colourfully dressed dancers performed in front of him, but he didn't pay them any particular attention. Everything about his posture and bearing suited the emperor he was about to become: confident, powerful, all-consuming—

Larger than life. That was how Cassius appeared – the effect his presence had on everyone around him. Being this close to him made my heart pound and sweat slick my palms, even as my body warmed in places it shouldn't.

It was difficult to believe he had once been mine. That someone so striking, who exuded such a potent sense of danger and control, had once held me with such tenderness.

Tell me you're mine, Mira. His words resurfaced, and for a second I was back at the lake, staring up into his hypnotic gaze. *Because I'm yours. In all ways.*

Was he still?

I swallowed down rising apprehension. Coming here was a risk – and it was beginning to feel like a monumental one. The last time we had met, I had been the one with all the political power. Now, he was about to inherit an empire.

All I had was my belief that his feelings for me had been genuine. My hope that those feelings hadn't shifted.

I drank him in, from the golden crown he wore to his fitted crimson doublet and bone-coloured breeches. My heart stuttered as one of the dancers approached, a seductive smile on her pretty face. She murmured something too low for me to hear. Cassius said something back, and her obvious disappointment made me smile. She slipped back into the crowd with diminished confidence.

And then Cassius looked up.

For a second, it felt as though my past and present had collided. But the prince who looked at me now wasn't the same one I had met in this ballroom over a year ago.

Cassius's midnight-blue eyes widened – with the kind of unfiltered emotion he never would have allowed me to see before. Even the nobles in front of him turned, curious to discover who had captured his attention so thoroughly. But he remained where he was, making no attempt to come to me. A challenging slant came over his lips; the kind of smile that should have made me very, very nervous.

But I hadn't come here expecting this to be easy. I had come here to finish the game we had started the night I entered this fortress.

And I had no intention of playing fair.

Neither did Cassius, it seemed. He leant further back on his throne, surveying me from beneath black lashes. 'Tonight's entertainment, I presume,' he said, and the dry amusement in his words – and the familiarity of them – made something in me relax. That, and the fact he hadn't thrown me out.

I glided across the hall towards him, nobles and dancers parting at my approach. Their stares meant nothing to me. All I cared about was Cassius's, boring into my face like a brand.

If he had looked at me this way during the first Trial, I would have been terrified. Right now, the intensity of his stare inspired very different feelings.

'Your Majesty,' I said, keeping my gaze fixed on his striking face. But I made no attempt to bow or kneel.

Gasps sounded around us as I slid boldly onto Cassius's lap. No doubt the courtiers were waiting for his reaction – and I braced myself for it too. My heart pounded a thunderous rhythm that I was sure he could feel as he drew me back against the warmth of his body. I jerked slightly in his hold as his hands skimmed tauntingly over my bare skin, in full view of his entire court.

'Oh no,' he murmured to me. 'You wanted to play this role. Now you have to see it through.'

This wasn't exactly what I had intended. *I* was supposed to be seducing *him* – but like this, he had all the control. And I could sense exactly how much he was enjoying it.

One hand played idly with my hair, the other tracing the sensitive skin just above the swell of my breasts. Light, languid touches that shouldn't have affected me as much as they did, making my breath hitch. His fingers inched lower, skimming over my beaded top and across my exposed navel.

'I thought you weren't coming to Ravalia.' His lips brushed against my ear, eliciting a shiver from me.

'I almost didn't,' I said honestly.

'Why did you?'

'For you.'

I felt him hesitate, disbelieving my words. I had pushed him away so many times that I couldn't blame him.

But Cassius's sharp eyes had always noticed every little detail, and I saw them notice those details now. My presence here, the red dancer's outfit I was wearing, the softness in my face.

I didn't need to say anything. I had already said it all. Except—

'I'm not a queen anymore.' A tiny part of me was afraid to say the words. Afraid that they would change his interest in me, even though he had told me it wasn't my crown that mattered to him. 'I gave up my throne. A council oversees Kalure now – a council made up of clansmen and shifters.'

I waited for his response, my heart in my mouth. Bracing myself for the dismissal, the sudden coolness—

It didn't come.

Cassius smiled – a real smile. Blinding in its magnificence. And I knew that he believed it. That he believed I was really here for him.

He helped me up and stood in a fluid movement. 'Shall we go somewhere more private?'

'Shouldn't we stay a little longer?' I asked Cassius. 'This is *your* party, after all. What will people think?'

'I don't care what they think,' he said lightly, but his grip tightened on my arm. 'I want you all to myself.'

His words were thrilling, exhilarating – and a little frightening.

Hundreds of eyes followed us as we climbed the stairwell. They lingered on me like a physical touch.

When we reached the end of a long hallway, the sounds of the celebration faded. I was acutely aware of Cassius's presence as the heavy wooden doors groaned open, granting me access to his private chambers.

They smelt like him: cedarwood and leather, masculine and yet somehow earthy. A perfect match to the floor-to-ceiling tapestries on the walls, their rich shades of green reminding me of ancient Kalurian forests. How strange it was to think I had once found these tapestries intimidating. Had looked at the hunting images as a demonstration of strength rather than seeing them for what they were: the few happy memories Cassius had of his childhood.

Cassius lit the candles in his bedchamber, casting the space in a warm glow. I crossed to the balcony, staring down over the firelit grounds far below. Remembering how afraid I had felt the last time I was up here. How certain that I was one wrong move away from death.

'Be honest,' I said, looking back at Cassius. 'Did you ever consider throwing me over?'

'Not even for a second.' His lips curved with silken amusement. 'You were always too intriguing to kill.'

One hand drew me to him, and the other cupped my cheek. There was something so intimate about the way he looked down at me, the moonlight softly illuminating his angular features.

'What now, Mira?' he asked, a challenge in his voice.

I kissed him until I was flushed and breathless, passion exploding between us like lightning. His soft laugh tickled my skin as I removed his clothing and pushed him back onto the four-poster bed, so that he was reclining against the mountain of satiny pillows, somehow still wearing his golden crown.

The soft light illuminated the chiselled perfection of his body – and the raised scar over his abdomen. My throat tightened as I recalled the goodbye on his face as he sank the dagger in.

'I thought I'd lost you,' I breathed, and I knew Cassius saw the true depth of my feelings then. Knew it, because I could hear the anguish and longing and *love* in my voice. A love that I had tried to bury in Kalure, only to realise that I was burying part of myself – and that Aric wouldn't have wanted that for me. He would have wanted me to delight in life, and everything it had to offer.

'You'll never lose me,' Cassius vowed as I straddled him, his fingers trailing across my exposed skin.

His hands went to my hips, bunching my skirt until it was up at my waist. And then his hands and lips were probing, exploring, *moving*, and I – I was burning, losing whatever vestiges of control I had left.

Cassius swallowed my moan with his mouth, his kiss searing through me. Setting my nerves alight.

And I knew that was what he had always done for me. Even when I had come so close to breaking, when I had been caged in numbness and fury, he had always kept me from drowning.

He had always made me feel alive.

His teeth grazed my neck as I drew him into me, and the sound of his groan . . . An animalistic side of me purred with the knowledge that Cassius – cool, composed Cassius – had lost his composure because of *me*.

I kept my eyes locked on his as I rode him, every wave of pleasure taking me higher, until our breaths were uneven and our bodies slick with sweat. Cassius cupped my breasts before his hands dropped to my waist, driving me against him in a thought-obliterating rhythm.

Passionate, forceful, urgent – our coupling was all of those things, and yet there was tenderness too. A desperate, aching tenderness that I would never get enough of. Just like I would never get enough of him.

Cassius's eyes blazed with blue fire in the candlelight, his grip tightening on me as though he couldn't bear to ever let me go. And when we both toppled over the edge, it was my name on his lips.

And his on mine.

For a few delirious moments, I could only lay against Cassius's chest, bathed in a lingering glow. Gentle fingers stroked my hair, and I felt my face flush as I looked up into his intent stare – filled with an openness that felt like a gift. Unexpected and infinitely precious.

'You'll always be a queen to me,' he murmured. 'But we can make it official, if you like.'

I didn't understand at first. Not until I saw him reach for—

'What are you doing?' I breathed.

'Rule Ravalia with me,' Cassius said with absolute sincerity. 'Not as my consort, but as my empress.'

Equal rulers. Equal partners.

I couldn't speak. I could only nod as I stared at the crown I had once stolen. The crown he was now giving me willingly.

'It was yours,' he whispered, 'from the night you took it from me. And so was I.'

Tears welled in my eyes as he placed it on my head, and no longer did its weight feel daunting or overwhelming.

It felt just right.

A desperate flurry of activity greeted me as I disembarked from the carriage the next morning, palace attendants ushering me away to prepare me for Cassius's planned coronation. A coronation that was no longer just for him, but for us both. A celebration of our unity as monarchs – and as husband and wife.

I rotated the engagement ring on my finger; a ruby set in a wreathed band of gold. The perfect tribute to both Ravalia and Kalure.

I had no idea *how* Cassius had sourced it for me, but somehow he had surprised me with it when I woke up in his arms. Then he had asked me how I would feel about making the coronation even more memorable.

And now here I was, being shepherded quickly through the gilded halls. Passing servants frantically carrying flowers and other wedding decorations into the throne room. I caught a glimpse of the grand ballroom: already filled with chairs and a beautiful flower arch over the dance floor.

Lillian was waiting for me inside Empress Ivalene's old chambers, holding up a stunning gown. Her other hand rested firmly on her hip as she said, 'It would be a shame to let it go to waste.'

Since not even Lillian would have had time to create such a master-piece, I knew exactly who this gown must have belonged to.

Even though I was tempted, I shook my head. 'It would feel wrong to wear it. Like stepping into Scarlett's life.'

To my surprise, Lillian only smiled. 'This arrived for you an hour ago,' she said, handing me a note.

I recognised the bold, elegant handwriting immediately.

Wear it well. With my blessing, and my love.
Scarlett

I turned it over, but there was nothing else. No mention of where Scarlett was, or if I would ever see her again. I felt a stab of loss, even though it was probably for the best. Part of me had always known that there couldn't be two queens, and crowned or not, that was what Scarlett would always be.

'It won't be forever,' Lillian said softly. 'I know Scarlett still considers Ravalia her home. And Severin is a powerful Artisan – if he Sees something important, I'm sure Scarlett will return.'

Lillian's words gave me some comfort, as did the knowledge that Severin must have Seen that Cassius and I would make good rulers. That Ravalia and the Elusive Isles would be in safe hands. Not to mention the Western Lands and Kalure, which Cassius and I had already discussed signing treaties with. That was the part of ruling I suspected Cassius was most excited for – the chance to visit other nations and establish diplomatic ties.

At my nod, Lillian helped me into Scarlett's coronation gown. It was obvious that it had been designed according to her exact specifications: the gold that made up the bodice was shaped like feathers, and they veered outwards like wings. A subtle tribute to Zandri.

The bodice flowed into an elaborate blood-red skirt with a waterfall of black beads painstakingly woven into the fabric. Its long train promised to make walking difficult, though Scarlett would have delighted in taking her time, gliding through the throne room while her nobles looked on.

'It's certainly . . . eye catching,' I said, surveying myself in the full-. length mirror.

Lillian bit back a smile. 'That it is. But by the time I'm done, you'll be able to pull it off.'

An attendant hurried up to me, dabbing some rose oil on my pulse points while her companions laid out sparkling jewels on the vanity table. I smiled and thanked them, still uncomfortable being waited on. My surroundings didn't help: the empress's chambers were large and echoey and overly opulent.

But Cassius and I had already spoken about remodelling a set of new chambers to share. Neither of us wanted the ghost of Emperor Kalias hanging over our reign.

'You're really okay with this?' I murmured to Lillian as she darkened my eyes with kohl. 'I know you always wanted me to marry Aric. I should have asked you before . . .' I glanced down at the ruby gleaming on my finger.

Lillian touched my hand gently. When I looked up at her, there was no trace of blame or hesitation on her face. 'Aric would have wanted you to find love. No matter who you marry, you will always be my family.'

I smiled back at her, more grateful than I could express. 'And you will always be mine.'

Lillian began weaving black pearls through the wavy strands of my dark hair. I tilted my head, admiring the way they caught the light. 'I'll always be happy to design clothing for you, Mira, and to visit the palace . . .' Lillian trailed off, as if she wasn't sure how to say what she needed to.

So I said it for her.

'But you don't want to be a palace dressmaker,' I finished. 'You want to open your own shop.'

Lillian's eyes met mine, and the spark in them – the excitement – made my heart swell. It had been a long time since I'd seen her look like that. 'Exactly. I'm sure I can lease a building in Ravalia, and in time, perhaps I can expand to Aldara. It would be nice to have an excuse to visit my mother more regularly.'

'Perhaps you can go into business with the weaver,' I said, and chuckled at Lillian's long-suffering expression.

'I just hope my mother doesn't start matchmaking again,' Lillian muttered. 'She made a point of telling me all about the eligible men in Aldara. I don't know how she's going to take it when I tell her I've decided not to marry.'

I blinked at my friend in surprise. 'When did you decide that?'

'I don't know exactly,' Lillian said, biting her lip. 'At some point I just stopped wanting the things my mother raised me to want – like a husband and children. I learnt to depend on myself, and I discovered that I liked the freedom of it.' She paused. 'Perhaps someone will come along who changes my mind, but I'm not relying on that. I want to focus on creating a business. Something that's all mine.'

Her words – and the conviction in them – affected me deeply. I hadn't noticed how much Lillian had changed until now. She still looked the same – pretty and seemingly delicate – but she was stronger and more independent than I remembered. I was glad something good had come from everything she had been through.

A fanfare of trumpets rang out in the distance. The signal that the ceremony was about to begin.

'I'll see you down there,' Lillian said. And then, with an impish smile, 'Your Majesty.'

She slipped out of the double doors, motioning for the attendants to accompany her.

I took a deep breath and straightened my shoulders. The young woman in the mirror stared back at me, no longer as naive or angry as the one who had first set foot in the Ravalian Court.

As I studied my reflection, I thought of how far I had come. And how far I still had to go.

I felt calmer and more centred when I turned and strode out into the hallway. I had thought my surroundings would bother me, dredging up memories of a past better forgotten. But that past had shaped me into the person I had become, forged in a crucible of fire. In many ways, I felt like I had finally found my purpose.

And the person I wanted to spend the rest of my life with.

Cassius was waiting for me at the bottom of the grand staircase. He was dressed in black breeches and a crimson high-collared top with accents of gold. A ceremonial sword gleamed at his side.

Our eyes locked as he turned, and I felt it again – that spark between us. Like an eternal flame, always burning, always drawing me back to him.

'Are you ready?' Cassius asked when I reached the bottom step. I heard the double meaning in his voice.

Was I ready to do this? To commit to ruling at his side – to commit to *him*?

I raised my chin and nodded. A slow drumbeat reached my ears as we approached the towering doors leading to the throne room.

A sense of rightness overcame me. Whether Cassius knew it or not, he had saved my life many times in the Ravalian Court. When I had needed it most, he had been there, offering me something to fight for. Encouraging me to do what was necessary to survive the Trials and achieve my vengeance.

I realised then that I couldn't have done it without him.

The guards pushed open the doors, exposing the colourful, buzzing crowd beyond.

But Cassius didn't have eyes for them. He only had eyes for me as he extended his arm.

This time, I recognised the gesture for what it really was, and what it always had been. A lifeline.

'Together,' he murmured, his voice silken.

'Together,' I echoed, and took hold of his arm.

Acknowledgements

I am deeply grateful to all the amazing readers who have helped make this possible. Whether you have read *The Order of Masks* or are just discovering this series, I'm so glad you're here!

The Order of Masks was a labour of love, and I wrote it not knowing (but hoping) that it would find its people one day. When I wrote *The Weight of Crowns*, it was even more special because I had all of you in mind. Thank YOU so much for your enthusiasm and support – and especially for falling in love with this world and its characters.

To my incredible author friends, Julie Eshbaugh, Morgan Watchorn and Natalie Mae, who kept me sane during the editing process: I am so blessed to have found you. Julie, thank you for reading so many versions of the middle section and helping me see the best path forward. Morgan, I treasure our chats and your advice on line edits was truly invaluable. Nat, I'm still pinching myself that one of my favourite authors read and adored this series. And a special mention to Marie Rutkoski and Samantha Sainsbury for your editorial and publishing advice.

Christabel McKinley and Josh Adams, thank you again for everything you do behind the scenes as agents. I always value our Zoom catch ups and appreciate having you both as advocates.

To my editors, Claire Craig, Belinda Huang and Molly Powell: it's been a delight to work with you and receive your editorial feedback. A special mention to Zoe Walton – your passion and excitement for *The Weight of Crowns* is fantastic, and I enjoyed reading your in-line comments. Thank you also to the amazing Sasha Coleman for creating the gorgeous header art for Mira and Scarlett's chapters and Marcela Bolivar for the stunning cover.

To my wonderful friends and work colleagues: you know who you are, and thank you for being in my life. I am also fortunate to have a very supportive (and creative) family, who understand what it's like to be fuelled by a passion for something and to feel the need to pursue that passion.

Thank you, Dad, for always being there for me. I don't know anyone else who would be willing to stay awake for over twenty-six hours, just to keep me company on the final night of my edit. I love you so much. Thank you also to Mum, for keeping the cups of tea coming, and to my furry companion Scamp.

I wish I could thank all my special reader friends individually, as you're very much the driving force behind this book. Please know that I see every single post, every review and every message, and it is such a surreal and special experience to connect with each of you. Thank you for being part of this journey and for championing Mira and Scarlett's stories.

And to future reader friends: feel free to connect with me on social media (particularly Instagram) under @alinabellwrites, where I share character art and book news. If you would like to be the first to know about upcoming releases and giveaways, the link to my newsletter is on my website alinabellchambers.com.

All my love,

Alina x